TAKARA'S LE

Angela's Hope

Bradley D. Warholm

 FriesenPress

Suite 300 - 990 Fort St
Victoria, BC, V8V 3K2
Canada

www.friesenpress.com

Copyright © 2016 by Bradley D. Warholm
First Edition — 2016

Editing by Mira Lea Revill-Tardiff

Proofread by Rosanna Evans

Tabitha Warholm
In His Image Photographic Services
Photography/Webdesign

All rights reserved.

No part of this publication may be reproduced in any form, or by any means, electronic or mechanical, including photocopying, recording, or any information browsing, storage, or retrieval system, without permission in writing from FriesenPress.

ISBN
978-1-4602-8540-4 (Hardcover)
978-1-4602-8541-1 (Paperback)
978-1-4602-8542-8 (eBook)

1. FICTION

Distributed to the trade by The Ingram Book Company

This book is dedicated to my beloved wife
Tabitha Warholm

*Through all the struggles of the first years of our marriage
you stuck by me even when I didn't deserve it.
I thank the Lord for giving me one of the most
beautiful, loving and patient women in the world.
Without the Lord's call for you to be my strength and support
this story would have never been written.*

Proverbs 31: 10-12
KJV

***Who can find a virtuous woman?
for her price is far above rubies.
The heart of her husband doth safely trust in her
so that he shall have no need of spoil.
She will do him good and not evil
all the days of her life.***

ACKNOWLEDGMENTS

I would like to thank my Mother-in-law, thank you for all those long nights of reading and editing it with me. I can only imagine that you have most of it memorized by now.

I must thank Mira Lea Revill-Tardiff, my Editor. The countless hours you spent reading and editing this book even during this trying time can't even be described. After what you went through to do all this work for me, I cannot thank you enough.

Thank you Kate Evans, my sister-in-law, for all the reading and feedback.

I would like to thank everyone who donated including: Trevor Norman, Russell Hilman, Carol Verge, Gary & Elaine Warholm, and Sherry & Eric Youngash.

Lastly, I would like to thank my parents, Rob & Deanne Warholm. Your caring words and encouragement helped to spur me on, and your support helped make my dream come true.

PROLOGUE
January 1986 — Japan

"Mother, it hurts!" cried Setsuko.

Hitomi held her daughter's hand, as the midwife talked Setsuko through her breathing. It had been a long labour already; she was nearly ten hours in, and there seemed to be no end in sight.

"Now, Setsuko, the cervix is almost completely dilated. It's safe to push now. You need to push on my word."

Setsuko nodded.

"Push!"

Setsuko cried out as she pushed through the contraction. When it passed, she gasped for air and her whole body trembled from the exertion.

"You are doing well Setsuko-chan, just a little longer." Hitomi brushed away Setsuko's tears and wiped her forehead with a cool cloth.

They were in the Fukui sitting room, which had been rearranged to accommodate Setsuko's delivery. Daiki stood silently outside the room with his head bowed. He felt disconnected from the world, and his hands went cold as he thought of what he had to do to save his family's honour. He lifted his head once again to watch his daughter's progress, and caught his wife's gaze. Her eyes were filled with a mixture of pain and joy at the birth of their grandchild.

From the day Setsuko had chosen to keep her child, her whole world had begun to collapse around her. Her pregnancy had destroyed her few friendships, and a rift had formed between her and her father. Another contraction gripped the girl, causing her to cry out, forcing her parents' attention back to her. As Setsuko's pain increased, panic set in.

"The child is crowning," said the midwife. "You must push now."

Setsuko gripped her mother's hand tightly and pushed with all her might. "The head and shoulders are out, now one more push," the midwife instructed.

Everything around Setsuko faded as she took a deep breath and pushed through another contraction.

"It's a girl!" Hitomi cried, beaming.

Bittersweet tears of relief streaked Setsuko's sweat-beaded face as she lay back to catch her breath.

Hitomi took the baby from the midwife, and beckoned Daiki into the room. Brooding and unmoving, he silently regarded the infant from where he stood, then turned away. Hitomi exchanged troubled glances with the midwife. She carefully lowered the newborn into a large basin filled with warm water and, humming a lullaby, laved the baby, soothing her. After she dried and swaddled the baby, she sat beside Setsuko.

"Look at your daughter, Setsuko-chan. Isn't she beautiful?"

Setsuko lifted her head to look at her daughter for the first time. Up until now, the pregnancy had been a surreal nightmare, something that would be her ruination. The realization that what she had brought into this world was a living being hit her full force. A mixture of emotions overwhelmed her. Tears welled up in her eyes as she looked at her child. Her daughter was indeed a beautiful baby.

Hitomi read the look in Setsuko's eyes, and placed her granddaughter into the girl's arms. Setsuko pulled away at first, but under her mother's tender encouragement, she finally relented and delicately gathered the little bundle to herself.

"What shall we call her?"

Setsuko studied the newborn. "I think I will name her Corliss, because she's breaking my heart."

Hitomi shook her head. "No, she needs a good name. How about Takara?" she asked. "Because she is a precious treasure from God."

Setsuko brushed a light finger against the baby's face. Unexpected feelings of intense love and tenderness washed through her being as a little hand grasped it. Setsuko smiled and nodded. "Takara, she will be my little Takara-chan."

Hitomi felt her heart sink when she noticed Daiki was no longer in the hallway. She left her daughter to the midwife's ministrations, and went to the family shrine in the tea room, just on the other side of the kitchen. This room was a quiet place of meditation, rites and worship. Daiki knelt on a cushion, his head bowed before the kamidana where incense and white candles burned. Sensing her presence, he raised his head slightly.

"It is over?"

"Yes."

"You know what we need to do."

"But Daiki, we can't, she is our grandchild!" she begged.

Daiki pierced her with a look of such intense anger it frightened her. Hitomi quickly took two steps back.

"You forget your place, Hitomi. If we do not do this, I cannot ensure the future of our family. I will not watch it all be destroyed because of a foolish indiscretion."

Hitomi met her husband's fierce gaze with a determined one of her own. "I wouldn't care, as long as we stayed together as a family."

Daiki swiftly rose and closed the distance between them. Hitomi flinched and quickly lowered her head before the heat of his anger.

"Why do you test me, woman? Your new faith in this Christian god has changed you! If this is how Christian women treat their husbands, then it has no place in my home! Do you understand me?"

Hitomi stepped aside to let him pass.

Unaware of her father's presence, Setsuko was studying the baby that slept in her arms. Daiki watched them, and a small part of him questioned his decision. He buried his doubts and entered the room to stand staring out the window near his daughter's makeshift bed of cushions and blankets. Setsuko held Takara close. She shut her eyes, hoping to escape what was to come.

"You may take care of the child for now, but we must be rid of her as soon as possible," he turned to face her, but she refused to meet his eyes. "I know it will be hard, but this needs to be done, Setsuko-chan," he said more tenderly. She began to weep and held her daughter tighter, which caused the infant to fuss.

"But why can't I keep her?" she sobbed.

"Haven't you brought us enough disgrace? Is it not enough that we let the child live? Or do you wish to bring even more shame to our family?" Without waiting for a response, he abruptly turned and stalked to the door, then paused. "I am doing this for your own good. One day you will thank me."

With that, he exited the room, leaving his distraught daughter to weep hopeless tears, alone.

CHAPTER 1
April 1983
Calgary, Alberta, Canada

Professor Lang gathered his papers for his first class of the day. It was nearing the middle of the second semester, and his workload had nearly doubled with the upcoming midterms. Fortunately, he had recently acquired a young teacher's aide to help with the workload.

Jonathan Hansen was a quiet, brilliant young man. Standing just over six feet tall, he had an average build, short brown hair and striking blue eyes. Attracted by his shy good looks, most of the girls on campus had noticed him the day he started his internship. His previous professor hadn't agreed with his Christian ideals, and had mocked them at every opportunity until, after one gibe too many, Jonathan had stormed out of the classroom. This only encouraged the professor to increase his attacks on Jonathan's beliefs, which resulted in more confrontations until Jonathan finally had enough and requested reassignment. When he heard of Jonathan's situation, Lang had petitioned to have him assigned as his aide; in his opinion, with a Bachelor's Degrees in Education and Journalism, Jonathan had the potential to become a great teacher — once he mastered his stage fright.

"Jonathan, are you ready?" Lang asked as he walked to the door. A thud sounded from behind, followed by the riffle of fluttering papers. Turning, he saw Jonathan trying to juggle the few things he had been able to hold onto. The young man gave the professor a sheepish grin and gathered the papers he had dropped.

Lang shook his head and held back a smile, "Don't worry about your notes and books; use mine when we get there."

Jonathan put the papers onto his desk and followed the professor to the auditorium. Lang took his place at the podium with Jonathan standing to his right. A potpourri of spicy cologne and flowery perfume permeated the air. The room resonated with animated conversation that was punctuated with bursts of boisterous laughter. The cacophony subsided as the students noticed the new arrivals.

Heat rose from Jonathan's collar. His mouth went dry before the assessing eyes of the students. He always had issues with public speaking, and it was ironic that he had chosen a profession that required it regularly.

"Jonathan, are you forgetting something?" The professor flicked a glance at the white board.

Jonathan almost tripped over his own feet as he reached for a marker to transcribe Lang's notes. Some of the girls tittered at his clumsiness. The rest of the English Literature class progressed smoothly, with Lang occasionally letting Jonathan take over the lecture. The young man sometimes stuttered and lost his place; nevertheless, he knew his Literature and was able to engage the class throughout the lesson. At the close of the lecture, Lang handed out the required readings as the students filed out. While Jonathan cleared the whiteboard, two young women approached the professor, who greeted them with a smile.

"What can I do for you young ladies?"

Jonathan looked around to see who Lang was talking to, and promptly dropped the eraser. As he stooped down to retrieve it, he stumbled and lost his balance. The young women tried unsuccessfully to stifle their laughter. Abashed, Jonathan hastily stood up, and joined the professor. Lang's lips twitched. He raked his fingers through his thinning grey hair.

"Stephanie, Angela, this is my aide, Jonathan Hansen; he will be helping me for the rest of the semester,' he said. 'Jonathan, this is Stephanie Marshal and Angela Boisclair.'

Jonathan could only nod. Stephanie was a tall, shapely brunette with soft blue eyes. In contrast, Angela stood a head shorter than her friend, was slimmer and had long curly blonde hair. What held his attention were her striking emerald-green eyes that held him transfixed.

"You know, young man, it's not polite to stare," Lang murmured. Angela blushed and looked away. Stephanie hid her smirk behind her hand. Lang reiterated. "What can I do for you?"

"Oh. Yes. We wanted to know if you had any homework for us while we are away."

"Sorry girls, I had completely forgotten." Lang rubbed his brow. "Is there any way you two can swing by my office tomorrow to pick it up?"

"That's the problem; we will be leaving tomorrow morning," Stephanie said and smiled mischievously at Jonathan.

Lang looked at Jonathan and chuckled. "I will have to prepare it. I'm sure that Jonathan will be happy to deliver your homework to your home," he said, patting Jonathan on the shoulder. "I will leave you to work out the details."

"I, uh, well I guess I could come and drop the homework." Jonathan swallowed hard and looked once more at Angela, who quickly ducked her head to hide her blush.

The Marshal house was located in Calgary's Northwest quadrant. Compared to Jonathan's childhood home, the two story structure, with its attached garage, trimmed hedges, immaculate lawn, and flower beds, was imposing. Jonathan's nervousness intensified and his palms began to perspire as he pulled up to the curb. He collected the books that were stacked on the passenger seat, checked the address again, and mentally rehearsed what he was going to say. He mustered his courage and stepped out of the car.

He made it to the front steps and hesitated. A part of him wanted to turn back, but his desire to see Angela again was stronger. He took a deep breath and swiftly walked to the door. He pushed the doorbell and stepped back. Several long seconds passed before the door was opened by a lovely older woman who greeted him with a smile.

"You must be Jonathan. I'm Mrs. Marshal, Stephanie's mom. The girls said you were coming by; please, come in." she waved him in, called up to the girls to come down.

"I ..."Jonathan stammered. Just then, Stephanie, clad in light khakis and a snug white top, appeared at the head of the stairs and smiled down at him.

"It's about time you showed up."

As she bounded down the stairs, Jonathan's head swam, and his nerves rendered him tongue-tied. He had always been awkward around girls. The fact that the one standing before him was beautiful didn't help.

Stephanie's smiled broadened as she noticed his disconcertment. "So what do you think of the house?"

"It looks good, that is ... well ... I haven't really seen much."

"Why don't you show Jonathan around the house while I get ready" Stephanie's mother stifled a laugh. Stephanie wasn't as successful at hiding her amusement.

The tour took about ten minutes and it made Jonathan feel uncomfortable. By the time they returned to the main entrance, he felt completely out of place, and a little disappointed that Angela was not there.

As he was preparing to leave, he started to ask Stephanie where they were going, when movement behind her drew his attention to the staircase. He froze. His entire body tingled as he watched Angela glide down the stairs. She was wearing a cream coloured dress and her hair cascaded down her back. Angela froze also as their eyes met, and colour flooded her cheeks. Her meek and gentle beauty overwhelmed him, her emerald eyes held him spellbound. Everything about her was golden. Truly an Angel, he thought, awed.

Stephanie groaned in mock annoyance, breaking the tableau. "We do have plans to go out and eat, unless you two would rather stare at each other all night."

The pair looked away, embarrassed. At that moment, Mrs. Marshal walked up and asked which restaurant they preferred. Jonathan headed for the door, fully intending to leave the others to their evening out. Mrs. Marshal forestalled him with an invitation for him to accompany them. His attempts to politely decline were no match for Stephanie's persistence. He eventually relented, and he and Angela were ushered to the back seat of Mrs. Marshal's car.

Mrs. Marshal was driving, which left Stephanie free to skilfully probe for details about Jonathan's life. He told them of how his parents had died when he was a child, of how his Aunt Kathy and Uncle Bill had raised him as their own. When he told them that he had recently graduated from the University of Calgary with two degrees, the girls were surprised to learn that he was only twenty-eight and had already achieved so much. Stephanie pointed out that she and Angela were only in their early twenties, and still didn't know what they wanted to major in. Angela had spent most of the ride listening in silence, head bowed. Whenever she glanced at Jonathan, their eyes would meet, and she would blush and duck her head.

At the restaurant they requested a corner table where they could talk in relative privacy. During the course of the meal, the conversation shifted to the girls. Stephanie's parents divorced when she was ten. Her father had left with his secretary to Ontario; her mother was awarded the house, and worked as a lawyer for a small downtown Firm. Stephanie and her mother met Angela and her grandparents at a Bible camp, and had become good friends. Angela's biological father had skipped town after learning her mother was pregnant. Her mother, in turn, abandoned Angela on her grandparents' doorstep when she was eight. Mrs. Marshal revealed that she considered Angela a second daughter, and had opened their home to her while she attended university. Both girls were brought up in the Church, but when it came to Sunday school and worship, Angela was more involved than Stephanie.

Angela remained silent throughout the conversation, intent more on playing with her food than in participating. When dessert arrived, Stephanie gently tapped her toe against her mother's ankle. In response to her mother's quizzical frown, she darted meaningful glances at their companions, and then inclined her head slightly towards the washrooms. Comprehension cleared Mrs. Marshal's eyes.

"If you will excuse us, we will be right back," Mrs. Marshal said.

Angela cast her friend a pleading look as the others stood up. Stephanie darted a sly look in Jonathan's direction and gave a little shake of her head.

Sitting alone with Angela was probably the most uncomfortable moment of Jonathan's life. He wanted to say something to her but she was so beautiful, her eyes so captivating, that he couldn't find his voice. Taking a sip of his drink, he wet his parched throat and found the nerve to talk to her.

"I'm sorry if I am imposing on your evening," he said. Angela's eyes widened in surprise and for the first time that night, she didn't look away from him. "It's just—" the words caught in his throat as he was once more captivated by her eyes. With an effort, he broke eye contact and regained his composure. "I was just thinking that you probably had plans before I got involved, and I must be intruding on your time together."

"No, you're not, it's just that Steph can be so pushy. I tell her something in confidence, and she decides to do something about it."

Jonathan blinked in surprise. Her voice was so soft and lyrical it made his heart race. "What was she trying to do this time?"

"It was nothing. I tell her that I think I like a guy, and she takes it as an opportunity to—" she began, then clamped her mouth shut. Jonathan felt butterflies in his stomach as he realised who 'that guy' was.

"What is it about this guy that you like so much?" He feigned cool collection.

The question caught Angela unprepared. She took a moment to formulate her words before answering.

"I think he is really cute and sweet," she said with a smile, blushing.

Her words made Jonathan want to fly. Instead, he bumped the table hard enough to topple their drinks. Mortified, he snatched up his napkin to mop up the mess. Angela helped him, and their hands touched as they reached for the same glass. The contact was electrical. Jonathan felt his heart pounding, and Angela felt her heart leap. They were so caught up in the moment that they didn't notice that the Marshals had returned.

"Well, what have you been up to since we left?" Stephanie asked. She and her mother exchanged knowing glances.

Jonathan and Angela quickly drew their hands back and returned to their seats.

Jonathan drove home that night with an intense feeling of accomplishment and anticipation. He couldn't wait to see Angela again.

CHAPTER 2

Setsuko
December 1984 — Japan

It was the final days of school leading up to winter vacation, and the students of Higashi High School were all abuzz with their plans for Christmas Eve. It was a time of excitement and great stress for the junior students, for as the next and final semester of the school year would determine their futures. Many of these young minds were already hard at work, preparing for the Entrance Exams for their final year, which would start in April.

One of these students in particular was looking forward to the freedom she would find heading into her post-secondary education. As the daughter of one of the wealthiest and prominent families in Japan, it was something she could only hope for. Often, the expectation of family position overshadowed any hopes of changing one's own path in life. Her hard work was paying off, though, and Setsuko was going to enter her senior year as one of the top ten students in the District. With this, she might be able to separate herself from the future her father had chosen for her. If not, all she would be was a wife to a powerful executive or partner in her father's company.

After the bell rang, Setsuko gathered her things. She checked her notes once more, realised there were some pages missing and checked her backpack. A thorough search turned up nothing.

Where could they have gone? She rifled through her bag once more. She sensed someone behind her, and turned sharply to catch Akari holding the missing notes.

"Akari, you brat! Can't you leave my stuff alone for once?" she grumbled, trying to grab the notes.

Grinning unrepentantly, Akari kept the papers just out of reach as Setsuko snatched at them. Only when she backed Akari against a desk was Setsuko able to retrieve her notes.

The girls had been friends since the beginning of high school. Both of their fathers worked as executives at their respective companies. Akari's father owned an expanding computer hardware business that specialized in developing new computer chips and processors. Setsuko's father was a powerful and well-established businessman who owned several companies, retail stores and food chains across Japan. Akari was a few months older, and the school socialite. She had a sense of entitlement and absolutely no ambitions for the future, and was content to squander her father's money on frivolous things: an attitude she had learned from her mother.

Akari's vanity prompted her to turn everything she and Setsuko did into a competition, even when it came to their appearance. Both had long silky black hair, but there all similarities ended. Akari was five-three, with a slim, willowy figure, while Setsuko was slightly taller and voluptuous. Where Akari was attractive, Setsuko was striking; she was the envy of the girls and desired by most of the boys, which was a source of irritation to Akari. Once, Akari had challenged Setsuko to compete in a school beauty contest. Setsuko had won, with Akari placing second. Akari never forgave her for that. Setsuko could also become just as much the self-centred child whenever she let her popularity go to her head.

"Sorry, Setsuko-chan, I was just checking to see if you actually took notes, or if you were daydreaming about Hicharo again," she said, and snickered. Glaring at Akari, Setsuko shouldered the backpack and followed her out to the school entrance where their friends, Natsuki and Misayo, waited.

Misayo ran up to meet them. "What do you want to do during the break?" she asked.

"Like I said before, Misayo-chan, it is extremely important to maintain our GPAs, and I can't squander my time with pointless activities. Some people are working their way towards a higher education," said Natsuki.

"Oh, get off it, Natsuki-chan. You could afford to take a few days off and have a little fun now and then. What about you Setsuko-chan? Do you have any plans with Hicharo?" Akari insinuated.

"No, it's over between us. Besides, Natsuki is right, you should focus more at school," replied Setsuko, adding with a knowing grin, "Hasn't Hashida-san been after you to bring up your grades?"

Akari glowered, "Not everyone needs top grades to make it big, you know. I, for one, am going to marry a gorgeous rich man and spend all of his money. I most certainly won't be working at some menial job the rest of my life."

"I take it I will be all alone Christmas Eve?" Misayo pouted. "And just when I thought we were going to actually have some fun this year."

"Oh, I'm sure we will have plenty of time for fun over the holidays, Misayo-chan, but unlike some people, the rest of us need to worry about our educations." Setsuko cast Akari a side-long glance.

Akari grinned cheekily as she headed outside with Natsuki in tow. Misayo walked alongside Akari, chatting about some cute boy, and their plans for the holidays. Natsuki and Setsuko followed close behind in silence.

Although there had been no precipitation in over two weeks, the temperature had hovered not far above the freezing mark, forcing the girls to take the train. The mercury had climbed a few notches that morning, and it was a welcome treat to finally have one semi-warm day where they could enjoy walking home.

Setsuko could see Natsuki was deep in thought. She was their group's Intellect, whose focus was on getting into university and becoming a chemist like her father. At five-eight, with short black hair and boyish features, she intimidated most boys with her intelligence and height. She and Setsuko had been close friends since elementary. They shared everything from their academic accomplishments to their future aspirations to leave Japan and travel the world; Setsuko hoped that would never change.

Misayo was the chatty one. She was average looking and petite, and her cheerful personality drew people to her. She wasn't particularly close to Setsuko and Natsuki, preferring to spend her time talking with Akari. Her parents owned a small bakery not far from the school, and her grandfather, a former Cabinet Minister, had pulled strings to get her into the private school. She didn't appear to be interested in academia, but, when called upon, she regularly astounded her friends with her knowledge and phenomenal memory.

"I will see you later," Misayo said when they reached her turn-off. "Don't make yourselves too busy to hang out, okay?"

Waving goodbye, the other girls continued on their way. Setsuko took a taiyaki out of the outer pocket of her backpack. She took a bite, then offered some to Natsuki. Just as Natsuki reached for it, Akari snatched it out of Setsuko's hand.

"Sorry Natsuki-chan, too slow for your own good," Akari said as she began to nibble on it.

Setsuko angrily snatched the treat back. "You don't have to be such a jerk, Akari-chan, you could have asked," she snapped.

Akari shrugged. She turned around and began walking away.

"Where do you think you are going?" demanded Setsuko.

"I'm apparently not wanted, and I have better things to do than wait around for you two," Akari said without looking back.

Setsuko looked at Natsuki, who was gazing pensively after Akari. Sensing Setsuko's curiosity, Natsuki continued on her way. Setsuko hurried to catch up.

"What was that about?"

Natsuki quickened her pace. Setsuko quickly cut in front of her friend, and turned to stop before her, effectively blocking her escape. Vexed, Natsuki stopped walking.

"What?"

"Do you know something about Akari?"

Natsuki met Setsuko's gaze. "Look, you can't tell a soul, what I am about to say might not be true." Setsuko's eyes widened with anticipation as she leaned in close. Checking to make sure Akari was out of sight, Natsuki whispered, "I heard this from someone in Akari's class. If the rumour is true, then her family is destitute."

"What, you mean ... Akari has no money?" Setsuko gasped.

Natsuki glanced around nervously. "Her father made a mistake when he pushed through some new products. He didn't test them before sending them out and it cost the company millions. The board had a meeting the following month and bought him out. He still works for the company but only as a manager."

Setsuko covered her mouth, shocked. If this was true, then Akari's father would never be allowed to run a company again. They could lose everything. The expensive cars, house, and the luxurious life they enjoyed.

"Did they lose everything?"

Natsuki shook her head. "I don't know, but with the way she's been acting out lately, I wouldn't be surprised."

"When did this happen?"

"I'm not sure. You have to promise me you won't say anything!" begged Natsuki. "If she finds out, she will know it was me, she knows that I tell you everything."

"Of course, your secret's safe with me," Setsuko promised.

The pair walked on in silence. Setsuko knew that pressing Natsuki for further information would only stress the girl out, and decided things were best left alone until verified. When they reached the two stone dragons that flanked the gate to Setsuko's house, she said goodbye to her friend and began the long walk up the serpentine driveway.

Setsuko's father, Daiki Fukui, was a man of wealth and high status. He had spared no expense in the creation of his home. Set on a ten acre parcel in Tokyo's Nerima-ku Ward, the house was completely surrounded by a ten-foot stone wall that isolated it from the outside world. Japanese holly bordered the cobblestone driveway. Immediately behind the holly, tall evergreen hedges outlined the gardens, which could be reached through either the wrought iron gate next to the house's front door, or the back doors that opened onto the patio. Providing shelter to the front porch was an impressive Yoshino cherry tree. The house itself was a large three bedroom kurazukuri with all the modern Western amenities her father enjoyed. Set slightly apart from the house, a three car garage housed Daiki's luxury cars.

When she reached the house, she found Suzaku Ikeda sweeping the walkway. Suzaku was a tall, handsome young man with short black hair, and alert black eyes that missed nothing. Born to a poor family, he had lost his parents at a young age. When he was seventeen, he had been hired on by Daiki to take care of the house and grounds. In return, he was fiercely loyal to Daiki and his family. Daiki's wife, Hitomi, doted on the boy like a surrogate mother. Setsuko teased him shamelessly.

"Hello, Suzaku-san," she chimed with a broad grin.

Looking up, he bowed respectfully, "Hello, Setsuko-ojousama, I hope you had a good day at school."

"I did, but my back really hurts. Do you think you have time to give me a massage later?"

As always, the young man blushed. "I'm sorry, Setsuko-ojousama, I cannot. You know what your father would do."

"Oh, Suzaku-san, you are so cute when you're flustered."

Setsuko laughed, and ducked into the genkan before he could say anything more. She set her boots in the getabako, stepped into her house slippers and headed for her room. Her route took her through the sitting room that was overlooked by prints of Azuchi-Momoyama period paintings. Two rare Morimachi originals hung above the sofa. She slowed just enough to make sure they were hanging straight. She could hear her mother humming a tune in the kitchen as she prepared the evening meal.

Hitomi was a gentle, soft-spoken woman content with her role as a mother and housewife. Her days revolved around cleaning the house, preparing meals for the family, and working on her expansive garden. When Setsuko was younger she looked up to her mother. As she grew, she began to realise that she was offended by her mother's unquestioning acceptance of her father's belief that a woman's only duties were to have children and be subservient to her husband. Setsuko wanted more than that. She wanted to create her own life, where she could travel the world and make her own decisions. She wanted her freedom, and the only way she knew to achieve that was to excel in school. "Knowledge is power" one of her teachers had told her, and with power, she knew she could create the life she dreamed of. All it was going to take was some time and a lot of effort, but eventually, it would all be hers.

In her room, she dropped her leather backpack in the corner and flopped onto the bed. She smiled up at her collection of posters of famous American actors. California was definitely on her list of travel destinations. A glance at the clock told her she had time for a nap before supper. But sleep would not come. Her thoughts kept shifting between what she wanted to do for winter vacation and what Natsuki had told her. After an hour, she gave up all attempts to nap. With a groan, she dragged herself out of bed to change out of her school uniform.

"Setsuko-chan, are you home?" Hitomi called from the kitchen.

"Yes, Mother, I am in my bedroom," she called back.

After a moment, Hitomi stepped inside. "How was your last day of school?"

"It was good, I got a ninety-five on my last exam and I brought home some books to study and prep for this year's Finals."

Hitomi grinned, and gave her a hug. "I am so proud of you. You have worked so hard, and it's paying off."

"Thanks, Mother." Setsuko smiled back. "I can't wait to finish school and get on with my life. I'm thinking of taking some business courses after high school, and maybe even moving out on my own." She paused as Hitomi pursed her lips. "Is something wrong, Mother?"

Hitomi hesitated, then said, "No. I just remembered that I forgot to get something from the Market." She turned to leave, then added, "Oh, before I forget, wear something nice for supper tonight."

"Oh? Is it a special occasion?"

Her mother returned to the kitchen without replying, leaving Setsuko wondering.

At forty, Hitomi looked like a woman of twenty, and was often mistaken for Setsuko's older sister. The daughter of a rich and powerful financier, Hitomi was well-known in high society, not just for her family connections, but also for her beauty. The year before she met Daiki, she had won a beauty contest which shot her into stardom. Overnight, reports of her beauty spread, and she became one of the most sought after girls in all of Japan. Men from all walks of life came to her father to ask for her hand, but he rejected everyone. Everyone, that is, except Daiki Fukui.

When Daiki arrived with his proposal, he had already replaced his father as the owner of one of the largest construction companies in Japan. His business success and ambitions were enough to make him worthy in the eyes of Hitomi's father; that same night he announced his daughter's betrothal.

The announcement came as a shock to Hitomi who, at the time, had been seeing a young man who worked at the local market. When she objected, her father threatened to disown her. Faced with the reality of losing everything and bringing dishonour to her family, Hitomi left her first love and married Daiki.

For the first two years she hated him, and made sure he knew it. With Setsuko's birth, everything changed. Looking at her baby, and seeing the love her husband had for their little girl, she began to realise how wrong she had been. In time, she began to discover things she respected about her husband, and that respect gradually turned into love.

Hitomi checked the time. In a few minutes Daiki would be home, wanting dinner. "Setsuko-chan?"

"Yes, Mother?"

"Please help me set the table," she said, then paused as Setsuko walked out wearing a T-shirt and skirt. "What do you think you're doing?"

"What?" asked Setsuko looking herself over, "It's not that bad."

"No, you go back into your room and put on the kimono your father bought you for your birthday."

"Oh, come on, Mother, what's going on? Why am I getting dressed up?"

"Setsuko-chan, don't argue with me. Get changed right now." Her mother's tone brooked no argument.

With a groan, Setsuko returned to her room and quickly changed. As she gathered her hair into a bun, she scrutinised her image in the full-length mirror, and decided to buck tradition and leave her hair down. She walked back to the dining room, where her mother was talking with her father.

Tonight Hitomi had prepared Udon soup and tuna Sashimi, two of her father's favourites. Taking her place on her father's left, Setsuko looked up at her mother, who raised a questioning eyebrow at her hairstyle. Smiling, Setsuko bowed her head as she and her father murmured 'Itadakimasu' in thanks for the food.

As Daiki began to eat, Setsuko noticed her mother still had her eyes closed as if in prayer. Her odd behaviour puzzled Setsuko, but she didn't question it. She waited politely until her mother was finished before asking why they had dressed up for dinner.

"What's the special occasion, Father?"

"I am not sure myself." Daiki gave Hitomi a sidelong glance. Surprised, Setsuko looked to her mother for an answer.

Raising her head, Hitomi took a deep steadying breath, "I wanted to..." she paused, and took another deep breath, "What I ... was trying to ... say ...."

Setsuko and Daiki stared at her, confused. Hitomi froze. She had spent all day going over what she wanted to say, but now under the quizzical eyes of her family, she felt her resolve melt away. As the silence lengthened, Daiki became annoyed.

"Is there something you wanted to share or are we going to dine on cold food tonight?" he asked quietly.

Hitomi bowed her head. "I'm sorry Daiki. I seem to have forgotten."

With a little grunt, Daiki returned to his meal as Hitomi sat shaking. Annoyed by the way her father belittled her mother, Setsuko alternated her gaze between them. Daiki noticed her aggravation.

"Is there something you would like to share with us, Setsuko-chan?"

"No, Father."

"Might I also ask as to why you are pestering Suzaku again?"

Setsuko smiled. "I was just having a little fun."

Hitomi made a vexed sound, "Setsuko-chan, leave him alone. He is not here for your entertainment. If you bother him again, you will be punished."

Setsuko pouted in mock petulance. "I'm sorry, Father. I promise I won't do it again."

Daiki scowled, but didn't press the subject, knowing that Setsuko was baiting him. They finished their meal in silence.

After the weekend, Setsuko spent some time with her friends. They were even able to persuade Natsuki to join them. It was the day before Christmas Eve and many of the stores were open late. The girls met at a nearby mall in the mid-afternoon to shop, and stayed out into the evening. Natsuki complained that she would have rather stayed home than waste her time shopping; however, she didn't seem to have any problems with Setsuko buying her things. Splitting up, Akari and Misayo continued shopping, while Setsuko took Natsuki out for something to eat.

"Are you feeling a bit better, Natsuki-chan?" asked Setsuko.

"I'm fine," Natsuki said as she picked at her food. "I just wanted to get a start on next year's lessons."

"You know, the others do have a point. We can't always be studying. Sometimes it's good just to get out and enjoy ourselves, don't you think?

Natsuki considered Setsuko's words before responding, "The senior year is important; it will determine the rest of our lives. If we don't buckle down now we will never make it into a prestigious university or college. I want to go to a university in the United States, so I need to keep focussed."

"Is that you talking, or your mother?" Setsuko asked.

Natsuki didn't say anything; she didn't have to. Setsuko knew exactly how much was expected of her friend, and how hard it would be to meet her mother's high expectations to become an accomplished Chemist, like her father. It was something they both shared, but in their own way. Natsuki's mother wanted her became an independent woman; Setsuko's father had a more traditional role in mind her, one that Setsuko was determined to avoid, no matter what.

"Are you coming to meet that boy Misayo and Akari were talking about?" Natsuki asked hopefully.

"My father has a meeting tomorrow with some business associates, and they have decided to make it a family lunch at a fancy restaurant. I am required to attend," she said, pushing her plate aside.

"Maybe you could ask your mother about coming?"

"My mother?" Setsuko laughed, "Not likely, she bows down whenever my father looks in her direction. Plus I would get a lecture on the duties of a daughter in the Fukui household."

"Oh," Natsuki said in disappointment, "I thought we could hang out while Misayo and Akari made eyes at him."

Setsuko smirked, "I thought you were too busy with studies to waste any time on extracurricular activities."

Natsuki's cheeks coloured, "My mother said I need to get out of the house more often, so Akari offered to take me with her."

Setsuko didn't feel like wasting time on a boy. Though, she did feel a little guilty leaving Natsuki to deal with Akari and Misayo on her own, with a boy there to flirt with, it wasn't likely that the other two would pay her any attention.

"I can't promise, but I will ask if I can leave early and meet up with you."

Natsuki beamed at the news, "Thanks, Setsuko-chan. Who knows? Maybe the boy is as cute as Akari says."

Setsuko was doubtful about that. No matter how cute this boy was, she wasn't about to fall all over herself for another one.

The incessant buzz of the alarm rudely pulled Setsuko from a deep sleep. She hit the snooze twice before accepting that resistance was futile. She kicked off the blankets and grabbed her housecoat. Half-asleep, she reached into the closet for her school uniform. Realising her mistake, she pushed it aside. She took out a white kimono with a cherry blossom pattern and gold trim, and made her way to the bathroom to perform her morning ablutions and make herself presentable for the planned luncheon. Twenty minutes later, her hair and makeup perfect, she went in search of her parents. She found her mother in the utility room, ironing one of her father's shirts.

"Mother, is Father sleeping in this morning?" she asked.

Hitomi exhaled in frustration, "There is some natto and miso soup in the kitchen for you. Your father is currently speaking with an investor on the phone, so we won't be leaving for a bit."

Setsuko went into the kitchen to get the bowl her mother had prepared for her, and slipped back into her room. When she finished eating, she pulled out a romance novel that was hidden between the bed and the wall, and settled back to read while she waited. She had just reached an intense part of the story when the sound of her bedroom door opening startled her.

"Setsuko-chan, didn't you hear me?" Hitomi asked as she stepped in. Setsuko casually slipped the novel back into its hiding place and sat up. "What are you waiting for? Let's go."

Setsuko obediently followed Hitomi to the front door, where she gave her father a small, courteous bow, "Good morning, Father."

Daiki grunted. "Let's go before we are late," he said as he herded them out the door to where Suzaku had the car waiting.

Whenever there was a special business meal or a gathering, Daiki always chose the venue, which was usually one of the many restaurants he owned. This time it was an older restaurant that he had brought the best designers from the United States over to update and turn into yet another five-star establishment. She had been to this particular restaurant before, as it was one of her father's favourites.

The Host immediately led them to a private dining room that overlooked the restaurant gardens. The guests rose and bowed. Setsuko recognized many of the people in attendance as trusted friends and advisors who worked with her father, and several had their families with them. Many of the young men were clearly captivated by the beauty of the Fukui women. A few grinned hopefully when Setsuko looked their way, and it was all she could do to keep from rolling her eyes. Every time she attended one of her father's functions, she felt like she was on display. The thrill of being the cynosure of all eyes had worn off many dinners ago, and she hoped this one would end quickly so she could leave and go somewhere where she could enjoy herself.

The host escorted them to the head of the table. Before sitting down, Daiki greeted everyone with a bow and took up his cup. Those gathered followed suit.

"Today we are here to celebrate one of the most profitable years for our company," Daiki announced, and then launched into one of his grand speeches.

When he had finished, everyone took a drink from their cups and sat down. Hitomi and Setsuko sat on her father's left, while

Mr. Asato and his family sat on his right. Mr. Asato was one of Daiki's oldest and most trusted business associates. He handled many of the smaller details of the family business, leaving Daiki free to deal with the management of the growth of the company. Mr. Asato had a wife and two young daughters. His wife was a vile woman who took pleasure in using her husband's position to lord over others. The few encounters Setsuko had with her hadn't been pleasant, and she had the distinct feeling the woman despised her and her mother.

Setsuko didn't know much about the rest of the guests, which suited her just fine, for it meant that she didn't have to be overly sociable. Everyone, for the most part, kept to their little groups and talked amongst themselves. Hitomi made a few attempts to strike up a conversation with Mrs. Asato, while Mr. Takeda talked with Setsuko. If there was one person she didn't mind talking with, it was Mr. Takeda. He reminded her of a kindly grandfather.

"How is school going, Setsuko-ojou?" he asked with a smile.

"Good, Takeda-sama." she smiled back at him.

"Good? That's not what I have heard from your father. He says you are one of the top ten students in the District."

To hear that her father took pride in her intellectual accomplishments came as a shock. Daiki never praised anyone, at least not openly. She glanced in her father's direction

"Did he?"

"Your father speaks highly of you, and he should. You are a beautiful and intelligent young woman." This from anyone else she would have taken as sycophantic flattery. Setsuko blushed at the compliment.

"Thank you."

She turned her head to hide her smile. She looked out the large windows facing the gardens, and saw her friends, Natsuki, Misayo and Akari. But the person who really caught her eye was the handsome young man who was with them. She leaned closer slightly for a better look.

Exasperated over her inability to carry on an intelligent conversation with Mrs. Asato, Hitomi turned to her daughter, only to notice her staring outside. Curious to see what had caught her attention, Hitomi followed her gaze and quickly spotted her daughter's friends. Looking back at Setsuko, Hitomi could see that she was anxious to go outside.

"A little preoccupied, are you?" she asked quietly.

Quickly straightening in her seat, Setsuko forced herself to focus on the people who were seated with her. Mr. Takeda was talking to her, but she couldn't concentrate on his words. Her gaze kept straying to her friends outside. She began to fidget. Understanding her daughter's distraction, Hitomi discreetly drew her husband's attention.

"Daiki," she said quietly into his ear, "do you think Setsuko could escape for a bit after lunch?" With a slight inclination of her head, Hitomi indicated the four people outside.

Daiki regarded the group in the garden, then studied his daughter's hopeful countenance. After a moment's consideration, he nodded.

"Setsuko-chan, you may go out for a bit after lunch if you'd like," he said, then returned to his conversation with Mr. Asato.

When lunch was served, Setsuko ate as quickly as decorum permitted. Before her father could change his mind, she excused herself from the table and headed for the garden. The stone path she followed took her to where her friends were laughing at something the young man had said. He turned at her approach and Setsuko froze. He stood just under six feet tall, with piercing blue eyes, tanned chiselled good looks and a muscular physique. His dirty-blond hair was styled in the mullet that was favoured by many Western celebrities, but none of the stars in the posters that adorned her bedroom walls compared to this stunning creature. He smiled at her, and Setsuko's breath caught in her throat as he raked her with an appraising look.

"Hello, my name is David," he said with a bow.

Surprised to hear a foreigner speak fluent Japanese, Setsuko forgot to reply. Natsuki nudged her.

"Oh, uh, I'm Setsuko, Fukui Setsuko," she stammered, trying to bow in return, making the girls laugh.

"That's a beautiful name," he said, still smiling. "We were just about to go get some food, would you like to join us?"

She felt the heat rise in her cheeks and her pulse race under his gaze. She wondered if this was what it meant when the romance novels talked about love at first sight.

"I would love to," she replied, impulsively.

"Setsuko-chan, won't your father be upset if you leave without asking?" Akari asked, clearly jealous that she had stolen David's attention.

Annoyed by Akari's tone, Setsuko turned on her friend. "It's none of your business Akari-chan. I can do what I want."

Akari jumped to her feet. "Let's go already," she snapped, "before anyone else decides to tag along."

The small group followed her, with Setsuko and David bringing up the rear. Setsuko's heart pounded in a mixture of fear and anticipation. She knew that sneaking off would get her into serious trouble, but if it meant spending time to get to know David, she didn't care.

Hitomi's heart sank as she watched the girls leave; she knew how angry Daiki would become once he discovered Setsuko had left without his consent. She closed her eyes and murmured a prayer for her daughter's safety. She gave a little start as Daiki touched her hand.

"What are you doing?" he asked just loud enough for his wife to hear.

"Nothing." She shook her head. "I was just thinking."

She could tell by the look in Daiki's eyes that he didn't believe her. Hitomi had never been a good liar.

"I think we will have a little chat when we get home," he said with a frown. Hitomi nodded nervously before returning to her desert. He was definitely not going to be in a happy mood tonight, not after he heard what she had to tell him.

As the company luncheon came to an end and the last of guests filed out of the room, Setsuko managed to return unnoticed. Fortunately, her father was preoccupied with something else, for he didn't scold her for her lengthy absence. Happy to have escaped his wrath, Setsuko kept quiet on the ride home and went straight to her bedroom.

As Setsuko hurried into the house, Hitomi stayed outside with her back turned to her husband.

"Are you planning on telling me what's going on with you?" Daiki asked.

Raising her head slowly in fear she turned to face him. "I ... It wasn't an easy decision. So much has been going on, but I didn't choose this to spite you ... it's just that ...."

Daiki's impatience grew. His nostrils flared and his eyes narrowed. The rest of what she was trying to say caught in her throat.

"You must understand this doesn't mean I don't love you. I believe ..." She closed her eyes and drew a deep, steadying breath.

"Speak, woman, before I really lose my patience," he growled.

Mouthing a small prayer, she finally looked directly into his flashing eyes. "I met with a group of young Christian believers several months ago and they challenged me to seek the Truth. Shortly after that I dedicated my life to Jesus Christ and became a Christian. This is what I have been wanting to tell you."

His eyes widened as he backed away from her, lips curling into a snarl. "That's why everything has changed? That's what's been going on with all your silent prayers and your Sunday excursions."

"I'm sorry, Daiki," she supplicated, and moved towards him, "but this doesn't have to change anything between us."

He snorted contemptuously. "No, this changes everything!"

Trembling, she tried to slip into the house, but he moved quickly to pin her against the door.

"Why would you do this to me?" he demanded in a menacing growl. "As long as you are in my house you will not speak a word about this god of yours, do you understand?"

She didn't dare say a word, fearing it would only enrage him further. She nodded her head emphatically. Daiki pushed her aside. Before going inside he turned to her, adding, "You can do what you want, but if you corrupt my daughter with that garbage, I will cast you both out forever."

Hitomi nodded in response. She waited for him to go inside before crumpling onto the porch, weeping disconsolately. In her heart she knew she had done the right thing, she only wished that it hadn't cost her so much.

CHAPTER 3
Angela
Calgary — 1983

The last week took forever to be over. Jonathan had been on tenterhooks all weekend, and he had never been so happy to see Monday. Angela's flight had landed late Sunday night and she had called to ask him if they could get together Monday evening for dinner. Jonathan felt his heart begin to flutter at the thought of seeing her again, and he couldn't get his head out of the clouds.

Angela's class was at one-thirty. The morning dragged and Jonathan spent most of his time watching the clock instead of working. At one o'clock, he gathered his things, and spent the next half hour pacing the office. Lang couldn't help but wonder at the young lad's distraction, and the pacing began to grate on his nerves.

At one thirty, they headed for the auditorium and Jonathan had to remind himself to walk, not run. When they entered the room, he forced himself to focus on the task at hand. He stepped up to the whiteboard and looked into the sea of faces, searching.

There she was, sitting in the tenth row, close to the middle. Stephanie was with her, but his attention was directed fully at Angela. She smiled at him and his heart skipped a few beats. It was as if she had become even more beautiful. Angela gave him a small wave while Stephanie told her something that made her blush.

A cough from Lang brought Jonathan back to reality. He quickly copied down the information from his notes while the professor talked. For the first time in his life, he felt confident and it was showing. Even the professor noticed the difference in him. When Jonathan's turn came to teach the class, he taught as if he had been teaching his whole life. He exuded a self-assurance that told everyone present that he owned the room. Lang was so surprised by the change, he forgot to take over to wrap up the last fifteen minutes of class. Instead, he watched the typically shy and socially awkward young man, amazed.

After class, Stephanie and Angela approached Jonathan, who smiled and began nervously rubbing the back of his head. The young man's newfound self-assurance suddenly made sense to Lang, and he was reminded of his early years and the way his life had changed after meeting his wife.

Angela smiled. "You seem to be getting better."

Jonathan laughed nervously. "You really think so? I guess I am finally getting comfortable."

"You could call it that, but from what I saw, all your attention seemed to be on a certain someone." Stephanie smiled at her friend, who blushed in response.

"Oh, I forgot!" Jonathan turned to Angela. "You left me a message about getting together for dinner."

Angela twisted her fingers nervously. "Yeah, I wanted to talk to you about something ... that is if you have time tonight."

"I am not sure, it might have to wait—" Jonathan stopped as Lang placed a hand on his shoulder.

"It's okay. You two enjoy your evening, I'll take care of preparations for tomorrow's class," Lang said.

Jonathan picked Angela up at seven. They vetoed the restaurant in favour of take-out so they could enjoy a stroll through

Confederation Park. As they walked, they shared the past week's activities, then sat down at a picnic table to eat in the shade of a cluster of venerable poplars. Jonathan noticed that Angela clearly had something on her mind.

"Is something wrong?" he asked.

"No, it's nothing, it's just …" She stopped to set down her utensils. "We need to talk about what we expect out of our relationship."

Surprised by her bluntness, Jonathan met her gaze. "Sure, if that's what you want to talk about."

She took a deep breath, and said, "I want you to know that I do not enter into a dating relationship casually and that I have some expectations."

"Okay, you do know that I believe in the same things as you. I would abide by the rules laid out in the Bible, like not having sex before marriage."

She shook her head. "It's not just that, I have some special requirements for the man who may one day marry me." Angela paused to give Jonathan time to respond. When he just stared at her, she continued speaking.

"First things first, if you decide to date me, I want you to know that it won't be typical. Actually, I prefer to call it 'courting' rather than 'dating'. You see, if you really want to go out with me, understand that this won't be a casual relationship. I am in this for the long haul. I want you to understand that if you decide to go out with me, that I am doing this with the goal of marriage."

She half expected him to leave, or at the very least tell her that he wasn't interested. The last time she told a guy something like this, he laughed and told her she was crazy. After a few moments, Jonathan smiled again and nodded.

"I think I understand. Actually, what's funny is that I want the exact same things. Well I guess not exactly the same, but nevertheless, I have prayed that God would show me the woman he wants me to marry."

Her heart skipped a beat. Could he be the one she had been waiting for? Jonathan had the same desire to serve the Lord, and he wasn't brash or cocky, like most other young men. His shy and gentle nature was what had attracted her to him, and now his willingness to respect her wishes drew her even closer. "So, you don't think I'm crazy for expecting this, then?"

"Of course not," he said. "It's definitely not what I had expected, but there is nothing wrong with what you want."

She couldn't believe her ears. Everything she had ever wanted in a man was sitting right in front of her. They continued their conversation at length. After they had eaten, they resumed their walk and Jonathan worked up the courage to hold her hand. As the sun began to set, they returned to the car. Angela knew that it was time to go, but as Jonathan drove her home, she longed to stay with him. At her doorstep, she thanked him for the wonderful evening, and he said they should do it again sometime soon. As he was leaving, she stopped him.

"Before I forget, I have one more request."

He looked up at her. "Yes?"

"Please don't kiss me. I made a promise to God that the man who gave me my first kiss will be my husband. So if you decide this isn't for you, then promise me that you will refrain."

Jonathan grinned. "It'll be hard, but I think I can do that."

As Angela and Jonathan's relationship blossomed, Lang realised that he was not the only one who noticed. Concerned that certain people at the university would make the couple's life difficult should they discover that one of the TAs was dating a student, he cautioned Jonathan to make his nascent relationship with Angela less obvious.

The following day, Jonathan quietly took Angela aside.

"I'm not sure if it is a good idea to go out publicly, because we might attract unwanted attention."

"Oh," Angela said, disappointed. "Will we ever see each other outside of class?"

"Yes, we can do other things."

Stephanie, who had a penchant for popping into their private conversations, chose that moment to join them. "Like what?" she asked with a wink.

"That's not he meant, Stephanie! It's just complicated with Jonathan teaching here."

"We need to keep our dating quiet," Jonathan and Angela said in unison.

"How cute. You're finishing each other's sentences," Stephanie said, earning a scowl from Jonathan. "I'll tell you what, how about I help? I can tag along as your chaperone, but I require a guy to look at while you two are making eyes at each other."

Angela and Jonathan looked at each other. Jonathan didn't seem as convinced. "If those are the terms, then he can't be one of my students."

"What about Kyle from our History class?" Angela suggested. "He's that cute football player,"

Stephanie thought for a moment. "Cute but dumb. I don't know, could I really stand him for that long?" she looked at Jonathan. "I guess he doesn't have to be smart, just pretty. Where should we go, then?"

Jonathan sighed. "I don't know, but we can't hang out on campus."

"How about 'Gustav's Steak House and Pizzeria'?" Angela suggested.

"That might work," Jonathan mused.

"Okay it's settled, then. We'll meet Friday night, seven o'clock at Gustav's. Now just to land the guy," Stephanie said with a smile.

Friday night saw Jonathan driving up to Gustav's. Jonathan decided to arrive separately to avoid suspicion. When Angela spotted him as he entered, and waved him in with a grin. Worried that someone from campus would recognize him, Jonathan gave her a small smile. He sat down and surreptitiously checked out the other patrons.

"What are you doing? Just relax, please," Angela whispered, "You're going to attract attention."

Kyle raised an eyebrow and asked, "Is there something about this guy I should know about? I only hang out with guys who are totally awesome."

"No, he's cool, Kyle," Stephanie said.

Kyle continued to study Jonathan, "Don't I know you from somewhere? You look familiar. I know, you're in my chemistry class right?"

"Ah, yeah. My name's Tim," Jonathan said, extending his hand.

"Oh, I thought this chick said your name was Jonathan. Whatever. Cool."

Stephanie shook her head and patted Kyle on the shoulder. "Pretty, right?"

They ordered a pizza, and Kyle expatiated on football for the better part of the evening. Stephanie kept touching his shoulder and would ask questions about his workout routine or his football practice. She wasn't particularly interested in him or football, but she wanted him to have a good time on their date. At the end of the evening, the girls went to freshen up while Jonathan and Kyle went to pay their bills. While they waited at the till, Kyle turned to Jonathan and said, "We have two bodacious babes tonight. I'm looking forward to the rest of my long night, ya know what I'm sayin'?"

Jonathan stared at him, shocked. "You know that they aren't those types of girls, right?"

Kyle leaned closer to Jonathan, intimidatingly. "I don't know about a prudish guy like you, but this guy gets what he wants. Besides that Stacey girl was all over me tonight."

"First of all, her name is Stephanie, *not* Stacey. Secondly, she's not some tramp that you can have your way with. She's a bright and valuable young lady who deserves better."

"Whatever, man! Her loss. Since she's so valuable, here's her bill." With that, Kyle turned and left.

Jonathan was shaking as he paid the bills. He couldn't believe that anyone could be that crude and disrespectful towards any woman, let alone his own date. As he put the change into his wallet, he turned to discover Stephanie standing there, looking shaken and hurt. Angela walked up behind her, and noticed immediately that something was amiss.

"Are you okay, Steph? What happened?" she asked, looking from Stephanie to Jonathan.

"Nothing," Jonathan replied. "Come on, I'm taking you girls home."

Stephanie was atypically quiet during the ride home, despite Angela's puzzled questions. When they reached their house, Jonathan walked them to the door. He gave Angela a kiss on the cheek and thanked Stephanie for her company. Angela walked in, and turned when Stephanie didn't follow her.

"Are you coming in?"

"Yeah, in a moment."

"Okay," Angela said, giving them both an uncertain look, "I'll see you in there."

Once Angela was inside, Stephanie turned to Jonathan.

"Thanks for defending me. Guys are always saying things about me and treating me like a piece of meat. It's nice to be treated like a human being for once not some dumb 'bodacious babe'."

"Anytime. Steph, you're not dumb"

"Thanks," Stephanie said, shyly.

"Well, I have to go. I have to prep for Monday's class."

As Stephanie watched Jonathan go, she could see what Angela saw in him. As she was thinking about the evening, she realised that this was the type of man she wanted, and how lucky Angela was.

CHAPTER 4
Calgary — 1983

Jonathan and Angela's courtship continued through the summer, and as their relationship grew, so did Angela's desire to meet Jonathan's family. For some reason he didn't feel the same way. Whenever she brought it up, he changed the subject or pretended he hadn't heard her. She and Jonathan were at restaurant when she broached the subject for the third time. He predictably dodged the issue. Frustrated by his evasiveness, she refused to back down this time.

"Jonathan David Hansen, I swear I will break up with you if you dare ignore me one more time," she said as he tried to escape to the washroom. Everyone's eyes turned to them as he slunk back to the table.

"What?" he said in surprise.

"You heard me," Angela replied.

"Bu-but why—what? Well, it's just you see … my family is sort of *special*." At her confused look, Jonathan took a long drink of water, and explained further. "It's just that … some people don't know how to take my aunt."

Angela met his gaze with a level stare. "First of all, I'm not 'some people' and besides, if we desire to work towards a future together, we need to get to know each other's family."

Jonathan expelled a ragged breath. Seeing that he wasn't going to dissuade her, he relented. "Fine, I will call my Aunt and see when she's got time for us to visit."

Angela patted his hand, "I will also make plans for us to visit my grandparents. They would love to finally meet you."

Jonathan had hoped they would have had more time together before he introduced her to his aunt. Aunt Kathy was a caring, gentle woman who was also outspoken and painfully honest. While some people find her frankness refreshing, she often made people feel uncomfortable. He had lost count of the times her candour had created mixed reactions amongst those around her. For the most part, it was comical to watch how people reacted; Kathy was usually spot-on with her observations and comments. But after an incident with one girl his cousin had brought over, Jonathan dreaded the day Kathy would get her hands on a girl he liked. He only hoped that Aunt Kathy wouldn't scare Angela too much, and that Angela's grandparents approved of him.

When he dropped Angela off at her door, she invited him in to use the phone to call his aunt.

"Right now?"

"Why not, we have tomorrow free after church."

"I ... I guess," he replied, feeling trapped.

He had postponed the inevitable meeting with Aunt Kathy and had been able to find valid reasons not to contact her. Now Angela had caught him unprepared and he knew the game was up. He followed her inside to the kitchen.

"I am going upstairs to see what Steph is up to, let me know if it works for tomorrow before you go, okay."

"Sure."

He waited until he heard Angela's footfalls overhead before slowly walking over to the phone. He picked up the receiver and hesitated, racking his brains for a solution to this problem. He depressed the disconnect button and dialled his aunt's number.

"Hi, Aunt Kathy, how are you?" he spoke into the dead air. "I was calling to see if you and Uncle Bill are available tomorrow night? ... You're not? Well, that's a shame, do you think you guys will be available anytime soon? ... Well, when do you think you would have time for a visit? ... No, if it doesn't work, that's all right, call me and let me know when you will be available. ... Yes, Angela is looking forward to finally meeting you, too. I will tell her. We look forward to hearing from you soon. Love you, too, Aunt Kathy. ... Yep, bye."

Well, that was easy, he thought. He turned around, and started as he saw Angela and Stephanie standing just inside the kitchen door, watching him.

"Oh, Aunt Kathy said they will be out of town for a while, but they'll let me know when they get back." As soon as the words left his mouth he knew they had seen through his prevarications.

"You talked with your Aunt on our broken phone?" There was a note of irony in Stephanie's tone.

"The phone is broken?" Jonathan asked, surprised.

"Yeah, and you would have noticed that if you had actually tried making the call. That's why we came down."

"Angela, I'm sorry, I just—" Angela stalked off angrily. Jonathan pushed past Stephanie and hurried into Mrs. Marshal's office where Angela was waiting for him. "Angela, please, let's talk about this."

"I'll talk, you'll listen." Angela picked up the receiver. "Dial the number, Jonathan."

Jonathan reddened under her glare as he dialled his Aunt's number. Angela held the receiver to her ear and waited for the call to go through.

"You're in the dog house now," Stephanie chided from the doorway.

Jonathan ignored her as he listened to the one-sided conversation between Angela and his aunt. He felt a sense of dread as he listened to her make dinner arrangements for the next evening. The date was set, and there was nothing he could do to prevent the inevitable; all he could do was pray that Aunt Kathy didn't send Angela running for the proverbial hills. He tensed as she hung up the phone and cast him an angry look.

"Your Aunt says she hasn't heard from you for weeks. Were you ever planning on calling her?"

Jonathan glanced around the room like a trapped animal seeking escape, then lowered his eyes. "I didn't want you to meet her yet, she tends to scare people," he confessed.

"I guess we will find out tomorrow, and don't you dare invent some excuse not to go. The only way you can get out of this one is if you are dead, understand?" At Jonathan's nod, she concluded, "I think we are done for the night. You should go home, because at this point I don't know if I can look at you anymore."

She walked past Jonathan without looking at him, leaving him feeling like a child who had just been reprimanded by his mother. He quietly left the room and slipped on his shoes. He could hear Angela and Stephanie whispering in the office and knew they were talking about him. Feeling deeply ashamed by his actions and wishing he could undo what he had done, he left the house without saying goodbye.

The next morning Jonathan met the girls at their church, which he had been attending since he and Angela began courting. Relieved that she was no longer angry with him, he was able to enjoy the service that she helped lead. When he had started attending, he was surprised that Angela had such a big role in the church. When she took the stage, the typically quiet and shy woman transformed into a confident, strong leader. The metamorphosis brought to mind actors and their ability to transform themselves to suit their various roles. Even though each persona was different, the actor was still the same person.

It wasn't just her ability to lead the choir that impressed him. Her voice filled him with awe. It was like listening to birdsong in the morning. Her beautiful melodic voice sent chills down his spine as it washed over him with praises to the Lord. It made him wonder if this was what it was like to hear angels sing.

When church ended, they stayed behind with a few others to help with the clean-up. The church itself was made up of only thirty members who gathered at the Forest Lawn Community Centre. The majority of those who attended were elderly, with a few young families balancing out the other side of the spectrum. Holding it all together from the middle was Pastor Jim Winter, a middle-aged man in his fifties. He was a kind man, with a heart that belonged to the Lord.

"It's always so good to hear your sweet voice, Angela. Your voice always brings me to tears as we sing to our Lord," the Pastor lauded.

"Thank you, Pastor Winter," Angela said modestly, embarrassed by the praise.

"What are your plans for the afternoon?" he asked.

"We are off to visit Jonathan's aunt and uncle."

"Introducing her to the family before you pop the question, hey Jonathan?" Pastor Winter chuckled.

Taken aback by the comment, Jonathan nearly stumbled over the chairs he was carrying.

"It's not like that, we just—"

"We decided it was time to get to know each other's family, Pastor," Angela interposed.

"I'm sorry, I guess I was presuming a little too much," Pastor Winter said apologetically.

"It's all right, we are courting for the purposes of marriage."

There was a lull in the conversations as they loaded the stacked chairs onto a dolly to transport to the storage room.

"You two should get going before it gets any later. I will take care of the rest." Pastor Winter waved them away.

"Are you sure, Pastor? It won't take long for us to help you finish," Jonathan objected.

"No, no, no, I shouldn't keep you two if you have plans."

Jonathan was about to protest, but one sharp look from Angela silenced his objections. In the car, Jonathan ran a hand over his hair and muttered something about fools and angels.

Angela grinned at him from the passenger seat. "Nice try," she said, giving his hand a playful squeeze.

"I was just trying to—"

"To stall." She cut him off abruptly, buckling her seatbelt. "I'm sorry, but you are not getting out of this."

Jonathan started the car and began the hour-long drive east to the rural town of Strathmore where Kathy and Bill Karisson lived. Angela read while Jonathan concentrated on the road and prayed under his breath, asking God that He protect Angela from his aunt's sharp tongue.

They arrived at the Karrison's shortly before two. The house was a blue and white bungalow with a detached garage and an immaculately maintained lawn. A small flowerbed beneath the bay window, and two planters of tulips on the porch added a profusion of colour to the scene. Jonathan wasn't looking at the pretty picture that the property presented. His palms were sweating and his heart was pounding. The last time he felt this nervous was when he had taught his first university class. He took his time getting out of the car.

"I don't have a choice, do I?" he asked.

"No, you don't," she said with a smile. "Besides, it would be rude to cancel when we have only just arrived."

Jonathan took her hand and they walked silently to the house: Angela with quiet excitement, Jonathan hoping fervently that no one was home. They were greeted at the door by a ruggedly handsome young man with lively brown eyes and short brown hair. Dressed in faded jeans and a blue shirt buttoned over a white t-shirt, he exuded masculinity. He was the type a girl would run away with without first introducing him to Dad, and he knew it. His smile broadened as he swept Angela with a roguish look that made her move closer to Jonathan.

"Well, if it isn't my favourite cousin!" the young man stepped forward to embrace Jonathan. "And look at who you brought home."

"I am your only cousin," Jonathan said drily.

Jonathan didn't know how he felt about the way Alex looked at Angela. He wasn't worried that she would be interested in his cousin and Alex was harmless, for the most part. It was just the way he eyed her that made Jonathan feel uncomfortable when Alex gave her a friendly hug.

"You must be the lovely Angela we have been hearing about. I'm Jonathan's cousin Alex." He winked at Jonathan. "How did he happen to stumble upon such a beautiful girl?"

Angela blushed and looked away, flustered. Jonathan chuckled. "I'm not entirely sure, it's definitely not for my looks," he said.

"Is Aunt Kathy home?" Angela interjected, wanting to change the subject before she became more embarrassed.

In response, Alex called down the hallway, "Mom! It's Jonathan and his girlfriend, Angela!"

The clanging of multiple objects hitting the ground resounded throughout the house. Moments later a middle-aged woman with long red hair appeared in the doorway and pushed Alex aside.

"You came!" Aunt Kathy grinned. Her hair was in disarray and there were white paint blotches on her face and clothes.

"What are you doing in there, Aunt Kathy?" Jonathan asked curiously.

"Repainting our room." She wiped the paint off her hands with a rag she had draped over her shoulder.

"Isn't that Uncle Bill's job?"

Aunt Kathy snorted in derision. "I'm lucky if your uncle gets around to half the chores around this place. He's been so busy with his business that we usually don't see him until things calm down in winter."

The group at the door fell into an awkward silence, which Aunt Kathy eventually broke. "Well, are you going to introduce us, or shall we stand like this all day?"

"Oh ... yes," Jonathan stammered, "She is ... I mean her name is ... I—"

"My name's Angela Boisclair. It's nice to finally meet you," Angela said, holding her hand out.

"Sorry, dear, but we don't shake hands around here," Kathy said with a laugh as she embraced Angela.

"Unless we don't like you, that is," Alex interjected with a cheeky grin. Aunt Kathy shot Alex a dark look, grabbed Angela's hand and took her inside, leaving the men standing at the door.

"Don't I get a hug, Aunt Kathy?" Jonathan called after her.

"You can help your cousin bring some lawn chairs from the garage!"

"Boy, is she mad at you." Alex chuckled as they headed for the garage.

Jonathan was surprised to see Alex there. Due to Alex's wild lifestyle, things had been strained between father and son for several years. Whenever Alex was out of cash, he'd return home. His father would read him the riot act and give him one month to get a job. Invariably, he would lose his patience before the month was up and kick Alex out. It was a repetitive cycle that, Jonathan knew from experience, wasn't going to change any time soon.

"What are you doing home?" Jonathan asked.

"You know, the usual, out of gas and cash."

"Uncle Bill has you doing odd jobs again?"

"Nope." Alex handed Jonathan some boxes that were piled up against the garage wall as he cleared a path to the chairs. "Mom got me a temporary job at the local food market."

Alex handed him two chairs while he took another pair. "What did Uncle Bill say when you arrived back home?"

Alex ignored the question. "I have to admit, that girl of yours is one hot babe, you lucky dog," he said as they carried the chairs out.

"She is beautiful," Jonathan agreed, his attention focussed on Angela and his aunt who were talking on the deck.

"You got any plans on marrying the girl?" Alex whispered.

"We have talked about it, but that's a long way off."

"Really?" Alex asked.

Jonathan shot him a quizzical look, but said nothing.

"Wow, Mom is right, you really are dense, aren't you?" Alex laughed. "So, how have things been going? What have you been up to since the last I saw you?"

Jonathan's tension and discomfort melted away as he brought Alex up to date with what he had been doing. As he spoke, he kept a watchful eye on Angela, and was relieved to see she was enjoying herself. Both she and Kathy were clearly discussing something particularly humorous, for it was making Angela laugh so hard she nearly spat out her tea. When the men had the chairs set up, Aunt Kathy asked them to go to the store to buy some drinks and snacks. She held out the keys for Alex to take. Reluctant to leave Angela, but hearing the order hidden in the request, Jonathan went along for the ride.

"Oh, get off it, Jonathan," Alex said, shaking his head as they unloaded their cart at the till.

"Get off what?"

"You're all stressed over those two meeting for the first time."

"I am not," said Jonathan.

"Don't deny it. I saw the way you were watching them. What are you afraid of?"

"Afraid? You have got to be joking, you don't remember?" Alex raised an eyebrow as he paid the cashier. Jonathan added, "Your girlfriend, Michelle?"

"What about her?" Alex asked as they walked out with their purchases.

"Who do you think had a conversation with her before you two split up?"

"So?" Alex opened the van's side door and placed the bags inside.

"So?" Jonathan echoed. "You can't be serious. She's the reason you two broke up. She's also the reason why that guy Derrick stopped hanging out with Rachel. Are you really that blind?"

Alex closed the door with more force than was necessary. "First off, Michelle and I were over long before she met Mom, and second, that Derrick guy was a real creep, even you would have to agree."

Jonathan looked at Alex in disbelief. Had he imagined everything, or was his cousin in complete denial? "What about the things she says?"

"So, Mom doesn't have a mouth gate. Would life be as interesting if she did? Sometimes when we are younger we see things differently." Alex tried to reassure him. "Besides, Mom is a lot better than what she used to be."

Unconvinced, Jonathan decided to keep his scepticism to himself. The conversation shifted to Alex's current girlfriend, a woman two years his senior who he had been seeing for the past two months. By the time they reached the house, Jonathan had decided that she sounded nice, and perhaps a little mature for Alex.

"I guess the only hang-up is that she already has two kids," Alex said as they stepped out of the van.

"Children?" Jonathan repeated, nearly dropping the bags he was carrying. "You have got to be joking."

"No, I'm not." Alex said, and added in a low tone, "And if you have some sense, you won't say a word to Mom, all right? She'll kill me if she found out."

"No kidding," Jonathan said, earning an irritated glare from Alex. He matched the other's quiet tone as they entered the kitchen. "Didn't she tell you when you started dating?"

"No."

"And you still want to go out with her?"

"Why not?" Alex replied as they began unpacking the chips and pop.

"She's hot, isn't she?" Jonathan drawled.

Alex grinned. "Of course, would I have it any other way?"

"How old are her kids?"

"Her daughter is four and her son is two. They are really cute, you would like them. Hey, maybe we should go out on a double date sometime, what do you think?"

Before Jonathan could respond, a noise startled them. They turned sharply as a young woman with short brown hair and sparkling brown eyes stood up from her hiding place behind the island.

"Eavesdropping again are we, Rachel?" Alex growled.

"Ooops," she drawled and flashed them a devious smile.

Rachel was a slim, athletic girl of eighteen. Like her older brother, she was bold and fearless, always testing her boundaries as well as her parents. Today, she was wearing a pair of short shorts and a white shirt knotted just above her midriff, which she knew full well would anger her father.

"Don't worry I won't tell Mom, that's as long as you keep to your promise," she insinuated.

Alex sighed in exasperation. "Look, I told you we will go next week, you just have to keep your mouth shut until then."

"Where are you two going?" Jonathan asked, his curiosity piqued.

"Alex promised to take me to Jimmy Dean's as a late birthday gift."

Jonathan looked at Alex in disbelief. Alex waved dismissively and rolled his eyes.

"You really are asking for a death sentence aren't you?" Jonathan asked sotto voce.

"She caught me in a moment of weakness."

"In other words, you were drinking."

Alex shrugged non-committally, and headed off to the basement. Jonathan decided to stay out of the matter; digging too deep would only cause more trouble than it was worth. He just hoped that Alex had enough sense to talk his sister out of going to the nightclub before things got out of hand.

He gave Rachel a questioning look, but she only smiled and pulled him to the front door. As they entered the dining room, Jonathan looked through the bay windows overlooking the back yard and saw Angela and his aunt chatting over tea on the deck. Rachel hurried outside to join them. Jonathan remained where he was as memories rushed to the fore. They were welcome memories of his childhood in this house, of his parents, of the kindness and dedication of his Aunt and Uncle who had taken it upon themselves to ensure that he had a home and a family, and was loved and treated as one of their own.

His uncle was a stubborn, brusque man, but he had a tender side that became more evident when he was with Jonathan. As the head of the household, he was Jonathan's surrogate father and male role model. As had Jonathan's mother, Aunt Kathy had strong biblical values that she strove to pass on to her children. Jonathan held fast to them, for they gave him a connection with his parents who also had been strong leaders within their church. Jonathan's father had taken Bible Studies for the first two years of his secondary education before going to university to become an engineer. His mother had been a youth leader for their church for many years, and had been an outspoken Evangelist in their Community. They had planned to become Missionaries and travel, but those dreams had never come to fruition. His aunt was the only one who would talk to him about his parents. His uncle could never bring himself to discuss them, preferring to let his wife answer the boy's questions. Jonathan's mother had been Uncle Bill's baby sister and his brother-in-law his best friend. He was never the same after he lost them.

With another look around the quaint little home, he stepped out onto the deck and was greeted with silence as all eyes turned to him.

"Hi," he said uneasily.

"Come join us, Jonathan. We were just talking about you." Kathy cast a knowing look to the others. Angela blushed slightly and beckoned him to sit beside her. Just then, Uncle Bill stepped onto the deck. When Rachel saw him, she jumped up and ran to give him a hug.

"Hi, Daddy!"

"Hello, Princess. What in the world are you wearing? Whose house do you think you live in? Go put a sweater on."

Rachel pouted like a petulant child, but her dad was not swayed. Grumbling something about being an adult, she stomped inside to change.

"Princess, I'll treat you like an adult when you stop pouting," Bill called after her. He turned his attention to Alex, and asked, "Do you have a place of your own yet?"

Alex sighed. "I'm working on it, Pops."

"Mmmhmm" Bill he pursed lips and shook his head. His demeanour brightened considerably when he noticed Angela. "And who is this lovely young lady?" he asked.

Jonathan took Angela's hand and introduced Uncle Bill to her. This proved to be an invitation for his family to share with Angela his life stories.

"Remember the jungle gym?" Bill asked innocently.

"Not that one!" Jonathan moaned.

"I remember it like it was yesterday," Kathy said.

"You weren't even there, darling"

"Oh, be quiet and let me tell it." Kathy turned to Angela. "When Jonathan was three, Bill took him and Alex to the park. Alex wanted to play on the swing, Jonathan wanted to play on the jungle gym. While Bill pushed Alex on the swing, Jonathan climbed to the top of the gym, and called out, 'Uncle Bwill! Look!'.

"Bill thought he was going to slide down the pole, so he watched him, fully expecting Jonathan to hold on. Instead he jumped, and fell hard on his little tushy. Bill ran over, picked him up, dusted him off and asked him if he was okay. Jonathan just stood there shaking, with his hands balled in little fists, face beet red. He looked Bill straight in the eye and exclaimed, 'You dithguthst me!'. He was so angry that Bill didn't catch him, that was all he could say."

Everyone burst out laughing. When Jonathan saw how much Angela was laughing, he couldn't help but join in. The rest of the visit was spent filled with laughter and reminiscence and, to his surprise Angela seemed comfortable around his family.

"So, did Aunt Kathy have anything interesting to say when she had you to herself?" Jonathan asked as they drove home. Angela averted her face to look out the window. Jonathan frowned. "Okay, what did she say?"

"It's nothing she said, it's what she asked." Angela fiddled with a pleat in her skirt.

"Oh, and what was that?"

Angela hesitated again and smoothed her skirt. She lowered her head as heat flooded her cheeks. "She asked how far we had gone, and wanted to know if we were waiting for marriage. If not, she asked if were we at least being safe."

Jonathan almost swerved into oncoming traffic and had to pull over to regain his composure. "You can't be serious?" he said.

Angela could only nod. When his aunt had asked her, she had almost choked on her tea, which only made Kathy laugh. Angela felt her heart pound in reaction to Kathy's questions. Jonathan's aunt was a peculiar woman who seemed to find nothing wrong with asking the most embarrassing questions. Her frankness and casual attitude was the complete opposite from what Angela had expected in most women, but it was also something she enjoyed about Kathy and what had allowed Angela to open up to her.

"What did you tell her?" he squeezed her hand and she lifted her head to meet his gaze.

"That you where being a complete gentleman and you have decided to honour me by waiting until we are married."

They both laughed, and it took everything Jonathan had to stop himself from kissing her. It was then that he knew she was The One, the one woman he wanted to spend the rest of his life with.

A week later, Jonathan and Angela made the trip to her grandparent's farm just outside the town of Olds, which was about an hour from the city. As they drew near, Angela pointed to a shelter belt of blue spruce to the right of them.

"There it is," she said.

This time it was Angela's turn to feel anxious about the visit. When their daughter had left Angela in their care and disappeared, they had adopted the child and raised her as their own. Where her grandmother was a compassionate, pleasant woman, her grandfather had a gruffness that put most people off. Which was probably why she hit it off so well with Jonathan's uncle; the two men were a lot alike. She just hoped his overprotective nature didn't take over.

As they pulled up to the farm, Jonathan surveyed his surroundings. The farmhouse that stood to the left of the gravel driveway looked a little rundown with chipped white trim, and peeling light brown paint that was fading in areas. The roof was in need of repair. The only thing that appeared to have received recent attention was the freshly painted porch. Further down the driveway stood a large barn with a tall gambrel roof and two large sliding doors with a man door off to the side. Jonathan assumed it was where the farm equipment and machinery were stored. Standing opposite were several smaller buildings and a chicken coop. Just beyond the line of outbuildings was a large silo, and beyond that a large pasture where cows grazed. Jonathan felt oddly at home.

As they walked to the front door, they heard a loud clanging of metal on metal, followed by a man's angry bellowing.

Angela identified the cause of the commotion as she opened the screen door. "That must be Grandpa working on the tractor again."

Jonathan squinted as he looked towards the shop, but he couldn't see anything through the barn's dusty windows, at least not from where he stood. He followed Angela into a large mudroom filled with cabinets, chairs and other pieces of furniture. The mudroom opened onto a small landing with two sets of stairs, one leading up and one down. They removed their shoes and placed them on a small rack beside the door.

Angela put a hand on railing. "I'm home!" she called to the house in general.

They heard a muffled voice above them. As they ascended the stairs, the smell of freshly baked bread greeted them, making Jonathan's mouth water. The upper level opened up into a large area that contained the living room, dining room and kitchen. Jonathan waited between the kitchen and dining room as Angela followed the voice. As she reached a doorway to the right of the kitchen, a slender, elderly woman wearing faded blue jeans and a purple button-up shirt and holding a phone to her ear stepped into view.

"I know that, Jen, but you know how Jim is. When he has made up his mind, that's it," the woman said as she checked her baking. "What did you expect when you married him? He's just like his brother. I can't tell you how many times I have tried to change Stan's mind, and every time he digs in his heels and refuses to budge. They are as stubborn as mules those two." Closing the oven door, Angela's grandmother turned around and nearly had a heart attack when she caught sight of them.

"Oh, good heavens!" she cried, "Jen, I got to let you go, Angela just came in." She hung the phone up without bothering to say good-bye and ran over to hug Angela.

"Oh, my little girl! Let me see you," she said looking her granddaughter over. "As skinny as a rail, like always," she chided hugging Angela once again. "And who might this be?" she asked taking a few steps towards Jonathan.

"Grandma, this is Jonathan, the one I was telling you about. Jonathan, this is my grandmother, Jean."

"Jonathan." Jean smiled broadly as she gave him a warm hug, "It's nice to finally meet you. Angela has told us all about you."

"She has?" Jonathan said in surprise.

"Yes, she has. Every time we hear from her, all she talks about is you. You've made quite an impression on our little girl." Jean grinned, making Angela blush.

"I have?" It was now Jonathan's turn to feel self-conscious. He wondered what exactly Angela had told them. Obviously, it was good enough for her grandmother to greet him amicably.

"Have you two eaten?" Jean asked as she hurried back to the kitchen. Jonathan noticed that Angela didn't even bother telling her grandmother that they had eaten with Stephanie before coming over.

"Sure, maybe something small," Angela replied as she motioned Jonathan towards the kitchen table. No sooner had they sat down when they were given bowls filled with homemade soup and fresh baked bread.

"Thank you." Jonathan looked into his bowl, wishing he had eaten less at the restaurant. Angela had warned him that they would be fed, but he hadn't realised how much.

"Jonathan, how do you like being a teacher?" Jean asked.

"I like it a lot," he replied, taking small spoonfuls of soup, "It's a bit difficult to get used to, but it definitely is something I want to do for the rest of my life."

"When Angela told us she was seeing a teacher, we had visions of someone much older. I'm thankful to learn otherwise, but aren't there rules against teachers dating their students?"

"Not really," Jonathan replied, "It's not something that's generally accepted. Yet, on the same token, there is nothing that they can do about it if it does happen. So, we've decided to play it safe and keep our relationship under the radar for now."

"I see." Jean whistled softly as she sat across from them, "All I have to say is welcome to the family, Jonathan."

Jonathan was thankful that Angela's grandmother seemed normal compared to his aunt. He felt a bit more at ease until a tall, burly man came up the stairs. Looking up, Jonathan felt every ounce of his confidence evaporate at the sight of such a goliath of a man. Standing over six feet with a barrel chest and large muscular forearms, Angela's grandfather was in good shape for his age. He wiped his hands on a rag before walking over to them.

"Grandpa!" Angela leapt up from her chair to give him a hug.

Jonathan watched as the man's embrace enveloped Angela's petite form, and he had a fleeting fear that she would be crushed by those massive arms.

"You made it," he said with a grin, "and I see you have brought the young man you have been telling us about." He reached a hand twice the size of Jonathan's and introduced himself, "You must be Jonathan. My name's Stan."

"N-nice to meet you," Jonathan stammered as he stood up.

As he shook Stan's hand he was surprised at how gentle the man's grip was. Jonathan was tempted to grip a little tighter, but quickly reconsidered. Stan had sun-leather skin and short salt and pepper hair, but what drew Jonathan's attention were his piercing green eyes.

"So, Angela gets her beautiful eyes from you," he said, unconsciously. Everyone smiled at this, including Angela who was now blushing. He felt a small bead of sweat run down the back of his neck.

"I'm s-sorry," Jonathan stuttered, unable to hide his embarrassment.

Stan patted him on the shoulder. "Why don't we sit down and get to know each other for a bit?" Jonathan sat back down, and took a sip of tea to steady his nerves.

"I hear you're interested in teaching, and that you also have a degree in Journalism," Stan said as he poured a coffee for himself. "Have you made up your mind what you want to do once you finished your internship?"

"I think I'm going to teach," he replied, rubbing the back of his head "I do like to write, but I feel my passion right now is in teaching."

Stan nodded. "I'm glad you have options, it's always good to have multiple skills." He studied Jonathan as he took a seat at the kitchen table. "What do you believe in, Jonathan?" he asked, brushing nonexistent crumbs from the table.

"Now, Stan," Jean admonished, "you be nice. He's come to visit and get to know us, not be interrogated."

Stan ignored her, and waited patiently for Jonathan to answer.

"Well, I'm a Christian, of course, so I believe what any other Christian believes in." Jonathan swallowed hard under Stan's scrutiny, hoping his answer was good enough.

"Like what?" Stan said. He set his cup down and gave Jonathan his full attention.

Jonathan tugged at his collar as he detailed the basics of his belief from the Trinity, to salvation through Christ and faith, and how faith without works was dead and vice versa. He quoted many pieces of Scripture, from the Gospels to James, bringing in many different aspects of the Christian faith. As he spoke, Angela held his hand and smiled her encouragement. Stan didn't look away from him once, but listened carefully to Jonathan's every word. Whenever Jonathan slipped up and said something that was incorrect or misinterpreted, Stan was quick to correct him. Jean kept a watchful eye on her husband and acted as his moderator whenever he sounded too harsh, but for the most part remained silent. At the end of Jonathan's response, his palms were clammy, and he hoped no one noticed the damp patches under his arms.

Stan nodded, thoughtfully. He finished his coffee and refilled his cup. "Are you up to giving me a hand before you guys leave?"

Still recovering from Stan's catechising, Jonathan was caught off guard by the question. "With ... what?"

"I need an extra set of hands while I work on the tractor."

Before Jonathan had a chance to respond, Angela's grandmother cut in. "Now, you better take it easy on him, Stan. He doesn't look like he can handle as much hard labour as you."

Jonathan felt a sense of panic come over him as he looked from Jean to Stan. The older man just smiled and motioned for him to follow. Jonathan stood up, giving Angela a worried glance.

She gave him a hug, and whispered, "It will be fine; he's a big teddy bear once you get to know him."

Despite her reassurances, Jonathan was doubtful Stan would go easy on him. This was the man who had raised Angela; he would want to know everything about her boyfriend. He wiped his hands on his shirt and walked to where the older man waited in the mudroom.

He had to pick up his pace as he followed Stan to the barn, for one stride of the Stan's was Jonathan's two. They entered through the man door, and once Jonathan adjusted to the dim lighting, he looked around curiously. The front part of the barn had been set up as a workshop. A large yellow tractor with its hood tipped open was parked next to a work table where an assortment of tools and engine parts were neatly laid out. Stan walked over to the tractor, gave the engine a thoughtful perusal and picked up from where he had left off. Unsure of what he was expected to do, Jonathan waited by the door for instructions.

"Well, are you going to stand there all day? Pass me that blue wrench."

Jonathan hurried over, and after a quick search for what he hoped was the right tool, he handed it to him. They rapidly fell into a routine where Stan worked on the tractor and Jonathan handed him the tools and parts as needed. As they worked, they chatted about life. Stan was full of questions about Jonathan's family, faith and future goals, and was particularly interested in his views about marriage. Jonathan felt that the older man was warming up to him, and even though he didn't know much about mechanics, he enjoyed the time they spent working together. It was nearing seven when Angela came into the barn. The men didn't notice her as they worked on tightening some bolts.

"Jonathan, Grandpa are you two almost done?"

Both men jumped, hitting their heads on the hood.

"Sorry Angie, I guess we got carried away." Jonathan hesitated as Stan raised a quizzical eyebrow. "Oh, it's only a nickname I ...." he trailed off feeling uncomfortable under Stan's gaze.

"Grandma and I will get the table set while you two get cleaned up." She stepped back outside and closed the door behind her.

Stan grabbed a rag and wiped the majority of the grease off his hands. Jonathan watched him closely. From the moment they met, he had been working up the courage to ask the man the question that had been foremost on his mind for the past week. He cleared his throat.

"I have been meaning to ask you a question. I ...." Jonathan looked up, hoping to make eye contact, but Stan kept his back turned to him. This was it. Jonathan had to ask him. "I want to ask if I could have Angela's hand in marriage."

Jonathan saw Stan's back tense, and instinctively stepped back. Stan drew a deep breath and set the rag down. He leaned on the worktable and gazed through the window into the sky. He had heard many wonderful things about Jonathan over the past few months. Now that he had met him, he knew that this was the right man for his granddaughter and that he truly loved and respected her. He turned to place a hand on Jonathan's shoulder, and was not surprised to feel his slight trembling.

"Why don't you give me a week to think about it, and then we'll discuss it?"

Jonathan quickly nodded "Yes sir, I would be happy to help you fix your tractor again. I mean talk about it ... the thing that is ...," he floundered.

Stan smiled down at the young man. "Let's go inside and enjoy the meal our better halves have made for us."

With that, both of them walked back to the house in silence.

CHAPTER 5
Setsuko
Japan — 1984

Hitomi had been waiting nearly two hours for Daiki to get off the telephone and leave so she could go out. She had hoped to slip out earlier, but was surprised to find him still home. They hadn't shared anything over the winter break other than curt exchanges of 'hello' and 'thank you'. Every time she tried to speak with him, a dangerous look entered his eyes, silencing her. She didn't want to admit it, but she was afraid of him now, just as she had been during the first years of their marriage. Memories of those days came flooding back. She rubbed the scar on her shoulder as she recalled the last time he had been violent towards her, and the promise he had made that day.

He had struck her repeatedly in one of his explosive rages, when six-year-old Setsuko had run to her mother's aid. She had grasped his arm mid-swing, and had been inadvertently thrown against the wall hard enough to be knocked unconscious. In that moment Hitomi's maternal instincts kicked in. She struck Daiki, forcing him back as she defended their daughter. Cradling Setsuko in her arms, she swore that if he ever struck their child again, she would leave with her and nothing on earth would ever find them. Shaken and shocked by the enormity of his actions, of what he had done to a child — *his* child — Daiki had backed off, ashamed. He promised to never again hurt her, or their daughter.

To this day he had been true to his word; in return, she was a faithful and obedient wife. It was not completely by choice, but because their family status required it. It had only been recently that her heart had changed on the matter. She wasn't his footstool, but his helpmate, and it was her job to help him be the best he could be. She was proud of him and how hard he worked to support his family. Moreover, she was proud that he had grown to become a kinder, more temperate man. She could only hope that one day God would open his heart to His word.

Hitomi checked the time. It was almost ten, and if she didn't leave soon she was going to miss more than the service. She folded her hands and prayed that God would find a way for her to make it to church without experiencing an uncomfortable argument with Daiki. As she prayed, she heard the sound of a car pulling out of the driveway. A peek around the curtains confirmed that the Eldorado was gone.

"Thank you," she whispered, relieved and happy her prayer had been heard.

She called a taxi and collected her coat and bag. As she stepped out of the house, Setsuko suddenly appeared behind her.

"Where are you off to, Mother?" her daughter inquired, slipping on her own coat. "If you are heading into the city, can I join you?"

Hitomi wasn't too sure what to say. Should she tell her the truth? Should she disobey her husband and incur his wrath? Would she even believe her? Hitomi followed her into the taxi and gave the driver her destination. Setsuko raised an eyebrow at the unfamiliar address.

'Where are you going?'

"I'm off to visit an old friend," Hitomi replied, banishing any ideas of telling Setsuko the truth.

Hitomi was relieved that she didn't question her further; yet, she felt guilty that she had lied. The more she dwelt on it, the worse she felt. She took a few deep breaths and tried to gather the courage to speak, yet when she turned to Setsuko, Daiki's warning silenced her. Why was it so hard to share something so important? Didn't God promise to be there in difficult times? Wasn't He supposed to provide her with the courage she needed in order to speak?

She lowered her head to pray for guidance, and God's word spoke softly into her mind: *For whoever is ashamed of Me and My words in this adulterous and sinful generation, the Son of Man will also be ashamed of him when He comes in the glory of His Father with the holy angels.*

Why must it be so hard to do the right thing? Why was it so hard to follow the right path? She felt a twinge of pain knowing she wasn't acting like a true follower of Christ. She began to pray silently for the Lord to give her the words she needed to reach her daughter, and the strength to overcome her fear of her husband. After a few more moments of silence, she decided to take the chance.

"Setsuko-chan? I was wondering what you thought about ...." her voice trailed off when she noticed Setsuko wasn't paying attention. She followed her gaze to a large group of shoppers that were gathered at a small street market. "Setsuko-chan, are you even listening to me?"

Her daughter snapped out of her reverie and turned to her, "Mother, is it okay if I go talk to someone while you go off and do your own thing?" The words Hitomi had been about to say stuck in her throat and fear held her back once again. "Oh, sorry, Mother, I have to go. I'll meet you later at home, okay?"

Before Hitomi could stop her, Setsuko stepped out of the taxi, darted out amongst the shoppers and into the crowd. Hitomi sat staring after her, wondering why she hadn't said anything to make her stay. Ashamed of her cowardice, she asked the driver to continue on to their destination. She prayed she would have another chance to reach out to her daughter.

Setsuko made her way through the shoppers to where David was scanning the contents of a magazine rack. She stopped a short distance from him, her heart racing in reaction to this unexpected encounter. Captivated by his gorgeousness, she couldn't help but stare. So intent was she on the young man, she failed to notice a boy on a bike headed her way until she stepped into his path. With a shout, the boy cranked the handlebars sharply to the right, narrowly missing her. He slammed into a nearby table, knocking it over and spilling its contents onto the street. Setsuko quickly helped the boy up and tried to comfort him as the table's owner berated them. Embarrassed by their clumsiness and the attention they were drawing, Setsuko and the boy apologised profusely and knelt down to gather the scattered merchandise.

"Are you okay, Setsuko-san?"

Setsuko froze and she swore her heart stopped. She kept her eyes downcast to hide her mortification. She slowly began to rise, and hesitated as David knelt next to her and helped pick up the items.

With the extra pair of hands they had the table was righted and restocked in short order. Setsuko watched in amazement as he spoke with the vendor and smoothed things over by offering to buy some of his merchandise. The vendor started to suggest some items, when he noticed something that had held Setsuko's attention as she was returning it to the table. He motioned for David to follow him. When he returned, Setsuko looked up in time to catch him tucking a small box into a pocket.

"What do you have planned for today?" he asked.

"Nothing in particular. I do have some studying later on, but that can wait."

"Do you think you would enjoy going to a small get-together with a few of my friends tonight?"

She considered the question. It had been a long time since she had gone out with a boy. Her last dating experience had ended on an awkward note when her father had caught them making out; her father had taken the boy aside for a private talk, after which the lad never came near her again. It frustrated her that most boys were too intimidated by her father to ask her out, but she was older now, and here was an opportunity to start anew. This was not a boy, but a young man who excited her and made her feel amazing every time he looked at her.

She took a small notebook from her purse, wrote her address down on a leaf and gave it to him with instructions to pick her up around six. He flashed her a wide grin and offered to walk her to wherever she was headed. As much as she wanted to be with him, she declined. On the long walk home, there was a skip to her step and she couldn't contain her excitement.

Hitomi was humiliated by her cowardice. Whenever she thought of her inability to tell Setsuko the truth behind her outing, her mouth went dry. Fear — no, terror had silenced her, and she didn't know why.

She lightly rubbed her knees and looked about the small office as she sat quietly waiting for the pastor. The office had a small wooden desk, and the walls were adorned with a collection of photographs. She was able to place the subjects of some of the pictures, but many were of faces and places she had never seen or visited before. In one corner of the room stood a large filing cabinet with a small map of the world taped to the side of it. There were two more chairs next to her, and next to them was a small end table with a beautiful ornate dragon and phoenix tea service set on it.

As she scanned the room, her gaze kept returning to one picture. It was of her pastor and his wife standing with an older Caucasian man. They were all smiling happily at the camera, but the smile on this one man stood out from all of the others. There was nothing particularly exceptional about him, but the light of the Spirit emanated from him. The door next to her creaked open, making her jump. She quickly regained her composure as the pastor entered the room, and she stood up to greet him with a respectful bow. He gave her a shallow bow of greeting in return before he walked around the desk and sat down.

Hikaru Ichinose had been the Bokushi-sensei of her church for almost a year before she had started attending. They had met by chance at a market near the church, and what he had said during their brief exchange had piqued her interest in learning more about her Lord and Saviour. He was young, but his eyes belonged to someone with experience beyond his years. He was a short, thin man whose preaching was a testament to his passion, and when he spoke, he captured and held the attention of the entire congregation. He had a spiritual strength about him that did not come solely from his own being, but from his faith in the Lord. It was the strength and courage that Hikaru-Bokushi possessed that she desired most: the ability to speak the words that transformed men's hearts and lead them to follow the Lord.

"How are you doing, Hitomi-san?"

"Not bad." She quickly averted her eyes. "No, I guess that's not entirely true."

"What seems to be bothering you?"

"I can't seem to find the strength to be a good witness." She closed her eyes to fight back the tears before continuing. "Today I had the chance to share with my daughter, but before I was able to, fear stopped me." She hid her face as the tears began to fall.

Pastor Hikaru got up from his desk and knelt beside her, taking her hand in his.

"Hitomi-san, it's a long process before someone can find the strength to share what they believe. This isn't Canada or the West where people share their faith and it is culturally acceptable. The one weakness our people have is that we keep our beliefs to ourselves and do not feel comfortable sharing them with anyone else. The Enemy attacks us and tries to either prevent or discourage us from doing what is commanded."

She raised her head and faced him. He had look of genuine love and concern that gave her a surge of hope.

"Pray with me and we will ask the Lord to give you the courage and strength that is needed, as well as the words needed to reach your daughter's heart."

He continued to hold her hand as they prayed, and gave her a warm hug and words of encouragement before she left. As she made her way home, she felt a new lightness and a comforting warmth that spread throughout her being. She couldn't wait to speak to her daughter.

Setsuko checked her reflection in the mirror. The red cocktail dress hugged her body and accentuated her curves. Pleased, she fussed over her hair that refused to cooperate with the curling iron. After a few more minutes, she finally achieved the style she was after. With a satisfied sigh, she touched up her lashes with mascara and applied red shimmer gloss to her lips. She studied her reflection once more, and smiled.

"I hope he likes what he sees."

The sound of a car pulling into the driveway filled her with nervous anticipation. She grabbed a small red purse and slipped on a pair of red sequinned high heels before heading out. Her eyes widened when she saw the fully-loaded blue Supra that idled in the driveway. David was leaning languidly against the fender, casually jingling his keys. When he saw her, his eyes widened involuntarily. He looked her up and down with a look of lust and approval as he stepped over to the passenger door and opened it for her.

"Your chariot awaits, m'lady."

"Where did you get this car?"

"I borrowed it from a friend," he said nonchalantly.

Once they were in the car, they peeled out of the driveway. David weaved in and out of traffic with the precision and confidence of an Indy driver, making it obvious that he was familiar with high performance vehicles. At first Setsuko was apprehensive, but after a few minutes, she started to feel thrilled. At one point, he took a corner too quickly and nearly sideswiped another vehicle, causing her to reflexively grip the dash.

"Whoa, that was a little too close."

The smile on his face faded slightly, and he slowed down for the final leg of the drive.

They pulled up on front of an apartment building. Setsuko felt a little nervous as she realised that they were in one of the city's more seedy neighbourhoods. The melodic, robotic rhythms of the Yellow Magic Orchestra blared through an open window from unseen speakers. Girls in heels and miniskirts danced and mingled in small groups and chatted gaily amongst themselves, looking up often to laugh coquettishly in response to the cat calls and whistles that were sent their way by the men who were smoking and drinking on the balconies. David stepped out of the car and opened her door for her, but she held back, unwilling to leave the safety of the car.

"Are you okay?" he asked. She smiled uncertainly. "Don't worry, they are good friends of mine, and I would never take you somewhere that would be dangerous."

He took her hand as she stepped out of the car. Some of the men who were harassing the women turned their full attention to her.

"Hey David, why don't you bring that cutie over to my place tonight?"

Setsuko self-consciously tugged her skirt down. She dare not look in their direction, knowing it would only make her blush more. David led her up a flight of stairs to the second level and followed the music to the last apartment. He pounded his fist on the door in order to be heard above the music. After a brief wait, the door was opened by a short, muscular young man whose arms and wrists were covered in intricate wabori tattoos. He had two missing teeth and was missing the top of his left ear. Without hesitation, he stepped outside to give David a hug. He started to ask him something, but stopped when he saw Setsuko. Clearly impressed, his eyes glowing with interest, he gave her a frank appraisal that left her feeling violated.

"Nice work, my friend. She is definitely a ten."

"Setsuko, this is my friend, Tetsuya. We go way back."

She shook his hand and wrapped her arms around herself, trying to hide what cleavage was showing. Tetsuya ushered the two of them into the crowded, dimly lit apartment. The air reeked of alcohol and was hazy with cigarette smoke, which made it difficult for Setsuko to breathe. There wasn't much furniture. Those who weren't sitting were forced to stand along the walls or gather in small clusters wherever they could. Any remaining free surfaces were occupied by overflowing ashtrays, and beer bottles and cans in various levels of fullness. For the most part, the men were dressed in styles ranging from khakis, casual blazers over polo shirts, and L.L. Bean Duck shoes, to expensive Levi jeans, leather jackets over t-shirts, and Nike trainers. The girls were all dressed in mini-skirts and skimpy tops that showed more skin than they covered.

The glares she was receiving from some of the women and the leers the men were sending her way made Setsuko tug at her skirt's hem, even when it wasn't riding up. What made her even more uncomfortable was how much older the guests were; most of them appeared to be in their mid to late twenties. David took her to the kitchen where he was given two drinks. He offered one to her. She politely declined, which elicited chuckles from those in the room. Setsuko did her best to keep her eyes on David and Tetsuya without being too obvious. The group of young men they were with talked about work and the girls they had been with, as well as some of the scrapes they had gotten into. It was in one of these fights that Tetsuya lost his teeth and the top of his ear. He proudly pointed these things out as if they were badges of honour.

From what she was able to ascertain, Tetsuya belonged to a gang that owned most of the apartments in the area. Their rivals were in another nearby Ward and, for the most part, they kept out of each other's territory.

She spun around as a hand groped her buttocks, and she came face to face with a tall, muscular man with a long scar across his right cheek. Before she could react, a young woman came up and slapped him and began to yell at him and call him horrid names. Shocked, Setsuko began to laugh, which earned her a sharp look from the infuriated woman.

"As for you!" she seethed, "Don't get any ideas. Just because you are a hot young thing doesn't mean you can get any guy you want."

Setsuko couldn't believe the woman's audacity. She had done nothing to encourage the man's licentious behaviour; to have someone insinuate that she had invited the man to grope her was the last straw. She tugged on David's sleeve in an attempt to get his attention.

"David."

He ignored her and continued to talk to Tetsuya, so she grabbed his arm and forced him to face her.

"David, I want to go home!"

"Setsuko, is that you?" a voice squealed from directly behind her.

Setsuko turned sharply. Standing in the kitchen doorway stood a short, slim young girl. At first glance she didn't recognize her, but when she got a better look, a name came to mind.

"Kyo!"

The young girl unexpectedly wrapped her arms around Setsuko, causing Setsuko to stumble back. "I can't believe you're here. Tetsuya, usually never lets me invite anyone, and I never expected someone like you to be here." Kyo's gaze singled out David, who waved. "She must have come with you then, David."

"Yeah, she is my date for tonight." His smile broadened as he placed an arm around Setsuko's waist. Setsuko pushed his hand away and stood beside Kyo.

"Maybe you can show me a good time. It seems that David only brought me here to show me off."

"Now, now David, that's no way to treat a girl of Setsuko's class," Kyo admonished. "If you don't mind I would like to borrow her for a bit?"

David opened his mouth to protest, but was too late. Kyo disappeared, taking Setsuko with her. The two girls pushed their way through the crowd to a room in the back of the apartment. Closing the door behind them, Kyo ran across the room and jumped onto the bed where two girls were playing a board game. The girls yelled at her for jostling the board and displacing the pieces.

Kyo introduced Setsuko to Nami, who appeared to be about her age, and Miya, who was older. The girls gave her friendly smiles and invited her to join them. Setsuko hesitated, then decided that hanging out with them promised to be more interesting than being put on display as David's trophy date in a room full of strangers.

"Is Miya your sister?"

"No," Kyo said with a giggle "Well, maybe not in the way you were thinking. She is my brother's fiancée."

"Brother?"

"Tetsuya."

Setsuko gave Miya an odd look, wondering how someone so beautiful could consider Tetsuya attractive.

For the next hour the girls played the game and talked. As they played, they talked about boys and school. Setsuko hadn't had so much fun in years. Over the past year, Akari had been digging for dirt on her, which kept Setsuko constantly on guard and unable to fully relax with others. Unlike Akari, Kyo and her friends didn't have any ulterior motives. It felt more like the times she had with Natsuki, who seemed to be the only true friend she had, and with these three, she felt she could be open and speak her mind without fear of reprisal. As she opened up, she felt as if a great weight had been lifted off her shoulders.

At some point during their talk, Miya brought them something to drink. Kyo complained that there was no alcohol, but a stern look from Miya silenced her. After the death of Kyo's parents, Miya, whose own mother had died giving her life, had become her self-appointed guardian and watched over her whenever her brother was gone, which was often. As for Tetsuya, he had turned to the local gang and, in them, found the leadership he had lost with his parents. Miya understood his actions, for her father had died shortly after she had moved out on her own. Theirs was a shared pain that brought Miya, Kyo and Tetsuya together. When it came time for her to tell them about herself, Setsuko explained how her father was a corporate chair of many companies, and her mother was a homemaker. Where the others were impressed by her father's status, Kyo was more interested in her mother, and commented on how Hitomi sounded like her own mother.

When Miya went to refresh their drinks, Setsuko checked the time to discover, with a sense of panic, that the evening had slipped by and she had only an hour before her curfew. She said goodnight to her friends and went to find David. After a frantic search, she finally found him out on the balcony, drinking with Tetsuya and their friends.

David gave a big grin when he saw her. He sauntered over and exclaimed, "There you are! Where have you been?"

Before Setsuko had a chance to respond, David pulled her close and kissed her soundly on the mouth. The mixture of alcohol and cigarettes made her gag, and she pushed him away.

"What's your problem, babe, you don't like being kissed?" David asked, miffed.

"Not if your mouth tastes like a sewer!" she spat back.

David's friends howled in laughter while David grabbed her arm and roughly pulled her to the side. "We are supposed to be having a good time," he said through gritted teeth.

"Well, I'm not! I want to go home."

Setsuko tried to pull free. David smiled at his friends and pulled her close while they cheered him on. Setsuko instinctively fell back on the defensive moves that he father had taught her. The next thing David knew he was flat on his back, dizzily looking at the night sky. Setsuko stormed out of the apartment, ignoring the jeers of the men around her. She threw on her coat and stalked off in the direction she thought led home. Such was her rage, she did not notice the chill in the air while she strode down the street. She was so lost in her thoughts and self-recrimination that she didn't hear the car that was driving slowly beside her.

"Get in!" David commanded.

Setsuko pulled her coat closer around herself and walked faster. David parked, slammed the door and started to follow her. Setsuko stopped and swung around to face him, annoyed.

"You ignore me the whole night, and you didn't even come to see if I was all right. When I did find you, you treat me like a commoner. Don't you know who my father is?"

David brushed her cheek with his thumb. "You are a prissy thing, aren't you?" he said with an unrepentant grin.

Setsuko wanted to pull away, but despite her anger something made her want to stay. Was it the way his look made her melt? Or how his touch made her warm inside? She didn't know. All she knew was she suddenly wanted this moment to last forever. She wanted to feel his gentle caress.

"How about I make it up to you?" David asked gently, drawing her close. "Would you like to do something this weekend?"

She thought for a moment. A part of her still wanted to leave, but a stronger part wanted to give in. Looking up at him, she met that intense gaze that made her melt.

"Do you promise?" Setsuko asked, leaning against him.

Laughing, David planted a gentle kiss on her lips. "I wouldn't have it any other way."

CHAPTER 6
Japan — January 1985

The winter holidays had come and gone, and David was nowhere to be found. He had cancelled their plans three times, and then had completely disappeared, leaving Setsuko wondering if he had been leading her on. Her mind kept playing different scenarios that did nothing to ease her fears: Could he have just up and left? Was he seeing someone else? Was she not hot enough? She could have played the guessing game all morning, but she was running late for school, and couldn't afford being late the first day back. With a growl of frustration, she grabbed her bag and dashed out of her room.

"Setsuko-chan, why are you so late?" Hitomi asked as she came out of the kitchen.

"Sorry, Mother, I slept in," she said as she slipped on her boots and jacket.

"Setsuko-chan, your lunch," Hitomi called after her.

Setsuko ran back and snagged the bag from her mother, "Sorry, I really got to go." Hitomi waved her out the door, scooped her own bag as she locked up after them. Suzaku waited patiently, the car already running.

"Hitomi-sama." He bowed respectably.

"That's fine, Suzaku-san." She shook her head, smiling. "When Daiki's not around you don't need to be so formal."

"I'm sorry, Hitomi-sama." He bowed again, brow furrowed. "But, it is my duty, and I do it out of respect for you and your husband."

"And Setsuko?" she asked.

With a slight clench of his jaw he tried to hide his annoyance. "Setsuko-ojousama, as well," he murmured.

"She's been bugging you again, hasn't she?" Again, Suzaku refrained from incriminating the girl, but she could tell by his rigid stance that she was right.

"I will talk with her again," she promised. "Now, shall we be off?"

Bowing once more, Suzaku opened the door for her and helped her in.

"To Fukui-kacho's office?"

"Yes, as always, Suzaku-san, thank you."

Every second Wednesday, Hitomi would go and visit her husband at work. They would enjoy her homemade lunches whenever she came to see him; this time he was taking her out. It was nice to have him dote on her. It wasn't often that he showed his affection towards her, but when he did she was reminded that he still loved her.

"Has Daiki given you time to go to church lately?" she asked, knowing the answer.

"No, Hitomi-sama, he keeps me busy doing work for him all the time now."

Hitomi was powerless to help. If she asked Daiki to give Suzaku Sundays off, he would realise that it was the boy who had introduced her to Christianity, which would make things difficult for him. She cared about Suzaku, and there was no way she would make him a target for Daiki's wrath. It was better that Daiki took his anger out on her.

"I will pray that God makes it possible for you to go."

"Thank you. I appreciate it, Hitomi-sama."

Suzaku took the expressway heading towards central Tokyo. They travelled in silence. Hitomi hoped that their lunch date meant that Daiki was no longer angry over her conversion. She longed for reconciliation and a chance to restore their relationship. Her thoughts turned to Setsuko. She needed to reach her daughter and show her how much Jesus could change her heart and make her life more meaningful. She wanted her daughter to understand that she needed Jesus like a skydiver needed a parachute.

Just then, God reminded her of Proverbs 18:10: *The name of the Lord is a strong tower; the righteous run to it and are safe.*

If only her Setsuko would find sanctuary in the saving grace of God.

"Hitomi-sama, have you had an opportunity to read your Scriptures lately?" Suzaku broke the silence.

"Whenever I can." Hitomi sounded a little downcast in her response. "I am always afraid that Daiki would see me reading and push me further away. Also, I am unsure how I am going to reveal my faith to my daughter. What it comes down to is I am afraid to share my faith."

"Hikaru-Bokushi has told me that sometimes the hardest people to share with are the people closest to you. When I first spoke to you about Christ, I was terrified that you would tell Fukui-kacho and he would cast me out. That fear nearly paralysed me from speaking and sharing God's word with you. I spent much time praying with Hikaru-Bokushi for an opportunity to speak with you. Finally God gave me an opportunity to show His law and leading into His salvation through Christ."

"I'm thankful that you were faithful, and that God used you to bring me to Him. I just pray that He draws the rest of my family to Him and is able to use me."

"I will continue to keep your family in my prayers."

"Thank you," Hitomi said, and they spent the rest of their drive in companionable silence.

Hitomi waited patiently for Daiki to arrive. He had a private table for the two of them at the back of a high-end restaurant. The lights were dimmed for a romantic setting, with luxurious furnishings, fine china and elegant silverware. Many of the tables had couples enjoying lunch, and she felt a little awkward sitting by herself. The waiter had already refilled her water three times, and she was perturbed by her husband's tardiness.

"Shall I have something brought out to you while you wait, Fukui-sama?" the waiter asked as he filled her glass once again.

"No, thank you. Has my husband called to give any indication why he has been delayed?"

"I'm sorry, we have not. I am sure Fukui-kacho is in a meeting. He should be along soon."

"I hope so, thank you," Hitomi said, taking another sip of her water. A moment later, she looked towards the door and saw her husband. Relieved, she stood to greet him, and gave a small bow as he reached the table.

"I almost thought you forgot about me," Hitomi said as they sat down. She regarded him through her lashes. Daiki had a pleased grin on his face.

"I had to iron out the details of a deal that will secure all of our futures," he said without looking at her.

"Oh, and what deal would this be?" Hitomi asked, her curiosity piqued.

"I have arranged for our daughter to be married to the son of a business partner. It will secure her position and maintain this family's status and legacy for generations."

Hitomi's throat tightened and her heart raced. After a moment, she was finally able to speak in a tight voice. "Arranged marriage, are you sure about this? I thought we were allowing her to choose her own future and I thought we would discuss this. Most people nowadays marry for love, not for a business proposal."

Daiki lowered his menu and narrowed his gaze. Anger coloured his cheeks and enmity his eyes.

"Your father chose me and look at the life I've given you." Hitomi shrank back from his glare. "Besides, this is *my* daughter's future we are talking about. She's not some common village girl. She is meant for something greater."

"Is this boy someone whom she can grow to love, who will treat her with tenderness and whom she can partner with? Will she be as happy with him as I am with you?"

Hitomi hoped that she was able to diffuse the rage that was growing inside of Daiki. She loved her daughter and wanted the absolute best for her, and she didn't think that an arranged marriage was what Setsuko wanted. Hitomi knew that her daughter would feel as trapped as she had, with no choices of her own.

"We all must do what is needed for the wellbeing of our family. Setsuko will learn to respect this man, and may one day come to love him as you say you love me."

He could see that his comment hurt his wife. Feeling a little guilty, he ordered Hitomi's favourite meal and decided to send her favourite flowers when he returned to the office. They ate in relative silence, while Hitomi wrestled with how she was going to prepare Setsuko for the last thing she wanted in life.

Setsuko was leaving her math class when she spotted David leaning casually against the opposite wall. His eyes lit up when saw her, and her heart skipped a beat. As she closed the distance between them, she became furious.

"Where were you? Where have you been?"

David shrugged a shoulder, "Sorry, babe, I've been around. My dad has business throughout Japan and that means I'm sometimes gone."

He stroked her hair back and cupped her cheek. Setsuko pushed his hand aside and glared at him. "You could have at least called, I deserve that much."

She suddenly became aware that the other students were staring at them, no doubt wondering what a Western boy was doing there. She clutched her books and stepped back.

"What are you doing here anyway? How did no one see you? You can't just wander around the school halls."

David took her hand and guided her to a stairwell that lead outside the school. When he opened the door, she pulled her hand free. "What are you doing?"

David flashed one of his charming smiles and looked into her eyes, making her feel flush.

"It's not like we can have fun here, plus I have a date to make up, don't I?"

"Wh — what, now?" Setsuko asked in surprise.

"Why not?"

"I've got class. I can't leave."

David gently stopped her and brushed the hair from her face. Leaning forward, he gazed at her, eyes dark and warm, and gently placed a kiss on her lips. The kiss was so gentle that it caused Setsuko to catch her breath.

"Do you really want to stay here? I thought you would like to have fun," he said in a rich, silky voice.

Setsuko hesitated for a moment, but still feeling the heat from his lips, she threw caution to the wind. They quietly slunk through the courtyard and jumped into his vehicle.

Chilled by the winter air, Setsuko's teeth chattered. "I should have grabbed my coat before leaving."

David put his arm around her and drew her to him. He gave her a deep kiss that heated her entire body. "Don't worry, I will keep you safe and warm."

David put the car into gear, and sped off. Setsuko was caught up in the thrill and excitement of the moment. The car's speed kept climbing as David weaved in and out of traffic, narrowly missing cars. Setsuko's heart pounded with a mixture of fear and exhilaration. She wondered what dangerous and exciting things he had planned for her. As they pulled into a cinema parking lot, she scanned the signs above the entrance, disappointed. "Is this it?"

"What, you don't like movies?"

"I thought that you would take me somewhere a little secluded. This feels kind of ... lame." She scrunched her nose in distaste. David gave her a wry smile and winked at her.

"Really, being in the back of a dark, quiet, nearly empty theatre with me isn't exciting enough for you?" He placed a hand on her knee. Setsuko started to tremble under his touch, and she felt an unreasonable desire to do whatever he wanted.

"I guess it would."

Throughout the movie, David was a gentleman. He made sure she wasn't too cold and had whatever she wanted from the snack bar. He wasn't all over her, but still made sure that he held her, whispered sweet words in her ears, or found a reason to brush his hand against hers. Occasionally he would tip her chin towards him, stroke her cheek and give her a soft promising kiss. The whole time she was left breathless and unable to concentrate. By the time the movie had ended she couldn't remember what the story was about. When they left the cinema, David took her across the street to a restaurant where they enjoyed a late lunch.

After their meal, Setsuko checked the time, and exclaimed in alarm, "I've got to get home!"

David eased himself out of the booth and cupped her cheek and kissed her. "Don't worry, babe, you'll be home before anyone misses you," he assured her.

After he paid the bill, they returned to his car. When they reached her house, he kissed her goodbye. Setsuko slipped inside, hoping that no one noticed. As she closed the door quietly behind her, she almost jumped out of her skin when she saw Hitomi from the corner of her eye.

"Setsuko-chan, where on earth did you go?"

"I was at school and I got ride from a friend."

"A friend? Does a friend take liberties with my daughter and kiss her?"

Setsuko went crimson as she realised that her mother had seen them. She snatched her bag, slung it over her shoulder and tried to push her way past her mother. Hitomi grabbed her arm and looked her straight in the eye.

"Who is he, and what are you doing with him?"

"He's no one, Mother. Like I said, he's just a friend. Now can you leave me alone?" Setsuko tore her arm free from Hitomi's grasp, and stomped towards her room.

"Setsuko-chan," Hitomi called after her, "the school called and informed me that you had left this morning. I suggest you think about how you respond to me and how you and I can explain the call to your father."

Setsuko stopped in her tracks and paled. Turning around, she went back to her mother and bowed. "I'm sorry, Mother, I won't do it again. I will be sure to make up my studies, and I will never skip class again."

Hitomi knew she was being manipulated, but with Daiki's news foremost in her mind, she knew this wasn't the time to address it. Now she needed to deal with the complication of her daughter falling in love with someone not of her father's choosing. She watched her daughter walk away, and was at a loss of how she would inform Setsuko of her upcoming marriage.

CHAPTER 7
Angela
Calgary — 1983

Jonathan had been staring at his breakfast for the past five minutes as he tried to think a way to prove to Angela's grandfather that his heart was in the right place. A knock on the table startled him, causing him to drop his fork. He met Lang's gaze, and realised that the other had been speaking. "Sorry, my mind has been somewhere else this morning."

"Apparently" the older man growled. "You have been out of it for the last few days, my boy, and if you don't get your head back into the game soon, I cannot give you a good evaluation. You are so close to finishing your internship, and once you are done you will have the freedom to apply at for any job, whether that be journalism or teaching. So, I need you to start paying attention. Besides, what could be bothering you so much, anyway?"

Jonathan had drifted again, lost in his own thoughts, and was shocked when Lang slammed his hand on the table, drawing the attention of those around them.

"You know what? If you wish to throw away your hard-earned schooling and waste your time as an intern, that's up to you, but I think I have had about enough." Lang stood up to leave just as Jonathan spoke.

"I want Angela's hand in marriage, but I can't seem to get the okay from her grandfather."

Lang studied him carefully before sitting down again. "Well, that explains everything. Why didn't you say something earlier?"

"I've always had someone digging me out of a fix when I was growing up. There was always someone there to help me, or people took pity on me because of my parents' death. Just for once, I would like to do something on my own, without someone having to step in and help."

Both men sat there for a time in quiet contemplation. "What have you done to prove your good intentions?" Lang asked.

"That's the problem, I have been going over to her grand-parent's place for the last few weekends, but I haven't made any headway."

Lang rubbed his chin thoughtfully. "Have you asked him what he expects of you?"

"Yes, but he only tells me to return in a week and he will think about it."

"So, you go over weekend after weekend to ask him the same question?" he asked, confused.

"No, not exactly. Every time I go over he has some chores for me to help with. He usually has me working until late at night and when I ask anything, he says that we have too much work to do for me to waste time asking pointless questions."

"Maybe he just wants to use you for slave labour and has no intention of giving you Angela's hand."

"I am beginning to wonder that myself, but as we work he has no problem questioning me." Jonathan rubbed his face with his hands. "I don't get it. He seems interested in me enough to interrogate me about my life and faith, but doesn't seem to want to give me an answer to my question."

"Don't give up, I think you may be on to something."

"What? If you know something let me know. I am almost at my wit's end with this whole thing."

Lifting his cup to his lips, Lang hid a small smile. "Just a hunch. Now, finish your breakfast. We have a class in two hours."

The rest of the day was spent in lectures, and grading assignments. The last lecture of the day was with Angela's class. Jonathan smiled whenever their eyes met, but he made sure he focussed less on her and more on assisting the professor.

Angela did her best to pay attention to the lecture, but her gaze invariably came to rest on Jonathan. She was perplexed by his evasiveness over the past few months. It wasn't that he refused to spend time with her, but lately he seemed to disappear on Saturdays and would appear exhausted when she saw him at church on Sundays. Whenever she brought up the subject, he always had an excuse or would sidestep the question. It was beginning to worry her. She knew full well that there were many eligible young women that were more beautiful than she was. When she felt a hand squeeze hers, she turned her head and caught Stephanie smiling at her.

"What?"

"Nothing, I just think it is cute the way you two look at each other."

Angela smiled back, but it was half-hearted. Stephanie started to ask what was up, but Angela quickly shook her head, mouthing, 'Later'.

Still struggling to focus on the lecture, her mind went over the many different possible explanations for Jonathan's erratic behaviour. Nothing that came to mind soothed her concerns, but brought on other, more worrisome possibilities. Maybe he is seeing Stephanie on the side. Angela shook her head, knowing she couldn't let her thoughts continue in that direction. She closed her eyes and began to pray that the Lord would clear her thoughts and give her peace.

Class ended with another reading assignment. Hanging back, Angela explained to Stephanie that she was worried about Jonathan. When her friend pressed her for more details, Angela got flustered and asked if she could have some time to herself.

Knowing that pushing Angela would get her nowhere, Stephanie reluctantly said goodbye and disappeared down the hall.

After what felt like an eternity to Angela, Jonathan finally left the classroom and walked over to give her a hug. Angela pulled away and looked up at him to ask the question that was nagging at her.

"What's happening?"

"What do you mean?"

"I mean what's happening between us?"

Jonathan rubbed the back of his head. Confused, he furrowed his brow, trying to figure out what she meant.

"I don't understand, I thought things were going great. I know that we haven't had as much time with each other as you wanted but—" Angela placed a silencing finger on his lips.

"You seem so far away at times. You also have been spending a lot of your Saturdays somewhere else, and you don't feel it's important to share with me."

He swallowed hard as he looked into to her eyes. He didn't realise that his recent absences caused her so much distress. Her imploring eyes searched his, and he felt his resolve begin to slip away. He loved her, and didn't like seeing her this upset. There had to be some way he could explain what he had been up to without giving away his secret.

"I have been spending a lot of time on the farm with your grandfather. He wants to get to know me better." It was the truth, and he hoped it was enough to allay her fears. Still staring into his eyes, it felt like she was searching for a hint of deceit. For a moment he was starting to wonder if he was going to have to tell her the whole truth.

"From the way you look most Sundays, it's obvious he has been keeping you busy with the chores."

He laughed nervously. "Well, to make it up to you, how about we go out for supper tonight? I'll come over and pick you up when I'm done work."

She smiled. "That would be great, I will see if Stephanie can chaperone us."

Angela watched him walk back to his office. She felt a little more relieved, but she had a sense he wasn't being fully honest with her. She turned and headed for the parking lot. She stopped in her tracks when she caught the sight of Stephanie trying to make herself look inconspicuous at a bulletin board.

"Are you planning to take Eavesdropping 101 as an elective?" Anger reverberated in her voice, causing Stephanie to freeze on the spot.

"Sorry," Stephanie replied, "I wasn't trying to pry, I was worried, nothing more."

"Worried?"

"Yes." Stephanie looked down the hall where Jonathan had disappeared. "You know that he wasn't being completely straight with you, right?"

Angela sighed. "I was hoping that it was just me." She wrapped her arms around herself. "What's wrong with me?" she asked. "Do I have some a sign on my back that says 'sucker'?"

Stephanie came up and embraced her friend. "You can't think like that. I am pretty sure he loves you, but he definitely is hiding something, and we need to find out what. I have a plan, why don't we stake out his place this Saturday and find out what he is really up to?"

Angela looked at her friend. "I don't know. Do you really think what he is hiding is that bad? Maybe it's like he said, all he is doing is hanging out with my grandfather."

"Have you asked your grandparents?"

Taking a moment to think, she couldn't recall in any of the recent conversations any mention of Jonathan visiting the farm. Then again, it was her grandmother she usually talked to, and maybe she hadn't said anything because she thought Angela already knew. But then, why hadn't it at least come up in conversation?

"Look, all we have to do is see if he really is going to your grandparents' place, and if he has been, then what do you have to worry about?"

Angela slowly nodded, still unsure if this was the right thing to do, yet needing to know what it was that Jonathan was hiding.

The atmosphere of meal they shared was strained. Angela wanted to ask why Jonathan felt he had to hide things from her; Stephanie was finding it hard not to ask him straight out. She made a few attempts trying to steer the conversation towards what he was up to at the farm, but Angela silenced her with a swift kick to the shin. Jonathan was beginning to feel a little uncomfortable with Stephanie's allusions to his work on the farm. The realisation that she might be catching on to what he was doing made him uneasy. He decided to give Angela a hint of what he was up to in hopes it would satisfy her curiosity and buy him more time.

After dinner, he took her aside and explained that he was planning a surprise for her, and that her grandfather was helping him. Intrigued, Angela asked if it had anything to do with her upcoming birthday, which gave him the perfect excuse. He decided to go along with it. She seemed happy with the explanation, which put him at ease, but he was worried that Stephanie might keep digging. As they left the restaurant, he hoped that Angela would be able to dissuade her friend from pursuing the matter.

Jonathan had to return to the office to get material for next week's classes, so Angela rode home with Stephanie. They barely said a word for most of the drive. Stephanie began to fidget, like she always did when she had something on her mind.

Angela sighed in frustration. "Just say it, already."

Stephanie couldn't hide her sly smile "Did you get it out of him?"

Angela felt her anger get the better of her. "Look," she said a little too forcefully, turning her full attention on her friend, "I don't want you sticking your nose where it doesn't belong. He said he was doing something for my birthday, nothing more. Now if you would please excuse me, I think we are done talking."

Stephanie scrunched her nose, bemused. "Don't you think it's odd that he has spent the last few weeks on the farm preparing for this surprise? Aren't you at least a little curious to see what he has been up to?"

Angela closed her eyes, wishing she could shut out her friend's voice. Stephanie was far too meddlesome, and her desire to dig into people's personal lives got her into trouble more often than not. Yet, that didn't seem to deter her. It seemed like a way for her to deal with the turmoil of her parent's divorce and their constant fights. Stephanie flashed her friend an impish smile, but Angela refused to let her gain any ground. She wanted to give Jonathan the benefit of the doubt, even if, deep down inside, she had her own concerns about what he was really up to.

A few more weeks passed with Jonathan spending his Saturdays at the farm. The anticipation was beginning to drive Angela crazy. With Stephanie's constant prodding to go spy on Jonathan, it was almost too much for her. She trusted Jonathan and was satisfied when her grandmother validated everything that he had told her, except for the birthday part. When she asked what time she needed to arrive for her birthday surprise, her grandmother was unaware of any plans and stated that all they had planned for was to come into town and take her out for a birthday meal. Her grandmother hated surprises, even when they weren't for her, so if it wasn't something for her birthday, than what was it? It was bugging her that he was lying, but when she confronted him again, he stuck to his story.

"What's up with you?" Steph asked, looking up from their studies.

Angela hadn't realised she was biting her nails until that moment. She picked up some notes and began to read them aloud. Stephanie snatched the papers away and placed them beside her books.

"You're not going to read another word until you tell me what's bothering you."

Angela wrinkled her nose in frustration. "I don't get why Jonathan can't tell me what's going on. My grandmother doesn't know a thing about a birthday surprise. I have this funny feeling my grandfather knows what is going on, but he refuses to tell me anything. I don't know why it's bothering me. It's not like Jonathan's messing around, but I can't shake the thought that he is lying to me. My grandparents always taught me the importance of being truthful. Why can't he open up to me?"

Stephanie felt a little bit guilty. She knew how much Jonathan loved Angela, but in a small way she wished he had noticed her instead. She had felt thrilled the first time he had touched her. His scent filled her senses, and sometimes all she wanted was to be with him. She knew what she felt wasn't right; Jonathan had chosen Angela, not her. But, why hadn't he pursued her when she was prettier than Angela? She looked at her friend and read the answer in her eyes. Angela's eyes were windows that revealed her compassionate nature. Doubtless, these were the things that drew Jonathan to her. Stephanie pushed her feelings for Jonathan aside.

"I am sure what he is doing stems from his desire to make you happy. You are just going to have to trust him."

Angela nodded. She started to put her notes away, and as she packed her books into her bag, she gave them an odd look.

"I don't believe it."

"What?"

"I left my English Lit textbook at the farm."

Stephanie regarded her for a moment, then she smiled happily. 'Well, I guess we're going to Olds."

Stan took a freshly baked bun from the tray that was cooling on the kitchen counter. Jonathan was outside painting the new barn doors they had just installed. Stan was heading back out, when Jean stopped him. She looked at him sternly. The garden dirt that was smudged on her face made her look intimidating.

"You still haven't said yes yet?" Jean raised an eyebrow.

"I was just about to, but—"

"After all we have learned about him, he still hasn't met your requirements? Or are you just planning on leading him on and have him as free labour until he's had enough."

Stan looked at her sheepishly. Jean placed a gentle hand on his arm.

"Stan we can't keep her forever. You know she will get a place of her own. Maybe she'll be fortunate and meet her perfect husband. Maybe that young man is outside right now, but we will never know unless we give him a chance."

Stan knew she was right. He couldn't keep procrastinating, but he was reluctant to let go of his baby girl. As he walked back to the barn, his mind wandered to a memory of a blonde child picking daisies in the yard. He smiled as the image brought back intense feelings of love. At the thought of her leaving, he began to tear up.

A crash shattered his reverie. Jonathan had stepped into the paint tray and, as he moved to step out of it, he knocked over the ladder, toppling the paint can and dumping its contents over his head and shoulders. Outraged, he cursed under his breath as he tried to wipe it off his face and hair with a rag. Stan couldn't contain his laughter.

"There is no point in getting angry, what's done is done. Now, what were you doing with the paint can on top of the ladder?"

"I forgot to take it down when I finished the trim." He threw the rag down, and clenched his fists. "I can't do this anymore."

Stan looked at him, confused. "What do you mean?"

"I feel like Jacob! You use me as slave labour for the work here, then interrogate me and send me on my way, while refusing to respond to my request. At the end of the day, the only thing you tell me is to return the following week. When will it be enough? Should I just give up and go home? Am I wasting my time?"

Stan recalled his own response to Jean's father when he had him jumping through hoops in order to earn his blessings to marry his daughter. Jonathan had worked hard on the farm, and Stan knew he couldn't have done all this work without his help. When it came to his granddaughter, the boy had good intentions. The more they talked, the more Jonathan had shown him how much he truly loved Angela. The young man had answered all his questions, and from what Stan could tell, he had an impressive understanding of the Bible. He wasn't completely sure if Jonathan's expressions of faith came from the heart, or if he was answering by rote. He started to answer, then glanced over Jonathan's shoulder.

"When it comes to your request, why don't you ask her yourself?"

Jonathan turned, and his jaw dropped in surprise when he saw Angela and Stephanie regarding him sceptically from a safe distance.

Angela looked at the overturned paint can, then at his face. She pursed her lips to prevent herself from laughing.

"Ask me what?"

"I wasn't trying to make you worry, it was supposed to be a surprise for your birthday."

"What kind of surprise?" Angela looked quizzically at her grandfather. Stan shrugged his shoulders and smiled.

"Why don't we go inside so Jonathan can prepare for your gift?"

Stephanie and Angela followed him inside. Jonathan hurried to the side of the house and tried clean up with the hose, which only served to spread the paint and make him a sopping mess. He shook off as much water as he could, then retrieved a small box from the car's glove compartment. When he returned to the house, all attention focussed on him. Angela and Jean gasped while Stephanie and Stan tried to stifle their laughter.

"What were you doing out there, taking a shower?" Stan roared.

Angry and embarrassed, it took everything in Jonathan not to snap back. Going down on one knee front of Angela, he pulled out the box. Angela's eye lit up and she began to tremble as a mixture of excitement, joy and pure love washed over her.

"Is that a ring?" she muttered, not realising she spoke out loud.

Smiling up at her, Jonathan took her hand. He wanted to say 'Angela, you are the love of my life and I know that God wants you to be my help mate. I want to wake up every morning and look into your beautiful green eyes. From this moment forward, I want to spend every breath I have loving you. Angela Boisclair, will you marry me?'.

Instead, his carefully planned proposal fled the scene and what came out was: "Angela, would you marry a man covered in barn paint?"

CHAPTER 8
Japan — April 1985
Setsuko's Senior Year

The aroma of food and the cacophony of voices filled the cafeteria as the students gossiped and laughed over lunch. The girls claimed a table towards the back. Setsuko poked at her katsudon as she pondered last night's events. Since the incident at the party, David had made an effort to put his best foot forward. He had been sweet, buying her flowers and going on walks through some of the local gardens and temples. He had even made a picnic lunch that they shared on a hill overlooking the ocean, and had presented her with the bracelet of cute cat faces that she had seen at the Market when he had helped her sort out the table that had been knocked over. She hadn't known that he had noticed her admiring it.

Their romantic encounters had become more affectionate over the past few weeks, and sometimes a little intense. On several occasions, passersby had caught them making out in the park. David promised that she would never be put in an embarrassing situation like that again, but it had been an empty promise. She was angry with herself every time it happened, but whenever she made an effort to control herself, all it took was a caress or tender look from him and she'd lose it.

She paid no attention to Misayo's updates of the school gossip. Akari seemed to be in an exceptionally pleasant mood today, and she even complimented Natsuki on her new haircut. She chatted endlessly with Misayo, and her giddy demeanour was beginning to grate on Setsuko's nerves.

"What's got you in such a good mood today?" asked Setsuko.

Akari beamed as the attention of the table turned to her. "Oh, it's nothing."

"Oh, come on, Akari! Tell us!" Misayo pleaded.

Akari gave a coy shrug, then expelled a deep sigh. "I bumped into him again about two weeks ago and we have been going out ever since."

"Really? Two weeks ago? Well, tell us, then. Who this charming guy?" Setsuko asked, her curiosity aroused.

"Do you remember that guy we met during the holiday break?"

"You mean David?" Misayo squealed with delight at Akari's nod.

"Yes, he asked me out after and we hung out for the afternoon."

Setsuko's eyes widened and she felt her entire body go numb. She listened as Akari related the details of her past few weeks with David, and wondered if she had somehow stepped into an alternate reality. Natsuki noticed Setsuko's dumbfounded expression.

"You okay?" she whispered.

Setsuko sat frozen in a state of denial; what she was hearing couldn't be true. She stared at Natsuki, speechless. When she was finally able to reply, she heard something that pushed her over the edge.

"You kissed him?" Misayo squeaked.

Akari nodded, unable to contain her excitement and she squealed with Misayo. To the astonishment of the girls, Setsuko cursed and abruptly stood up.

"What's wrong with you?" Misayo asked.

"Nothing, I just remembered that I forgot to finish my math assignment."

She stormed off, ignoring Natsuki who tried to grasp her hand. Her eyes stung with unshed tears. She walked aimlessly from hall to hall, taking no notice of the figure that shadowed her. Trying her hardest not to cry, she wiped her eyes, but nothing seemed to staunch the flow of tears. The sound of approaching footsteps startled her. Wiping away her tears, she spun around to see who there. Natsuki came to a halt a few feet away.

"Is everything okay, Setsuko?"

"Can you just stay out of my business? Just because we are friends that doesn't mean I need to share every intimate detail of my life." Natsuki flinched, and Setsuko immediately apologised. "I am sorry. I didn't mean that."

Natsuki gave her a quick hug and held her at arm's length. "Now, what's wrong? I haven't seen you like this in forever."

"Akari is not the only girl going out with David."

"You're kidding me, he's going out with you, too?" At Setsuko's nod, she asked, "What are you going to do? You need to let Akari know about David."

Setsuko couldn't agree more. "I think it's time for his little game to come to an end."

As she made her way back to class, she swore she was going to make David pay for humiliating her.

The last class of the day was interminable. Mr. Yoshida was going over a review of their last math exam, asking students at random to answer the formulas he would write on the chalkboard. Setsuko's attention was focussed on the clock above the door. She watched as the seconds slowly ticked by. The slow movement of time was gnawing at her nerves. She knew she had to end it with David, but the more she thought about it, the more she dreaded the thought of being without him. She found herself thinking about his touch and how he made her feel.

"No!" she said aloud.

Mr. Yoshida abruptly stopped and turned to look at her. Setsuko's mouth went dry and, feeling trapped, she looked at her classmates.

"It seems Setsuko-san has found an error with my equation." He frowned down at her and held out the chalk. "Perhaps she would like to instruct the class today."

"I apologise, Yoshida-sensei," she said, her words coming out clear and strong, belying her nervousness, "I had just realised I made a mistake taking notes. I did not mean to interrupt you."

She waited for him to call her on the lie. He regarded her coolly for a moment before returning to his lecture. With a sigh of relief, she lowered her head and pretended to take notes. *Why do I have to act such a fool whenever David is involved?* When class was dismissed and the room cleaned, she gathered her books and made a mad dash to the school's main entrance, intending to catch Akari on the way out.

Akari was standing in the corner of the genkan, talking to a classmate. Setsuko took one step forward but stopped, as a voice whispered in her mind, IF YOU DO THIS YOU MAY NEVER SEE DAVID AGAIN. She struggled inwardly, once again the feelings she had for David made her question her resolve. She took one more look in Akari's direction. IT'S NOT LIKE SHE WILL EVEN KNOW, AND YOU CAN ALWAYS TELL NATSUKI TO KEEP IT A SECRET.

Akari noticed her and beckoned her over. Setsuko smiled back even as her heart sank. She walked to her friend. Every step was an effort where she fought the voice that kept telling her to stop. Akari met her halfway and hugged her. Feelings of tenderness and kinship once shared between the two welled up inside Setsuko. They were accompanied by a strong sense of guilt. When she looked into her friend's eyes, she knew she had to do the right thing and tell her about David.

"Akari, I need to speak to you."

"What's going on?" Akari responded, still beaming like she had during lunch.

"It's about David." Setsuko hesitated, unsure if she could continue.

Akari gave her a peculiar look. "I really don't have time to be lectured about 'being safe', I have heard enough from my parents to last me a lifetime." She turned to leave.

"He's been with me, too," Setsuko blurted.

Setsuko's words stopped Akari cold. A few moments passed before she turned to look at Setsuko, her eyes seething in rage. For some time the two of them stared at each other, unmoving, both hesitant to say anything.

"You know what, you really are pathetic."

"What?" Setsuko blinked, flabbergasted.

"You can't handle someone having something better than you!" Akari hissed. "Your perfect life, house, and family are not good enough, you have to come and steal my man!"

"Now, hold on a moment," Setsuko protested. "First of all, I did not steal your man. Second of all, he came to me."

Akari's eyes flashed and she began to say something, but bit her tongue.

Setsuko sighed, "Look, I don't want to fight. I was only trying to be a friend, you know, looking out for one another."

"A *friend*?" Akari scoffed, "We haven't been real friends for almost a year. The last time I checked, that lanky mouse was your best friend."

"What's that supposed to mean?"

"You are always with Natsuki, and you never come to me anymore. Now you come invent this lame story to try to gain my friendship by telling me you're chasing after the boy I like."

Setsuko was angered by the accusation and by the quandary she suddenly was in. She wanted to be friends with Akari, but didn't want to let go of David. "That's not fair!" she fumed.

"I think it's perfectly fair. Since you obviously think David will choose you, let's make a wager and let him decide. I bet he'll be with me by the end of the week."

"Fine!" Setsuko raged. She slung her bag over her shoulder. With a toss of her hair, she turned and didn't look back as she stormed out.

Setsuko came home to an empty house. Her mother had gone out while her father had meetings all evening, which left her to her own devices for the next few hours. She went straight to her closet.

David had already made plans to pick her up that evening. Setsuko took out the red dress she had worn on their first date. She began to undress when a picture on her desk caught her eye. It was a photo of her and Akari taken at the mall. She mentally replayed the day's events, Akari's harsh words, and realised that Akari was right. Their friendship was over. Any guilt she felt over letting a boy destroy their friendship evaporated. She was going to win this battle.

"If you really want to fight, Akari, get ready to lose," she said to the photograph and placed the picture face down on the desk.

Setsuko returned to the closet, searching for the perfect outfit. She selected a tight white button-up shirt and a black mini miniskirt. She stood in front of the full-length mirror, admiring herself, and then sat down on a small chair at her dresser to skilfully apply makeup and eye liner. Lastly, she curled her hair, adding an exotic look to her appearance. Prepared for the evening, she went the sitting room, and sat on the sofa to wait for David.

David was running late. Setsuko stood at the sitting room window, watching for his car. Her heart beat faster when the familiar roar of a car engine reverberated through the air. She quickly ducked into the hallway. The sound of a car door closing and the footsteps that followed caused her heart to skip a beat. The front door creaked open and David stepped into the genkan. He looked into the vacant sitting room, and was about to call for her when she stepped in view and leaned against the wall seductively.

"I was getting worried that you weren't going to make it," she purred.

David's eyes widened and he consumed her body with his gaze. He felt his mouth go dry as Setsuko slowly walked over to him and took his hand to guide him to the sofa. She leaned against him, giving an ample view of her bosom.

"What's this all about?"

"I want to show you what you were missing."

"Missing?" David gave her a wry grin. Setsuko wrapped her arms around his neck and placed her mouth close to his ear. The heat of her breath made his heart race.

"Let's just say if you play along I will reward you," she whispered.

"What's gotten into you?"

"Nothing, I just want you to promise that I will be the only one."

"The only one?"

"I heard about Akari, but you are going to understand that I am the only one." Setsuko felt her self-control begin to falter. In contrast, David appeared calm and cool, but there was a hit of something in his eyes.

"So, what will it be, me or Akari?" she asked.

David stroked her cheek. "I'm sorry. I know you're angry at me. I promise you, I wasn't trying to hurt either of you."

Setsuko took his hands, and placed them on her waist. She leaned against him.

"I will forgive you, but you need to promise me that it's over between the two of you. That way we can be together, isn't that what you want?" she asked as she batted her eyes coquettishly. David could only nod, his eyes filled with desire. Setsuko gave him one more kiss before turning around and walking away.

"Where are you going?" David asked.

Setsuko gave him a coy smile over her shoulder. "You wouldn't expect me to go out in this outfit would you?"

His eyes wandered over her once more and he gave her a cheeky smile. "I wouldn't mind. We could go somewhere private, if you'd like?"

Setsuko continued to her room where she slipped into the red dress. When she returned, David looked a little more composed.

"Come on now, you didn't think I was going to be that easy did you?" Setsuko smiled seductively. "We have a deal don't we? If you pull through with your end, I may give you something in return."

For a brief moment his eyes flickered with burning desire. That night Setsuko made sure to do her best, being seductive when she needed to be, slowly enticing David with the promise of intimacy. She knew if she played her cards right Akari wouldn't have a chance, and she was going to win, at all costs.

The next day both girls kept to themselves, giving each other wary sidelong glances that put Natsuki and Misayo on edge. Misayo became reclusive, not wanting to pick sides, while Natsuki stuck by Setsuko, trying to convince her to make up with Akari.

"I don't want to talk about her," Setsuko growled. "She called me a spoiled little brat. She thinks I have this picture-perfect life, but she has no clue."

Natsuki grew quiet, she could see Setsuko's mind was set, and she was less likely to make Akari change hers.

"Please promise me you two won't be too rash with each other?" Natsuki pleaded.

Setsuko looked over to Akari, who was seated with one of her classmates on the other side of the cafeteria. "Maybe you should go talk to her and tell her to get her head out of the sand. Now if you don't mind, I would like to eat my lunch without mentioning that putaro's name. Just thinking of her makes me sick."

Natsuki looked over at Akari, who was laughing at something a classmate had said. Sadness filled her as she thought of the happy times they had shared as friends. She turned her attention to Misayo who was sitting by herself, raising her gaze periodically to stare thoughtfully at Akari and Setsuko in turn. Natsuki pushed her bowl aside and stood up.

Setsuko looked up from her notes. "Where are you going?"

"I thought I might sit with Misayo, she looks all alone over there."

"Yeah, what's with her anyway? It's not like she hasn't seen us fight before."

"I think she feels like she is stuck between a rock and a hard place," Natsuki responded. "She doesn't want to choose between her friends."

Setsuko said sincerely, "Tell Misayo I am not mad at her and if she would like, she can come sit with us."

Natsuki nodded before moving to the seat next to Misayo.

"You okay?" she asked.

Misayo raised her head. "Is Setsuko going to try to make up with Akari?" When Natsuki shook her head Misayo let out a small sigh. "Do you think we will ever be able to all be friends again?"

Natsuki looked at her thoughtfully. It was moments such as these that endeared the normally boisterous girl to her. "Maybe, but all we can do is wait and pray."

Misayo looked up at her "Have you told them yet?"

Natsuki shook her head, "No, and if I told them right now, I fear Akari would use it to her advantage. But, whatever happens, at least we will stay friends, and I think that Setsuko would love to have us as well."

Natsuki darted one more glance at Setsuko as she spoke, knowing that this fight was not going to end well for any of them, especially not for Setsuko.

CHAPTER 9
Japan — April, 1985

The next few days passed without incident, and Setsuko was beginning to wonder if David was ever going to break up with Akari. It was Thursday afternoon when she got her answer. She and Natsuki were walking down the hall and chatting as they made their way to the lunchroom when a furious Akari stormed through a classroom doorway. She thundered like a tempest as she tore down the hallway towards them. Her visage was filled with anger and hate, and it was all directed at Setsuko. Natsuki stepped back in fear, while Setsuko stood her ground and did her best not to show how intimidated she felt.

"You witch! You Kijo!" Akari shrieked. All eyes turned to the two girls, and those around them stopped to watch the drama unfold.

"What's gotten into you?" Setsuko demanded.

"You know what?" Akari was spitting mad. "You couldn't leave it alone! You had to, didn't you?"

Setsuko's confused looked was replaced by a defiant smirk as she realised what had transpired. She held her books to her chest. "I don't think I know what you are talking about. Why don't you enlighten me?"

Natsuki whispered to Setsuko to stop, but her friend was enjoying the power she had over Akari. Akari went into a rage. A string of obscenities left her mouth. She threw her books down and poked a finger at Setsuko.

"You knew I liked him, you knew it and you stole him from me, you little tramp." Akari's voice shook.

"I didn't need to steal him, he simply chose someone who had a little more to offer," Setsuko said, gloating, her eyes meeting Akari's.

Natsuki nearly fell over at the last comment; she knew Setsuko could be harsh, but this was a little much even for her. Misayo came to stand by Natsuki. Both girls exchanged nervous glances, unsure if they should intervene.

Akari lowered her hand and balled it into a white-knuckled fist as she stared wide-eyed at Setsuko. The students who had stopped to watch began to file out of the hallway when Principal Akio Sato and the Teacher Advisor, Mrs. Jin Kichida, appeared.

"What is all the commotion about?" demanded Mrs. Kichida.

"Nothing, Kichida-Hojokyoyu." Akari overrode Setsuko's response. "I just found out my best friend betrayed me, and now I am letting her know that we are no longer friends." With that, she picked up her books and shoved past Setsuko, earning more than a few surprised looks with her rudeness.

"Twice in the same week you and Akari-san have made a disturbance in these halls, Setsuko-san," said Principal Sato.

"I'm sorry, Kocho-sensei. It won't happen again." Setsuko bowed.

Principal Sato dismissed her before walking down the hall with Mrs. Kichida. Setsuko turned to Natsuki and Misayo who were looking at each other in mystified disbelief.

"What's wrong?" she asked.

"You didn't need to be that mean" Natsuki replied.

"I just give her what she wants, then? She wins and I get nothing because she can't handle the fact he chose me instead?"

"Why do you always have to fight? Why can't we be friends like we used to be?" Misayo cried out.

"It wasn't me, David was dating me first before Akari came around. She's just jealous. Give her some time and she will be back to her normal devious ways, you'll see."

"Did you ever think David is playing you two against one another?" Misayo ventured.

The thought had crossed her mind, but the animosity between Akari and herself had pushed her to make decisions that may have destroyed their friendship. She recalled what Akari had said, 'A friend, we haven't been friends for a year'. Setsuko had a stubborn set to her jaw as she pulled back from them.

"She was never a friend to begin with," she spat.

Natsuki's eyes widened in astonishment "Setsuko, you don't mean that."

Did Akari turn them against me? Is she really that jealous that she's willing to tear apart our entire group of friends to get what she wants? Setsuko stepped back, shutting them out.

"I can't believe you would side with her after all that she's done to you, Natsuki," Setsuko said, and turned to Misayo. "What about all those times she has ditched you? Or when she told you not to go out with Akihiro and when you did, she tormented you until you dumped him, just because she didn't like him? Or how about how the way she treated your brother, Natsuki, when he dared ask her out? She was relentless when she dragged him through the mud after that one date. You two are willing to forgive her, but when I make the decision to keep one thing to myself instead of letting her talk me out of it, like always, you two side with her and gang up against me.'

"No, it's not like that, Setsuko, we just don't want you two to fight, we need to forgive each other just like—" Natsuki clamped her teeth over her lower lip.

Setsuko's brow furrowed. "What are you talking about? When did you start believing in forgiveness? Didn't you say you would never forgive your father for leaving your mother for a younger woman?"

"I did," Natsuki began, "but I have learned a lot since then, and I know now that living a life of hate only makes you a prisoner of regret."

"Where is all this coming from?" demanded Setsuko.

Misayo lifted her eyebrows at Natsuki, who nodded before responding.

"I—I am a Christian."

"You've got to be kidding me!" Setsuko laughed derisively. "So, you believe in some Jesus and poof, your troubles go away. So, let me ask, did your father come back?"

"No," Natsuki replied quietly. "That's not how it works."

"Then how does it work exactly?" Setsuko snarled "I'm supposed to believe in your god, then all of a sudden it becomes okay for Akari to treat us like garbage?"

"No, I didn't say that. You haven't let me finish." Natsuki's voice shook from the doubt that was welling up inside her.

"You know what, if believing in this god of yours means I am supposed to tolerate what she does, then I don't want anything to do with it. What about you, Misayo? Do you believe in this nonsense?"

Misayo looked from Natsuki to Setsuko before shaking her head. "I don't believe, but I have considered what she has to say, and I—"

Setsuko raised a silencing hand, her face twisted with hurt and bitterness. "No, I don't want to hear it. If this is truly how you two feel, then so be it. You go and continue to grovel at her feet, but I refuse to play her game."

Her voice trembled under the weight of her sadness. She clutched her books tighter and hurried down the hall. Misayo and Natsuki called after her but she ignored them.

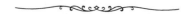

Setsuko avoided her friends for the rest of the day. When she got home, she marched past her mother without saying a word and went straight to her bedroom. She tossed her backpack into its corner and threw herself onto her bed. She grabbed a pillow and screamed into it.

There was a soft rap at the door. "Setsuko-chan, is everything all right?"

"I'm fine, Mother," she mumbled into the pillow.

Hitomi entered the room and sat down beside her. She gently rubbed Setsuko's back. Setsuko felt the tension from the day start to ease with every stroke of her mother's hands. Ever since Setsuko was a little girl, her mother would rub her back and listen to her woes. Setsuko lay still, lulled by the soft calm tenderness of her mother's voice as Hitomi sang softly. Setsuko hung on to every word, feeling her heart rise and fall with the song. When Hitomi had finished, Setsuko tilted her head so she could look at her.

"So...?" Hitomi let the unasked question hang between them.

"It's like I said, Mother, I'm fine, I had a little argument with my friends."

"It would seem it was more than a little argument."

"Could we not talk about this right now?"

Hitomi removed her hand from her daughter's back. Setsuko had always been able to confide in her, but Hitomi had noticed that she didn't open up as often lately. Setsuko had almost completely shut her out, just like Daiki had. Now Hitomi faced what felt like a mountain of problems and unresolved issues. She reflected on what Pastor Hikaru had told her, and said a silent prayer. She looked at her daughter and carefully considered her next words.

"Setsuko-chan?"

"What?" Setsuko replied warily.

"What do you think about Christians?" her voice quivered from nervousness.

"Christians?" Setsuko snorted derisively, "Why are people so interested in Christianity these days?"

Hitomi's mouth fell open, and her words and confidence died. Raising an eyebrow, "Why do you ask?"

Hitomi stared at her daughter, one part of her trying to regain her courage, the other part terrified of losing her daughter. *This is your chance Hitomi, I will give you the words to say.* The small voice helped her regain her confidence, but when she went to speak, her fear overwhelmed her.

"Never mind, I was just making conversation." She was discouraged to know that she had failed once again to share the Good News. They sat in an awkward silence that was finally broken by Setsuko.

"What are we having for supper, Mother?"

"Oh no!"

Hitomi hurried to the kitchen. Setsuko followed close behind and was quick to help Hitomi get things started for supper. If her father came home and found that supper was not ready for him he would lose it, and they would have to endure an evening of him berating and belittling her mother. As Hitomi hurriedly prepared the meal, Setsuko noticed the amount of food she was making was way more than the three of them normally ate.

"Are we having guests?" Hitomi was so focussed on the task at hand that Setsuko had to poke her to get her attention. "Mother, who's coming over for dinner?"

"I forgot—" she began, and took her by the arm and almost dragged her back to her room. She ignored Setsuko's questions as she rummaged through the closet. Setsuko fell silent as her mother pulled out the mini skirt that she had worn for David. Hitomi waited expectantly for an explanation. Her mind racing, Setsuko snagged the skirt from her mother.

"I was holding it for Akari," she squeaked.

Hitomi was not fooled. She selected her best kimono and silently handed it to Setsuko. She went back to the kitchen and ignored her daughter, who was watching her from the doorway. After a few minutes of silence, Hitomi looked at her, "You need to get dressed. Your father has a colleague coming over, and he is bringing his son."

Setsuko gave a decided click of her tongue showing her distaste, earning a sharp glare from her mother.

"I get to play trophy daughter again," Setsuko snarled, her frustration and anger colouring her voice.

"I don't have time for this, Setsuko-chan. Get yourself ready and I don't want to hear any more complaints."

Setsuko stomped back to her room. Hitomi closed her eyes and whispered a small prayer, asking the Lord to calm her nerves, and to give her the wisdom to speak to her daughter about dressing appropriately.

Daiki came home around seven. He looked questioningly at Hitomi when he found her still preparing supper. She glanced in the direction of Setsuko's room, and he nodded in understanding.

"I think things will be a little different after tonight," he said with a smile.

Before gathering the last of the plates, Hitomi quickly went into Setsuko's room, hoping to catch her before she came out to join them. While Setsuko was primping, she turned her head slightly as Hitomi slipped into the room.

"You don't need to hold my hand mother. I am dressed and ready to take my place as one of Dad's trophies." Setsuko turned to leave the room but Hitomi stopped her. Grabbing hold of Setsuko's arm, Hitomi pulled her close and spoke quietly into her ear.

"You will not disrespect your father in front of me ever again, you hear me?"

"Anything else I can do for you?" Setsuko asked sullenly.

Hitomi was so shocked by the disrespect it set her back on her heels. An overwhelming anger raised her hand and she struck her daughter across the face. Setsuko staggered back and she raised a trembling hand to her cheek. Staring back at her mother, she began to tremble in anger as she fought back tears.

"Setsuko, I'm—I'm sorry," Hitomi stammered, unconsciously wiping her hand on her kimono

Rubbing her cheek, Setsuko pushed passed her mother, leaving Hitomi shaken. Moments later, Daiki poked his head into the room.

"What happened?" he asked.

Hitomi quickly regained her composure and turned to him. "We had a disagreement."

Daiki didn't press any further and allowed her to go back and set the table. Minutes after the meal was ready to be served, a knock at the door broke the uncomfortable silence. Daiki greeted the two men at the door. The first to enter was a heavier set balding man, followed by a young man closer to Setsuko's age.

Daiki introduced his associate, Mr. Michio Hashida, and his son, Ryota, to the women. Ryota greeted Setsuko with a polite smile and a respectful bow. Setsuko didn't return the gesture, which drew a disapproving glance from her father. Ryota took a seat next to Setsuko, while Mr. Hashida sat beside her father. Her mother sat across from her and refused to make eye contact. During the meal, the men discussed business and what was happening in the world. Ryota was respectful, and a bit timorous. He was average looking and quick to oblige his father. She mentally compared him to David. Where David was handsome, charming and charismatic, Ryota was average, awkward and nervous. Setsuko could never be with someone so pathetic. She wanted to be independent, but she also wanted a man who knew what he wanted: a man like David.

Throughout the meal her father kept glancing in her direction and smiling. Setsuko could feel her fury rise as she once again felt like a pawn in her father's quest for prestige. What did he have planned for her this time? When she rose to help her mother clear the table Daiki stood up and motioned them to sit down.

"I have a special announcement to make," he began.

Hitomi's heart raced; it was like stepping back into the past. Her father standing just like Daiki was, a smile on his face as he announced her arranged marriage to a stranger. History was repeating, only this time it was her daughter who was being given away, and the news would devastate her. Hitomi had planned to prepare her, but the afternoon's conversation had distracted her. Setsuko was about to receive the shock of her life, and she was in no way prepared to deal with it.

"After much consideration, Mr. Hashida and I have come to the agreement over the future of our two children."

Setsuko's eyes widened and her heart sank. *What is he talking about?* When she saw the look on her mother's face, she knew. She stared at her father in shock. Her hands went cold and she felt the blood drain from her face.

"We would like to announce that we have arranged the marriage of Ryota and Setsuko, to take place in the summer."

Marriage! Setsuko felt her heart begin to break as all feeling left her body. She didn't even look up when Ryota nervously presented her with white and gold fans. *Marriage?* Her whole life was slipping away and she was powerless to stop it. Once again she found herself controlled by her father, and this time he had taken the freedom she had planned for herself. All her hopes and dreams had been dashed by one simple word, 'Marriage.' The rest of the night was blur as Mr. Hashida and Daiki drank and celebrated. Ryota whispered something about taking good care of her, but all Setsuko could think about was David.

The night ended, leaving Setsuko haggard and trembling. Hitomi wanted to comfort her daughter, but knew it would draw unwanted attention from Daiki, who would not tolerate disrespect from either one of them. She would wait until he went to bed and then she would talk to her daughter; but what was she going to say? When Daiki had fallen asleep, Hitomi slipped from their room and went to Setsuko.

"Setsuko? May I come in?" she whispered, not wanting to wake her husband. When no reply came she opened the door to find an empty room. The kimono was on the bed and Setsuko was gone.

CHAPTER 10
Japan — April, 1985

Setsuko ran as if her life depended on it. She ran even as her legs burned from the exertion. She needed to get away, from her life, her parents, to anywhere where she was in control.

A left, a right, then another left: she ran and ran until she began to stumble from exhaustion. She finally collapsed onto the hard ground of a vacant alley. Her stomach wretched and she felt like she was going to vomit. Everything was happening so fast; first the fight with Akari, then Natsuki and Misayo abandoning her, and now this. Her world was coming apart at the seams and she felt her life spiralling out of control. When she regained her breath, she stood up and leaned against a nearby fence and closed her eyes. Bitter tears cascaded down her face.

Her heart ached so badly that her chest hurt under the strain of her sorrow. Her clothes were wet from a mixture of sweat and damp air, and she was chilled to the bone. She looked at her surroundings, trying to determine where she was, but her vision was blurred by the tears. She slowly made her way to the end of the alley. When she reached a main street, she searched frantically for a familiar landmark that would tell her where she was.

The few people who were out at that late hour gave her the briefest of glances in passing. Setsuko wrapped her arms around herself as she shivered. The pain of loneliness and sadness threatened to swallow her whole as her emotions teetered on the edge. She took another, clearer look around and realised she was lost. She looked back the way she had come, uncertain whether or not to continue or turn back.

"Hey there, Ojousan. What are you doing out so late?" asked a voice that nearly sent her scurrying back to the darkness of the alleyway.

"Who—who's there?" She was unable to make out the person approaching her.

"It's me, Miya," said the slender young woman who appeared under a streetlight several feet away. She was carrying several grocery bags. "What are you doing out here?" she asked again, curious by the state the girl was in. Setsuko quickly straightened and steadied her demeanour.

"N—nothing, I felt l—like going for a w—walk." Setsuko tried to sound confident, but the cold made her teeth chatter.

"So late at night?" Miya inquired. When Setsuko didn't respond, Miya walked over to her and handed her two bags before draping her coat over the young girl.

"Why don't you come with me? Let's get you out of those wet clothes and cleaned up, and then you can tell me what's really going on."

Setsuko hesitated, but she was too cold to argue. She longed for a hot bath and dry clothes, so she nodded and followed Miya down a maze of small streets to her apartment complex. Miya ushered her into her Unit, dropped the grocery bags off in the kitchen and led her down the hall to the bathroom.

"You can get undressed, I will get you some towels and find you something to wear while you take your bath."

Miya's motherly tone was comforting. Setsuko started running the bath, and let the steam from the water ease her tension. When the tub was full, she slipped out of her clothing and settled into the soothing water. For the first time that day, she felt the pressure start to lift, and she began to doze off.

"Be careful, we don't want you to drown."

Miya closed the door behind her and set the towel and dry clothes on the vanity. Surprised by the unexpected voice, Setsuko started violently. Miya placed a steadying hand on her shoulder and brushed back the lock of hair that hung in the girl's face. She gave her a warm smile.

"You look better already."

Setsuko leaned her head back, closed her eyes and sighed bitterly. Miya drew the curtain and sat down waiting for Setsuko to speak. Feeling more comfortable, Setsuko began to ramble on about the week's events leading up to the shocking marriage agreement. Miya listened intently and, when Setsuko had finished, she gazed pensively into the distance.

"It looks like you are in a bit of a mess," Miya stated. "As for David, I am not surprised. He has always been a bit of a player. I'm sorry that he came between two good friends."

"But, what about this marriage?" Setsuko asked, trying to hold herself together.

"An arranged marriage isn't all bad," Miya said. "My parents had an arranged marriage, and from what I remember they really did love each other. I think when it comes down to it, love is really a choice, and one that we all make day after day in the way we treat others."

"But I don't even *like* him, he's just going to be doing whatever his dad tells him to do. He has no confidence, he will be a weak man and I will be the pawn of three men," Setsuko whinged.

"That may be, but you might be surprised. You may be the one to inspire this young man's confidence. In time you may learn to love and respect him," Miya said.

"Did you like Tetsuya when you met him?"

"No. When we first met I thought he was a jerk and a pig, always making cat calls whenever I came around. He would make comments about my body that would make a girl die of embarrassment."

"What changed?" inquired Setsuko.

Miya reflected for a minute, then replied, "It was the way he treated his sister. I was coming back from work and two boys about your age where harassing Kyo. The poor girl was crying, and I was about to step in when Tetsuya came up and gave those louts a thrashing. After he had knocked them around a bit, he made them apologise to his little sister and warned them the next time he wouldn't be so nice. After seeing that, I knew he couldn't be all bad. That night, I went over to his place to see how his sister was doing. We struck up a conversation, and that's when he asked me out. At first I wanted to say no, but I made the decision to give him a chance. I chose to look past his faults to find the man he truly was."

Setsuko sat silently, trying to imagine life married to Ryota, but the thought was inconceivable. She could never marry a complete stranger. David was more of a match in her mind than Ryota would ever be, and though he was rough around the edges, he could be kind and gentle when he wanted to be.

"You get dried off and dressed, I will see if Tetsuya can take you home," Miya suggested.

Setsuko reluctantly eased herself out of the relaxing water, and put on the clothes left for her. The clothes were a little tight, but at least they were dry, and she was relieved to see her undergarments there. Once dressed, she stepped outside and followed the soft voices to the kitchen. Miya was leaning against the counter, talking to Tetsuya, who had not fully woken up yet.

"Setsuko, Tetsuya said he is going to take you home, that way you don't have to walk all that way so late at night," Miya said.

"Hey, what's going on?" asked a voice from behind Setsuko, sending a thrill down her spine.

David stood in the doorway of one of the rooms. He met Setsuko's wide eyes and, with a smile, drew her into a warm embrace. Setsuko's heart sped up at the contact. Wherever his skin touched hers, she felt as if it was on fire.

"Hey, beautiful, I wasn't expecting you to be here. How are you doing?" he asked gently as he stroked her cheek. Setsuko looked down and her mouth quivered as she fought another swell of emotions.

"She's had a bad night, David. Tetsuya is going to take her home," Miya stated flatly.

"What happened?" he combed his fingers through her silky hair and framed her face with his hands.

Setsuko felt her sadness disappear and felt flushed and warm under his touch. In that moment, all she wanted was to be in his arms where it was warm and safe. "I—I had a disagreement with my parents. Miya found me when I was walking around trying to clear my head."

"So far from home?" David raised a brow.

"It doesn't matter. Setsuko, we should get you home. Tetsuya, could you get the car started?" Miya asked as she tried to regain control of the situation.

"Why don't I walk her home?" David inquired.

"I don't know if that's a good idea." Miya eyed Setsuko warily.

"Why not?" asked Tetsuya "It would save me the trip and it's not like this lazy louse has a job to go to tomorrow."

"I just don't think that—" Miya cut herself short, trying to find the words to delicately state the obvious without starting a fight.

"Look, let David take her home, he can then stop at Naoki's place for a snooze before his father comes back tomorrow."

Miya knew having David walk Setsuko home was a bad idea. She'd rather Tetsuya drive her, but could find no viable reason why David shouldn't. She nodded reluctantly.

"She better go straight home, and you'd better act like a gentleman, David," Miya said with a dark edge to her voice.

"Sure thing, *Mother*," David said with a laugh.

He took Setsuko's hand and they walked in silence, following the same route that Miya had taken. Setsuko took advantage of the silence to analyse what Miya had told her. The woman's advice made sense, yet Setsuko was repulsed by the thought of Ryota as her husband. Her heart was breaking and as they drew closer to her neighbourhood, her pace slowed to the point where

David finally drew them aside. Concerned, he lifted her chin to search her dark eyes that were glistening with unshed tears.

"What's wrong?"

"I don't know," she said, averting her eyes.

"Well, something is obviously wrong because you seem very reluctant to go home."

He brushed his fingers across her cheek. His touch caused her heart to skip a beat, and she felt warmth course through her. Turning her face and taking his hand into hers she kissed it, and then in a moment of passion she stood on her tiptoes and kissed him deeply. David's breath caught and her body nestled into his as he took her into his embrace. Setsuko felt her body grow warmer as she lost herself to her desires. David pulled away with a gasp, and tried to catch his breath.

"What was that for?" he asked shakily.

"I don't want to go home," she said, "I want to be with you."

David was doubtful, but when he met her entreating eyes, he ceded. "We can go to Naoki's, he has a sofa, and an extra bed if you'd like?"

Setsuko nodded enthusiastically, and she felt her pulse race as they walked back towards the hill and took a turn down a small path that meandered through several housing complexes. They stopped at the back of a large apartment building. David led Setsuko around the back of the building, and rapped lightly on the door of one of the units.

For long moments, they waited. A light lit up a window and the door creaked open just enough to allow a pair of beady black eyes to assess them.

"David?" asked the deep voice behind the door.

"Hey, Naoki, is it okay if I stay at your place tonight?"

"What? Tetsuya got sick of you lounging out at his place?"

"Yeah, something like that." David shrugged, giving Setsuko a wry grin.

"I guess it's okay, but what's with the girl?" Naoki grumbled.

"She's a friend. Her parents kicked her out for the night, so I told her you might have a bed for her."

Naoki's eyes looked Setsuko up and down before turning back to David. "Nice catch, do you have protection?"

"It's not like that," David sighed, "I will take the sofa, if it's all right with you."

"Sure, sure." Naoki smiled as he opened the door for them. "But if you need anything, I keep some in the spare bedroom on top of the book case." Setsuko blushed, which only made Naoki's smile broaden. "In case of emergencies." He winked at her and took them to the spare room.

"Sorry about that," David apologised when Naoki left.

"It's okay." Setsuko smiled up at him before giving him lingering kiss. She felt his muscles tense under her hands as she slowly slid them up and down his back. Once more, it was David who stopped and tried to pull away, but Setsuko wasn't going to let him go as she gripped his head in a passionate kiss.

"Setsuko," David gasped, suddenly nervous, "do you really want to do this?"

Not knowing what had come over her, Setsuko didn't even bother to respond before she pulled him into the room.

Setsuko slid out from beneath David's naked body without waking him. She located the bathroom and stepped into the shower. Her hands trembled as she gripped the faucets, and the sudden rush of water over her body made her cry out in shock. She could hear Naoki's voice call out to see if everything was okay, but she ignored him and sat in the shower shaking and sobbing. Placing a hand on her belly she felt an instant sense of terror.

What have I done? she asked herself. Why do I feel so empty inside? I thought the good feelings I had were supposed to last, but all I feel is more emptiness and pain.

She did her best to cry silently. Her mouth twisted in anguish as she took the soap and began to vigorously scrub her body clean. No matter how much she washed, the feeling of being dirty wouldn't go away. Her mother's words of warning to save herself for marriage echoed in her mind. Chucking the soap, she covered her face and wept more bitterly than she could ever remember. Even when the water turned cold she didn't stop crying, the tears and mourning she felt seemed endless. For her first time, she didn't experience what many of the other girls at school had talked about, but when the initial pain subsided she had experienced some pleasure for a fleeting moment.

Oh no, the protection! She panicked. A wave of dread fell over her with the realization that she might have conceived. Saying a silent prayer, she dressed, collected herself and sat in the living room until first light. She didn't even wait for David to wake up before leaving. She followed the path they had taken earlier, and traced her way back to an area she recognized and found her way home from there.

She walked stealthily up the driveway, every sense alert for the sound of her father's car. Her father always checked up on her before leaving; if he were to find her missing, it would mean the end of her social life, and any possibility of seeing David again. When she reached the bend she stuck her head out just far enough to see the garage. To her relief, the El Dorado was parked in front.

She slipped through the gate to the gardens and made her way to the back of the house. Her bedroom window was still ajar. She cautiously peered over the sill to make sure the room was empty, and carefully eased herself through the opening. She toed off her shoes, dropped her bag of clothes on the foot of the bed and, without bothering to undress, burrowed under the covers. Moments later, there was a light rap on the door and the sound of it creaking open.

"Setsuko," her mother whispered. "Where have you been? I was worried sick."

Setsuko pretended to be asleep, but Hitomi wasn't having any of it. She promptly ripped the blankets off her daughter.

"Setsuko, whose clothes are these, and what's that bag?" Hitomi demanded angrily. When her daughter refused to respond, Hitomi grabbed her chin and forced her to face her.

"Now, you listen. If your father finds out you were out all night he will lose it." Hitomi's eyes studied her daughter while Setsuko stared defiantly back at her.

"I don't want to talk about it." She curled into the foetal position.

Hitomi shook Setsuko roughly "What's wrong with you? Don't you know how much it scared me to find you missing last night, and what about your father?"

"What about my father?" Setsuko challenged defiantly. "Oh, that's right. I need to be the dutiful daughter and obey without question. Did anyone think of asking me what I wanted?"

Hitomi's hand flinched back. Setsuko had never spoken so disrespectfully to her. It shocked her that her once cheerful and carefree girl could act this way.

"Why is he so determined to keep me under his thumb? What is it with him that he has some need to control my life and run it the way he sees fit? Don't you understand that I have dreams and aspirations, or maybe I should be more like you and give up on all of that so I can sit at home and be the submissive housewife?"

Setsuko regretted the last words the moment they left her mouth. Her mother's expression changed from shock to hurt. Wounded by the verbal blow she had been dealt, Hitomi stepped back to leave the room.

"Mother, I'm sorry!" blurted Setsuko.

Hitomi paused at the doorway to look back at her with teary eyes. "I'm sorry I am such a disappointment to you. Perhaps one day you will think better of me. Now, get dressed for school or you will be late."

All Setsuko could do was watch her mother walk away. Filled with a strong sense of self-pity, she sat on the edge of her bed. She wanted to cry, but tears wouldn't come. She felt trapped. Everything was a complete mess, and she had no idea how to clean it up.

CHAPTER 11

Angela
Calgary — September 3, 1983

The last few weeks leading up to the wedding blew by like a whirlwind. The list of tasks required to be completed before the wedding made Jonathan's head spin. On the eve of the wedding day, he felt the strain of the previous weeks had come to a head. After several stress-filled days and sleepless nights, The Day was finally here, and now all he could do was hope that everything went well.

When the procession began, he prayed for the strength to stand up in front of their guests. He felt weak from nervousness, and the feeling intensified when his bride made her appearance in her stunning wedding gown. Jonathan was so eager that he didn't even wait for Stan to hand over the bride, and instead found himself standing confused and flustered as Alex directed him to where he belonged. All those in attendance laughed at his enthusiasm and Stan shook a warning finger in his direction. Angela's soft laughter drew his focus back to her. Pastor Winter went through the account in Genesis and spoke about the first husband and wife, Adam and Eve. He explained that marriage was the union of one man, and one woman. He moved on to speak about the husband's role as it was written in Ephesians and First Peter. Then talked about the wife's roles in a marriage found in

Titus and again in First Peter. After they exchanged rings, Pastor Winter talked about the different aspects of love, and encouraged the couple to seek after God's heart in all matters.

When it was time to kiss the bride, Jonathan's breath caught as he lifted the veil. Angela was radiantly beautiful and her eyes sparkled as she looked at him. Never in his life had he seen someone so delicately and exquisitely beautiful as his new bride. Their kiss made his heart pound, and he felt the same electricity dance between them as it had on the day they first touched.

The Reception was held in an elegant plaza. The tables were draped in royal purple. White and lavender rose petals had been artfully scattered around the fine china and silverware. White organza was wound and wrapped around the arches and were draped across the walls, giving the room a sense of majesty. The Head Table was covered in white Irish Linen and trimmed with lavender ribbons and royal purple bows. In the centre, two paper doves marked the bride and groom's place of honour.

During The Dinner, family and friends took their turn at the podium to congratulate the pair and make speeches. Alex was the first to go up. He began with a few jokes, poking fun at his cousin, then shared how Jonathan was more a brother than a cousin whom he admired and looked up to. Jean and Stan gave their tear-filled anecdotes of Angela's life and how much they would miss her. Rachel gave a small speech and tried to steal the spotlight from her brother, but her jokes didn't land as well as his. Kathy and Bill were up next and Kathy couldn't hold back the tears when she talked about how much she had enjoyed raising Jonathan after his parent's death. Bill was brief and to the point, as always, and told Jonathan how proud he was of the man he had become. Stephanie was the last to speak. She guided everyone at the reception through Jonathan and Angela's time together, from the fateful moment they first met, to their first date, to Jonathan's hilarious proposal. When she spoke about Angela, she spoke of a loving sister and her dearest friend, someone who had been there through the turbulent times of her life and who, no matter what happened or how far apart they were, had always found a way to be close to her. Her speech moved everyone in the room to tears, and Angela joined her at the podium and embraced her.

The Speeches were followed by The Dance, where Angela quickly discovered that Jonathan couldn't dance to save his life. She was patient with him, even when he kept stepping on her toes. Jonathan was a quick study and had most of the steps mastered in short order, and they danced until they were the only ones left on the floor.

While bride and groom danced, Stan noticed Stephanie watching them, drink in hand. Something about the way she looked at Jonathan caught and held his attention. He excused himself and made his way over to join her in watching his children.

"Is something bothering you?"

Stephanie started as her thoughts were interrupted. "It's nothing," she said as she set her drink down and quickly wiped a tear from her eye.

"They are a beautiful couple, aren't they? Stephanie, I know that you love Angela, and all you want is for her to be happy. You will find your own prince too, some day."

She smiled up at him, and Stan gave her a fatherly kiss on the forehead before returning to his table. She returned her attention to Jonathan and whispered to herself, "I know. I just wanted it to be him."

Jonathan and Angela cut their cake and Angela smeared it all over Jonathan's face. Afterwards, Angela called the single women over so that she could throw the bouquet. All but Stephanie crowded and shouted around Angela, but she overshot and the bouquet landed in Stephanie's lap. Everyone cheered and clapped as Stephanie sardonically waved it in the air. It was almost midnight before they left for their honeymoon. The wedding day had ended, but the memories of what they shared that day would last a lifetime.

It had been almost four months since the wedding, and the new couple were settled in their basement apartment in the city's Southeast. At first it was difficult for Jonathan. His day was done at three, and he was accustomed to heading straight home after work; Angela's classes ended at five. Add to that the two hour bus ride she would have to take, the earliest she would get home was seven thirty. So, he waited the extra two hours to drive her. He passed the time by checking out the parts of the city that were within walking distance of the university, or finding quiet places to read on campus. When the weather forced him to stay inside, he waited for Angela in his and Lang's office. In a surprisingly short time, he read their combined book collections, and the titles that caught his fancy at the university library. He began to pester Lang about his life and family, which only led to more personal questions about relationships until, one day, Lang handed Jonathan several books about learning Japanese. When Jonathan asked what they were for, the older man mumbled something about a hobby and walked away.

After two years of General Studies, Angela decided to change her major to Paediatrics. When she told Jonathan, he was a little shocked. He warned her that it would be almost ten years before she graduated, and that the tuition fees were exorbitant. She countered with the information that she qualified for several educational funding programs offered by the government, and that she could take a part-time job to ease the load. Jonathan was a little disconcerted by the idea but, unwilling to rob her of the opportunity, agreed to support her in her pursuits. Angela was so excited by the idea she called up everyone she knew. Her grandparents were happy for her, but warned that Paediatrics was a hard row to hoe, and that they couldn't afford to put her through that many years of school. She assured them that she was going to use government grants, and student loans if needed. Stephanie and her mother were genuinely excited for her. Mrs. Marshal told her if she found it hard financially, to let her know and she would try to help. Angela, determined to make it on her own, respectfully declined. Stephanie was a little sad, as they wouldn't have the same classes. Angela pointed out that she wasn't leaving the campus and that they could always hang out when they had free time.

The rest of the year passed by quickly as the newlyweds adjusted to married life and each other's idiosyncrasies. Jonathan was a morning person; his morning started early with a run followed by a small but nourishing breakfast; any change to this routine made him cranky. Conversely, Angela routinely hit the snooze button four times before getting up; consequently, her mornings were often rushed and hectic. At first, Jonathan would get frustrated when they left fifteen to twenty minutes later than he wanted to. He once mumbled something about her needing to make it a priority to wake up early enough to leave on time. This brought on one of their more significant arguments within the first year of their marriage. Jonathan learned that the mornings were not a good time to pester her for anything, and to keep his comments to himself.

Angela learned that, because Jonathan was accustomed to having his aunt pick up after him, he habitually dropped his jacket and suitcase in the front hall, and left his laundry on the bathroom floor. He once told her to pick up her clothes when she accidently dropped a pair of panties, and then became annoyed by her attitude when she hurled the garment into the basket with a waspish 'Like *this*, your Majesty?'.

Angela decided that, since Jonathan didn't appreciate her cleaning, she didn't have to clean. For the next two weeks she scaled the housework down to the bare essentials, and afterwards explained to him that she wasn't his maid. He finally understood. She also discovered that preparing supper after a long day of classes was something Jonathan expected of her when they got home. At first Angela felt a little put upon. But after letting Jonathan try his hand at cooking a few meals, she quickly discovered it was probably safer if she ruled the kitchen.

At the end of the school year, Jonathan passed his Review, only to discover that all teaching positions had been filled. When he enquired about continuing as a Teacher's Aid, they told him that as much as they appreciated his help, with the latest Government cutbacks, the position was no longer available. Jonathan was devastated. He had hoped to continue teaching at the university. As luck would have it, this happened on the same day Angela signed up and paid for her first semester in Paediatrics. When she came home excited, Jonathan didn't have the heart to tell her he lost his job. In the weeks that followed, he sent out resumes to as many schools as he could find. When it came time for the interviews, he found the common theme was they were looking for someone with more experience. After the twelfth rejection, he decided that he would apply at the local newspapers. He was asked by one of the larger city papers to present an article of his choosing along with his resume, but when he was called in, they told him his writing was a little too flowery for their liking. Disheartened, Jonathan returned home and finally broke the news to his wife.

Angela was understandably hurt that he hadn't told her right away, but to his surprise, she took it quite well. She had the summer free until her first semester, so she found a fulltime job for herself and encouraged Jonathan to not give up. Jonathan continued to look for work; as the month came to a close he still hadn't found a job. They would soon be out of funds and he knew that if he didn't find something soon, they wouldn't be able to afford Angela's tuition, and she would have to cancel her enrolment. Jonathan wasn't willing to crush her dreams. A week into August, Jonathan went to work for a construction company as a labourer.

The work was hard, but Jonathan didn't mind. The men he worked with were a little rough around the edges, but they all seemed to like him, all except for one young man named Doug. For reasons known only to himself, Doug had it out for him. Every time Jonathan turned around Doug was dropping garbage on the ground for him to clean, calling him vulgar names, and blaming him for things that were not his fault. After one particularly rough day, Jonathan came home so stressed that he felt ill.

"You need to give it to the Lord," Angela advised.

"I've been trying, but nothing ever changes," grumbled Jonathan.

"Have you tried talking to your boss about it?"

"I can't. When I mentioned going to the boss, one of the guys told me that Doug was his son."

"I am pretty sure he would understand if you talk to him."

"It doesn't work that way. Apparently Doug has done this before to other people he doesn't like, and when they tried to deal with it, all it did was get them into trouble. Sometimes I want to smash him in the face, he gets me so angry," Jonathan growled.

Angela sat beside her husband in thoughtful reflection, then softly quoted, "'But you, Israel, my servant Jacob, whom I have chosen, you descendants of Abraham my friend, I took you from the ends of the earth, from its farthest corners I called you I said, "You are my servant"; I have chosen you and have not rejected you. So do not fear, for I am with you; do not be dismayed, for I am your God. I will strengthen you and help you; I will uphold you with my righteous right hand'."

Perplexed, Jonathan looked at his wife, "Where in the Bible did you find that?" he asked, smiling back at her.

"Isaiah forty one, verses eight to ten. It's one of my grandmother's favourite verses. God was telling Israel that no matter how the other nations treated them, that He was the Lord of all and their strength. He is never going to abandon them. I know that the same is true for us as long as we seek after Him with all our heart," Angela said reassuringly.

"What would I do without you?" Jonathan's smile widened. "I don't think I could live without you."

"You mean the Lord, right?"

"What?"

"The Lord, you can't live without the Lord," Angela said softly, her brow creased with concern.

"Yeah, I guess," Jonathan replied, rubbing the back of his head like he always did when he was uncomfortable. Angela looked into her husband's eyes, and she was afraid — not for herself, but for him — for in that moment she realised that she was his whole world, and that scared her. He had known all the words to say, all the things to do, but not once had she called it into question or considered that he had never truly given his life to the Lord. Now the truth was staring her in the face; if Jonathan had never fully repented and trusted in Jesus, he didn't have salvation, and that terrified her.

"Jonathan, I can't always promise that I will be with you—" she began, but when Jonathan stared at her in shock she quickly eased his fears. "I am not cheating on you. I want you to understand that as much as I love you, one day I might die."

Jonathan laughed nervously "Well, if statistics are true, women tend to outlive men, so what are you worried about?"

"I don't want to be the centre of your world. That's God's place, not mine. 'Love the Lord your God with all your heart and with all your soul and with all your mind and with all your strength.'"

Jonathan nodded thoughtfully, "I know what it says. I just can't see my life without you."

Angela felt at a loss. She wasn't sure if she could reach him, but she was determined to not give up.

School came so quickly that it felt like they had missed summer entirely. Angela was so thrilled to be attending medical school, she could barely contain her excitement. At the end of her first day, she collapsed onto the sofa and fell asleep as soon as she lay her head down. Jonathan let her sleep, and ordered Chinese take-out. After her nap, Angela told him the amount of homework she already had and how heavy the semester's course was. Concerned, Jonathan asked if she was going to be able to handle the workload. She smiled and assured him that everything would be okay

Things seemed to go well for the both of them during the months that followed. Angela's course load kept her up studying until all hours of the night. Jonathan began to prepare the meals but needed a little help from Aunt Kathy, who came over whenever she was free to teach him the basics of cooking. The first few meals he made were barely edible, and Angela began to worry that, along with her schooling, she would have to take over meal preparation, but after a while Jonathan began to show progress with his cooking skills.

Nights were a little lonely for Jonathan with Angela staying up to study. He made up for it on the weekends by taking her out on dates, and in a short time, they finally found their rhythm and things began to look up.

CHAPTER 12
Calgary — 1984

Jonathan's life at work became more complicated when his foreman was sent to another site and one of Doug's friends was put in charge. One Thursday afternoon, while Jonathan was helping unload some material, a co-worker, Jim, came up to him looking grim. He told Jonathan he was needed at the 'white house', the head offices of the project managers and site superintendents. When Jonathan asked why they wanted to see him, the older man said he wasn't too sure. Jonathan felt jittery whenever he had to make a trip there, and this time was no exception. He had a gut feeling that something bad was going to happen. At the office, the receptionist asked him to wait in one of the conference rooms down the hall. The minutes dragged on and Jonathan's nerves began to get the best of him. The instant the door opened and Jonathan saw Doug following the foreman, Kevin, into the room, he knew something was up. Jonathan felt like he had been put on trial in absentia and was about to be handed the verdict. Doug stood smirking at him while Kevin took a seat across from Jonathan.

"Jonathan, did you leave plywood sheets on top of the building without tying them down?" Kevin asked, his tone was dark and accusatory.

"What? I don't understand, I haven't been up on the roof in weeks, and I would never leave plywood that high up without tying it down first."

"Don't lie, I saw you do it, and you obviously never listened to me when I told you to tie them down. Now we have an accident on our hands and police reports to fill out because, once again, you don't think before you do." Doug's face grew gnarled and venomous as his accusations flew. Stunned and bewildered, Jonathan felt the blood drain from his face. An allegation like this would cost him his job and he was afraid to think of what the legal ramifications would be if the company decided to implicate him.

"But it wasn't me, you can ask Jim. He knows what I have done these last few weeks. I promise you, I didn't do it," he pleaded.

Sighing, Kevin looked resigned as he sat back and folded his hands on his lap, "I guess that Doug and several others were seeing things, then?"

Doug's eyes never left Jonathan as his mouth began to curve into a smile. Jonathan was dumbfounded and at a loss. Doug had finally found a way to get rid of him. Hanging his head despairingly, he awaited to hear his fate.

"The company is going to pay for the damages to the vehicles hit by the flying sheets, but as for you, well I am sad to tell you that we are letting you go. Your past history and consistent mistakes have made you a liability and a risk to all those around you. So, I will ask you nicely to gather up your things and remove yourself from site. Your cheque is waiting for you at the front desk." Without another word, Kevin stood up and left the room.

Jonathan sat frozen. His whole world was destroyed in a matter of minutes, and he had Doug to thank for it. The young man smiled at him maliciously as he walked to the door, telling him to suck it up and get out of here. Grabbing a pencil off the table Jonathan whipped it at Doug, just missing him.

What was he going to do? What was he going to say when Angela found out? Jonathan gathered his belongings, and as he headed for his vehicle, Jim stopped him and asked what happened. When

Jonathan informed him of his wrongful termination, Jim shook his head, cursed, and spat on the ground. Jonathan shook the older gentleman's hand and thanked him for all his help over the last few months. Jim regarded him sadly and told him to keep his chin up and not to worry, promising that one day Doug would meet his Waterloo.

Jonathan was so stressed he could barely drive. As he set out for home, he felt his stomach lurch. He pulled over to the side of the road and vomited until all he could do was dry heave. When he got home he slouched in the sofa and hung his head back, feeling his pulse pound in his ears. It was quarter to one and Angela wasn't due home until six. He mulled over what to do, but was too stressed to think. Laying his head back once more, he closed his eyes and focussed on the low hum of the kitchen ceiling fan.

Jonathan awoke to the tantalising aroma of bacon. He went into the kitchen and where Angela was preparing BLT sandwiches.

"You're awake," she exclaimed happily. "I can't wait to show you what I got on my exam, you will be so proud of me." She practically danced across the room and snatched up a small envelope. She carefully withdrew the paper folded inside and presented it to him.

"See, it's my first ninety-seven, I can't believe it. I thought I would never get above a ninety, but a ninety-seven!" She squealed with glee. Jonathan scanned the paper, feeling guilty as he read the breakdown of the test and saw how well she had done. Angela made the first two BLT's and lifted the plate up to Jonathan. She froze when she saw his troubled expression.

"What's wrong?"

Pressing his lips into a tight line, Jonathan felt the stress build up inside again and struggled to control his shaking.

"I—" he licked his lips and cleared his throat before continuing "I lost my job today."

Angela dropped the plate she was holding and it shattered on the floor.

"What? You lost your job, but how?"

Jonathan gave her a concise account of the day's events that led up to his dismissal. Angela stared at him and, for the first time since he had known her, he saw a small flash of fear cross her face. They stood there, silent and unmoving, both stuck in their own thoughts. Angela was filled with anxiety, frustration and fear. This change of events affected everything, including her ability to pay for school.

Angela slowly started to clean up the kitchen. Jonathan continued to stand there silently, unwilling to look her in the eyes. He felt ashamed. He was the man of the house and was unable to provide for his wife. Feeling utterly defeated he started towards the entrance, when Angela took his hand.

"Wait," she said calmly, "It's not over yet, maybe we can ask one of our relatives for money, and you still have time to get another job."

Jonathan shook his head. Even with Angela's Scholarships and loans covering her tuition, on Jonathan's income, they barely covered bills, let alone rent. He couldn't afford not having a job. As for borrowing money, her grandparents were maxed out with the enrolment cost, they also owed both his Aunt Kathy and Mrs. Marshal for the school books as well as for covering some of their bills. Downcast, Angela realised that the only thing they could do was have her quit school.

"I'm so sorry. I didn't mean to lose my job, it just happened. I wish there was something I could do," Jonathan said, frustrated.

Angela looked him straight in the eye and shocked him with a tearful smile. "It's okay. I was worried this might happen, but it's like Grandpa told us, life will not be easy. We need to make the best of things. As for my school, I will finish this semester, and after that I will get a job so we can start saving money."

Jonathan started to protest, but she hushed him. "I know that you want me to finish, but we can't afford it right now. Maybe in a few years I will reapply, or maybe I will take something else instead. As for now, we need the money and stability; that's way more important than trying to continue my schooling with no money or a place to stay. All I want is for us to live happily together, and if that means that I have to give up something in return, then so be it."

When they went to bed, Jonathan couldn't help but feel he had destroyed Angela's plans for her future. Yet, she found no fault in him; nevertheless, he felt he had failed her. If he hadn't lost his job at the university, she wouldn't need to take a bus to school, and if he hadn't lost his job at the construction company she would have been able to continue her schooling. He couldn't find a viable argument in his defence proving it wasn't his fault, and Angela's assurances to the contrary did nothing to appease his guilt. Angela kissed him and caressed his face. Comforted by her touch, he drew her into his embrace and stroked her hair until she drifted into a deep sleep. She had been excessively tired lately, he realised as he studied her angelic face. The stress of her classes and late night studies were taking their toll on her. Perhaps leaving university until she could return without the financial stress weighing her down was a good thing.

As Christmas approached, Jonathan went to the university to ask Lang for some advice. The professor was surprised to see his former Aide at his door, but gladly welcomed him into his office. The professor chatted about the goings on in the university, the large overturn of faculty staff due to budget cuts, and the new computers that were driving him nuts. Lang could have prattled on forever about all that has happened since Jonathan left, but he could tell the young man had something on his mind.

"What is it, Lad?" he asked.

Jonathan took a moment to get over his nervousness. "I was wondering if you had any leads on some jobs I could apply for."

The professor thoughtfully sipped his coffee. "I'm not sure, there is nothing that really comes to mind. Have you tried applying to different local Papers?"

Nodding, Jonathan exhaled slowly, he was rapidly running out of options and time. They had to come up with some money soon or they might be depending on family for a place to live. "Well, thank you anyway, I thought I would at least ask."

"Hold on a minute," exclaimed the professor as Jonathan got up to leave. "You only came to me for a job, is that it?"

"Well no, I mean yes. I thought you might know someone I could talk to, I didn't mean any disrespect." stammered Jonathan.

"No, it's fine. I was hoping you actually wanted to see me, not because you had an agenda. You young kids tend to forget us older folk when you go out on your own, it's just like my kids. They only want you when they need something," Lang grumbled, adding, "Now that I think about it, a friend of mine said that schools where he lives are looking for western English-speaking teachers. Let's see if I can find that letter. Ah, here it is."

Jonathan's hopes were raised. A teaching job? Something he was actually interested in? Standing beside the professor, he leaned in to read the letter he was talking about.

"Japan!" he exclaimed.

"Yes, Japan. My friend still teaches there. I still wonder sometimes what my life may have been like if I had stayed."

"You lived there?" Jonathan asked incredulously.

"Yep, I was just a little older than you, but it was one of my first teaching experiences and one of the best times of my life. It was a huge culture shock when I got there. School is a child's top priority, and there is a lot of pressure from society and parents for excellence."

"But why me? Not to say I am not thankful for the consideration, but you know how I am in front of crowds. If I go, I will be standing in front of an entire class all by myself. I don't know if I am ready to teach in a foreign country."

Lang smiled, "Don't sell yourself short. By the end of that last semester you were doing pretty good on your own. Besides, with how quickly you went through those Japanese language studies

I gave you, I am sure you should know enough that you won't sound like some bumbling Western idiot."

Jonathan recalled the books the professor was talking about; in his opinion, he had only been able to retain the very basics of the language.

"Well, since you are so unsure of yourself, let's try a basic conversation and I will let you know how well you did." Lang placed his hands behind his head and began asking Jonathan some generic questions in Japanese: what his name was, where he lived, et cetera. At first, Jonathan was tripping over his own tongue, but as he felt more comfortable, he began responding with greater ease. Lang said that he was fluent enough that he shouldn't have too many problems speaking to Japanese students.

"You really think I should do it?" Jonathan asked hopefully.

"It is an option, but I think you need to talk it over with your wife before making your decision."

Jonathan thanked Lang profusely before heading home.

By the time he made it through the front door, he was beyond excited and couldn't wait to tell Angela the good news. He started by telling her that going to Japan was something they should seriously consider, and that rapidly transformed into them actually going. He prattled on about the different places they would see, all the people they would meet, and began discussing what they needed to do before leaving.

Angela listened to his news in silence, stunned by Jonathan's announcement. He didn't seriously intend to move them halfway across the world for a job — did he? What about their family and friends? What about her returning to school? Her heart sank, but she couldn't say anything. He was so thrilled by the prospect of having a real teaching job, she couldn't bear to tell him she didn't want to go. When Jonathan was finished, he sat at the table to make a list for the move, leaving his wife feeling crushed. She knew he was excited to teach again, and she didn't want to stand in the way of his career. The bottom line was, they needed the money. She had cost them considerably when it came to finances, and even though Jonathan hadn't seemed frustrated by it, he made it hard not to notice the hole they had dug for themselves. The more she dwelt on her failings, on everything Jonathan had given up to help her, their financial problems, and all that they owed, the more depressed she became. Angela sank into a chair, feeling the weight of her circumstances smothering her.

"What's wrong, honey? Is everything all right?" Jonathan asked.

"Nothing," she said. When he raised a questioning brow she just shook her head and smiled, putting on a brave face.

"Okay, then. We need to call your grandparents to see if they can store some of our belongings in one of their empty sheds until we return."

Return? Somehow, she had feared that they would never return from this trip, she would forever be trapped in a foreign land, with foreign people. Come on, Angela, he gave you support for what you were doing. Why can't you reciprocate?

Angela picked up the phone to call her grandparents. She struggled with every press of a button as an inner battle waged on inside her over what to do. Was she going to pack up and leave everything behind, or did she have the courage to tell Jonathan what she felt and take the chance that he may have to give up on his pursuit in order to make her happy?

CHAPTER 13
Calgary — January 1985

Their announcement came as a shock to their family. Everyone tried to persuade Jonathan to at least take some time to reconsider his decision, but Jonathan had his mind set and there was no talking him out of his decision. When anyone asked Angela what she felt about it, she would tell them that she supported her husband in any decision he made. This didn't sit well with Stan, and he tried to dissuade Jonathan, without success.

Unaffected by the opposition he was receiving, Jonathan began making the arrangements with Lang. A month later, they received a confirmation letter from a school in Tokyo. When the contract was signed, Angela discovered that they would be required to stay for at least a year and that all living expenses would be covered by the School Board. Even a year felt way too long; Angela hoped this trip would make Jonathan realise how much they needed their family, though it was doubtful he would at this juncture.

They were set to leave near the end of February. The school year in Japan started in April, which gave Jonathan some time to train and prepare ahead of time. The days leading up to their departure flew by, and before Angela knew it they were at the airport saying goodbye to family and friends. Before leaving, Stephanie made her promise to call her at least once a month so they could keep current on one another's activities. Through tear-filled eyes, Angela gave her friend one final hug goodbye.

During the flight, Angela wanted to sleep but found it impossible as the hum of the engines was too loud to ignore. Jonathan spent the time catching up on his studies of Japan's culture and people, and took breaks to practice his linguistic skills in Japanese. Angela closed her eyes and imagined she was flying back home, with her family waiting for her return. Her heart already ached for the sound of her grandmother's voice, or the laughter and stories of Aunt Kathy and her kids. She longed for Stephanie's endless chatter and warm friendship, and the smell of her grandparent's farm. As each face took form in her mind she felt herself begin to drift away to sleep.

A hand gripped her shoulder, shaking her awake.

"Angela, look!" Jonathan's voice shook with excitement. "We're here! I think that's Tokyo!"

Wiping the sleep from her eyes, Angela raised her head to find Jonathan peering out over the city that sprawled below. The city was a much larger than she had expected, spreading out as far as she could see. Mount Fuji stood tall and proud, a silent sentinel sixty miles southwest of Tokyo, yet clearly visible. The city was unlike anything she had come to expect. Calgary had a central downtown where all the office buildings and its largest towers resided. It was hard to tell which area of Tokyo was residential or business, as it seemed to be one large conglomerate of towers that spread themselves across the entire city.

The pilot's voice came over the PA and announced that they would be landing in a few minutes. Jonathan couldn't wait. He began telling Angela about all the sights they would see and the interesting people they would meet. Every word seemed to drive home the feeling that she would never see home again. As much as she tried to keep up the appearance of a loving and supportive wife, she was finding it a struggle to hold in her deep-seated regret.

All too soon, their plane landed and the pilot announced their arrival at Haneda Airport. This being their first flight, they were confused about where they needed to go. An airport attendant noticed them and graciously escorted them to Immigration, where their documents and Jonathan's work visa were thoroughly examined before they were granted entrance into Japan. When they had finally made it through, they joined dozens of new arrivals who were waiting for their rides to arrive. Jonathan and Angela were confused and a little nervous, as they didn't know who was supposed to meet them.

Jonathan caught glimpse of two men holding up a sign with his last name written in both English and Japanese. He and Angela wound their way through the milling throng to the pair. Jonathan gave the two gentlemen a low bow which brought a small laugh from the younger one.

"Sorry, did I do it wrong?" Jonathan asked.

"No, it's quite all right, Hansen-san. During your stay with us you will learn how to properly greet someone, but that is a lesson for another time. I am Kato Katsunori. I work for our international exchange program, and this is one of the members of our student council, Iida Genji. He attends the high school where you will be teaching."

Genji offered to help with their bags, and helped Jonathan load them onto a waiting trolley. Mr. Kato guided them to their vehicle, while Genji followed with the luggage. Mr. Kato quietly quizzed Jonathan on Japanese etiquette, and was happily surprised to discover that he already had a working understanding of most of the customs. Angela remained silent, sticking close to her husband as they made their way through the airport's multitudinous throng. Many men, both young and old, cast her admiring glances, making her wonder if her short skirt and blouse may have been a bad choice in travelling attire.

Feeling a little safer when they reached their ride, she was surprised when Mr. Kato offered his hand to help her into the vehicle while Jonathan took their bags and put them in the trunk. That was one thing she did notice, how respectful and polite these two men were. It felt strange, but somehow refreshing to find people with such decency and common courtesy.

They were driven to the Shinagawa District where Jonathan was scheduled to meet the heads of the School Board. Mr. Kato talked at length about the training Jonathan was to receive, and told him of some of the lovely sites they might like to visit while during their stay. Jonathan was then asked a question in Japanese. Caught off guard, he stumbled over his reply. He tried again, this time a little more fluently.

"That was really good, Hansen-sensei," Genji said, impressed. "Does your wife speak Japanese as well?"

"No, sorry. I haven't taken the time to study it like my husband, but I'm pretty sure he will be giving me lessons while we're here," Angela said.

Jonathan gently squeezed her hand, grinning. Their first stop was at the high school where he was going to be teaching. Genji and Mr. Kato guided Jonathan and Angela inside where they were greeted by the school trustee, Mr. Adachi, and his assistant, Mr. Ueda. They were then ushered into a small private office where Jonathan was handed a copy of his work contract and several other documents that required his signature. They discussed the terms of his work contract and confirmed how much he was to expect to be paid.

"You will be meeting with the school's Principal, Kagawa Kocho-sensei, tomorrow morning. Mr. Kato will show you his office before you leave. As for living arrangements, we have set you up with a teacher from the United States. She will meet with you at your apartment complex after our meeting here. In conclusion, we would like to welcome you to Japan and we look forward to working with you, Hansen-san." Mr. Kato showed Jonathan the location of Mr. Kagawa's office before rushing them out the door. "I apologise for the rush, but your flight was later than expected," Mr. Kato said, getting into the car.

They drove a short distance to their apartment complex. When they entered the foyer, they were greeted by a delightful and charming young woman with a Western American accent.

"Hi, my name is Kate Walsh and I will be helping you during your stay in Japan," the slim brunette said, shaking their hands.

"I'm Jonathan, and this is my wife, Angela."

Angela was happy to have a woman to talk to. Kate's energy and infectious exuberance reminded her of Stephanie, and she was just as chatty and opinionated. The similarities made her miss her friend even more and drove home that she was far from the friends and family she had left behind.

Mr. Kato asked Genji to help them with their bags while he went to make a quick call. Genji graciously offered to take the heavier bags, much to Jonathan's discomfiture. The young man told him it was an honour to help his new teacher. Jonathan was taken aback by the respectfulness and thoughtfulness of the young man; back at home some of the students he had worked with were polite and helpful, but nowhere near this level. He had heard a lot about the consideration and courtesy the Japanese people showed foreigners, but to experience it firsthand came as quite a shock.

After setting their luggage in the apartment's genkan, Genji told them that he had to leave. Jonathan thanked him and moved to shake his hand. Caught off guard Genji froze for a moment before extending his own hand.

"Oh, sorry. I guess I should have bowed?"

"It's all right, Hansen-sensei, I am sure you will catch on soon enough before classes begin," he said with a firm handshake, and left.

"Where do you two come from?" Kate asked Angela as they set the lighter bags next to the luggage.

"Calgary," Jonathan responded.

"Texas?"

"Alberta, Canada. Where are you from?"

"San Francisco, California. I came here with my boyfriend, but we ended up splitting."

"I'm sorry to hear that. Are you working at the same high school as Jonathan?" Angela asked.

"No, I teach at an elementary school, but the same group that recruited you hired me. I love to teach and I wanted adventure, so I packed my bags and dropped off a resume. The next thing I knew, I was working as an elementary teacher in a school only a few blocks from yours."

Kate showed them around their apartment, which was large, by Japanese standards. The genkan opened up to a large furnished living room with a sofa and a recliner opposite a small television. Next to the television were sliding glass doors that opened onto the balcony. The hallway at the other one end of the living room led to a small bathroom, a smaller water closet, a linen closet and two bedrooms. The bedroom closets held futons and extra bedding. Through the archway on the right of the living room was the kitchen and a small dining nook. The kitchen had a small refrigerator, a microwave, toaster oven, two burner gas cooking table and was stocked with dinnerware settings for six, eating and cooking utensils, a rice maker and, to the left of the cooker, a lower cupboard contained stainless cookware. The only thing missing was food.

Kate took them to the market where they picked out some interesting local fruits and vegetables. Jonathan wasn't so keen on the selection, but Kate pointed out that beggars couldn't be choosers. At the bakery, they bought bread, beef and pork buns, and a few tasty and curious looking pastries. On their return, they made a slight detour to see where Kate lived on the level below. Once the groceries were put away, Angela brewed a pot of genmaicha tea and she and Kate sat at the dining table, where they laughed and talked at length about their families and friends. Comfortably ensconced in the recliner, with tea and tea cakes to fortify him, Jonathan listened intently. An hour later he succumbed to jet lag and fell asleep. The girls continued their chat as they sampled the goodies.

"Shoot," Kate exclaimed in surprise, "it's coming up eleven and I haven't prepared for tomorrow's class. I am so sorry for keeping you two up; I'm glad I finally have someone to chat with, though."

"So am I. I look forward to spending some more time with you. We should have you over for dinner some time."

"Yes, and I should show you how to cook some easy meals you two might like. Beef is a little pricey over here, so it would be wise to adjust your palates to the local produce and seafood." Kate put on her shoes and shook Angela's hand, "Well, you should get your husband to bed. He has a long day tomorrow. Make sure that he wakes up and meets me for nine. I will meet him in the lobby."

Jonathan was fast asleep. His snoring was so loud Angela was surprised it didn't waken him. She shook him awake and helped him into bed. She was a little restless, so she brewed a fresh pot of tea and stood out on the balcony. The air was humid and thick with the smells of car exhaust, rain, rich earth, and sea salt. Looking out over the lights of the city, she still couldn't believe how large it was. She wondered if she would ever get used to living in such a large metropolis and being so far from home, but for her husband's sake, she was willing to try anything.

Jonathan was scheduled to arrive at the Kasuhiro High School at ten, but both he and Angela forgot to set the alarm. When Jonathan woke up it was nearing nine-thirty, which barely gave him any time to get ready or eat. He showed up twenty minutes late for his appointment with Mr. Kagawa. The office contained one large oval table and chairs opposite the large rectangular desk where Mr. Kagawa sat. Jonathan bowed nervously. Mr. Kagawa looked up from his paperwork, his gaze narrowing as he scrutinised Jonathan. He pointed to a book on the corner of his desk and went back to his work. Jonathan picked the book up and leafed through the first few pages. Most of it was written in English and spelt out several of the school's guidelines and rules, and the last few pages held his class schedule for the next few months.

"I hope that today is not an indication of things to come, Hansen-san." Before Jonathan could say anything Mr. Kagawa raised his hand. "In Japanese please."

It took a moment for Jonathan to remember the words. "No, sir. I'm sorry, Kagawa-sama."

Without raising his head, Mr. Kagawa told him that his Japanese needed work, and dismissed him. When Jonathan left the office, a young man in brown slacks and black vest jacket rose from a chair across the hall and introduced himself as Mr. Matsuno.

"I have been assigned to you as an aid during your stay with us, Hen ... Han ... son-san." Mr. Matsuno tried to sound out the unfamiliar name.

Mr. Matsuno's English was good, but his sentences were disjointed. He gave Jonathan an extensive tour. The school was unremarkable, designed more for function than style. It was similar to a Canadian high school, but with two key differences situated immediately inside the entrance: the long rows of box lockers that were stacked six high, and the genkan opposite with its rows of open cubicles that stored the outdoor shoes of everyone who entered the building.

Each classroom was the same rectangle with windows on one side and a door opposite. It held a chalkboard, and one small desk for the teacher facing double rows of wooden desks for the students. Mr. Matsuno advised that each pair of desks be occupied by a boy and a girl. He explained that each class was assigned its own room, which the students were expected to clean at the end of the day, and it was the teacher's responsibility to take their material to each class.

When they had finished the tour, they returned to the teachers' room to go over the Teacher's Guidebook. They went to a group of desks at the end of the room where Mr. Matsuno detailed the responsibilities of the teachers and students. He handed Jonathan the textbooks he was required to teach from. It was his responsibility to familiarize himself with them and use the examples from the teacher's guide to structure his lessons. Jonathan asked if he was permitted to use supplementary texts and was told that he could, so long as he followed the sequence of material in the school's textbooks and the Teacher's Guidebook. Mr. Matsuno jotted down a quick note for Jonathan and told him to meet him tomorrow in the specified classroom.

When Jonathan got home, he could hear Angela moving around in the kitchen. He sat at the table, pulled out his books and began leafing through them. The amount of information he needed to absorb was daunting. He was beginning to feel nervous at the prospect of teaching a group of students by himself.

"How was your first day?" Angela moved his book and placed a plate of food in front of him.

"A little intimidating."

"I'm sure you will be fine, I have faith in you, and so does Professor Lang. If he didn't, he wouldn't have given you this opportunity."

"I know." He eyed the food distastefully. It was salmon sushi, something he didn't care for.

"Sorry, I know you don't like this, but there isn't much in the fridge. We need to pick up more groceries."

Jonathan picked up his chopsticks and attempted to pick up a sushi roll. Just as it reached his mouth, he dropped it.

"Wow, and I thought I had problems," Angela said with a laugh as he blotted soya sauce off his shirt.

"Yes, well, let's hope no one takes us out for dinner." He picked up the next sushi roll by hand and carefully removed strip of raw salmon from the centre before eating the rice roll.

"We still haven't prayed over this place, so why don't you take a break?"

"I wish I could, but I have so much to do to get ready for my classes."

"You can't take even a couple minutes?"

Jonathan was getting annoyed, "Look, I'm sorry, but this is really important. I need to prove myself to them and that means I need to spend as much time as possible preparing. I'm sure God will bless this house, whether we do it together or not. Why don't you get started and if I get a moment, I will join you."

Angela watched him dejectedly as he leafed through his books and jotted down notes. Back in the kitchen, she leaned against the counter and thought again about all those she had left behind.

"Please, Lord, help me, give me the strength, help me to respect my husband and help him persevere." Wiping away a tear, she decided to start in the kitchen and then go room to room, praying over their entire household.

Jonathan never once got up from the chair as he pored over his texts, trying to map out a syllabus that conformed with the school's curriculum. He didn't even notice his wife in the room. Angela continued through the house until she finished in their bedroom. Once she was done, she decided to see if Kate was up for a visit. She grabbed her purse, quickly looking back to see if Jonathan noticed her. He was so absorbed with his work he didn't hear the door open or close with her departure.

Kate's apartment was down one level and three doors from the stairs. She rapped twice on the door and anxiously waited.

"Who is it?"

"Angela."

"Come in!"

Angela opened the door and stepped inside. Kate poked her head around the hall corner, her hair soaking wet. "Give me a second to get some clothes on. Make yourself comfortable."

Angela looked around the room as she headed for the sofa. A collection of paintings and drawings adorned the walls. The detail of some of the works was incredible, and in one the birds and trees were almost lifelike. The paintings were outstanding and the vivid colours brought them to life.

"What do you think?"

"They're amazing," Angela stammered, startled by Kate's sudden appearance.

"I took art classes when I attended university. It's more of a hobby. I had been offered money for some of them, but I just never had the heart to part with them," she said, lightly brushing some of the paintings with her fingertips, and straightening the ones that were crooked. "How was Jonathan's first day? I'm sorry I couldn't wait for him."

Angela assured her that sleeping in was a rarity for Jonathan, and attributed his atypical lateness to Jet Lag. They talked about many things, from Angela's reluctance to come to Japan, to the differences between Japanese and Western culture, to religion. When Angela mentioned that they were Christians, Kate told her of a small church that one of her students attended. Shintoism was the largest practiced religion, followed by Buddhism, and were considered to be intrinsically connected yet mutually exclusive. Even after living in Japan for two years, she couldn't understand how their beliefs worked. As for religion as a whole, her mother had been all fire and brimstone, which was the main reason Kate was an atheist and didn't put much stock in a god or higher power.

"I think that the biggest difference between Christianity and the other religions, is that we don't work our way to heaven."

"How so?" Kate asked a little perplexed and interested. "My mom always harped on me to say my benedictions, and confessions or I will surely go into the lake of fire."

"Confession without repentance and good works protects you from judgement as much as giving to charity after you commit a crime prevents you from going to jail. According to the Bible we are all worthy of God's judgement. None of us have kept His Commandments and He says that if you break even one then you break them all."

"This God of yours sounds like a tyrant, I thought he was a god of love?"

"He is, but He is also just. Would you expect a good judge to let a murderer go because the judge was 'loving'? That would make him a bad judge and unjust."

"So, you are saying that if someone steals, even once, they burn?" Kate asked, feeling quite indignant.

"God is perfect, and therefore His laws and justice are perfect. If I steal from a homeless person, likely nothing will happen to me. On the other hand, if I embezzle money from the government, I will be tried and sent to jail. When I commit a sin, even something as *small* as stealing, I am committing the offence against the One who created everything, including me."

"So, there is nothing we can do, we all just go into the everlasting inferno?"

"If we are to get what we deserve, we would. God loved us so much that He graciously sent His Son, Jesus, to live a perfect life and He chose to suffer a criminal's death on the cross. Then, three days later, He rose and conquered death all in order to pay your debt." Kate looked at Angela, puzzled. Angela elaborated. "Okay, let me take you back to the courtroom. Let us say that you decided not to pay your taxes, were caught and told that you either had to pay a huge sum you couldn't afford or go to jail. Your only recourse is to go to jail, but at the last minute, someone comes in and pays your fine."

"All I have to do is accept Jesus and everything is all right?" Kate asked, still a little confused.

"No. You need to confess your sin, and repent, which means completely turning away from that behaviour. Then you need to make Jesus as your number one priority and ruler of your life."

"That's an interesting perspective to think about." After an awkward silence she asked, "Was there anything else you wanted to talk about?"

Thinking for a moment, Angela shook her head. "No, I just felt like talking to someone."

"Is something going on between you and hubby?"

"No, it's nothing." She wanted to open up to Kate, but with their difference of beliefs she wasn't too sure Kate would understand.

"Are you sure?" Kate asked, concerned. "You can tell me if he's done anything. I won't say anything or judge you."

"I'm fine really, he has never been abusive. I guess we simply don't always see things eye to eye."

"That's marriage, I guess. Part of the reason I will never tie the knot."

Still feeling a little awkward after their talk, Angela excused herself, explaining that she had to get supper ready.

When she had returned home, Jonathan was still working. If she didn't make him something to eat soon, he would go the night without food and then complain about being hungry the next morning. Sometimes she wondered if he would work his life away. He was so involved that it appeared that the only thing he actually cared about was his job.

She prepared a dish of rice and fried fish with some buttered bread. A simple enough dinner and she knew it was something he would actually eat. When supper was ready, she had to practically tear him away from his books. Dinner was eaten in silence, and Jonathan continued working, completely ignoring her. After dinner she cleaned up and headed to bed, asking Jonathan if he wanted to join her. He mumbled something about needing to get some reading in before the night's end. Angela sighed and told him she loved him before heading to bed.

CHAPTER 14
Japan — 1985

In the weeks before school began, Jonathan pored over his notes and the material he had to teach from. He found that the material didn't cover the English language in as much depth as he'd like, so he pulled out some study aids that would give the students a broader understanding. He spent hours compiling the information and material he had collected to make up several months' worth of information for the students to absorb. Mr. Matsuno made sure he received as much in-class training as he needed to feel confident.

With all of Jonathan's time and attention focussed on his work, Angela had to find something to occupy her time. One day she decided to go out for a walk and check out neighbourhood. The city streets were filled with people bustling around, but unlike what she was used to back home, the only noise that could be heard was that of the traffic. The sidewalks that bordered the roads were much larger than those found in Calgary. Bus stops were located at regular intervals with maps that marked out the bus routes as well as several key locations. One thing she couldn't help but notice was the large amount of bicycles and bike racks. She had to dodge a few cyclists who nearly clipped her when she wasn't paying attention. The city moved at a steady beat, like an efficient and well-oiled machine. Everyone walked with purpose as if every step counted.

When she had walked several blocks, the aroma of fresh baked goods drew her to the marketplace that Kate had taken them to on their first day. The first shop she looked at carried fresh fruits and vegetables, some she couldn't identify. She wanted to pick out some items but she wasn't sure how their currency worked. She became nervous when the elderly vendor eyed her suspiciously, so she moved on to the next table. She could still feel the old man's eyes on her, but when she looked at him surreptitiously, he was busy dealing with a customer.

"Are you looking for something?" a young man wearing an apron asked, as he emptied the basket of fresh bread he was carrying.

"Uh no, well maybe," she floundered, startled by the unexpected interruption.

He smiled, picking out some baked goods. He handed them to her. "Here, this you might like. If you want, it only nine hundred yen."

"Nine hundred yen!" She inspected the items dubiously. "That sounds like a lot of money."

Puzzled, he took the bag back from her. "It's good price for these."

He held the bag open so she could get better look. Flustered, Angela tried to remember the value of the individual coins and bills Jonathan had given her. She remembered him showing her how Japanese currency worked, but in that moment she couldn't bring it to mind. The young man watched her puzzle over the money, and understood the nature of her problem.

"Here, I show you."

He smiled and took her to the till where he explained the price of each of the items and the associated yen coins and bills. He then had her select some items and match the price given with what she had for money. On the third try she finally understood it.

"Oh, thank you so much!"

With a small bow, he took her money for the items he had picked out for her. "If you need help, just ask, some of the others not know English well, I can translate for you."

"I will keep that in mind next time I shop here, and thank you again." Pleased with her purchases, she checked the time. It was coming up one o'clock and she wanted to look around a bit more before she had to get home.

"My name Noguchi Eiichi."

"I'm Angela Hansen, my husband and I have just moved to Japan."

"I welcome you to Japan, Okyakusama. I am happy to serve you, may you have good day." Eiichi gave her a small nod, and turned his attention to the other customers who had lined up at his till.

Angela resumed her tour of the market. One vendor sold paintings and oriental tea cups, another had toys and other novelties. She watched a little girl with her grandparents browse through the selection of toys. The grandfather was trying to draw the child's attention to a ceramic tea set, but she was more interested in a selection of robotic action figures. She picked up one of the small figures. When she noticed Angela smiling at her, she hid her face behind the toy and peeked around it. Angela grinned at her, making her giggle. The grandmother murmured something into the girl's ear, and picked her up. The girl wrapped her arms around the woman's neck and giggled once more, waving goodbye. Angela's heart melted at the sight, and she realised that she longed for a child of her own.

Angela picked up the figure and studied it, mentally envisioning a child of her own playing with it on the floor while she prepared supper. She could see the child's face light up when Jonathan came home from work. The fantasy came so easily to mind, and was so clear, it made her wonder if now wasn't the time to start their own family. Stephanie would tell her she was crazy. What about Jonathan? She speculated that he would say they couldn't afford a child just yet, and point out that neither of them had established themselves in their chosen careers. As she worked through the list, the cons began to outweigh the pros, and she was feeling disheartened. What if they were never ready to have a child?

Time slipped by and before she knew it, it was almost four and she needed to get home. She travelled back, but got lost when she didn't recognized an intersection. Looking at her surroundings, she could not make out which way to turn. Going back she stopped at another intersection, but still couldn't figure out which street to take. What am I going to do now, Lord? Angela watched people as they passed her on the street, and feelings of isolation and fear welled up inside of her. A moment later a slim brunette caught her eye. It was Kate coming back from the market with groceries in hand. Thank you, Jesus!

"Kate!" Angela cried. Looking about, Kate caught sight of Angela. She stopped and waited for her.

"Going my way?" Kate asked. "I was just headed home."

Angela nodded, thankful that she didn't have to admit that she had gotten lost. They walked to the intersection where Angela had gotten confused the first time and this time took the right turn. As they walked, Kate asked her how things were going between her and Jonathan. Angela was hesitant to disclose too many details, not wanting to cast Jonathan in a bad light. She did point out that he had developed the habit of becoming so involved in his job that he would shut everyone else out, even her.

"I know how that feels, it was part of the reason why my parents split. My dad lived to work, and when my mother would tell him he needed to spend more time with the family, he'd simply shrug his shoulders and say we were needy." Angela couldn't imagine someone ever being so callous.

She and Kate walked by a park where several children and their mothers had gathered to enjoy some playtime. There were some tables set up where several people played a game using black and white stones on a wooden board with a grid painted on it. Angela watched curiously as the two players seemed to be trying to surround one another's stones with their own while trying to cover the board with as many of their own stones as possible.

"What game are they playing?" she asked Kate.

"That game is called Go. It's a popular abstract strategy game, similar to chess, only the object is to create rather than to destroy. A few of my students who I used to teach made a club at our school just to get together with others who played the game."

They watched the game for a few more minutes before continuing on their way. Angela's grandparents had instilled a joy of board games in her at an early age, and she loved playing them as a child. Whenever she tried to play with Jonathan, he would complain as soon as he began to lose. The only time he had fun was while he was winning, or when he played chess — which she sucked at. She was a little disappointed that they didn't share that in common, but it didn't stop her from trying to get him to play a game of chess once in a while. This game wasn't chess, but seemed similar, and she thought it might help him to relax and refocus on their relationship.

When they arrived back at the apartments, Angela declined Kate's invitation to stop in for coffee, citing the need to get supper on before Jonathan got home. Once again Jonathan spent the night immersed in his work. When she asked if he really needed to work so hard on his syllabus when school didn't start for another two weeks, he explained to her that his goal was to provide his students with the best lesson layout possible. When she realised that he was probably right, Angela called it a night and climbed into bed with a Christian romance novel. As she got settled, she remembered that she had promised to call Stephanie back a couple of days ago. Mindful of the eight hour time difference, and that Stephanie had taken the next few days off for her grandmother's funeral, she hoped Stephanie would be up.

Stephanie answered at the fourth ring.

"Hey Steph, it's Angela, sorry I didn't call back until today."

"Oh, my goodness, Angie. Hey Mom!" Stephanie covered the receiver so she could talk to her mother, then said to Angela, "We have about an hour to chat, a little short for my liking but at least it's something. So, how are you doing? Something's wrong. Is Jonathan treating you okay? If he's not, you can tell him I will kick his butt when you guys come back home."

Angela laughed, she didn't realise how much she missed Stephanie's brashness. "No, the only thing he's doing that's bothering me is putting work before family."

"You're the one who married a teacher." Stephanie paused for a moment. "If you can't sort it out, then you'll just have to live with it. He may have been cute and perfect when we were in school, but he sounds like more of a pain in the butt than he's worth."

Angela wanted to agree but, in her opinion, pessimism was counterproductive, and talking negatively about her husband was ungodly. "I know he can be, but he's worth it. I only wish he would take some time out for us and realise that there is more to life than school. Speaking of school, how are your studies going?"

Stephanie was in her last term and was trying to decide which grade she wanted to teach. Angela suggested elementary level, as she loved young children. Stephanie had to agree that shaping the minds of children eager to learn was preferable to being ogled by hormonal teenaged boys. When asked what Japanese schools were like, all Angela could tell her was that the Japanese school calendar had classes running year-round with three semester breaks and that the students were under a lot of pressure to excel.

The conversation shifted to the death of Stephanie's grandmother and how it was affecting her mother. The loss was extremely hard on Mrs. Marshal, and what puzzled Stephanie was how her mother wished that her ex-husband were still there.

"I don't get it. Wouldn't you write Jonathan off if he had run off with his secretary?"

Angela thought about it for a moment. "I take it that you have never forgiven your father?"

"It's not like I haven't tried," Stephanie said after a brief silence. "I just can't get over how much he hurt her."

"I know, Steph, but God tells us that we need to forgive one another, no matter how we feel."

"What about your husband, then?" Stephanie shot back.

"Even my husband, as much as he drives me nuts." Angela ignored the barb. "It's different when you truly love someone, Steph. I know that if it happened to me, it would be hard to remove myself from the deep feelings of love I have for Jonathan. Even though that person really hurt you, the love you feel sometimes never really goes away. You really need to forgive your father. He still loves you." Angela could imagine her rolling her eyes.

"I know, it's just hard to get past his floozy," Stephanie said with a sigh. "I get so mad when he brings her around."

"Then tell him how you feel instead of holding it in."

"Only if you talk to Jonathan."

"Agreed."

"Angela, I really miss you."

"I miss you, too. I will try to call you in a couple of weeks, but I should let you go so you can get ready."

"Okay. Tell Jonathan I told him he has to start paying attention to you."

Angela checked the time and saw that they had been talking for almost an hour. She called out to Jonathan to ask if he was coming to bed. He told her he only had to finish a few things and that he would join her soon. Angela opened her book and began reading. Before long, she began to nod off, and realised that Jonathan was not coming to bed any time soon. She'd talk to him in the morning before he left for work, she decided and turned off the light.

It was almost ten in the morning when pain awoke her. Her mind was fuzzy as she made the transition from sleep to full wakefulness. She gasped as she felt a sharp pain in her abdomen once more. She waited a moment for it to subside; once it did, she waited a little longer to see if it would come back. 'Female problems' is what the doctor had called them during her last physical before leaving Calgary. She shrugged them off and looked over to Jonathan's side of the bed; the covers were undisturbed.

She donned her robe and padded to the living room. It was vacant as well; Jonathan had gone to work without wakening her. Ever since he had started this job, he had become totally obsessed with perfecting his syllabus. It was like when he worked at the university, only worse. She knew that moving so far away from home would take some adjustment, but she never imagined that she would be left completely on her own. Remembering her conversation with Stephanie, she tried to calm down, but after weeks of being ignored, she couldn't take it any more and her body shook from the mounting hurt and frustration.

That's it! She fumed. If he thinks he can drag me half-way across the world without considering my feelings and then turn around and abandon me, he's got something coming.

She decided not to do anything that day but relax and read. When Jonathan got home, arms full, he walked to the nook and set his load of texts on the table. He noticed the breakfast dishes on the counter. He looked at Angela, who was curled up on the sofa, reading.

"What's for supper?" he asked.

Angela didn't look up. Jonathan waited a moment to see if she would respond. When she didn't, he hung up his coat and swapped shoes for slippers.

"In two more weeks, I will be teaching my own class," he said. "Mr. Matsuno says my Japanese is a lot more fluent. After a few weeks of practise in front of a class, he believes I should be good enough to teach on my own."

Sitting beside Angela, he leaned in for a kiss. Angela shifted away from him, her attention riveted on her book. Jonathan tickled her sides. She pushed his hands away. She stood with a scowl and went to the kitchen to put the kettle on. Confused, Jonathan followed her.

"Angela?" Her disquiet was starting to aggravate him. "Did I say something wrong?"

Angela looked at him in astonishment, and wondered how he could be so daft. She pushed past him to retrieve her book and went to the bedroom. Jonathan watched her go, bewildered.

At a loss, he took it upon himself to make supper. He determined that fish and rice was the safest dish to prepare. While the rice steamed, he fried the fish. He liberally seasoned it with the few spices he could find, rationalizing that the spice would mask the fishy taste. The end result was burnt fish and undercooked rice. He considered binning it and making another dish. A rumble of his belly made him decide otherwise, so he prepared two plates before going to the bedroom.

Angela was lying on her side with the blankets pulled up. The lights were off and Jonathan tripped over a pair of slippers that had been left out.

"What are you doing?" Angela muttered, poking her head out and turning on the bedside lamp.

"You seem a little upset, so I made supper." Jonathan came over to her side and put the plate on her nightstand.

Angela wrinkling her nose at the conflicting aromas that emanated from the dish. She slowly sat up and gave the food a dubious look.

"What is it?"

"Fish and rice. Sorry about the rice, but you know how bad I am at cooking." He took a forkful of fish.

Angela took a small sample of the fish and sniffed at it. She took a tentative taste. The flavour of fish was impossible to distinguish from the other flavours that overwhelmed her mouth. Each brought forth its own version of the good, the bad and the burning. Angela pondered the many horrible insults a meal like this would inflict upon her intestines. Watching Jonathan, she couldn't believe he could eat this abomination with such zeal.

"Jonathan, what spices did you use?"

"Most of them. I thought that mixing them would give it an interesting flavour. It's at least better than the actual taste of the fish."

Angela wasn't sure about that. She put the plate back onto the nightstand, and gave her husband an apologetic smile. "Jonathan, I appreciate the gesture, but I can't eat this."

"That bad?"

"Worse." She gave him a warm hug. "It was a nice gesture, but let's leave the cooking to me, okay?"

She got out of bed and took their dishes to the kitchen. The kitchen was a war zone. Bits of rice had been strewn about, and drippings of grease mottled the counter. Angela cleared off the counter, cleaned the rice cooker, and put the pan and utensils into the sink. The spices he had used had been left out. She was astonished by how many different spices he had used on the fish; no wonder it tasted so awful. In short order she had an edible batch of fish and rice on the table and they shared their late supper in thoughtful silence.

Later, as they prepared for bed, Jonathan took her hand and said earnestly, "I'm sorry. I know I can get so caught up in my work that I tend to forget about everything else. Even you, my heart and my strength. I can't keep on doing this to you. I will do better, I promise."

"We need to share more quality time," she said. "Why don't we start with you coming to church with me?"

"Church?" he repeated.

"Yes, church. Over the past year you have practically stopped attending, and when you do go, it's only after I hound you about it." She gave him a searching look. "Kate gave me the address of a small home church in another district. I was planning to go this weekend. I want you to accompany me."

"I only have two weeks before school starts an—" he cut off short as Angela drew back. Grasping at her hand, he pulled her back, "Look, I will see what I can do. I promise I will make more of an effort to join you when I can."

Nodding, Angela slid under the covers and gave him another kiss. She reached for the bedside lamp to turn it off, but stopped as a nagging question came to mind.

"Jonathan, why do you always seem to find a way to skip out on church?"

"I don't see how going to church makes you a Christian, it would be like saying eating at a burger joint makes you a double cheese burger."

"We can't forsake the fellowship of the saints. They are what build us and make us stronger in the Lord. If you stop attending church, how can you be the iron that sharpens iron?" She lay her head on his chest. "Please, come to church with me. You never know, you might meet some people you like."

He placed his arms around her, and kissed her on the forehead. "Like I said, I will try to make it as often as a can."

Angela could only hope that he wouldn't go back on his word, but only time would tell.

CHAPTER 15
Japan — 1985

Pastor Hikaru took his worn and battered Bible from his desk and tucked his sermon notes between the pages of scriptures he had planned out for the day. It was almost nine and he only had a few short minutes before his wife, Mai, would be opening their doors for the parishioners. He went downstairs into their basement where his sons were setting up the chairs.

"Good morning, Father!" his twelve-year-old son exclaimed, running over to give him a hug.

"Good morning, Haru, and how are you and Ichiro doing this morning?"

"Great! Everything is set up, Father."

"After church, do you have time to go over my math homework?" his older son, Ichiro, asked.

"Yes, I'm pretty sure there will be plenty of time for that," Pastor Hikaru replied before going upstairs. Mai was at the door, admitting an elderly couple. Pastor Hikaru greeted the couple and then turned his attention to his wife as their visitors made their way downstairs.

"Good morning, dear," Pastor Hikaru said and gave her a brief kiss on the cheek.

"You forgot your breakfast this morning, dear husband," she chided playfully.

"I know, but I needed to finish the sermon."

Pastor Hikaru slipped back downstairs to set up a music stand that he used as a podium. The boys were busy chatting with the elderly couple, discussing school and what they liked to do in their free time. When nine-thirty rolled around, the last of the parishioners took their seats and Mai seated herself at the piano to begin worship.

Pastor Hikaru loved to watch her play, her hands moved so gracefully across the keys, playing each note perfectly. His parents had tried to get him to play piano, but gave up after a few lessons when he showed no interest. Unlike most Japanese parents, Hikaru's didn't expect him to excel at everything he did, and instead encouraged him to pursue his passions. Mai, on the other hand, had been expected to succeed at whatever she was directed to do. After going to Canada through a university student exchange program, she met him and they began to date. A few months later, he had proposed to her, much to her parents' disapproval. Wanting her parents' blessing, Mai spent months trying to convince them that Hikaru was a good man. Her parents started pushing the young couple's wedding day further and further away. It took a year for Mai to realise that nothing they did would gain her parents' approval, so she and Hikaru took charge and were married in a private ceremony. It was difficult, but they made things work. When Hikaru finished Seminary, they felt led to come back to Japan and share the Lord's Word there. It took them nearly twelve years to get their church established. With a lot of hard work and prayer, God had answered them and provided a fellowship of thirty believers.

Pastor Hikaru espied Hitomi sitting in her usual seat at the back. When she had first arrived, her appearance had caused a little bit of a disturbance amongst the older members; even his own wife had reservations about her. He had been the only one who hadn't known she was the daughter of one of the most powerful men in Japan. Many were fearful of her father with his connections to the Yakuza. When she continued to attend, some of the elders requested that he try to persuade her to leave. Being led by the Spirit, he was compelled to do the opposite. Seeking to encourage Hitomi in her walk with the Lord, he began to counsel her.

Mai had become jealous, which was unusual for her. Once, she even implored him to ask Hitomi to leave, and when he refused, she didn't talk to him for a week. One day, Hitomi had come over, disrupting their dinner. Mai was so enraged, she began yelling at Hitomi. Pastor Hikaru had been downstairs when she had arrived. Hearing the commotion, he came upstairs and was shocked to see his wife consoling the older woman, embracing her like she would a friend. That was the first time Hitomi had revealed her husband's emotional abuse to anyone.

The next service she attended, Mai invited her to the front and sat beside her. This single gesture of love and mercy quelled all opposition against her. Shy and quiet, Hitomi preferred the seclusion of the back row. Even though no one spoke outwardly, the glares and silence she received from several in the congregation made it abundantly clear she was tolerated, not accepted.

Once worship was done, Pastor Hikaru stood up to deliver the message. Turning to John 21, he spoke about Jesus' question to Peter. Looking to the congregation, he asked what they thought the meaning was behind Jesus' inquiry. In the back, a few seats away from Hitomi, sat a young white couple he did not recognize. The young woman was listening to something her husband was telling her, nodding when he was finished, she said something back to him and he smiled at her. He wondered how he had not noticed them before.

Continuing with his sermon, he suggested that the passage was a redemption of Peter's denial of Jesus. Throughout the entire sermon, the young couple talked quietly back and forth; it took him a while before he realised that the young man was translating for his wife. He smiled, inadvertently drawing the attention of a few of the parishioners to what was going on in the back. The couple quickly averted their eyes, the young man nodding and smiling at those who looked their way, while the young woman stared straight ahead, blushing. Pastor Hikaru made sure to keep his focus away from the back, preventing further embarrassment.

After the service, Pastor Hikaru did his best to work his way through the gathering. He wanted to welcome the couple before they disappeared, but it seemed everyone was eager to have a word with him. While speaking briefly with one of the elders, he spotted them talking with a friend of his near the stairs. He was trying to keep one eye on them, while also trying to keep up with the conversation. Pastor Hikaru was startled when he lost sight of them. With a quick apology, he excused himself and ran up the stairs, hoping to catch them. Turning the corner at the top of the stairs, he found them talking to Hitomi who, much to his amazement, was speaking to them in fluent English.

"Hello, Bokushi," Hitomi chimed as he walked towards them.

"Hitomi, I didn't know you spoke English."

"You never asked," she replied.

Looking to the couple, he gave a small bow. "Welcome. My name is Hikaru Ichinose, I am the pastor of our small congregation here," he said in English.

"My name is Jonathan, Jonathan Hansen, and this is my wife, Angela."

"You must excuse me for earlier, I was not intending to embarrass you."

"It's all right," Jonathan said, giving Angela a small hug. "My wife doesn't know Japanese yet, so I translate for her."

"Yes, I thought that was the case. How long are you visiting Japan?"

"We aren't visiting, I have a job with a high school teaching English. A friend told my wife about your church and she wanted to come and check it out."

Looking to Angela, Pastor Hikaru smiled and nodded. "What did you think? Was it a good enough sermon that you might consider making this your fellowship while you're here?"

Angela bowed in return. "We would love to, Pastor Hikaru Ichinose."

"Hikaru-Bokushi. Bokushi will do," he said.

"The only thing I might have added, though, is that Jesus was asking Peter if he loved him not because of his rejection of Christ, but because Peter wasn't giving him the answer he wanted."

Pastor Hikaru wasn't sure how to reply. Hitomi seemed a little taken aback herself by Angela's bold response.

"I'm sorry — did I do something wrong?" Angela asked.

"No, no, it's quite all right. I just never thought of it, but how do you know he was responding incorrectly?"

"I am assuming that your Bible was translated from the English version, and seeing as there is only one word for love in English, we don't necessarily fully understand what Jesus was trying to say. If we look to the Greek, we find that Jesus was using the word *Agapé*, which refers to a complete, devoted, sacrificial love, the kind of love we attribute to God, while on the other hand, Peter used *Phileo*, which is the kind of love you would have between friends ...." Angela's voice trailed off, when she noticed that everyone was listening to her intently. "I'm sorry, I didn't mean to offend anyone," she said, moving closer to her husband in embarrassment.

"I don't think you offended anyone, hun. I think we are all a little surprised." Jonathan gently squeezed her hand. "Where did you learn all that?" he asked curiously.

"When Professor Lang overheard me and Stephanie talking about the Bible passage, he told us that sometimes, to understand the Word much deeper, you needed to understand the language and culture that it was written in."

"Your professor sounds like a wise man, Mrs. Hansen," Pastor Hikaru said. "He reminds me of a Bible College professor I had the privilege of learning from."

Jonathan checked his watch. "Oh! We've gotta go, hun, or we are not going to make it for the hike."

"Taking the guided tour up Mount Fuji, I take it?" Pastor Hikaru asked.

"Yes, I was hoping to take the earlier one and get the full tour, but we decided it was better we come to church instead," Jonathan replied. Angela resisted the urge to roll her eyes.

"I want you two to know that you are welcome to join us again next week, and I hope you enjoy your tour." Pastor Hikaru gave them the customary bow, which they reciprocated.

As they left, Angela and Hitomi exchanged goodbyes. "We will see each other on Thursday then?" Angela asked.

"I look forward to it," Hitomi said, waving to them as they left.

"It looks like you have a new friend, Hitomi."

"I suppose I do." She beamed.

The following Sunday, the Hansens didn't attend, much to Pastor Hikaru's disappointment. When he asked Hitomi how her day with Angela had gone, she revealed that the young woman was extremely fatigued, so they stayed in and had tea. He assumed she was down with a cold and didn't give it another thought. The next Sunday, Jonathan and Angela had arrived a little late and quietly sat down next to Hitomi, with Jonathan acting as interpreter, as usual. As Pastor Hikaru preached, an idea came to mind, something that would make it possible for Angela to enjoy the service without the need of an interpreter. He was so excited by the idea, it was all he could think about during the week that followed. Whenever he had a spare moment, he enlisted the aid of his son to put together what he had planned. Ichiro was confused at first, but when Hikaru explained the reasoning behind his plan, he was more than happy to help.

When the next church service arrived, everything was ready to go and Pastor Hikaru was on tenterhooks. He was excited to use what he knew had been God's idea to help Angela familiarise herself with their church. Sadly, they didn't show up. Feeling deflated, his normal exuberance diminished and he sorely lacked the bright, cheerful tone he used whenever speaking about God's Word. He once again asked Hitomi if she had heard from them, and was a little concerned when he found out that Angela had fallen ill again. Two weeks later, Angela and Jonathan made an appearance. Angela looked haggard and tired, but she put on a brave, smiling face when she came in. Overjoyed to see them, Pastor Hikaru greeted them when they entered and told them that he had something for them during service. Curious, both of them inquired what it might be, but Pastor Hikaru told them that they would know it when they saw it.

Mai lead them in worship and as they sang, Angela's eyes lit up. Using an old projector and some transparencies he dug up out of their closet, Pastor Hikaru and his son had put the words in English to both the worship and his sermon. Taking an old bed sheet and a large piece of cardboard, he created a screen for the projector and, with the use of one of his wife's easels, he was able to have it sit high enough that Angela could see it from the back. His two boys took turns changing the transparencies as they went along. Angela face filled with a brightness and joy as she sang with all her heart. Her melodic voice caught the attention of everyone around her, drawing several surprised and awed glances her way. By the last song, almost everyone had taken notice of the young woman and her singing talents. Even if she didn't speak the same language, the beauty of her voice had captivated everyone. As the singing came to a close, Angela finally realised that all eyes were on her. Blushing furiously, she tried to hide her face behind her husband. Pastor Hikaru stepped up to the stand and began his service. Thankful that she was no longer in the spotlight, Angela happily read the transparencies as Pastor Hikaru spoke. Following the service, everyone went up to greet and welcome the new couple, showering her with their praises of her wonderful singing. Angela was made a little self-conscious by the recognition she received, but she thanked everyone.

"Knowledgeable in the Word *and* an amazing singer, that's a wonderful combination," Pastor Hikaru said.

"The voice is not from me, I just sing, it was given to me by God." Angela humbly shook her head.

"Well, in either case I am happy that you two made it."

"Thank you, and thank you for the projector and transparencies, that was a Godsend."

"God gave me the idea, I just followed through with it." Pastor Hikaru grinned. "Are you two staying for tea and snacks, or are you off again?" he asked.

"We don't have any pressing matters to attend at the moment, so we would love to stay," Jonathan said.

"Glad to hear it, maybe you two can convince Mrs. Fukui-sama to stay as well," Pastor Hikaru said, nodding in Hitomi's direction.

"I will go and talk with her," Angela said. She walked across the room, catching Hitomi who was headed for the stairs.

"How have your first few weeks of teaching gone, Hansen-san?" Pastor Hikaru asked.

"Pretty good. It was a rough start, but I think I am finally getting the hang of it. There have been a lot of adjustments I've needed to make, as school is conducted differently here."

"Yes, it can be quite a culture shock." Pastor Hikaru stopped at the snack table and quickly filled a plate with some of his favourites, "Any plans of staying long-term?" he asked hopefully.

"I am not sure about that yet," answered Jonathan, grabbing a couple snacks himself. "We are playing it by ear for now."

The men's gazes turned to Hitomi and Angela chatting and laughing at the base of the stairs.

"How is your wife doing?"

Eyeing her worriedly, Jonathan shook his head. "Not good. She has been complaining of exhaustion and abdominal pains."

"Nothing serious, I hope." Pastor Hikaru felt ill at ease. Something about Angela's illness didn't sit well with him. "Have you taken her to a doctor?"

"I did, but all we were told was that she might be acclimatising to the change in food, sea level and climate."

Watching Angela, Hikaru was reminded of an elderly member of his father's church who had shown similar symptoms.

"I know it can be a scary thought, but have you asked to have her checked for cancer?" Shocked at the mention of such a devastating illness, Jonathan put down his plate, and the pastor hastened to add, "I'm sorry, I'm not trying to worry you needlessly. I'm thinking it may explain why she has been so sick."

Jonathan considered the possibility, and was reminded of the times over the past few weeks when she had complained about fatigue and pain. Never once had he contemplated something so severe. Looking at it from this new angle, from what little he knew about the disease, all the pieces seemed to fit, and that scared him.

"Look, don't think about it too much. You never know, maybe she is just suffering from a longstanding flu or something," Hikaru said reassuringly, but the seed of doubt and fear had already been planted.

Angela led Hitomi over to the two men. "Jonathan, Hitomi has offered to take us to lunch, may we go?"

Jonathan didn't answer at once, his thoughts on what the pastor had said. The happy light in Angela's eyes reminded him that she was longing for a friendship with someone like Hitomi. He pushed aside his concerns and accepted the invitation.

"You and your family are welcome to come, Bokushi," Hitomi said.

"I wish I could, Fukui-sama but my wife has plans to have someone from the congregation over for lunch," he responded.

With polite bows, Hitomi, Jonathan and Angela left for the lunch engagement. That night, Hikaru couldn't shake his uneasiness regarding Angela's wellbeing. Guided by the Spirit, he knelt at the side of his futon.

"Oh, please, Lord," he prayed, "I ask that you watch over the Hansens, please help them in any trials that come their way. Lord, I ask that you send your Holy Spirit to dwell upon them in what awaits them. Guide them into Your eternal mercy and rest, no matter what comes."

When his wife entered the room, she saw that he was in deep prayer. She waited until he had finished. Something about his demeanour concerned her.

"Is something wrong?" she asked him as he rose up off of his knees.

"I'm not entirely sure. Maybe."

"What do you mean, 'maybe'?" she pressed him.

"When I was talking with Jonathan today, something struck me about his wife." He sat beside Mai and took her hand. "I was worried, and had suggested that she may be sick with something more severe than a flu."

Nestling her head on his shoulder she could see that what he was thinking about was burdening him. "What do you think it is?"

Hikaru sighed uneasily, "There was one elderly man in my father's church back in Canada. He started getting sick. He always seemed tired and in pain. One day, he collapsed and was rushed to the hospital where he was diagnosed with cancer, but it wasn't diagnosed early enough. By the time they caught it, it had spread throughout his body. After a long stint in the hospital and on heavy drugs that made him feel even worse, he passed away suddenly in the night."

"So, that's what has been bothering you?" she asked, placing a comforting hand on his cheek.

Hikaru nodded. "I have a bad feeling. It might just be nothing."

"Or it could be everything." Taking both his hands in hers, Mai knelt down beside the futon as he had before, "We should pray about it, and ask for the Lord to help her."

Looking down at her, he felt a sense of pride. This wasn't just any woman, this was his wife, and she was one of the wisest women he knew.

CHAPTER 16
Japan — April 1985

Jonathan held his wife's hand as they waited nervously to be seen by a doctor at a local clinic. He had spent the last two weeks trying to persuade her to see the doctor, but she was just as stubborn as her grandfather. All that changed couple of days prior to their appointment, when she awoke to find Jonathan shaking her. She had asked him why he was still home and was alarmed to learn that she had slept for the entire day. After that, Angela didn't need any persuasion to make an appointment.

While they waited, Angela watched the few children in the waiting room play quietly. A young boy and his sister were playing with two stuffed animals, as they acted out a little story they made up together. Their mother was mindful of them as she waited to be called in for her appointment.

The woman smiled as she noticed Angela's preoccupation with her children, and asked quietly in Japanese, "Are you expecting?"

Unsure of what she was asking, Angela turned to her husband, who responded, "No, but we have thought about it."

That wasn't entirely true, they had discussed the possibility of having a child, but had only given it fleeting consideration. Given that his wife was so taken by the children, he wondered if they should visit the idea again, as long as everything was all right.

When the nurse called them and took them to an examination room down the hall, Jonathan helped Angela onto the table.

He sat in the chair next to it and held her hand, as much for his comfort as for hers.

Doctor Ishida came in moments later and listened attentively as Jonathan described Angela's symptoms of fatigue and pain. He jotted down notes as he fired a barrage of questions at Jonathan, who acted as Angela's interpreter. By the end, Jonathan felt like he had been the one under examination. Dr. Ishida checked her pulse one more time before calling for the nurse. Jonathan looked at his wife. She smiled at him, but her ashen face revealed the strain she was under. A small knock sounded at the door, and the doctor went outside to give his nurse some instructions before returning.

"Do you know what's wrong with her?" Jonathan asked him.

"I can't say for certain. I will be sending you to the nearby hospital for some tests. I need you to explain to her that she needs to keep up with her vitamins and eat a lot of fresh foods." Dr. Ishida walked with them to the nurse's desk where he grabbed a chart from the pile and called his next patient.

"Well, that was short," Angela said shakily. "Did he find anything?"

Jonathan shrugged his shoulders. "They aren't entirely sure, he wants you to go in for some tests, just to be safe." Giving her a hug, his heart sank as he felt how frail she had become. *Oh please, Lord,* he prayed silently, *let there be nothing wrong with her.*

The receptionist handed him a piece of paper with the address for the hospital, appointment time, and the name of the specialist. The appointment was two days away. When Jonathan asked for today off, Mr. Matsuno had offered to cover his classes, much Mr. Kagawa chagrin, who had grumbled about Westerners being lazy. Now Jonathan was going to have to ask for another day, which was not going to look good in the eyes of his superior. When he asked if he could get an appointment later in the day, he was told that the earliest date for an afternoon appointment was three weeks away. Jonathan was not about to wait that long for a diagnosis.

"Is something wrong?" Angela asked as they left the clinic.

"I need to take another day off." When she began to protest, he added, "It will be fine, it's only one more day and this will all be over."

He kissed her on the cheek, and helped her into their rental car. Angela fell asleep during the short drive home, which only added a sense of desperation to Jonathan's fear. When they reached the apartments, he carried her to their suite and encountered Kate, who had the afternoon off and had stopped by to visit. Kate prepared a pot of tea while Jonathan got Angela undressed and tucked into bed. When she asked about the appointment, Jonathan told her that they needed to run some tests.

"Hopefully they don't find anything serious," Kate whispered at the bedroom doorway as they watched Angela sleep. "Have you told her family?"

"No, I haven't even thought that far ahead," he admitted, not sure how to broach such a sensitive subject. "What can I say? 'I'm sorry, but after taking your granddaughter away, she has become ill.'? I'm terrified. Our pastor thinks it may be cancer."

"Does her family have a history of cancer?"

"Her grandfather does." Jonathan closed the door behind them as they left the room. "He had colon cancer several years back."

"Who knows, Jonathan? This could be nothing more serious than mono."

Jonathan nodded, but the hope seemed faint. Kate gave him a hug before leaving, telling him there was no point in stressing out before the tests were run. When she had left, he went into the kitchen and poured a cup of tea. He stood staring at the phone, undecided. After a few minutes, he picked up the receiver and called Stan and Jean.

"Doggone it!" Stan shouted as the hammer slammed down on his thumb.

"What's going on up there?" Jean called from downstairs.

"Nothing, I seem to like to hit my fingers," he barked sarcastically.

"Well, don't do that, it hurts." Jean laughed.

Stan couldn't help but grin. His wife could be cheeky when she wanted to be. He had been at work on the upstairs guestroom wall since morning. Winter was coming to an end and the flurries were being replaced with unusually high winds and powerful thunderstorms. The last storm had ripped open a section of the roof above the guestroom during the night. Next morning they were greeted by a sopping wet floor and bulging walls. It took him over a week to repair the damage to the roof, then another couple of days to get the initiative to go into the attic and replace all of the wet insulation. Dipping into the cash they had set aside for a rainy day, he went into town and picked up the materials he needed to build a new wall. The only problem now was his shaky hands. He lifted a two by six and nailed it into place. When it was secure, he looked outside to see the sun begin to sink below the horizon.

"It's about time for supper, why don't we call it a day, Chico?" he said to the cat that was stretched out on the floor, watching him curiously. He picked up the cat and was headed downstairs to wash up, when the phone rang.

"That's wonderful, well I'm glad everything's going well for you two." Jean was saying as Stan walked into the kitchen. "So, what's school like?"

Stan poured a coffee and sat at the table. He turned on the television to the CFCN News. Gord Kelly was giving an update about the Lord's Day Act that was being deliberated in the Supreme Court where there was a debate over whether or not the Bill violated Canada's freedom of religion. Watching the news half-heartedly, he kept his ear on what Jean was saying.

"That's wonderful. How's Angela doing?"

The name of his granddaughter was enough to draw his complete attention. He turned the volume down so he could hear the conversation. Without even looking at Jean's face, he could sense her mood had changed. Her back was to him, her shoulders slumped as she steadied herself with one hand on the counter. Stan felt a knot form in the pit of his stomach as she turned to face him, her face grave.

"Has she gotten checked yet?" she asked Jonathan. "You let us know as soon as you find out." Her voice trembled slightly as she tried to compose herself. "Tell her that we love her and she is in our prayers. Let us know if you kids need anything, okay? We love you, Jonathan. Call us as soon as you hear anything."

"Jean, is everything okay?" Stan asked, getting up from the table.

Jean hung up the phone. Her face was pale and her hands shook. "Angela is sick, and Jonathan is worried that she might have cancer."

"Cancer!" The mere mention of the disease set him back on his heels. It had been years since his own battle which had nearly cost him his life. "Is she all right? What are they doing about it?"

"I'm not sure." Jean shook her head weakly. "All he said was that they are not sure, but she is going in for some tests soon and he will let us know as soon as he knows."

"Has he talked to Kathy yet?"

"He's calling her right now; I'm sure we will hear from her as soon as he has told her."

They sat in silence, supper forgotten, as they waited for Kathy's call.

A cancer survivor, Stan knew that if Angela had cancer, there was the possibility that she would not survive it. Jean prayed quietly, tears rolling down her face. Stan reached for her and pulled her close as she nestled her head on his shoulder.

"If she has cancer, what are we going to do, Stan?"

"I don't know, but we can't give up on her." He kissed her on her forehead. "She will make it through this, I promise. She's strong, just like I was, and I have a feeling that God's not done with her."

The phone rang minutes later with Kathy on the line. Jean talked with her at length as they planned a course of action. In the end, it was decided that Kathy would fly them all to Japan so they could be there to help their children. Stan could only listen as the women worked out the details. He was thrilled that he was going to see his granddaughter again. He hoped it wouldn't be for the last time.

CHAPTER 17

Jonathan threw the last of the dirty clothes into a basket and tossed it into the bedroom closet. As he picked up the dirty plates and cups he, he took a mental note of anything else that needed to be cleaned before their guests arrived.

"Angela, what are you doing?" he cried.

Stooped over the coffee table, she was sorting Jonathan's papers before filing them into his briefcase "I just thought I'd—"

"The doctor said you need to take it easy."

"I know, I just feel bad that you are doing all this work." She wrinkled her nose, surveying the disastrous condition of her household.

"I didn't mean for it to get this bad," he apologised. "I guess I just let things get out of hand."

"You think?" She laughed a little, watching her husband scramble to make the place presentable.

Jonathan was happy to see his wife so cheerful and bright. Things had begun turning around for her two days ago when Aunt Kathy had called back to inform them that she, Jean, and Stan would be coming to visit.

The news had revitalised Angela's spirits and she had found the strength to get up and walk around. He understood her desire to help clean. Both knew how much of a neat freak his aunt was, and were reluctant to let her see their house in such a state. How did I let it get this bad? he wondered.

Aunt Kathy had advised them to take a Limousine, as they charged a flat rate and were about twenty-five percent cheaper than a standard taxi. It was due to arrive at ten, and — he checked the time — it was already ten.

"Shoot, we have to go." He snatched the papers out of Angela's hands, gathered the rest of his books and school papers, and stuffed them into his briefcase. Struggling with the clasps, he gave up after a few tries and shoved it under the sofa.

"Jonathan Hansen," Angela said in a stern voice, "is that where it goes?"

"I know, I know," he said, exasperated, trying to rush her to the door. "I'll take care of it before Aunt Kathy sees it."

Jonathan helped her with her shoes as she struggled for balance. He handed Angela her jacket, quickly shrugged on his own, and laced on his shoes before rushing out the door. The Limousine was waiting at the curb. The flight was due to arrive in an hour; fortunately, the roads were clear for the most part, and they reached the airport with time to spare. Jonathan located a nice sitting area for Angela before continuing to Arrivals. The flight was delayed, so he kept her company until it touched down. When the plane landed at eleven fifty, he met up with the driver that Kathy had arranged to meet them at the Arrivals Gate. The three visitors looked tired, but relieved to see him.

"Hi there, honey." Aunt Kathy gave him a big hug. "Where's Angela?" she asked looking around intently.

"I got her to sit down while I waited here for you."

"You are a good husband," said Jean as she gave him a hug. "We have been so blessed to have you as part of our family."

Jonathan blushed slightly at the compliment, which made Stan chuckle.

"Now, now, dear, stop it before you embarrass the boy any further." Stan reached out for a handshake. "How are you doing, Son?"

"Not bad, but we should go. I am sure that Angela is getting anxious."

After they transferred their luggage from the carousel to a trolley, Jonathan led them to where Angela patiently waited. When she saw them, her face shone with joy. Jean and Kathy ran up to embrace her. It was a tearful reunion, and even Stan's eyes shone with unshed tears at the sight of his granddaughter. As the women began talking amongst themselves, the men followed them with the luggage.

"How has she been?" Stan asked quietly.

"Her energy is coming back, but I have this feeling that the worst is yet to come," Jonathan replied.

Stan placed a comforting hand on the young man's shoulder. "She's strong, I'm sure that she will make it."

"That's what I am worried about, the test results I mean. She told me that the pain and exhaustion began shortly after our wedding." Looking at Angela, he added, "I just hope it's not too late, I don't know what I would do without her."

Stan understood all too well. It had been the same for Jean when he had been sick; she had felt a sense of hopelessness and a premonition of loss.

"Other than what I have heard from Jean, how are things going with work?"

Jonathan's face lit up at the mention of his job.

"Really good. The students are great, my fellow teachers are great, and it's been a few weeks since I have needed help interpreting."

"So, you love teaching, then?"

"Yes, it's so exciting to help guide the minds of tomorrow and seeing their eyes light up when they finally understand. I do find that teaching here is different than it is back home. The students here are like sponges, trying to soak up every little bit of information you give them. In a few short weeks they have burned through about an extra week's worth of teaching material. I find it hard to keep up with them."

Stan laughed. It was good to see that his grandson-in-law was adjusting well. "I take it there are no plans on coming home after you're done?"

Jonathan sobered. "That depends on whether they will renew my contract and if the government allows me to stay. I also would have to discuss it with Angela first, but there's no point in worrying her with that now."

Stan nodded in agreement. Right now, they were here to support Angela, and pray for God's guidance. They followed the driver to where his Limo was parked, and the men helped him transfer the luggage from the trolley to the spacious trunk.

"Well, why haven't you?" Kathy demanded.

Until this point Jonathan and Stan had shown no interest in what the women were talking about, but something in Kathy's tone told him it was an issue that included Jonathan.

"Why hasn't she what, Aunt Kathy?" Jonathan asked.

"Why haven't you two discussed having a family yet?"

"A family?" Stan choked.

"Yes, it would be nice to have some great nieces and nephews. Most people your age are already having kids, so what's stopping you two?" Kathy questioned pointedly.

"Jonathan wants to get his career moving," Angela said, "and I would like to go to school and finish my doctorate."

"Look, there's no need to rush into things. These kids still have a lot of growing up to do," Stan interposed.

"Don't wait too long. Before you know it, your cousins will be having kids. Then, when you finally settle down and turn forty, you will be too tired to run after the little ones, what will you do then?" Kathy chided.

There was a brief moment of silence as they got into the Limo. No one was really sure what to say, it was a touchy subject and something that Jonathan wished his aunt would have brought up privately. Sensing the mood, Kathy changed the subject.

"How is your work going?"

"It's going well. I teach several classes a day, and the kids soak up the lessons faster than I can prepare them."

"Do you have any favourites?"

"Favourites?" Jonathan had never considered any one of his students better than another, but there were some that stood out from the rest. "I have never given it that much thought. I guess when it comes down to it, there is one girl in my afternoon classes. Her name is Ayako. She is enthusiastic about learning English, but that is because she wants to attend a university in the West."

"Ahya- Ahy- Aya-ko." Kathy fumbled with the foreign name. "That's an interesting name, what does it mean?"

"It means 'pretty child'."

"Do all Japanese names carry specific meanings, similar to most European names?" asked Jean.

"Yes, and the meanings can differ, depending on what character and alphabet they choose from. Japanese is a complex language for most people to learn."

"It looks like you have adjusted to it well enough." Stan smiled proudly. "And what about you, Angela? How's your Japanese coming?"

Angela grimaced, embarrassed to acknowledge the fact that she didn't understand Japanese at all. "I haven't begun learning it yet."

"Why not?" Stan asked, looking to Jonathan for an explanation.

"Jonathan's been so busy with school, I felt bad about asking him," she said. In truth, she had no desire to learn the language, but she felt guilty letting Jonathan take the blame for her inaction.

"If you learned the language, you might—"

"That's enough Stan," Jean interrupted. "Lay off the kids, already. We're here to give support, not interrogate them."

Stan caught the look in his wife's eyes, and knew not to push his luck. Annoyed, he folded his arms and stared out the window, while Jean and Kathy continued to probe for answers to all their questions. When the Limo pulled up to their apartment, Angela got a little worried.

"Jonathan, honey, did we miss a stop?"

"No, not that I can think of, why?"

"How are we going to fit everybody into our apartment?"

"There's plenty of room, we have a spare room, and a sofa that we could use for a bed."

"What about the mess?" she whispered.

"Oh, I forgot!" He mentally cringed. "See if Kate's up for a visit. She said she wanted to meet them."

She gave him a quick kiss and led their party to Kate's apartment.

The driver unloaded the luggage and, with Jonathan assisting, took it up to the apartment. Jonathan thanked him profusely for his services, and set to work making the apartment more presentable. He stowed the dirty dishes under the sink, quickly wiped down the stove and counters, ran a dusting cloth over every flat surface in the living room and gave the bathroom a last minute spot check.

"Is everything all right?" Kathy called from the front door as she walked in with Stan and Angela. "Your neighbour Kate has a lovely collection of art."

"Really?" he said in surprise. "I didn't know she was a collector."

"No, she's an artist, honey, not a collector. I thought you knew that." Kathy gave him a big hug. "It's a cute little place you have here."

Angela was surprised to find that Jonathan had cleaned up the mess so well — until Stan and Jean sat down on the sofa.

"Your furniture seems to be printing class agendas here," Stan declared, pulling some loose-leaf out from under the cushions.

"Still the last minute cleaner, I see." Kathy laughed, helping Stan remove the papers from the sofa.

Jonathan blushed hotly. "I lost track of time, with Angela being sick." He shrugged his shoulders in embarrassment.

"I guess we should stay out of the cupboards and closets, then," Jean said with a smile.

Angela started to help, but Stan motioned for her to sit down. "Don't worry about it, honey. We'll help you two clean up and then we can sit down and chat."

While they got the apartment sorted, Kathy shared some embarrassing, but hilarious stories from Jonathan's childhood. By the time she was finished, everyone was laughing so hard they could barely breathe.

Angela held Jonathan's hand, while wiping away tears. "You guys have the best childhood stories."

"Yes, they were all interesting characters growing up." Kathy nodded. "What are you two planning to use that spare room for?"

"It's being used for storage right now, but I thought I might turn it into a study," Jonathan said.

"You could always make it into a nursery," Kathy said.

"Nursery?" Jonathan exclaimed incredulously, "I thought we went over this. I think that it's a little early for that."

Angela listened to this byplay silently, and she unconsciously touched her belly. In her heart, she knew she wanted a child of her own, but she hadn't been sure if Jonathan was of the same mind. His reaction revealed his feelings on the matter.

Stan caught his granddaughter's subtle reaction to Jonathan's response, and tactfully steered the conversation to safer waters. "This place reminds me of the little shack we started out with."

"I can't believe you could compare that shack to this at all," Jean said derisively. "This would be like Buckingham Palace in comparison."

"It was nice, and I remember you were just as excited to have a place of our own as I was."

"I was just happy to finally be out from under my parents. Trust me, I was not thrilled when I saw what you called our 'happy little home'."

Jean gave her husband a meaningful look. Stan responded with a grin that made them both burst out laughing. The atmosphere became more relaxed and they discussed that day's itinerary. The first thing on the agenda was booking a couple of rooms for Stan, Jean and Kathy at a hotel that was within walking distance to the apartment, followed by getting something to eat, and then taking a tour of the neighbourhood. Five hours later they were back at the apartment, relaxing over late night coffee.

"Are you sure you don't want to stay and save some money?" Angela asked, hoping that they would.

"Your aunt was gracious enough to pay for the hotel and wouldn't hear anything about payment in return." Stan was obviously uncomfortable with the idea of having someone pay their way.

"It's no problem at all, besides it will take some of the burden off of you kids anyway," said Kathy.

"It wouldn't be a burden," Jonathan interjected, "we have plenty of room for you, if you'd like to stay."

"No, I think that you need to get some rest," Kathy said, shaking her head. "It's only a ten minute walk from the hotel. We'll come to visit tomorrow evening."

While Jonathan saw their guests out, Angela was overwhelmed by the weariness and exhaustion that she had been holding back. She slowly shuffled over to the sofa and lay down. What's wrong with me, Lord? she wondered, although deep down she already suspected that everyone's concerns were correct. But she wanted to hold onto hope, she needed to.

She closed her eyes and, placing a trembling hand on her belly, imagined a small little boy or girl being held in her arms. She could almost make out the baby's face. As she envisioned what her child would look like, she slipped into a deep sleep.

Jonathan watched the taxi drive off into the night before returning to the apartment. Seeing the joy on Angela's face eased the heaviness of his heart and brightened Jonathan's day. He thought back to the comment his aunt had made about children. He had caught the flicker of sadness in Angela's eyes when he had negated the idea, and it occurred to him that she had been entertaining the thought of having children. Children? he thought. Not until she is better.

Angela was sleeping on the sofa when he entered. As he watched her sleep, he heard a small still voice within cry out, *Something's wrong!*

He placed a hand on her shoulder and shook her. "Angela?"

Nothing. Her breathing was laboured. Further inspection revealed she was pale and her lips thinned. Panic took over and he pulled her to him.

"Angela!" he shouted, "Wake up!"

Again, no response.

His hands trembled as he gathered her in his arms.

"Angela!"

Her body was limp and unnaturally light. He got the front door open wide enough to shoulder his way through, and ran down the hallway to the stairs. Several other tenants poked their heads out to investigate the commotion. Jonathan ignored them. He hurried down the stairs, nearly toppling at the bottom, and ran to Kate's apartment. Using his heel, he kicked on the door.

"Kate!"

Terror had stripped him of all reason as he kept kicking on the door. All he could think of was getting to Kate.

One elderly woman who had followed him downstairs called out to him in broken English, "My husband call ambulance. Is she all right?"

Not taking notice of her, Jonathan kicked on the door once more, "Kate, please! Something's wrong with Angela!"

A bony hand reached around him and took Angela's.

"She is very ill." The woman looked up at him compassionately. She said something he couldn't comprehend.

Just then, the door swung open to reveal a bewildered Kate. Her eyes widened when she saw Angela in his arms. She examined Angela's face and felt for a pulse.

"Angela — something's wrong — please, help me! Something's wrong!" he begged.

The woman said something to Kate in Japanese, but Jonathan couldn't focus his mind to translate what they were saying. "What's wrong with her?" Jonathan pleaded. Kate said something to the old woman, who nodded and gave Jonathan a sympathetic look before returning to her apartment.

"Jonathan, an ambulance is on its way. She's cold, maybe we should bundle her up." Whisking the two of them into her apartment, she quickly fetched a blanket and helped wrap it around Angela.

"What happened?" Kate inquired.

"I don't know," Jonathan said. "Everything seemed all right, she looked the healthiest she had been in a long time. I don't know what could be wrong with her."

"Why didn't you call the emergency transport services in the first place? I'm not a doctor."

"I don't know. I'm sorry, I can't think—"

Kate looked him straight in the eye. "Jonathan Hansen," she said in a commanding voice, "you sit down here and calm down and get control of yourself. You are no good to her if you can't even think."

Meeting her level gaze, he nodded and did his best to comply. Cradling his wife in his arms, Jonathan stroked her ashen face. She was so cold, almost lifeless, except for her slow, laboured breathing. How could this have happened? Why hadn't he seen this coming? He looked up and found himself alone; Kate was nowhere to be seen. Looking back down at Angela, he desperately wished beyond hope that, like in some fairy-tale, a kiss from him would somehow bring her back. He pressed his lips against her forehead, feeling his breath catch when he felt how cold her skin was. When he pulled back there were water marks on her face. Confused, he wiped them away, and that's when he realised that he was crying.

The sound of the ambulance brought him out of his daze. He carried Angela outside the apartment to the ambulance attendants who quickly secured her to the stretcher. Once they had her in the ambulance, the attendant began asking him questions, but Jonathan was so frightened he found it difficult to keep up with what they were saying. With Kate's help, he was able to give them Angela's medical history and explain what had happened.

With Kate's assurances that she would call work and explain the situation, Jonathan got into the ambulance. He sat beside his wife and held her hand, hoping and praying that she would be all right.

Jean and Stan followed Kathy into the hotel lobby. Kathy went up to the front desk and collected the keys to their rooms. When Jean turned around, Stan was nowhere to be seen. After a quick search, they found him standing outside looking down the road that lead back to the apartment block.

"Miss them already?" Jean asked, embracing her husband.

"What?" he asked coming out of his daze.

"Are you okay, hun?"

"Yes, well ... I don't know. I had a funny feeling a moment ago when I saw the ambulance pass by. Something is wrong."

Jean pulled back from him. "Stan, what is it?" she asked. Kathy wasn't sure what was going on, but Stan's tone gave her a sense foreboding.

"Do you think we should go back?" Jean asked.

"It feels as if the Lord is telling me to go back."

Without a second thought, Stan marched back into the hotel and went up to the front desk. "We need a taxi."

Startled at Stan's demeanour, the attendant looked puzzled. "You not staying?"

"No, it's not that, we just need a taxi, it's a family emergency." Stan tried to control the tension of his voice so he would not upset the young woman.

"Jean, what's he talking about? What's wrong?" Kathy asked.

"Sometimes, the Lord gives Stan an inkling when something is wrong. It doesn't happen often, but when it does, he's always right."

"Is he like a prophet or something? I thought you two didn't believe in that?"

Taking Kathy's hands, Jean tried to soothe her fears. "I'm not saying he can tell the future, but sometimes I believe that the Holy Spirit speaks to him. Not in the sense of some Old Testament prophet or one of Jesus' Apostles. It almost always has to deal with something that is happening to someone close to us."

"Angela, do you think that she—?"

"No, I don't think it's that, it's not like that with him. He can't predict someone's death, but he can sense at times that something is wrong."

"A taxi is going to be here any moment, we should wait outside," Stan said.

A few minutes later, a taxi pulled up and they got in. The driver's English was horrible, but he understood them well enough to get them to their destination. When they arrived back at the apartment complex, Kate was just going back upstairs when she saw them.

"Kate, where're Angela and Jonathan?" Stan asked frantically.

"How did you know they just left?"

"Do you know where they took them?" Stan asked.

"The ambulance is taking them to the hospital. I will tell your driver where to go."

Kate informed the driver and they quickly drove off, Kathy had tried to glean some information from Kate, but Stan was in such a hurry, she couldn't get the full story. When they arrived at the hospital, Kathy tried to figure out the cash for the taxi while Jean followed her husband inside.

"I need some help, my—our kids were just brought in, we need to find them," Stan asked the nurse behind the desk. She stared up at him, perplexed and responded in Japanese.

"Don't you have anybody who speaks English?" Stan snapped.

"Stan!" Jean squeaked.

"Look, I'm sorry. I need to find our kids."

Kathy came up and stood beside Jean. "Anything?"

Shaking her head Jean waited anxiously as the nurse got up and disappeared into a room. Stan began to pace as they waited, watching the time as if every second counted. Finally the nurse reappeared with a doctor.

"What seems to be the problem?" he asked them.

"Our granddaughter and her husband were brought in here not that long ago, their names are Angela and Jonathan Hansen."

The doctor relayed the information and the nurse picked up the phone and keyed a few numbers. "It will take us a few minutes, but we should be able to track them down, if you'd like to have a seat."

Stan nodded and reluctantly took a seat near the back of the waiting room, while keeping his eyes glued to the front desk. No one spoke for the next hour as they waited for news. Stan pestered the nurses every fifteen minutes, only to be told to sit down and wait. Just when Jean thought Stan was going to snap, a nurse came over and asked them to follow her. She took them up a few floors and then over to the west wing of the hospital. As they passed a nurses' station, they caught sight of Jonathan in a room just down the hall.

"Jonathan!" Kathy gasped when she saw him and ran to embrace him.

"Aunt Kathy? How did you know we were here?"

"It was Stan, he felt that something was wrong."

He looked incredulously at Stan, who shrugged, "It wasn't me, the Lord gave me a feeling you needed us."

"Thank you," Jonathan said.

The small knock on the door announced the presence of the attending doctor. "You must be the parents," he said in Japanese.

"Yes, they are, Oisha-san. What's wrong with her?" Jonathan asked, as the others waited for him to translate.

"She is extremely ill, and from the information we got from the clinic, there is a chance it is cancer. We can't be certain until we run some tests. For now, we have stabilized her and she will continue to rest until she is strong enough to wake up. As for all of you, we have visitor hours and we request that you go home and come back in the morning, I am sure you need your sleep."

Jonathan communicated the information to the others, and thanked the doctor before they left.

"Well, it looks like we won't be getting any sleep tonight, so why don't we go back to your place and help you finish cleaning?" suggested Kathy.

Jonathan nodded, and the four of them returned to his apartment. It was about two in the morning when they finished, Jean made coffee and tea for all of them as they sat in quiet contemplation. After drinking his coffee, Stan quickly fell asleep. Aunt Kathy tried to stay up, but began to doze off. Jonathan told her to take the bed, seeing as he couldn't sleep yet. Kathy told him she loved him and tried to encourage him, but Jonathan looked like a man who had lost all hope. Jean watched Jonathan solemnly. His disconsolate demeanour brought back memories of her own fears of when Stan had been so sick. Jonathan hadn't touched his cup as he stared off into space.

"Jean, how did you handle it when Stan had cancer?"

"I don't think I handled it much better than you have, to be honest. Stan has always been the stronger one, even in faith. I've always been thankful that Angela took after him."

As he listened, Jonathan began to shake as his emotions got the better of him. "She's going to make it, isn't she?" he asked.

Jean sat beside him and wrapped her arms around him. Jonathan rested his head against her as he wept. She wanted to tell him everything was going to be all right, but she didn't want to give him false hope.

CHAPTER 18

Angela cuddled her child in her arms, while she contentedly leaned back in the rocking chair on the porch. Out in the yard, Jonathan and her grandfather laboured in the midday heat, working on the fence while Jean was busy in the kitchen. She had never felt as happy in her life as she was at that moment with this new babe in her arms. The baby began to fuss and kick.

Smiling, Angela loosened the blanket from around her, "What's wrong, my little girl? Feeling a little confined?" As she gazed at her baby, she realised that her daughter resembled neither Jonathan nor her. Strangely enough, this revelation didn't seem to shock her. Suddenly, menacing clouds blotted out the sun as sheets of rain approached with alarming speed; the men continued working as if they hadn't noticed the sudden change in the weather. Cradling her baby close, she stood up and called out, "Jonathan, Grandpa, time to come in."

Lifting their heads, they looked toward her with sorrowful expressions. Disconcerted by the sadness on their faces, Angela hesitantly stepped back as fear began to build in her. Then, without warning, everything went black. Screaming, Angela shut her eyes tightly. When she opened them again, she found herself in a field beside a large pine tree. Looking down, she discovered her child was missing. Frantically, she searched nearby and tried to cry out for her baby, but whenever she opened her mouth to speak, nothing came out. Turning around, she began to run. She ran and ran but she didn't know where to or why. She was confused, baffled by what was happening. *Haven't I dreamt this before?* She halted, paralysed by fear.

She stood a short distance from a small stand of blue spruce on a ridge, and she recognized where she was. Without realising it, she was running again, but this time she was certain she would find her answers once she reached the trees. Nearing them, she found a small graveyard. *I've seen this somewhere before*, she thought, and came to a halt a few feet away as it dawned on her. *This is the small graveyard near my grandparents' place.* She felt compelled to enter, but couldn't figure out why. Hesitating, she was suddenly filled with fear. *What am I doing here? What's going on?*

She noticed some people gathering around a grave. One of the figures caught her attention. There, standing beside two older men, was a little girl with long black hair and an unfamiliar face. The girl was holding the hand of one of the two men and studying the gravestone. Angela tried unsuccessfully to make out their faces.

The man holding the little girl's hand turned to the child and quietly said, "Let's go home, Takara."

Angela's heart lurched, as she recognised the voice; somehow, though, she couldn't quite visualise its owner. She stepped forward to enter the graveyard. As soon as she took that step, the scene telescoped away from her. Surprised, Angela reached out, but it was too late; the world dissolved into nothingness.

"Angela," the man's voice called out in the darkness. "Angela, wake up, honey."

Opening her eyes, she winced at the piercing sunlight that streamed through the blinds. She was cold and she felt something odd draped over her. When she finally adjusted to the light, she saw Jonathan and the others standing around her. All their faces revealed the strain of their fatigue and worry. Jonathan looked particularly exhausted.

"Wh-what happened?" she asked groggily.

"Thank you, Lord," Stan breathed with relief. "You're looking better, for once."

"You have been asleep the last two days and had us all worried. I don't think poor Jonathan slept at all," Kathy said.

Angela looked into her husband's face, and watched the fear and stress of the last few days melt away at her smile.

"I'm so happy you're okay." His voice quivered as he leaned over and kissed her.

The smell of his cologne and the warmth of his touch made her heart soar. "I didn't mean to scare all of you. I guess I was really tired."

Before anyone else could speak, the doctor entered the room, "How is the patient?" he asked in perfect English.

"I feel fine. Tired, but fine." She tried a smile, and failed.

"If I could speak with you and your husband in private, we can go over the few tests we were able to run."

The others gave her a quick hug before exiting the room. Jonathan stood protectively at her side as the doctor went over the results. From what they were able to ascertain she had cancer, but they had to run a few more to confirm the diagnosis.

"How bad is it?" asked Angela.

The doctor scanned the lab results, and shook his head, "It's inconclusive at this point. We wanted to see how you were doing once you were awake."

"How long before we will know?" Jonathan asked.

"She is slated for a few tests today and some more examinations tomorrow. It may take us two weeks before we have the results. In the meantime, we want you to relax and get some rest. You will need your energy, so keep the visiting to a minimum, besides your husband, that is."

Angela felt disheartened. After all the trouble the family had gone through to come here, she was going to miss most of their visit.

"Are you going to put her on treatments?" Jonathan inquired.

"Not yet, once again we would like to wait and get a full diagnosis before we go ahead with any medical treatment." The doctor gave them the approximate time for her tests, but cautioned them that the time may change. "If she is doing well, we might discharge her within a few days."

"Now, that's some good news we'd like to hear," Jonathan declared with a deep sigh. When the doctor left, Jonathan gave her a gentle embrace, kissing her once more.

"It's going to be all right," Angela said.

She felt his back tense at her touch. The past few days had clearly been hard on him, and this news didn't help. She raised a shaky hand and caressed his face. Stan, Jean and Kathy came back into the room, all asking what the doctor had to say. As Jonathan relayed the information, each of them looked at her despairingly.

"They didn't say that I have one foot in the grave, I'm going to be fine. I'll make it, just like Grandpa did."

Not everyone was so sure about that. Stan, on the other hand, understood what his granddaughter was trying to say.

"She's right, the last time I checked she doesn't have an expiry date stamped on her foot, so why should we treat her as if she's already gone? I believe that just like God worked through my illness, He can work through hers. Psalm 34 tells us 'The eyes of the Lord are on the righteous, and his ears are attentive to their cry; but the face of the Lord is against those who do evil, to blot out their name from the earth. The righteous cry out, and the Lord hears them; he delivers them from all their troubles. The Lord is close to the broken-hearted and saves those who are crushed in spirit'.

"Times ahead may seem hard for all of us. We may fail in strength, but we serve a God whose mercy and power is beyond comprehension. He helps us in our weakness, and dries our tears in our sorrows. I know that without His strength, I would have never made the recovery I had, and I know that if we search out His heart, He will work all things in accordance to His good will. Why don't we all pray and ask that the Lord speed up Angela's recovery? We will also pray that no matter what comes, He will give us the strength to make it through the hardships."

Stan's words of wisdom struck a chord in all of them and they could not stop the flow of tears. With renewed spirits, they all gathered together and joined hands to pray. When they had finished praying, they stayed with Angela until visiting hours were over. Jonathan waited behind, afraid that if he let go of his wife's hand, she would fade away.

Angela sensed his misgivings. "I will be here when you come tomorrow. You need to go home and get some rest, my love." She stroked his face. Jonathan kissed her once more, and left.

Jonathan almost didn't go to work the following day, but the last thing he needed was to lose his job. His fears proved to be unfounded, for Mr. Kagawa called into his office first thing to inquire after his wife's health, and gave him permission to leave early if the situation warranted it. Jonathan didn't know what to say; even Mr. Matsuno was taken aback by the gesture. The staff and several students had gathered little gifts and homemade goodies for him to bring to Angela. Jonathan was overwhelmed with their compassion.

Whenever he was able to visit, he was with Angela. Stan and Jean spent a lot of time with her, as well. Kathy would visit for an hour or so each day and then spend the rest of the day preparing meals, cleaning house and washing clothes for Jonathan. Angela felt guilty that Kathy was doing so much, but Kathy refused to hear anything about it and told her she would do it for any of her kids.

By the third day, Angela's strength had almost completely returned along with her appetite, and she was beginning to look like her old self. Her returning strength had given her a resolve to fight to get better, and she had made up her mind to tell Jonathan about her desire to have children. Everyone else had decided to tour Tokyo for the rest of the day, so Angela knew she could speak without being interrupted.

"Jonathan, I've been wanting to say something for a while, but I wasn't sure how you would react."

Jonathan set aside the tests he was marking and went to her side.

"I want a baby," she said in a hushed tone.

"A baby?" Jonathan repeated.

"Yes, I want to have children. I want a little girl, or maybe a boy. I know we haven't discussed it, but I would like us to at least consider the possibility."

"Why not?" he asked.

Angela's eyes widened. "Why not? But I thought you—"

"I know what I said to my Aunt, but maybe I was a little premature in my decision. As you pointed out, we have yet to discuss it, but as far as I am concerned I am all in if you are."

Angela was overjoyed. "Thank you, oh, thank you! You are the best husband ever." He leaned over to embrace her and she wrapped her arms around his neck, squeezing so tightly he had trouble breathing. "I'm sorry," she said, "I'm just so happy."

Their excitement kept them talking for the next two hours, planning. Jonathan decided he would clean out the spare room and turn it into a nursery and they would try to conceive when she got better. The details of the nursery were made, and their excited conversation could be heard down the hall. They were asked more than once to keep it down out of respect for the other patients.

When it was time for Jonathan to go home, he couldn't sleep. All he could think about was babies and the nursery. After tossing and turning for several hours, he decided that he wasn't going to get any sleep until he did something with the spare room. He quietly got up from the sofa so he would not disturb Stan, who slept soundly on the recliner, and went to the spare room. The room was cluttered with a desk he had purchased but hadn't set up, some chairs, cleaning supplies, an empty bookshelf, a pile of clothes, their suitcases, and stacks of books. Undaunted by the size of the task before him, he buckled down and got to work. He was so intent on the task, he didn't notice that Stan had slipped into the room.

"What are you doing up so early in the morning?"

Startled, Jonathan dropped the books in his hand, tripped on an empty box behind him and would have crashed to the ground if Stan hadn't caught him. Stan let a curse slip his lips.

"Are you done making a racket? I don't think you've woken everyone in your complex yet," he whispered harshly.

"I'm trying to get some cleaning done before Angela gets home," Jonathan said in a hushed voice.

"Getting the nursery ready are we?" Stan asked.

"How did you—"

Stan pressed a finger to his lips and cocked his head towards the door. When no sound was heard he picked up one of the books and handed it to Jonathan.

"Jean sensed that Angela's been wanting a child since the day we arrived. She mentioned it to me and, after I saw you sneak off to this room, I put the two together. Now what exactly can I help you with?"

Jonathan and Stan worked through the rest of the early morning. They spoke companionably, mindful to keep their voices low. Stan talked at length about his battle with cancer and his road to recovery. Interested in what he had to say, Jonathan felt a reassurance he hadn't felt in a long time. He didn't know when, or how, but Angela was going to make it, and they would start a family. As the room became more organised, Jonathan began to ask what he needed to get in order to turn the room into a nursery. Stan was happy to oblige. He gave him a few ideas on what they could do to transform the room, but told him that Jean would probably be better at it than he. The men had cleared the room enough to get to the walls and started wiping them down when the smell of toast wafted into the room. Putting down their rags they went to investigate and were greeted by two plates of toast, eggs, and sausage.

"You two were busy last night." Jean set placemats on the table.

"Jonathan thought he should get a head start on that room." Stan winked at him before he took his plate and sat down to eat.

"Did you guys decide what colour you want to paint it?" Jean asked.

"Angela wanted honeysuckle, and she was thinking of painting some of her favourite childhood characters on the wall," Jonathan replied before taking a bite out of his toast.

"You might want to check and see if they will let you paint. Some apartments we had in the past wouldn't allow us to change anything," Kathy interjected.

Jonathan grimaced; he hadn't thought about that. He would need to speak to the manager before they did anything, but at least he could get some of the items Stan had mentioned, like a cradle and maybe some stuffed toys.

"I'm happy that you two have decided to have kids. I was getting worried that you would hold off until you got your careers going before starting a family. Trust me, having kids when you start heading into your late thirties can be hard. Your uncle and I have several friends who waited that long only to learn they had to adopt due to problems with their pregnancies," Kathy said between sips of tea. "What would you two like? A boy or a girl?"

"A girl. Then again, I guess we would be happy to have any child at this point. It's not like we can choose," Jonathan added.

"Well, girls can be a handful, so can boys I guess, but with boys you tend to only have to worry about one thing, and that's the girl he is with. Girls, on the other hand, you might as well go to bed with a bat in order to beat the boys away." Stan smiled at him. "I guess I must have misplaced mine when you came around."

They all laughed, and enjoyed the rest of the meal. Time flew by and before they knew it, Jonathan was running late. Jean offered to pack him a lunch, but he told her he would pick something up. Stan said they would visit Angela, and if they released her early, they would bring her home.

Jonathan ran as fast as he could, but he still missed the morning meeting. Mr. Kagawa was nowhere to be seen and

Jonathan was thankful for that. He gathered a few papers from his desk, and ran to make it to his first class. When he arrived, the sound of students rising to attention made him abruptly stop in his tracks. Looking through the door window he could see Mr. Matsuno greeting the students. Jonathan was unsure what to do, wasn't this his class? He didn't need to stand there long, as Mr. Kagawa stepped up beside him.

"Late, Hansen-san?" he asked.

Jonathan was embarrassed and a little unnerved by his presence. "I—I'm sorry, I didn't mean to. I mean, I had a late night and I was—"

Mr. Kagawa held up a silencing hand, and Jonathan's mouth snapped shut. "Come. Walk with me."

Every hair on Jonathan's body stood on end. Mr. Kagawa walked quietly alongside him and led him to the schoolyard were a class of students was stretching for a run. The Principal stood quietly watching the students. Jonathan took his place beside him and waited for the reprimand he knew was coming.

"How is she doing?"

"What?" Jonathan asked, startled by the question.

"How's your wife?"

Jonathan relaxed a little. "She's coming home today," he replied.

"How are you?" Something about the way the Principal was acting struck him as odd. The harsh, iron-fisted man had been replaced with someone Jonathan didn't recognize.

"I'm doing fine, I guess."

"You guess?" Mr. Kagawa raised an eyebrow, but still refused to make eye contact as he watched the students begin their run.

"I don't know, I guess as far as it goes, things could be a lot worse, but she's getting better, and that's all that matters to me right now."

They were silent for another few moments before the Principal spoke again. "I remember when my son was sick, almost like it was yesterday. Doctors told me he was so sick that they were not sure if he was going to make it. That nearly tore me apart from the inside out. Never had I considered the possibility of losing either of my boys. He was my eldest, and there was nothing I could do but watch as he wasted away from his illness. Before I knew it, the doctor told us to say our goodbyes."

Jonathan listened, transfixed. This was not what he had expected. He didn't know how to respond. What did one say to someone who had lost a child?

"That was long ago," Mr. Kagawa continued. "Now, I look back and wonder what my life would have been had he lived. Maybe my marriage would have survived, maybe my youngest boy would still talk to me." He turned his steely gaze to Jonathan. "Looking back prevents us from moving forward, and the choices we make back then shape us into who we are today. Don't let your past control your future. Move forward and keep moving. Don't let the weight of this world and its problems hold you down, unless you want to become like me."

Jonathan was not sure what Mr. Kagawa meant about the past controlling his future.

Mr. Kagawa turned and they walked back towards the school. "You indicted that your wife is coming home today?"

"Ah, yes sir."

"Then I suggest you go and be with her, make sure you are on time for class next week."

Next week? Was he being given the rest of the week off?

"Kagawa-sama," Jonathan called after the man, but he had disappeared through the school doors.

When Stan, Jean and Kathy arrived at the hospital they were surprised to find that Angela had visitors.

"Hello, you must be her grandparents," said the man. "I'm Hikaru-Bokushi. Your granddaughter has been attending our small home church."

"You speak English," Kathy said, surprised by his fluency.

"Yes, my father is the pastor of a small church in Alberta, near where you come from, I understand."

"Yes. I'm Stan Boisclair." Stan grinned, giving the pastor a friendly, firm handshake. "Well I'm glad our kids have found a place to worship while they're here."

When he looked up at the pastor's companion he was momentarily entranced by her beauty. Hitomi stood beside Angela, blushing a little at the sudden attention. Jean jabbed her elbow into Stan's ribs, drawing an annoyed grunt from him.

"My name is Jean, I'm Stan's wife. And this is Jonathan's Aunt Kathy," she said to the pastor.

"Oh, I am thoughtless. This is my good friend, Mrs. Hitomi Fukui, a member of our church and a good friend of Angela and Jonathan."

Jean gave her a quick hello, feeling a little envious of the woman's striking beauty. Wary of the women's' coolness towards her, Hitomi gave a small bow before excusing herself from the room.

"Oh, she didn't need to leave," Stan protested, but another nudge from his wife drew him back. Feeling the tension in the room, Hikaru regretfully watched Hitomi walk out.

"It's all right, she is shy around others."

"Grandma, you would like her very much. She is very sweet, and an amazing cook as well," Angela said.

Jean's apprehension dissolved into guilt over her atypical reaction. "I'm sure she is an incredible woman, maybe we should have her over for tea." She went to her granddaughter's side and gave a kiss on the forehead. "Are they discharging you today?"

"We are waiting for the doctor to return. He has to ensure all the test results are in before discharging her," said Hikaru as he put on his coat. "Well, I should be off, Angela, it was good to see you."

"You too, Bokushi, say hello to your wife and sons for me, and tell everyone I am doing fine."

Saying goodbye, Hikaru left to go find Hitomi.

Displeased by what had transpired, Stan turned to face his wife and growled, "That was a little rude."

Jean shook her head, feeling guilty. "I'm sorry Stan, I was just a little jealous by your sudden interest in her."

"I wasn't interested in her like that," Stan grumbled.

"I don't know, Stan," Kathy chided. "From your body language and how quickly you greeted her, it was as if she had become the only woman in the room."

Flustered and provoked by Kathy's jab, Stan proceeded to defend himself. "Look, there's nothing wrong in admiring someone for their—" Jean's glare cut him short before he made a big mistake.

"Come on, you guys came here to see me, not to squabble," Angela said. "Grandma, I am sure that Grandpa didn't mean to make you jealous, and I am sure that your response to Mrs. Fukui was one of friendship, wasn't it Grandpa?"

Ashamed by their actions, they turned to each other and apologised.

"I'm sorry, Stan, I know you weren't trying to make me jealous."

Putting an arm around his wife, Stan pulled her close and kissed her. "I'm sorry that I gave you any reason to doubt."

"And I'm sorry for fomenting trouble," Kathy muttered. "But you have to admit, she is gorgeous. No wonder we felt a little jealous of her."

Clenching his teeth, Stan knew no good would come from dwelling on the subject any longer. "What's done is done. Now, where is that doctor so we can get you out of here?"

As if on cue, the doctor stepped into the room, followed by a nurse.

"It looks like everything is in order," he said. "We won't have any affirmative information on the tests for another week or so. In the meantime, I want you to take your vitamins and eat as healthfully as you can until we get the results. If you would like, you may go home today."

Excited to be free, Angela thanked him, and with some help she was able to get up and go home.

Jonathan concentrated on understanding the instructions that were before him. Although his skills in reading and writing Japanese had improved, he still experienced difficulty deciphering some of the characters shared in each of the three Japanese alphabets and how they were used in a sentence.

He passed the bolt through the stand and crossbeam, and tried to attach the corresponding nut on the other side. Every time it seemed to go on, it became cross threaded and he would have to fight to remove it. When he turned the nut slowly, it eased itself on better than it had during his previous attempts. Finally, the two ends of the stand were put together. Now all he needed to do was assemble the basket. He consulted the diagram again, and struggled to find the screws he needed for the next part. As he sorted through the mix of parts before him, the sound of a door opening caught his attention.

"Hello?" came a voice. "Anyone here?"

"I'm in the study," he called.

Stan's head poked into the room, "What are you doing back so soon?"

"I was given the day off," Jonathan replied. "What do you think?"

Stan surveyed the chaos and could see that Jonathan had been hard at work trying to get things together before Angela came home.

"Well?" Jonathan prompted.

"It's coming along," Stan said tactfully. Two paint cans, a roller and paint tray sat in the corner of the room. Newspaper speckled with paint and dust debris protected the floor. There were several drip marks marring the fresh paint job and the original colour was showing through the new. Stan suspected that Jonathan hadn't primed the walls before painting. Two out of the three shelves he had put up were askew, and the drawings of teddy bears, trees and beehives looked like something a four-year-old had drawn.

"It's beautiful," Angela declared, entering the room with Jean and Kathy, who cringed at the mess.

"Need's a little TLC I think," Kathy sputtered, holding back her amusement. "Well, you might not be good with your hands, but at least your heart is in the right place."

Jonathan felt a little demoralised by his aunt's response. "I was hoping to have this finished before you got home. I've never done anything like this before."

"It's fine, Jonathan. You did a good job. I'm sure Stan wouldn't mind lending a hand to finish it up," Jean said, giving Stan small nudge.

"Sure I can." Stan gave Jonathan a pat on the shoulder. "In the meantime, let's get something to eat."

The others filed out of the room, leaving Jonathan and Angela alone.

"It's going to look amazing, I know it," she squealed, throwing her arms around him.

"I'm so happy you're home," he said softly in her ear and gave her a tender kiss on her neck. They stood there a while longer, silently holding each other. When they hadn't emerged from the room, Kathy came to check on them.

"Well, are you two coming?"

Jonathan helped Angela to the living room and set up a T.V. tray while Jean served her food. When they finished eating, Angela asked if they could sing together. Jonathan brought out two of the hymnals that Angela had brought from Calgary. Stan flipped to hymn number four hundred ninety eight, "Peace Like a River". The song was followed by "In the Garden" and "The Old Rugged Cross". Jonathan was elated to see Angela so cheerful; it was as if she had been given a new life.

Angela closed her hymnal and grinned. "I wish I could play piano again. I really miss it."

"You could always ask Hikaru-Bokushi. I'm sure his wife would be happy to take a service or two off and let you play," Jonathan suggested.

"I guess." Angela hid her face. "I don't know."

"Oh, come on now. I'm sure they would love to hear you play." Stan reassured her.

"What's the worst that could happen?" Jonathan asked.

Feeling emboldened, Angela agreed to ask Mrs. Ichinose the next time they went to church.

During the last few days of their visit, Angela was able to enjoy a little sightseeing with her grandparents, and go shopping with Aunt Kathy. When it came time for their return flight home, Angela was depressed and feeling homesick again.

"I'm going to miss you all so much," she said, giving her grandfather a lingering hug.

"I know, honey. Maybe you could persuade your husband to make a trip back home when he has time off."

"Yeah, I have two babies at home who would like to see their cousin again, if he ever decides to take a break," said Kathy in an authoritative tone.

"Yes, Aunt Kathy, when the next school break comes, I will see if we can afford to make it back home for a visit," Jonathan replied.

Angela and Jonathan walked with them to Departures and gave their final goodbyes. On the way home, Jonathan made a request for the driver to stop off at a small convenience store. Angela watched him enter the store. When he returned, he had flowers, a balloon and card in his hand.

"Are those for me?" she asked unnecessarily, opening the card. "What does it say?"

Jonathan read the poem to her. It was supposed to be a love poem, but it sounded more like something a stalker would write. Flustered, he quickly closed the card and shoved it back into its envelope.

"It looked good. The shop owner told me that you would like it."

"As long as you are my stalker I think it's wonderful."

They both laughed. Jonathan held his wife in his arms for the rest of the drive, looking forward to spending his next few days off with her.

When Jonathan returned to work, Mr. Matsuno and the rest of the staff welcomed him back with a small present for him and his wife.

"It's an Omamori." Mr. Matsuno held out the little decorative pouch, pointing to the Japanese symbols written on it.

"Oh, is this one of those good luck charms I have seen in the office?"

"Yes, this one is for a happy and healthy household."

"Thank you, I'm sure Angela will love it," he said.

Mr. Kagawa joined them and went over some of the day's events, including the preparations for the upcoming spring festival. Expecting to be asked to stay back, Jonathan waited after everyone else got up and left.

"Is there something I can do for you, Hansen-san?" Mr. Kagawa inquired.

"Uh, no, I just thought that you might want to ...." his voice trailed off and he felt a little foolish.

"You have a class to attend to this morning, it wouldn't be good if you were late."

Jonathan jumped up and stumbled out of the office, nearly bumping into Mr. Matsuno in his hurry. "Sorry, I didn't see you there," he apologised.

"It's all right, I got a little worried when you didn't leave right away. Are you in trouble?"

"No, no," Jonathan murmured in a daze. "I think everything's all right. Is he always like that?" he asked as they walked down the hall.

"Is he always like what?"

"I don't understand. He rode me so hard when I first arrived. The next thing I know he is trying to give me some advice. Then he turns around and he's back to his old self, I just can't wrap my head around it."

Mr. Matsuno waited for them to pass a couple of teachers before replying. "I think it's because you remind him of himself when he was younger. It's not well known, but a few of the teachers speak about a death that had torn his family apart. He's a little ill-tempered, but I think that's how he hides his pain. I was a little surprised by his response when you took off so much time, but if the rumours are true, he felt a kind of kinship with you during your troubles. One of the teachers mentioned that he had praised you and if you kept up the good work, he might consider giving you a recommendation."

"Really?" Jonathan said in astonishment.

"As rigid as he is, he does have a soft spot when it comes to family problems, but I wouldn't push it. I'm happy things are going better with your wife. If you need anything don't be afraid to ask."

They stopped off at the teacher's room to gather their materials. Jonathan had just enough time to go over the notes Mr. Matsuno had given him before heading off to his first class. When he entered the classroom, the students welcomed him back and were clearly happy to see him. Jonathan was happy to be back as well. The morning flew by as he concentrated on catching up on the lessons he had missed. By lunch time, he was already feeling a little anxious to get home, and by mid-afternoon he was counting the minutes. The afternoon class went by quickly enough and, instead of staying to do some paperwork, he decided to leave early and go home to his wife. He was greeted by Hitomi, who had stopped by for a tea and a visit.

"How was work?" she asked.

"Good to be back, but I am happy to be home now." He sat beside his wife on the sofa and he gave her a hug. "How are you feeling today?"

"A little tired, but better. I think the diet the doctor has me on is helping."

"I'm glad, do you two want some more tea?" he asked.

"I think we are fine for now. Hitomi said that she could take me to the doctor's appointment next week so you don't have to stay home."

"Oh, thank you," he said, a little disappointed. "Do they have your results?"

"They said that the lab results should be in by the end of this week."

"I like the nursery, it looks good," Hitomi said.

"Thanks, I got some help from Angela's grandfather to put it together. It looks better after he helped."

"You did a good job, honey, all he gave you were some pointers. I think the room is lovely."

"Do you want boy or girl?" asked Hitomi.

Jonathan looked at his wife. "We've never really discussed it."

Angela had wanted to say a girl, but she couldn't understand why she felt that way. She should be happy as long as the child was healthy. Maybe it had something to do with a dream she had, but her memory of it was too fuzzy.

"It's not like we can really choose. I will be happy with whatever we get, boy or girl." Taking Angela's hand, Jonathan smiled at her.

"Well, I should go, I must prepare supper for my family before it gets late." Hitomi set down her cup.

"Thank you for the visit, Hitomi. It's always nice to see you." Angela bowed her head.

"I liked the chat, as well." Hitomi bowed back. "Will I see you two at church this week?"

"Yes, we will be there, and I promise to bring her with me," Jonathan said with a smile.

Hitomi grinned. When she left, Jonathan prepared supper while Angela sat on the sofa and read one of her books. After supper, Jonathan sat with her while she read aloud. An hour later, he pulled out the work he had taken home and worked late into the night. When he was done he cleaned up and carried his sleeping wife to their room.

The rest of the week flew by and next thing they knew it was the day of the appointment. Both were a little nervous, but Angela did her best to stay positive and said that, if worse came to worse, she might have to take some treatments for a while to get better. Jonathan didn't find much relief in that, considering the treatment for cancer seemed as deadly as the disease itself. He hoped it was nothing, but the feeling of dread was tearing at him. At school he couldn't concentrate, all he could think of was how Angela was doing. He was so distracted that one of his students, Miss Fujino, had to repeat herself three times in answer to his question.

"Sorry," he apologised. "I have a lot on my mind today."

"It's all right," she said, her friends giggling making her blush.

When he was off, the uncertainty of what he would learn when he came home hung heavily on his heart. He was so distracted that he hadn't noticed Kate, and he nearly ran into her.

"Kate!" he yelped, startled at her sudden appearance.

"Hi, you okay?" she asked.

"Yeah, I'm sorry. Angela has an appointment and I've been in a daze all day."

"Why don't you pick her up something? Chocolate, flowers, maybe a sweet card. I'm sure she's been stressed out, too," Kate suggested, adding, "I'm on my way home and had to pick up a few things. You don't mind if I walk with you, do you?"

"No, of course not. Would you mind helping me pick out something for her?"

"Follow me," she said with a smile. "I know a small store around here that she would like."

She took him to a small family store nearby where he bought a small cake, some flowers, and a cute little stuffed bear. While they walked they talked about their jobs, what they liked and disliked, and she even shared a few of her bad dating experiences.

"So, are you seeing someone?" he asked.

"No, the last guy I dated was involved in a gang and he would always get jealous whenever I talked to other guys. We fought one night when I caught him with someone else, and I ended it then and there. For now, I just want to focus on work and my art. I have no desire to build a relationship." Looking up she saw that his mind had drifted off somewhere.

"What was that?" he asked coming out of it.

"Nothing," she said. "Well, we're here. Tell Angela I will try to visit her tomorrow night, and thank her for me."

"Thank her for what?"

"For what she had said last time. It made me think about things, and you know, she might be right. I talked to my mother for the first time in months and I was able to open up to her, it was the first time since I was a little girl I ever felt that I could share anything with her. It's all thanks to your wife. She's so kind and insightful, and her faith is genuine. I've never felt so comfortable talking about God or Jesus with anyone in my life. I'm thankful I met you two, and I hope that everything goes well with you."

Jonathan nodded, "I will tell her, and thanks for helping me today."

"No worries," she said walking ahead of him to her apartment. "Oh, and Jonathan?"

"Yes?"

"You're lucky to have each other. I hope that one day I can meet someone like you, maybe then I might settle down."

Jonathan watched her leave. He was lucky to have someone like Angela, and no matter what came of today, they would face it together. He opened the door to find the apartment silent and dark.

"Angela, you home?" he called out.

He was met with the ominous sound of silence, and the feeling of dread returned. He set the bags down at the door and walked towards their room. As he passed the nursery, he saw his wife standing there as if in a trance, gently rocking the cradle.

It was eleven forty-five, only fifteen minutes before Hitomi was to arrive. Angela fiddled with the pages of her book. She glanced every few moments at the clock. After getting up for the fifth time to see if Hitomi had arrived, she realised she was becoming frantic. She forced herself to sit still and, folding her hands, closed her eyes and began to pray.

"Dear Lord, I ask that You would still my heart. Bring me comfort, Lord, and help me through this. I ask that You give my husband and me peace and show us that You have Your hand in all of this. Let this come to the end You desire, and I pray that whatever I find out today, Lord, that You will give me the strength to overcome any obstacle. I ask this all in Your Son Jesus' name, Amen."

She felt a wave of confidence wash over her. She checked the time once more, and resumed reading. She hadn't read more than two pages when a knock at the door brought her back to reality.

"I'm coming."

She ran to the front and put on her shoes and coat. When she opened the door for Hitomi, she was surprised to see a young man standing with her.

"Hello, Angela." Hitomi bowed. "This is my driver, Suzaku-san. He will be taking us to the hospital."

Angela greeted him with a bow. "I didn't realise that you had your own personal driver," she exclaimed without thinking. "I'm sorry, that came out wrong."

"It's all right." Hitomi laughed. "Shall we go?"

"Yes." Exiting her apartment, she locked the door before following Suzaku and Hitomi to the car. When she saw the sleek black Cadillac with its chrome trim and tinted windows, she nearly slipped on one of the steps leading down to the parking lot. Suzaku instantly took her hand and helped her regain her balance.

"Are you all right?" he asked in Japanese. Hitomi said something to him and he smiled and nodded before letting her go.

"Th-thank you," she stammered. Angela wanted to ask Hitomi how she could afford so much, but she bit her tongue, knowing that Japanese didn't normally like to share personal matters.

The drive to the hospital rubbed her nerves raw. She didn't like good surprises, much less bad ones, and she could only hope that the doctor would give her good news. When they arrived, she was admitted almost immediately and taken to one of the examining rooms. She started pacing the room and biting her nails as her anxiety mounted. Each minute that ticked by brought her a deeper sense of foreboding. What's taking them so long? She jumped when the door suddenly opened. The doctor who entered was much older than the one who had seen her during her stay. Looking at the chart in his hands, Angela wished she had ex-ray vision to see what the chart said, but it would have been pointless as she couldn't read Japanese anyway.

"You Angela?" He spoke firmly.

"Yes." Her voice shook from the stress.

"I need you to sit down." His voice took on a grievous tone.

She felt her heart drop, and she sank onto the nearest chair. Her hands and feet turned to ice and she felt the blood draining from her face. The doctor took a moment to put together what he needed to tell her. He tried to be empathetic as he delivered the crushing blow.

"Endometrial cancer?" The words dug into her like claws into flesh.

He nodded, "Yes, it would seem your uterus lining is full of small tumours. We took a biopsy of one of the masses and confirmed the diagnosis. As far as we can tell, the cancerous growths are limited to the uterus and have not spread. When it comes to treatment we need a few more tests, but we are leaning towards the removal of your uterus." Angela nearly fell out of the chair and the doctor reached over to steady her. "I'm sorry, but there's no other way. If it is left for much longer you risk the chance of it spreading into the rest of your body."

The sheer devastation Angela felt as news of her illness settled over her was beyond what she had envisioned. Her mouth went dry and she felt as if she had left her body. The doctor laid out dates for her appointments so that they could determine how best to proceed, but at that point she was no longer paying attention. It was as if the whole world had darkened and she had just been stranded on a small raft in a sea of emptiness. There was no sadness, no sorrow, no pain, just a void. It was as if her entire being had been obliterated.

"Do you understand?" he asked, looking at her with compassion.

She could only nod.

Before the doctor left, he gave her some literature written in English. He told that she could stay for a while if she needed to. When he closed the door Angela wanted to scream or cry, but for some reason she couldn't. As she stood shaking, the feeling of nausea almost overtook her and she leaned over a nearby trash can. Holding herself up with one hand and covering her mouth with the other, she began to shake more violently. She slowly sank to her knees and curled up into a ball. Everything had been taken from her. There was nothing left. All her prayers, her hopes and dreams, were for nothing.

Hitomi became concerned when Angela didn't return after an hour. After fifteen more minutes, she was about to ask the nurse to check up on her friend when she saw Angela walking down the hall. Hitomi's breath caught when she saw her pale complexion and haunted eyes. She ordered Suzaku to start the car, and hurried to her friend's side.

"What's wrong?"

Taking Hitomi's outstretched hand Angela tried to say something but she froze. Placing one arm around her, Hitomi guided her out of the hospital and helped her into the car.

"Is she all right?" asked Suzaku, concerned.

The news had obviously been worse than Angela had thought. Hitomi shook her head. As they drove Angela home, Hitomi held her hand and began to hum one of the lullabies her mother used to sing to her. Angela stared at the floor, heartbroken and defeated. Once Angela was home, Hitomi asked Suzaku to wait at the car. With a low bow, the young man left them. When Hitomi turned around, Angela was nowhere to be seen. After searching, Hitomi found Angela standing alone beside the cradle in the nursery. In that moment, everything became clear.

"Angela, I'm so sorry," she said, placing a reassuring hand on her friend's shoulder.

"This was going to be the baby's room, we were going to try after I got better." She touched her belly. "Now we won't have *any* children, and it's all my fault."

Her small frame shook violently as she released the pain and sorrow she had been holding back. The news was devastating; Hitomi didn't know what to say. She stood beside Angela and put an arm around her as Angela buried her face in her hands, sobbing. Hitomi lost track of time as she tried to console her. Oh Lord, she prayed quietly, please help her through this.

Wiping her eyes, Angela shrugged off Hitomi's hug. "I think I want to be alone right now."

Hitomi opened her mouth to object, but the look on Angela's face told her this wasn't the time. "Let me know if you need anything."

She watched Angela from the doorway for a minute before leaving. Angela stood beside the cradle. She lifted a trembling hand she rested it on the basket's railing and began to slowly rock it back and forth.

Seeing her standing there in some sorrowful trance, Jonathan called softly out to her, "Angela, honey."

For a brief second she stopped rocking the cradle and raised her head a fraction. "I've ruined everything."

Grief stricken, she lowered her head into her free hand and wept. Jonathan gently took her into his arms and laid her head against his chest, and slowly rubbed her back to console her.

"It's not your fault," he said as a million different painful scenarios played in his head.

Angela melted into his arms, the agony she felt was so intense it made her body shudder. His heart ached in response to her pain. He brushed aside her hair and kissed her forehead.

"What did they say?"

"That I will never be a mother," she whimpered.

"There's nothing they can do?"

She shook her head. "It took everything from me."

Tilting her chin up a bit, he searched the emerald eyes that were now filled with tears, pain and sorrow.

"I know it doesn't change anything," he whispered, stroking her face, "but I want you to know that I will never leave you, I promise."

CHAPTER 19

Setsuko
July, 1985

Summer break was only a few weeks away, and Setsuko was already craving the freedom it offered. Her first term exams for her senior year were under way, leaving little time for David. Natsuki and Misayo were steadfast friends again. Akari had removed herself from the group, only keeping a tenuous relationship with Misayo. The animosity between Setsuko and Akari was growing and it was only a matter of time before it came to a head. Her relationship with David had grown closer, but more on a physical level, much to Setsuko's chagrin. Whenever she pushed for something other than sexual intimacy, David would become disinterested and distract her with a comment about how some girl had flirted with him. Whenever he made her angry, he would give her a disarming grin followed by a passionate kiss, and she was lost. Everything about him made him impossible to resist, and he knew it. Yet, whenever they were intimate, she felt as if she was giving him another piece of her soul.

Her obsession with David was affecting her schooling. She couldn't concentrate on her studies. For the first time, she was falling short of her teacher's expectations, and was dangerously close to being dropped from the top ten list of students in the District. Her lacklustre grades had caught the attention of the

Principal, but with some grovelling, she had convinced him not to report it to her parents. She had to catch up on her studies and ace the exams, but the chances of that were slim.

"Setsuko-chan," There was a light rap at her door and Hitomi opened it and looked in. "There's a young man here to see you."

"I'll be right out." Setsuko's heart soared. She pushed her notes aside and jumped up from her desk. She checked herself in the mirror. Happy with her appearance, she left to greet her visitor. Her breath caught at the sight of her Intended. "Ryota?"

He greeted her with a low bow. "Setsuko-san, I have come to ask if you would join me for lunch."

It wasn't David, as she had hoped, and her mother was standing nearby, waiting for her response. If she were to say no, her father would hear about it and that would cause more grief than it was worth.

Steeling herself, she returned his bow. "Give me a moment to get ready."

The young man's face became crimson. It had obviously taken a lot of courage for him to ask her out. Hitomi beamed at her daughter and told her to have a fun time.

Fun time? This is far from what I would call fun, Setsuko thought. She scooped up her small purse, and marched out the door. Ryota was unsure of how to proceed, but after a derisive snort from Setsuko, he quickly led her to their ride.

Mr. Hashida had arranged for his driver to take them. Ryota sat next to her in the back seat but kept a little distance between them. Setsuko was thankful for that. As they drove she stared outside, reluctant to make eye contact in case it would encourage him to strike up a conversation. Out of the corner of her eye, she could see him fidgeting in his seat whenever he looked at her. Her mouth curved into a faint smile. Even if she didn't like him, he was at least cute when he was flustered.

"Where are we going?"

"My driver said he knows of a nice little restaurant not far from here."

Turning to him she felt a twinge of regret. It wasn't his fault that their parents had decided to stick them together, so why punish him for it?

"You look very handsome."

"I ... I ...," he stuttered as he rubbed his hands on his trousers. "Thank you."

She waited for him to say something more, but she could tell he was too nervous. "What about me?" she asked softly.

"You look amazing." His voice shook.

"Amazing?"

"Yes, I mean, you look beautiful, as always. Well, more like gorgeous." The words came tumbling out.

He kept correcting himself and apologizing as he tried to work out a compliment he thought was worthy of her. For the first time since he met her, she blushed. Something in his genuine thoughtfulness and soft-spoken demeanour tugged at her heart. Maybe her father's decision hadn't been all bad; but she still wanted David. Taking the initiative, Setsuko slipped her hand into his and gave it a gentle squeeze. Ryota froze under her touch and she could feel the clamminess of his palm.

The restaurant was a little farther than Setsuko had imagined. When they arrived, the driver opened the door. Ryota stepped out and held out his hand. Setsuko took it and smiled up at him, which caused him to sheepishly avert his gaze. The restaurant was small but luxurious, and the waiter at the entrance greeted Ryota with a deep bow.

"Hashida-san, your table awaits."

"They know you here?" Setsuko asked.

"My father is friends with the owner, this is where he and my mother went for their first date."

When they were at their table, Ryota pulled a chair out for Setsuko before sitting down. The waiter handed them menus and listed off the specials. Ryota ordered one of the specials while Setsuko settled on a rice dish with calamari. Once Ryota had eaten a bit, he seemed to talk with more confidence and assurance. He told a few funny stories about himself and his father, while Setsuko reminisced about her childhood with her mother.

"You don't like talking about your father much, do you?"

Setsuko grimaced, "There's not much to say, really. He's a businessman and he proves that by putting it before anything else. Sometimes, I feel like I'm a pawn in a game he is playing. I grow tired of being under his thumb all the time, always needing to sneak around just to have a little fun." Placing her chopsticks down, she dabbed the corner of her mouth. "I guess that's something we have in common."

Ryota took a minute before responding. "I think we can perceive our parents as controlling us in a negative way, when in reality they only want what's best for us."

"You're joking." Setsuko threw the napkin onto her plate in frustration. "How can you say that when they are making all of the decisions for us?"

Ryota felt tension growing, and carefully considered his next words. "All I was trying to say is that parents sometimes make decisions regarding what they think is for our good. I'm not saying that they are always right, but I know that I can make some bad decisions because I lack the wisdom to foresee the possible consequences. That is why I think parents try to make some of the bigger decisions for us. They only want us to be happy and successful in life. Isn't that what you would want for your child?"

Setsuko couldn't find any fault in his logic, and that irritated her. She reluctantly took what he had to say into consideration, but that didn't mean she liked the choices being made for her. As she thought about it, a small knot formed in the pit of her stomach. When she tried to say something, that knot exploded into an intense feeling of nausea.

"Setsuko, are you all right?"

She couldn't respond, as any sudden movement would send her stomach over the edge. She took slow, shallow breaths, and closed her eyes and attempted to swallow, hoping it would calm the sensation. That was a big mistake. She quickly turned to the side and vomited onto the floor.

When her stomach had settled down, Ryota took her home. Embarrassed, she didn't say a single word to him other than 'thank you' before he left. Hitomi was cleaning the sitting room when her daughter came through the door, sweaty and pale. "What happened?" she asked, concerned.

"I don't know, I just felt nauseous all of a sudden." Hitomi raised a brow in question but Setsuko shook her head. "I'll be fine, Mother. I think I need to lay down."

"Maybe a little too much excitement?"

"Sure." She smiled wanly, and slowly walked towards her bedroom.

"I'm glad that you went out with him. He is a nice boy, and from a good family, too. It will be nice to see you both together."

Setsuko nodded. In truth, she couldn't picture herself with him. He was considerate and caring, but more in the way of a brother than her future husband. David, on the other hand, was gorgeous and exciting. In her room, she lay down on her bed and hugged a pillow to her abdomen. She wished David were there to hold her, and maybe tell one of his jokes that always made her laugh. As she lay there, she gradually fell into a deep sleep.

Her alarm woke her the following morning. Her nausea was still there, making it difficult for her to get up and ready for school. *Maybe I'm just sick,* she thought. Classes for the day were spent studying for exams and reviewing old material. Everyone was on edge as competition for top grades was intense. GPAs and entrance exams were the only two ways to get into university, so the pressure to perform had everyone stressed.

Natsuki was leading with the top GPA in the District, while Setsuko barely hanging on to tenth place. Misayo and Akari placed amongst the top twenty-five students, which gave them a future in an office or a management position. Students were so intent on their exam preparations that lunch time turned into an additional study period. Setsuko, Natsuki, and Misayo sat together during their spares and lunch, quizzing each other. Akari was spending time with her new friends and no longer acknowledged the girls. Relieved to escape the drama that was Akari, Setsuko couldn't be happier that her former friend ignored her.

"Hey Sestuko-chan," Misayo whispered.

"What?"

"Are you still seeing David?"

Setsuko sighed, "Yes, but we haven't really been seeing each other lately. He's been busy with his parents, and I have had to work like a dog to make up my grades. Why are you asking?"

"I was curious. I heard some rumour that one of the girls at school was dating someone who looked a lot like him."

Setsuko's gaze narrowed onto the table where Akari sat. He wouldn't, would he?

"I'm pretty sure it was some other guy, there are lots of Westerners that come overseas for business and school," Natsuki piped up. "Besides, we have to focus and study for our Finals."

Misayo rolled her eyes. "It would be nice to take a break every once in a while, Natsuki. I'm sure that someone like you who ranks number one in our district doesn't have much to worry about when it comes to studies."

"That's not true." Setsuko grimaced in disgust. "Everyone here is working hard to keep their grades up. One slip and you can find yourself running the family shop the rest of your life."

Misayo winced at the slight. "I wasn't trying to fight with you, Setsuko, I was just saying that maybe we could take a break. What's your problem anyway? You've been acting strangely over the last couple of weeks."

"I think the stress is getting to all of us, but Misayo you're right, maybe we do need a break. So, how about we get together this weekend and have a girl's night out?" Natsuki cut in before Setsuko lost her temper.

"This weekend!" Misayo slumped in her seat. "I was hoping for tonight."

"We can't. Just because you like to settle for top twenty five, that doesn't mean the rest of us have to," Setsuko growled.

Hurt by her friend's thoughtless words, Misayo picked up her books and left.

"Why did you have to say that?" demanded Natsuki.

"We can't afford to be held back because of her. If we don't make good grades now, the entrance exams will kill us," Setsuko spat back. When Natsuki stared at her wide-eyed, Setsuko felt guilty for her extreme reaction. "I'm sorry Natsuki, I guess I didn't realise how harsh I was being."

"What is going on with you?" Natsuki asked. Her friend's recent outbursts had been odd, even for her.

"Like you said, it's the stress of everything."

Natsuki reached over and placed a hand on top of Setsuko's. "Setsuko, it wouldn't have anything to do with David, would it?"

Puzzled by her friend's question, it took Setsuko a few moments to catch her meaning.

"No, it couldn't be! We've been careful and David made sure nothing would happen."

Natsuki didn't look convinced. Setsuko tried to think of another possibility, but everything that was happening lately brought her to the same conclusion. Suddenly irritated by her friend's touch, Setsuko jerked her hand away.

"If it makes you feel better, I will go apologise to her." She slammed her books shut, put them into her bag and stormed off.

She found Misayo outside, leaning against a wall as she stared up into the sky. "Misayo-chan!"

Closing her eyes, Misayo turned her back to Setsuko. "Leave me alone."

"Misayo, I'm sorry. I didn't mean it." She circled around her friend to face her. Misayo's cheeks glistened in the sunlight. "I'm sorry, I really am." Setsuko reached out for her friend's hand but Misayo pulled away. "Please Misayo, you have to forgive me."

Setsuko's eyes moistened, her chest hurt with the pain of an immense grief she couldn't explain. "I don't know. I—" Setsuko choked, covering her face.

"Setsuko-chan, are you okay?"

What's wrong with me? Setsuko wondered. One moment I'm happy, the next I am angry or an emotional wreck.

She bolted. Running past the school gates, Setsuko slowed her pace to a hasty walk. Her tears had subsided, but the nausea had returned. She felt her stomach lurch and, before she knew it, she was throwing up again. Holding her stomach, she stayed hunched over as she tried to steady herself. Passersby gave her room and ignored her, except for the occasional look of disgust. Her palms were clammy and her heart started racing. The realization that she may be pregnant sent chills down her spine. She stood up gradually, allowing her nausea to settle. She could hear Natsuki and Misayo calling her in the distance. No matter what, she was not going back, she had to make sure that this wasn't a reality. She turned down the nearest road and headed for home.

Setsuko slowed her pace as she approached the house. Suzaku was not there, which meant he was either picking up her father or driving her mother somewhere. Not trusting the silence, she sneaked in through her bedroom window. She stood motionless, listening for the slightest sound of movement. Reassured that she was alone, she set her bag down and emptied the contents of the nightstand's bottom drawer onto the floor. She opened the false bottom she had made and took out the small jewel box that was secreted there. Inside was a wad of bills that she had been saving for emergencies. She slid the money into her pocket, slipped out the way she came, and slunk back to the driveway.

Setsuko's nerves were already on edge, and by the time she reached the drugstore, her heart was pounding. Terrified by the thought of being recognised, she gave the store a quick scan, looking for any familiar faces. Seeing none, she kept her head down and quickly stepped inside. It took several minutes to locate the pregnancy test kits. As she reached for one, she froze at the sound of bells jingling. She glanced surreptitiously at the door and watched a woman walk over to the counter to talk with the clerk. Setsuko exhaled slowly and grabbed three different tests. The woman was still chatting, which distracted the clerk as he ran Setsuko's purchase through. Thankful that he hadn't recognised her, she slipped out and hurried home.

When she returned home, the car was sitting in the driveway. She wished she had kept track of the time, as coming home early would stir up questions. Just as she was about to turn back, Suzaku emerged from the garage. He caught sight of her, smiled and waved. Rolling her eyes, she begrudgingly made her way to the front door.

"Hello, Setsuko-ojousama. How was school?"

"Fine, Suzaku-san, would my mother happen to be home?" Her tone had a slight edge to it.

Suzaku bowed "Yes, we just got back from grocery shopping." When she said nothing further, he resumed cleaning the car.

She could hear her mother humming a song in the kitchen. With Ninja stealth, Setsuko made her way to the bathroom and closed the door. Shaking, she opened the tests and set them out on the vanity. She rested her head against the mirror and said a quick prayer before starting the tests. The instructions said she had to wait twenty minutes. Taking a seat, she took the first two tests and, shaking her legs restlessly, waited for the results. At the twenty minute mark, she tore her eyes away from her watch and checked the results.

Both were blue.

Her entire body went numb.

She dumped the tests, and reached for the last one. In her haste, she knocked it to the floor. She reached for it with her foot and sent it skittering towards the door. Lunging after it, and saw the shadow of feet beneath the door. Setsuko pulled herself back up but had no time to readjust her clothing before her mother opened the door.

"Setsuko!" Hitomi proclaimed in surprise. "You are home, what are you doing back from school so soon?"

Setsuko froze staring at her mother. Hitomi's eyes widened when she surveyed the disaster. Her gaze fell on the pregnancy test sitting at her feet. Dropping the eggs she had been holding, Hitomi covered her mouth in shock and stared back at her daughter.

"Setsuko, what have you done?" she gasped.

Setsuko's eyes glistened as she poured out her heart to her mother. Hitomi stood slack-jawed in disbelief. After everything she had told her about saving herself, her daughter had given herself away, and to a foreigner, no less.

"What am I going to do?" pleaded Setsuko.

Hitomi gathered the tests and their packaging and hid them deep in the kitchen garbage. She returned to the bathroom, only to find it vacant. After she had cleaned up the eggs she had dropped, she went to her daughter's room. Setsuko was sitting on her bed with her arms wrapped tightly around a pillow.

Hitomi stroked her tear-streaked cheeks. 'We will figure something out," she whispered.

As she stood holding her daughter's head against her and stroking her, a horrible idea came to mind. GET RID OF IT, NO ONE WILL FIND OUT. Hitomi's hand stilled, and she shuddered at the thought.

"'No' what, Mother?" Setsuko asked, confused.

Bewildered, Hitomi stared at her daughter, "What?"

"You said 'no'. What was it?"

Hitomi's squeezed her eyes shut. "A bad thought, nothing more."

"But if it helps, it can't be that bad."

She tipped Setsuko's chin and she looked into her tear-filled eyes. "We can't Setsuko, what you have inside of you is a child. It's unthinkable."

"An abortion?" she ventured.

Biting her lip, Hitomi nodded. Setsuko had taken the words right out of her mouth. "I won't allow it. You don't understand, that would be the worst thing you could do right now."

"But there are girls at school, I know a few of them, they've had it done and they're all right."

How could she explain to her the devastation a woman could feel after having something so precious torn out of her. She unconsciously stroked her own abdomen, then jerked her hand away, leaving Setsuko perplexed by her action. Taking her daughter's face in her hands, she leaned down.

"You must promise me you will never consider it. If you do, you may never forgive yourself."

The disheartened look on Setsuko's face made Hitomi question her decision. IT WOULD MAKE THINGS EASIER, whispered a voice in her mind.

No. After everything in her life, she would never make that choice again. She couldn't do it, and she certainly wouldn't put her daughter through it. Another thought silenced the whispers. What was she going to do about Daiki? He was going to lose it when he found out.

Hitomi knelt down and held her daughter's hands. "Leave everything to me, just go to school and don't tell anyone."

Setsuko hesitated before nodding. "I will, Mother, I promise. But what about Father, if he finds out—"

She placed a finger on Setsuko's lips and shook her head. "Leave that to me. I want you to focus on your schooling and bringing your grades back up."

Setsuko's eyes took on saucer proportions. "You knew?"

"I saw one of your test scores that you had left on your bed, but I assumed you had trouble with that one test. Then I saw you with that American boy, and I put the two together. Now we have this to worry about." Hitomi put her hand over her daughter's womb.

"I'm sorry, Mother, I didn't know this was going to happen. I've been working hard to get back on track but I wasn't planning on getting pregnant. I've ruined everything!" Setsuko wept, burying her face in her mother's shoulder.

Pushing her back, Hitomi took on a commanding tone. "Setsuko-chan, we cannot turn back time, so we must move forward. You need to keep up your studies. You cannot falter for even a moment, and you need to stop crying. You got yourself in this position, now you must deal with the consequences."

"I don't understand why I can't get an abortion, it would fix everything."

"Setsuko," Hitomi barked, "I will not allow you to entertain the idea, now get yourself cleaned up and get to your studies."

Setsuko flinched at the harshness of her mother's voice, but relented.

Hitomi felt weary and weak. "Oh, Lord, please help us through this," she prayed softly and a sense of peace settled over her. She went back to work in the kitchen as she contemplated their next move. It was a tense evening when Daiki returned home and the atmosphere felt strained.

"Has something happened that I need to know about?" Daiki asked. Setsuko froze, her eyes locked on her mother in fear.

"No, Daiki, everything is all right. Your daughter has been struggling with her studies and feeling the strain of her senior year." Looking at Setsuko, she nodded.

"Yes, Father, I just feel a little stressed."

Daiki nodded, but his eyes showed a hint of curiosity. "You will need to work harder to prove yourself this year. Top ten in the District is good, but you can become greater. I had better not hear of you slacking on your studies, do you understand?"

Setsuko nodded, "Yes, Father, I will do better, I promise."

Hitomi was happy when it came time for bed. But she had yet to sort out how best to help Setsuko, and how to explain her condition to Daiki.

Setsuko could not sleep. She tossed and turned, her heart pounding in her ears. Every time she tried to close her eyes, thoughts of aborting the pregnancy overwhelmed her. Before the sun began to rise, Setsuko slipped out of bed, dressed and went outside. She was thankful to find Suzaku's bike gone, which meant he was probably still at home.

She returned to her room as quietly as possible, and packed her books into her backpack before going back out. When she had closed the front door, she waited for the nausea to strike. The ginger tea her mother had made the night before seemed to have assuaged her regular morning sickness. Relieved, she broke into a run and raced down the driveway. Following the path she had taken many times to Kyo's place, she kept her head down and didn't stop for anyone. The air was cool and the streets empty except for a few early risers. Setsuko's pace slowed and her anxiety began to abate. I have to talk to David, she thought. He needs to know, maybe he can help me.

As she neared her destination, more and more people poured out of their homes. She caught a glimpse of the two young men who had harassed her. One of them noticed her and grinned, pointing her out to his friend. Halting, Setsuko debated going into a nearby alleyway to avoid them, but when she saw them make no move towards her, she crossed to the other side of the road to walk around them.

"What's wrong, you don't want to hang out with us?" one of them called.

"We won't bite, we promise. You never know, you might actually have some fun." The other chuckled.

Setsuko kept her eyes on the road and ignored their taunts. When their voices faded, the tension in her shoulders eased, but as the knot in the pit of her stomach loosened, the nausea returned. She slowed her strides as she neared Kyo's apartment. Walking through the small lot in front of the complex, she went up the stairs and a few doors down to the apartment. Raising her hand, she stopped short of knocking as nervousness took hold of her. Looking back, she considered turning around and go to school.

"Setsuko, what are you doing here?" a voice asked, startling her.

"Kyo, what are you doing here?"

The girl laughed. "I live here, silly."

"Sorry, I meant what you are doing up?"

Kyo raised her brow, "It's time to go to school, which brings me back to my first question."

Setsuko twitched nervously, "I came to see if David was over."

"David? No, we haven't seen him for the last week, he said his Dad had some business elsewhere and he wouldn't be back for a couple of weeks."

"Weeks?"

"Are you okay?" Kyo adjusted the backpack on her shoulders.

"Let's go." Setsuko turned around at the bottom step. "Are you coming or not?"

Kyo struggled with the door before running to join her. The pair walked side by side as Kyo rambled on and on. Setsuko clenched her jaw, angered by David's sudden disappearance. He hadn't said a word to her, and now he had just up and left? She was afraid, afraid of being alone and having this child, afraid of everyone finding out. What would Natsuki and Misayo think? What would her father do when he found out? She felt so much despair well up that she fought back a small whimper.

"What did you want with David?"

Setsuko felt her heart stop. What am I going to say? She forced a smile. "Nothing, I just wanted to talk to him before school."

Kyo didn't believe her, but she decided to not press the matter. When they arrived at school, she thanked Setsuko for walking with her and left to join her friends. Setsuko found Misayo and Natsuki waiting for her inside.

"Setsuko, what happened to you yesterday?" asked Natsuki.

Setsuko collected herself before answering. The turmoil she felt within was chipping away at her control over her emotions, and she wasn't sure how much longer she could hold it in.

She shrugged, and smiled insincerely. "I just didn't feel well. I didn't miss anything, did I?"

The two girls looked at each other uncertainly. "No, the last two periods were turned into study time. Are you feeling better?" inquired Misayo.

"Yeah, I'm fine, just fighting stomach flu." Setsuko hoped the lie would satisfy their curiosity. They didn't press the matter, but she could tell that they were sceptical. The rest of the day was one trial after another as she battled with her internal unrest.

At home she spent the night studying, eating supper with her parents, and then went straight to bed. Hitomi made sure not to bother her, knowing how frayed her emotions were. Instead, she made plans to talk with Pastor Hikaru the following day for guidance.

CHAPTER 20

Pastor Hikaru listened patiently as Hitomi told him of Setsuko's predicament. Her worry was tangible.

"Have you discussed other options?"

She shook her head slightly. "I couldn't think of anything. That's why I came here. I thought if anyone knew of a solution, it would be you, Bokushi."

Hitomi wasn't the only one in the church who felt that he had all the answers. It was frustrating that everyone expected so much of him, but such was the life of a pastor.

He not only had to compose a sermon every week and help his wife with the hymn selection, he also needed to be a counsellor, friend and advisor to his parishioners. With everyone having such diverse needs and desires, it was sometimes taxing to meet all the demands this job asked of him. Add the stress of his day job to the equation and he more than once found himself at wit's end. At those times he would pray that the Lord would have this cup removed, and would be reminded of what the Lord Jesus Christ had suffered and endured on his behalf. Even the King of Kings was told 'no' when He had asked to have the cup of suffering be removed, so why should he expect any better?

"What has Daiki said about all of this?"

Hitomi flinched. "I haven't told him yet. If he finds out he will demand an abortion."

Horrified by the thought, Pastor Hikaru looked to the Bible sitting on his desk as a myriad of passages about the sanctity of life came to him. It wasn't talked about, but it was a common practice for a woman, and sometimes even a Christian one, to abort an unwanted pregnancy. What wasn't common was the idea of adoption. It was difficult to watch people, who claimed to have Christ, make such a detrimental and immoral decision. It reminded him of the hypocrisy he had witnessed at his father's church back in Canada, and how much he had detested it. It wasn't until he matured and took a hard look at himself while in Bible College, that he realised that everyone struggled in one form or another with hypocrisy.

"What about adoption?" Hitomi's confused reaction told Hikaru that she had not even considered the possibility. "Don't decide right now, but there are children being adopted overseas. I know it isn't something that's promoted here, but it's at least better than the alternative."

Hitomi's uncertainty dissolved as she considered it. It wasn't a perfect solution, and Setsuko would be devastated of course, but at least they could save the child.

"It sounds like a good idea, but I don't know how I will be able to convince Daiki. He can be stubborn when he makes up his mind. I'm not entirely sure if I would be able to change his mind if he decides to make our daughter get an ... abortion." Her lips twisted in distaste as she spoke the word.

"Why don't we ask the Lord to do that for us? Remember that He does all things in accordance to His will. I'm sure that He won't let any harm come to this child and that, whatever is decided, He will ensure that he or she will be taken care of."

Hitomi was grateful for the encouragement and the prayer that followed. She thanked him for his time and asked him to keep her family in their prayers.

He saw Hitomi to the door, and went upstairs to refill his teacup. Mai was cleaning the upstairs bedrooms and the boys were at school. As he savoured the tea and the silence, he felt compelled to call the Hansens. They had not attended church for the last two weeks. Hitomi had kept him up to date with what was happening in their lives, and from the latest bit of news regarding Angela's illness, he knew that they needed all the support they could get. He returned to his office, and made the call. The phone rang several times before Jonathan picked up.

"Hello?"

"Hello, Jonathan, this is Hikaru-Bokushi. I thought I would call and see how things were going."

"Hikaru-Bokushi." Jonathan sounded surprised, "Oh, everything's all right, I guess. Angela is going in for an examination next week, and I am busy preparing exams for the next sesemestermester. I'm sorry that we haven't been to church, it's been really busy around here."

"I've heard. Hitomi has kept me up to date. How has Angela been coping with the news?

"Not well, I'm afraid." Jonathan laid out everything that had happened. Angela had taken the news hard and had fallen into a deep depression. She rarely got out of bed, and she would eat only a little when Jonathan made her. Hikaru was surprised to hear that she had resisted Jonathan's attempts to get her to go to church last Sunday. He felt his heart break for Angela.

"I'm so sorry for all that she has endured. I wish there was something we could do." As soon as the words left his mouth, inspiration struck him. "Jonathan?"

"Yes?"

"When they are done with the procedure, I am assuming they will remove all of the cancer?"

"Yes, why do you ask?"

"God may have provided the solution to your problem, but I would like to talk to you two in person. Do you think she would be up for a quick visit?"

"It's probably better that you come over. She doesn't seem to want to talk to anyone lately."

Hikaru checked the clock. He had just enough time to make it over and deliver the good news before his scheduled meeting with the elders.

"How does right now sound?"

"Any time works for us, Bokushi. I think she would really appreciate your encouragement."

"I'll be right over. You get her up and ready for when I arrive, and we will leave the rest in God's hands."

Jonathan went to their room and shook Angela, "Honey, we have a visitor coming over."

With her back to him, she shrugged under the covers and pulled the blankets more tightly around her, "I don't feel like visiting."

He stroked her back through the covers. "Honey, you need to get up, you can't spend the rest of your life hiding away."

"I said I don't want to visit with anyone. Please, leave me alone."

Jonathan's heart sank in response to her coldness. The once kind and compassionate young woman had become a hard, small shell of her former self. Jonathan had tried everything to make her happy again, but the knowledge that she couldn't bear children had darkened her heart.

With a firm hand, Jonathan rolled her over so she was facing him, "Angela, you are getting up. I will not hear anything else from you, do you understand me?"

Angela's eyes widened as she stared back at him, mouth slightly agape. He had never taken such a stern tone with her. For a brief moment, he worried that he had gone too far. Without saying a word, Angela sat up, put on her slippers and walked out of the room.

Jonathan went to the kitchen to put on some tea, then tidied up the apartment. When he had finished, Angela emerged from the washroom. She was still in her housecoat, but her hair was brushed and tied back in a ponytail, and she had applied a touch of make-up. The bones in her hands and face were more prominent, and her complexion was pale. He had done everything he could to get her to eat, but she often flat-out refused. At her last check-up, the doctor had given her strict orders to get her weight up, or they would have to cancel her surgery. Jonathan was running out of ideas and he hoped that whatever Pastor Hikaru was so excited about would be the catalyst that rekindled Angela's fighting spirit.

Pastor Hikaru arrived within the hour. Jonathan greeted him at the door and welcomed him in. Angela was sitting on the sofa with a teacup in her hands. She started to rise when Pasotr Hikaru entered, but he motioned her to sit back down.

"Hi, Bokushi, I'm sorry we haven't been to church," she apologised.

"It's all right, you two have a lot on your plate, so take all the time you need."

Jonathan took the pastor's coat and hung it up. Hikaru sat across from Angela and waited for Jonathan to take a seat next to his wife. Angela looked haggard and careworn, and her gaunt face wore a haunted expression. Jonathan offered him a cup of tea but he declined, saying he was only there for a short visit.

"When are they planning to perform the surgery?" he asked.

"She's scheduled to go in at the end of next month, but she needs to gain some weight first," Jonathan said on Angela's behalf.

Angela ignored his pointed look. "I'm assuming you came over to tell us something?" she asked, bitterness tainting her voice.

Jonathan almost dropped his cup. "Angela!" he exclaimed, shocked by her tone.

Unperturbed, Hikaru folded his hands in front of him and looked back at Angela. "What are your thoughts on adoption?"

It took a moment for both Jonathan and Angela to comprehend what he had asked. Looking at each other, Angela felt a glimmer of hope, while Jonathan was a little sceptical.

"I had thought about it, but I was afraid we couldn't, as we would probably have to go back home to adopt," Angela replied.

"I can't give you any more information for now. All I can say is that there might be a mother who needs to put her child up for adoption. I will tell you more when I get all the details together, but I felt guided to talk to you about it. Now, is this a possibility that you two are open to?"

"Of course, we would love to adopt a child," Angela said, excited by the prospect. She grinned broadly. Jonathan gave her a weak smile in return, but he couldn't help feeling a little apprehensive.

"Why don't I look into it some more and get back to you? Even if it doesn't work out with this mother, it opens another avenue for you both to explore. In the meantime, concentrate on getting better and we will leave the rest in God's hands."

Hikaru excused himself and Jonathan walked him to the door. Angela was thrilled and kept thanking him for the visit and promised that they would make it to the next church service. As the door shut, Angela squealed and wrapped her arms around her husband. "Jonathan, can you imagine? Adopting a child?"

Jonathan's feelings were mixed on the subject, and he couldn't return her enthusiasm. Part of him was happy to see her smile again, but another part felt a little cheated.

"What's wrong?" she asked him.

"I don't know," he said, "I feel a little odd about raising someone else's child."

The second the words left his mouth he wished he could take them back. Angela stepped back, her face stricken with confusion and hurt.

"You don't want to have a child?"

"No, it's not that."

"Then, what is it?"

Jonathan shrugged, "I don't know if adoption is what I think we are called to do."

Once again he regretted his choice of words as Angela's expression turned to anger, "What do you mean by that?"

Her eyes probed his, searching for an answer and moistening as her emotions welled up. The pressure was on, he had to tell her why he felt the way he did. He had grown fond of the idea of having their own child. Adopting someone else's felt odd; he felt like he was less of a man by their inability to have children on their own.

"I guess I wish we could do it the natural way like everyone else."

"So it's my fault, then?" Angela instantly put up the wall she had constructed around herself over the last few weeks and there was nothing he could say to tear it down again. "Well, I guess it is, seeing as I am the one with the problem!" She defensively wrapped her housecoat around herself and stormed off to their room.

"Angela, I didn't mean it like that." Jonathan followed her, only to have the bedroom door shut in his face, leaving him standing in the hall to dwell on what he had done wrong. Jonathan waited for a minute before opening the door.

Angela lay in bed, covers over her head with her back turned to him. Her shoulders shook and he could hear her sniffle as he slowly walked over to sit on the end of the bed.

"I wasn't trying to say it's your fault." He paused waiting to see if she would respond. When all he received was silence, he exhaled slowly and continued, "I can't get past the fact that it won't be ours."

Pulling the blankets down Angela popped her head out, her eyes red and puffy. She refused to look at him. "Since we can't have our own, you just want to give up?"

Reflecting on it, he realised how selfish he sounded. He tried to rub her legs, but she pulled them away.

"Are you going to be angry with me for the rest of our lives?" he asked, exasperated.

"Please, leave me alone." With that, she pulled the covers back over her head.

Jonathan could see that no apology would suffice as Angela was feeling far too hurt and betrayed. Leaving the bedroom he went to the living room and picked up the phone. There was only one person who would know what to say and do in this situation.

Stan had finished with the last coat of paint when Jean walked into the room. "Well, what do you think?"

"It looks amazing, honey."

The room was painted a light purple with white baseboards that made the room pop. The floor was covered with grey carpet that a friend had left over from a house renovation. Instead of a regular popcorn ceiling, Stan decided to go with a smooth finish and a white coat of paint. The windows had new trim and were the final detail that pulled the room together, making it the best looking room in the house.

"When are you going to get to the rest of our house?" Jean prodded. Stan ignored the question as he began cleaning the room. "Before you tidy up, Jonathan is on the phone for you."

"Jonathan?" he looked up at her.

"She's fine. They are having a little tiff and he was wanting your help."

"My help?" Wiping his hands with a rag he followed Jean downstairs and picked up the phone from the counter.

"Hi, Jonathan, so what's going on?"

"Hi, Stan, I need to talk to someone and the only one I thought could help was you. Do you have some time to chat?"

"Sure I do, let me grab a coffee." Jean handed him a fresh cup and he added a dollop of milk and a teaspoon of sugar before sitting down. Jonathan told him the exciting news about the possible adoption and how elated Angela had been after hearing about it. He then expressed that he felt uncomfortable about raising someone else's child and how Angela had taken offense. He rambled on saying that he wasn't upset with her. Stan could see why Angela felt hurt, but he also understood Jonathan's point of view.

"Do you two want a child?" he asked, taking a sip of coffee.

"Yes, of course we do."

"Other than that it won't be yours, what else is bothering you?"

There was a long pause on the other end while Jonathan gathered his thoughts and feelings. "I don't know why God is allowing this to happen. Out of everyone, why us? Why is God putting us through this?"

"Well, why not?" Stan asked.

"What?" Jonathan replied in surprise.

"Why does God allow us to suffer, even if we are his children?" Jonathan didn't have an answer.

"What about Job?" Stan asked, "He was a follower of the Lord and had a stronger faith than all those that lived during his time. Yet God allowed Satan to destroy everything he held dear and left him in ruin. What about Israel? There were many times in their history that God allowed other nations to conquer and rule over them. Then there is Ruth and Naomi. Ruth's husband died and Naomi lost not only her husband but her sons as well, and they were believers in the Lord. Why did they suffer?"

Jonathan's silence told Stan that this was something that he had never considered before.

"Think about it this way, Jonathan. In Job's case, God was allowing Satan to test him, just like He tested Abraham's faith and devotion. Israel was punished for their sins and their disobedience and were cast out of the land given to them by God, yet whenever they repented, He would bring them back home. As for Ruth and Naomi, God used their loss as an opportunity to return them home. Ruth then met her new husband, Boaz, and because of their union, we have the family line that led to our Lord and Saviour, Jesus Christ. In every one of these examples, God used the bad for His glory. So I ask you again, why shouldn't God use this as an opportunity for a child to have faithful and loving parents to raise her to be the best that she could be?"

Jean refilled Stan's cup. "Child? What child?" she whispered. Stan made a shushing gesture and mouthed, 'Later'. Overcome with curiosity, Jean sat in the chair next to him and listened intently to his side of the conversation.

"I guess I never thought of it that way, thanks Stan."

"No worries, Son. I'm glad you called. We have been worried about you two since the last time we talked. So, when is the surgery?"

"They want to get her in as soon as possible, but with her weight loss and lack of appetite, they are concerned. Right now, they are keeping an eye on her and will let us know when they think she is ready."

"Maybe this is a blessing. After all the loss she has suffered, God has provided in your time of need. Now all you have to do is be faithful, and He may bless you two with a child you both will love and adore."

"Thanks." Jonathan sounded relieved. "I knew there was a reason why I thought of calling you."

"You're welcome. Give her some space before talking with her again, and tell her when she is feeling better to give us a call. Or better yet, why don't you go out and get her some flowers and pick up some dinner to show how much you love her."

"I will, and maybe I might make something for her."

Stan cringed just thinking of the few meals Jonathan had tried to make for them during their visit. "Why don't you stick to take-out."

Jonathan laughed. "I guess you're right, thanks. I'm glad we could talk."

"Anytime, Son. We love you both and wish you the best. I will ask the elders to pray for you two, and we shall see where the Lord leads."

"Thanks. Oh, and Stan."

"Yes?"

"Why did you say it was a little girl?"

Stan wasn't sure why he had said that, it just felt right. "I'm not sure, I guess it's a force of habit for me."

"Who knows? Maybe it will be a little girl. Maybe God is telling you something."

"Maybe He is." Stan chuckled.

"Well, have a good night, I should get going and pick up something to eat. Tell Jean that we miss her."

"Will do, Son, will do. Send our love to Angela, and we will chat with you soon."

He hung up, and looked at Jean, who waited in anticipation in a chair beside him.

"What's going on?"

"It would seem that we have an answer to our prayer. God may have given them the opportunity to adopt a child."

Jean's eyes lit up, "You mean it? We are going to be great-grandparents?"

"We shall see," he said resting his hand on hers. "We shall see."

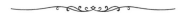

Jonathan picked up his coat. "Angela, I'm going to the Market. I will be back in a bit."

As much as he wanted to take Angela with him, he knew he would only be met with resistance. He locked the door behind him, and headed off to pick up some food and flowers.

Angela waited until she was certain Jonathan had left before she slipped into the living room and picked up the phone. She was still upset at him, and knew from what she had overheard that he had talked to her grandparents. She keyed Stephanie's home number and waited for an answer. Mrs. Marshal answered on the fourth ring.

Mrs. Marshal was surprised and happy to hear from her. After exchanging pleasantries, they chatted about her health and when she was expected to go in for surgery. Angela explained that they were waiting for her to get stronger. The subject shifted to how much she missed everyone, and of how she longed to be back home smelling the warm spring air and walking along the familiar dirt roads near her grandparents' farm. She never felt like Tokyo was where she belonged. The church was nice and the people were warm and welcoming, and Pastor Hikaru was easy to talk to. She had even made friends with Hitomi. Yet, there was the language barrier and cultural differences that prevented her from interacting with the people. Everything felt alien to her and, with every passing day, she felt as if their apartment was a cell and she was in Solitary.

Mrs. Marshal suggested they come home for a visit. Angela explained how Jonathan's job was pretty demanding. That school was year a year-round affair with only a few weeks off between semesters, and during that time Jonathan had to prepare for the next semester.

"I don't know when we will be able to make a trip home," she concluded.

"Well, that's no good. Now, I'm guessing you didn't call to chat with me all night."

"I like talking with you, Mrs. Marshal, and thank you for listening and for your concern."

"You're welcome, honey, Now, you do what the doctors tell you and know that we are all behind you. I'll get Stephanie to take the extension."

A few moments later, Stephanie picked up the other line.

"Got it, Mom," she said, and Mrs. Marshal hung up. "Angela, I'm so happy you called, I've got so much to tell you!"

Before Angela could say anything, Stephanie launched into a rant about being stuck with an annoying classmate for a partner on a project. Angela couldn't get a word in edgewise as Stephanie jumped from one subject to another. She talked about everything, from all of the cute guys she has met to the infuriating amount of homework she had to do in preparation for the exams. Angela waited until Stephanie paused for breath before jumping in.

"Stephanie, what would you think about me and Jonathan adopting?"

"Adopting!" Stephanie exclaimed. "You guys are looking to adopt?"

"Maybe, maybe not. We may have an opportunity to adopt a child, but there's only one small problem."

"What's that?"

In frustration Angela blurted out, "Jonathan."

"Jonathan?" Stephanie repeated, confused. "Does he not want to have a child?"

Angela gave her the pertinent details of their disagreement. When she was through, she was once again in tears and feeling angry.

"I don't get it! He wants a child, but only if it comes from us, so that means it's my fault we can't have children."

"Wow, I don't know what to say there, Angie. Guys can be the biggest idiots sometimes. I would've never thought of Jonathan being so insensitive."

"I know! Wouldn't an adopted child be ours? I don't get it, his aunt took him in when his parents died, but somehow adopting a foreign child doesn't appeal to him."

"Is he racist?"

"Jonathan? No, he fell in love with Japan the moment we arrived; it makes me wonder if we will ever come home."

"Didn't he say you two would come back so you could finish your schooling?"

"Yeah, he did, but things have changed. I've changed. I thought I wanted to go into medicine, but being here has made me realise that I want to be a mother."

"How are you going to change his mind?" Stephanie asked.

"I don't know. For now I have to focus on getting ready for surgery. Until I get better, there is no point in thinking about it."

"What do you have to do before they say you're ready for surgery?"

"I need to gain some weight."

"Gain some weight? What do you mean? Haven't you been eating, or can't you keep anything down?"

"I..." Angela took a moment to breathe. "I just haven't been eating as I should. It's been really hard and I've been feeling really down."

"Come on Angie, what would my life be like without you? You need to start eating. Don't make me come over there. I promise you, if I hear that you still aren't eating in a week I will strap you down myself and stuff your face for you. You can't do this to me, or to Jonathan."

It was odd, but Angela thought she caught a note of tenderness in Stephanie's voice when she spoke her husband's name. Deciding it was nothing, she brushed it off and let out a small giggle. "I'd like to see you try."

"Oh, you know I would."

They both laughed at that. Stephanie always knew how to get her out of her slump. In that moment she felt such profound love for her friend that she wished she could reach out and hug her.

"I love you like a sister, and as my sister, I want you to start taking care of yourself. Tell Jonathan to stop being such a jerk."

"I will." She looked around at the sound of the front door opening. "Steph, it looks like he's home. I will talk with you in a couple weeks."

"Sounds good. Love you, Sis."

"I love you, too." Hanging up the phone Angela looked up to see Jonathan coming in bearing flowers and some bags of food.

"Who was that?" he asked.

"Just Stephanie," she replied coolly.

Jonathan cringed. "Shoot, we need to be more careful with our phone calls. It's not cheap, you should have—", he cut his sentence off short as he caught the dangerous gleam in Angela's eyes.

"So, you can call my grandparents and tell them about our argument, but I'm not allowed to talk to anyone? Maybe I should file my feelings in the same folder as my inability to provide you with a child."

She was about to get up and go to their room when Jonathan groaned and called to her.

"Could we please stop fighting?"

She stood with her back to him and waited for him to continue, "I'm sorry, I know what I sounded like."

"Like a jerk," she snarled and turned to face him.

"Yes, like a jerk," he agreed. "I know how hard it's been for you to be so far away from home, with no family and friends, and then with all this. It's made things difficult, and I don't want to burden you with any more troubles. Are you still wanting to adopt?"

"Yes," she said, drawing the word out.

"Let's say if everything works out, we adopt the child and you get better. Would you like to move back home next year?"

"Home?" The word caught at the lump that formed in her throat. "Are you serious?"

"I have been thinking about it for a while, and I know how much happier you would be if you could see everyone."

"But, what about your job? Where would we live?"

"Professor Lang said he knows of a few schools that will need some teachers next year. As for a place to live, we already have enough saved up to get a small basement suite. I'm sure our family would help us out as much as they can."

"Won't you be missing half of the school year though?"

"Yes, but I'm sure if we count upon the Lord to make things work out in the end."

"Jonathan." Her voice quivered as an overwhelming sense of joy filled her. Running up to him she threw herself into his arms, making him drop his bags as he caught her. "I love you so much, you don't know how happy I am right now."

"I think I have an idea." He laughed, tilting her chin he kissed her tenderly.

CHAPTER 21

Setsuko spent the past two weeks waiting anxiously for David's return. Her mother had told her to keep quiet about her pregnancy, but she needed to tell someone before she went out of her mind. Natsuki and Misayo barraged her with countless questions, but she kept her condition under wraps. It was only Natsuki who she worried about. Her friend didn't say anything, but she could tell from the looks she received that Natsuki wasn't believing her excuses. She wanted to tell her best friend, but she didn't know where to begin, and she couldn't tell Misayo, for fear that Akari would find out. The thought of Akari learning the truth made her panic.

One day when Setsuko was leaving school with Natsuki and Misayo, Kyo came running up to them. "Setsuko-chan!" she shouted. Setsuko and her two friends came to stop and waited for Kyo to catch up.

"Setsuko," Kyo gasped, trying to catch her breath. "David's back."

Setsuko was filled with anticipation and hair-raising uneasiness.

"Back? When?"

"He came back last night, but he said something about needing to leave tomorrow night."

Tomorrow night? Alarmed, she dropped her bags and gripped Kyo by the shoulders. "Where is he?"

"Are you okay, Setsuko?" asked Misayo.

Setsuko shook Kyo, "You need to tell me, where is he?" Her voice rose with every word.

"He's visiting Tetsuya." Kyo tried to pull away. "What's wrong with you?"

Setsuko picked up her bags, slung them over her shoulder and sprinted towards Tetsuya's place. The others called out to her as they tried to follow. Setsuko ran on, tears burning her eyes as she cut through alleyways and small side streets. Her legs burned, but she ignored her discomfort and pushed herself even harder. *I need to talk to David*, was the only thing she could think, and it spurred her on.

As she rounded the last corner, Tetsuya's complex came into view. A sense of dread came over her as she caught sight of David standing outside, chatting with a few gang members. She slowed down and tried to regulate her breathing as she walked towards them. Her lungs burned and her heart pounded in her chest. A couple of the guys saw her and grinned. They said something to David as she approached.

"Hey, if it isn't my favourite girl." David smiled, walking up to greet her with a kiss. He brushed back a few strands of her hair. "What's wrong?"

"David, I need to talk to you," she said, giving the others a nervous glance.

David wrapped one arm around her shoulders and took her to a location where they could talk in private. He motioned for her to sit. "What's going on?"

Setsuko took a quick look around to make sure no one was within earshot. "I'm pregnant," she said faintly.

David stiffened and his voice became cool. "What?"

"I'm pregnant," she whispered a little more forcefully.

"Are you sure?"

"What do you mean, am I sure?" she asked incredulously, "Of course I'm sure, I took several tests to confirm it. Why would I lie to you?"

"I don't know, some girls say things so that the guy won't leave," he said offhandedly. Setsuko's jaw dropped. *What is he trying to say? That I'm making this whole thing up?*

He stood up and leaned against a wall, hands in his pockets, and looked into her eyes. "What does this have to do with me?" he asked nonchalantly.

Setsuko was too stunned for words. Did he think it was all her fault? Digging her nails into her palms, she strode up to him to stand toe to toe. "If you had worn something that first time, maybe this wouldn't be happening, did you ever think of that?"

He gave her a disarming grin. "You know, you're cute when you are angry." He stroked the side of her face with his fingertips.

Slapping his hand away, she stepped back, fuming, "You have got to be joking! After what I just told you, all you can think of is that."

David's expression was suddenly menacing, "Look, it wasn't me who decided to sleep around, now, was it? Who knows whose child that is, anyway? It wasn't that hard to get into your pants in the first place. The way you dress and act, how do I know I haven't been sharing you with others?"

Setsuko reflexively slapped him across the face. In an instant, David was on her and held her by the wrists. Setsuko's instincts kicked in and she tried to break his hold. She shifted her weight, but David anticipated her move and swung her around like a rag doll to pin her against the complex wall. He clamped his hand over her mouth as she tried to scream.

"You didn't think it was going to be like last time, did you?" he growled, spittle flying as he seethed with anger. Setsuko looked around in desperation for someone to help, but there was no one. Every time she struggled against him, he tightened his grip, nearly crushing her under his weight. "Now, be a good girl and don't you dare scream, or I swear you will not like what I do next."

Terrified, Setsuko nodded quickly, and gasped for air when he removed his hand. Setsuko fought the urge to cry out, fearing that David would live up to his threat. As she relaxed, he slowly loosened his grip on her until he finally let her go. Shaking, Setsuko didn't know what to do. A part of her wanted to run, but a bigger part desired to exact her revenge on him and strike back while his guard was down. Resisting the urge to do either, she stood there, rubbing her shoulders and fighting back tears.

"Good, it looks like you have regained your senses." David began to walk towards the parking lot. He motioned her to follow. Setsuko was too afraid to move.

"Don't just stand there. Let's get going. You want to take care of this mess, don't you?"

Considering her options, Setsuko decided it wouldn't be wise to run. She picked up her bags, which she had dropped during the scuffle, and followed behind him at a safe distance. Some of the guys David had been talking to were still there. A few of them gave her a cursory glance, but didn't seem to notice that something was amiss. Walking past them, David opened the door to a new BMW and waited for her step inside. Staring wide-eyed, she took a few steps back, unwilling to get in.

"Come on now, I'm not going to bite. Get in and let's go."

With the others watching her curiously, she decided to keep up appearances and accepted David's helping hand into the vehicle. He took her bags and tossed them in the back. Her heart jumped as he slammed the door shut. She warily kept David in her peripheral vision as she studied the roads he drove down, trying to get an idea of where he was taking her. The drive was nerve-racking. One road led to another and another. As they travelled farther away from her home, Setsuko became more uncertain of David's intent. When he turned down a back alley, everything became clear when she saw the words 'Medical Clinic' emblazoned on the back of a whitewashed building. Even when David came to a stop in front of the clinic, it felt so surreal that Setsuko had to ask the obvious.

"Do you want me to get an abortion?"

"Would there be any other reason for me to bring you here?" he asked while getting out of the car. He opened her door and held his hand out to her once again. She started to get up, but suddenly had misgivings about terminating her pregnancy.

"What's wrong?" David asked impatiently.

"I ... I don't know if I want to do this." Setsuko gripped the dash so hard that her knuckles were white.

Irritated, David leaned against the car door, his arms crossed. "I don't know what to do, then."

"We could do this together," she pleaded. Normally she would never act so weak, but her desperation was overriding her feminist disposition.

"Are you kidding me?" David scoffed. "You expect me to raise a child."

"I could raise the child, but we could at least be together."

What's wrong with you? screamed her inner voice. After everything he has done, you just want to waltz back into his arms? She couldn't argue with her rationality, but right now she didn't want to be rational, she wanted security and hope, something to hold onto that would give her the strength to get through this, and at that moment, all that came to mind was David.

"If you want a bed buddy, babe, I'm your man, but if you think I'll stick around because you decide to keep that thing, well, you are out of your mind. Now stop being a chicken and let's get this over with."

As desperate as she was, just thinking about what they would do to her made her feel sick to her stomach. Raising her hand once more to take his, she shuddered.

"Do we really need to do this?" she asked. It wasn't that she hadn't considered it, but she had heard about things that some girls went through after such a procedure.

"Look, everything will be fine, now stop stalling."

"But I don't have any money." That wasn't entirely true, but she certainly didn't have enough to cover a doctor's visit.

"Don't worry about it, my dad has connections. All I have to do is some sweet talking."

The way he had it thought out told her that he had done this before, but when and with whom? She looked at the building that cast its shadow over them, and began to tremble as she felt the nausea return.

"I don't know if I can do this, David," she said hesitantly.

"Stop being a coward, you will be fine. This is the only way you will be able to deal with this and no one has to ever know." His grip on her hand tightened as he tried to pull her along. That one word, coward, stoked a fire inside her and rekindled her resolve. She wasn't a coward, and no one, not even David, had the right to say that to her.

Ripping her hand out of his, she stood tall and defiant. "I'm not the coward, you are!"

A flicker of anger crossed David's eyes. "What did you call me?"

Standing strong, she refused to be bullied by him. "You heard me, you're a coward!"

"And what makes you think that?" he asked sardonically.

"You want to hide the fact that you got me pregnant by getting rid of it. It looks like I'm not the only girl you have done this to, am I right?"

A wry smile appeared across David's face. "I guess you caught on. It was only a matter of time, though. I'm surprised you didn't find out earlier." He closed the passenger door and made his way around to the driver's side.

Earlier? What does he mean by that? "Where do you think you're going?" she asked.

"Going? Well I am going to go have some fun, and I will leave you here to think about your decision. Maybe when you get your head out of the sand, we can do what needs to be done."

"You are taking no responsibility for what part you played in this?"

"I have. I offered you a way out, but you won't take it. Now it's your responsibility. You want to keep it, then keep it, but if you do, then you can say goodbye to any chance of us getting back together."

"Back together, but I thought you were leaving soon?"

David snorted. "So, the cat's out of the bag. Who told you? Kyo?" The thought of what David might do to Kyo held Setsuko's tongue. David gave her a scornful look. "It's not like it matters anyway. I got what I wanted, and you're getting, well — what you deserve."

The mocking smile he gave her made her want to slap him again, but the fear of his anger stayed her hand. How could someone so gorgeous be so vile? Didn't he have any shame, any remorse? It sickened her to think that she had ever let him touch her or that she had ever considered him worthy of her affection. The young man before her had transformed into a repulsive, contemptible, vulgar creature that didn't even represent a human being. As she was about to give her retort, she fell inexplicable ill. She leaned over the front of the car and vomited.

"Not on the car!" yelled David. Laughing inwardly, she grinned at him as she wiped her mouth, which angered him further. "You know what, you deserve whatever you get, but leave me out of this. It's all on you now, so get your hands off my father's car, I need to get it washed now that your dirty paws have been all over it."

Moving to the side, she gave him a scornful look while she motioned him to pass. After all that he had done to hurt her, he deserved much worse. Standing in the silence, she felt cold, not just externally, but an internal coldness as well. She watched the lights of his car disappear in the fading sun, and for the first time in a long while she felt free. She walked to the nearest bus stop, located where he had taken her and mapped out the three buses she needed to take to get home. As she stood waiting in the cold, she realised that she had left her bags in the car. After everything, he had the last laugh, for now she had no way to study for the Finals without her notes.

The ride home was quiet. The buses were full but no one was talking, which was nice. It gave her time to reflect on the revelation she had. It was almost eight before she reached home. A light came on as she walked up her front steps. Hitomi opened the door and gasped in relief. Reaching out she embraced Setsuko and held her tight.

"What happened? Where did you go?" Hitomi asked, her eyes searching hers.

"I needed to go for a walk," she mumbled.

"But where did you go, and why did David have your bags?" Setsuko was shocked to see her bags on the entrance floor. Why didn't he just keep them? Her mother's eyes were filled with fear as she added, "I talked with him, and he said something about a clinic?"

"I didn't do it," she responded solemnly.

"Oh, thank the Lord, thank You, Lord, for protecting my daughter and grandchild."

Just when Setsuko thought she couldn't be any more surprised by the day's events, her mother had said something that gave her chills. "Thank the Lord? Mother, are you one of those Christians?"

Hitomi struggled with her reply. She wanted so desperately to share all that Jesus had done for her, but the time had never been right. Her gaze flickered to the other end of the house. Daiki was in his office, but he was so light on his feet that he may appear at any moment. Taking her daughter's hand she stepped outside, quietly closing the door behind her

They enjoyed the night air and walked through the gardens. The lanterns her mother had set out illuminated all of the work she and Suzaku had done in the last month. Normally by this time, there would have been new growth and they would have been working hard to keep the gardens free from grass and weeds. This year had seen a long winter, making it a hard year for many gardeners, like her mother, to get their starts in the ground. Hitomi was renowned for her gardens. They were featured on the covers of many local and some international magazines. From the looks of things though, her mother and Suzaku would have the gardens up to snuff and flowering by summer. Setsuko had always loved playing in them when she was younger, hiding amongst the flowers and listening to the birds singing. She also loved laying under the cherry tree, watching the pink blossom petals dance in the wind. To this day, she still yearned to see what kind of beauty her mother could grow each spring with her gentle touch.

"We have a lot of work ahead of us if we are going to grow anything this year." Hitomi seemed a little discouraged at the lack of progress.

"I'm sure they will look as beautiful as they do every year, Mother."

The warmth of her daughter's kind words brought a smile to her face. "Suzaku is a good boy. He works so hard for your father and me. Sometimes he can be a little hard on himself though, always needing to have everything look perfect."

Hitomi bent over and brushed away some dirt that had fallen on one of the flowers. When she looked up, her daughter stared back at her, eyes searching, looking for the answers to her questions. Wiping her hands, Hitomi continued walking down the flagstone path that wound its way through the multitude of flower beds. Setsuko followed closely behind her, waiting silently for her to say something.

"We had been working all day in the sun last year, and poor Suzaku looked like he was going to faint from the heat. He didn't make a single complaint about all of the work, until he found that he had forgotten some plants in the shed. The funny thing was I had completely forgotten about them, too, but he refused to let me take the blame and kept apologizing. I have had people apologise to me before, but never had I experienced someone say it with such sincerity. After I forgave him, he worked extra hard to make up for his mistake, not out of fear or some sense of obligation, but because he felt compelled to do better. That's when we began to talk and he shared with me his faith in Jesus Christ."

Setsuko had heard of this Jesus Christ from Natsuki. He was some sort of teacher, or prophet spoken about in a book called the Bible, beyond that she didn't know anything else. As they walked, Hitomi came up to a wooden bench under the boughs of a pair of trees that shaded one end of the garden. Sitting down, she patted the seat and waited for her daughter to join her.

"Through Him I learned that we are all sinners and we are all in need of salvation. Jesus gives us the opportunity through His death to find forgiveness, but we must acknowledge that He is the Son of God and that it's only through Him that we can attain eternal life."

A funny expression touched Setsuko's face, prompting Hitomi to explain further. "In the beginning God created the heavens and the earth in seven days. On the sixth day He made the first man in His image and then gave him a helpmate, man's first wife, so that he wasn't alone. This first man was called Adam, and his wife was Eve, and they were given dominion over the Garden. The only command God told them was to not eat from the tree of knowledge of good and evil. During this time, Satan, the enemy of both mankind and God, entered the garden through a serpent and tricked Eve. In her foolishness, she ate of the fruit, and she beguiled Adam to eat from the tree. Adam's choice to completely ignore God's command cost them everlasting life in Paradise and they were cast out of the Garden."

Setsuko's eyes were like saucers as she tried to comprehend what she was being told. It sounded too fantastic, something she might have heard in a fairy-tale, but her mother seemed to believe it was true.

"Because of man's disobedience, even nature itself paid the consequences and all of Creation began to crumble and decay. Yet this was not the end for mankind but the beginning, as God had planned at the start to redeem His creation through His Son, Jesus Christ."

Hitomi took a moment to see if Setsuko wanted her to continue. When all she got in return was a blank stare, she felt a small twinge of fear begin to burn within her. *What if she doesn't believe? What if this is all for nothing?* As she took a moment to gather herself, she was reminded of second Timothy 3:16: **'Preach the word; be diligent in season, out of season; reprove, rebuke, exhort with all longsuffering and doctrine'.**

She knew she couldn't back down now. She not only had a duty as a mother, but as a follower of Christ to share the words of hope found in His Holy Book.

"Jesus came down in the form of a babe, to a young virgin woman named Mary. He was born and raised by his earthly father, Joseph. Jesus lived a sinless life, and ministered to His people. Some listened to what He said, while others didn't, and because of His teachings and the miraculous wonders He performed, His name spread far and wide. Then, during the Passover, He was accused of blasphemy by the religious leaders and was sentenced to a criminal's death. This happened so that, through His death and by His blood, all those who turn to Him could find salvation."

Setsuko was dumbfounded; she had never heard such a thing. A god who would sacrifice his own son to save his creation? It was a little hard to believe that someone, even a god, would go to such extremes in order to redeem a fallen world. The more she thought about it, the more the whole story behind it sounded hyperbolic and unreal to her.

"Do you understand what I am trying to say?" Hitomi asked.

"To be honest, I don't know what to think. So, as long as you believe in this dead son of a god, he will save you and let you enter heaven?"

"It's not quite so simple, you see." Hitomi began rubbing her legs nervously. She was about to continue when movement out of the corner of her eye caused the hair on her neck to stand on end. A shadowy figure moved towards them from the house. The light of the lanterns illuminated Daiki's face as he approached.

"What are you two doing out so late?"

"Just having a mother-daughter chat, Daiki." Hitomi smiled at her daughter.

"I was throwing some garbage out, when I came across something curious."

Setsuko panicked as he pulled his hand from behind his back. If her father had found the pregnancy tests, he would know they were hers. He held out his hand to reveal a crumpled letter. Confused, Setsuko looked to her mother.

"I was meaning to talk to you about that Daiki, Setsuko has been—"

Motioning for Hitomi to be silent, he turned his attention to his daughter. "What do you have to say for yourself?"

Say for myself? I don't even know what that letter is? She glanced at her mother for some hint as to what the letter contained, and was surprised to see how calm she was.

"Setsuko, are you going to explain to me about why I am just learning about this now?" He held the note up in the light. Setsuko recognized the school's letterhead, and sighed in relief.

Daiki's brow rose at her reaction. "I didn't realise that failing grades brought you such comfort."

"They don't, Father, I'm sorry." Setsuko did her best to look sorry, but Daiki didn't seem convinced.

"What are you going to do about this?" he asked, and waited patiently for a response.

"I will make up the grades, Father, and I won't let them fall again."

Setsuko rose to leave, but Daiki reached out and grabbed her arm. "Until this is resolved, you are no longer allowed to go out. I expect nothing but the best from my child, do you understand?"

"Yes, Father." She bowed slightly, and quickly made her way to the house.

Daiki watched her curiously as she left. "It was that boy, wasn't it?"

Hitomi got up and went over to stand beside him. "You remember what it was like, to be that young."

"When we were that young, you didn't want anything to do with me." Hitomi looked away, sensing the hurt in those words. Daiki turned to her, but she continued to avoid his gaze. "What was his name again? Makio, wasn't it? Yes, I remember. Your father chose me, but you wanted him. Funny how much you two are alike, hopefully your daughter finds some common sense, and makes the right choice."

"I chose you in the end, didn't I?" Hitomi asked, hoping to quell any misgivings he had.

"Yes, yes you did, but not before you were with him."

He walked away, leaving his wife standing there. It had been so long ago, but he still held it against her. She had always known there would come a day where she would have to face the consequences of her youth. How was she going to explain Setsuko's situation to him after what she had done?

CHAPTER 22

Pastor Hikaru was exhausted and frustrated. After all the digging he had done, he had come out empty-handed. With the current laws dealing with international adoption, there was no way the Hansens could adopt Hitomi's grandchild. It was a setback he had not anticipated. The other thing that bothered him was the very real possibility that if he didn't find an adoptive set of parents for the child, Hitomi and her daughter may resort to abortion to save themselves the shame.

Please, Lord, show me a way, he prayed silently.

He looked over the pamphlets and notes he had collected. Under the current adoption laws, only certain provinces within Canada had an arrangement with Japan for international adoption. Alberta wasn't one of them. He wasn't looking forward to telling the Hansens, especially Angela, about his failure. When they hadn't shown up at church, he had called and learned that Angela was feeling ill and Jonathan wanted to stay home to keep an eye on her. While they talked, Jonathan spoke about Angela's appetite returning, and her cheerful disposition. She was even making efforts to get up and go for walks to help improve her health. Now Hikaru was about to deliver a blow that might send her back into a deep depression. He looked up as Mai, loaded down with several shopping bags, walked into the room.

"The boys have some new shoes and I was able to pick up some new shirts for you." He nodded only half listening. Putting down the bags Mai came over and began rubbing his shoulders. "What's wrong?" she asked.

Taking a deep breath, Hikaru put down the pamphlets and leaned back in his seat, resting his head against her.

"I may have to tell the Hansens that they can't adopt, at least not from here. Then I have to still find a home for this child, hopefully before Hitomi's daughter makes the decision to terminate her pregnancy. What bothers me the most about this, is the fact I have this nagging feeling that God wants the Hansens to adopt this child, but I don't know how to make it work."

Mai looked at the pamphlets and notes that littered her husband's desk. "What about some of your contacts with the government? I'm sure they would be able to provide some assistance."

Hikaru shook his head. "I've already talked to them and, as far as they are concerned, rules are rules."

Mai leaned over and kissed him on his forehead. "Don't give up, I'm sure the Lord will provide a way."

The doorbell rang and their youngest announced Hitomi's arrival. Mai left to greet her friend, leaving her husband to gather his thoughts. There had to be a viable solution to this problem. What was the Lord trying to accomplish through this? Whatever it was, he hoped it would be revealed soon.

After a short conversation with Mai, Hitomi followed her downstairs to Hikaru office. Their parishioners didn't mind having Mai around when they spoke to their pastor, and for propriety's sake, she made it a point to sit in on a visit, especially when he was meeting with unescorted female members.

"It's good to see you, Hitomi." Hikaru motioned to the chair across from him. "Have there been any new developments since last night?"

Hitomi shook her head. "No, I haven't had another chance, but I keep praying."

"I am proud that you were able to share your faith, and I am happy that God gave you the courage to talk to your daughter about the Gospel."

Mai was a little perplexed. She looked at Hikaru questioningly.

"I asked him not to say anything, as I don't think I did that well sharing the Gospel," Hitomi said in explanation.

"I am sure that the Lord will use whatever you shared to help plant a seed of hope in your daughter's heart. You have done your job, now it's up to the Lord to call her to Him," Mai replied.

"Thank you." Hitomi blushed. "Is there any information when it comes to the adoption?"

Hikaru handed her the brochures. "As far as I can tell, there aren't too many options for adoption. If the child is put up for adoption, he or she may be stuck in the system for quite some time before someone may be able to adopt."

Hitomi frowned as she glanced over the brochures. "There isn't anyone who would want to adopt my grandchild? No Christian family at all?"

Hikaru clenched his jaw as Hitomi looked to him for answers. "I don't know if I should say this, but there was a couple that I was considering, but as it turns out, Japan's international laws on adoption prevent them from participating."

"There's no other way, then?"

"Not that we could find at least," Mai said. "You can't lose hope Hitomi, God will find a way to save your grandchild."

All three of them fell silent, then something came to Hitomi. "What if I could provide a way for this couple to adopt?"

Mai and Hikaru looked at her in surprise.

"What were you thinking?" Hikaru asked.

"I still haven't told Daiki."

Hikaru felt the air suddenly grow cold. "I don't understand how your husband's involvement would help."

"He has more connections through the government and a lot more pull than you do."

Mai's face lit up. "Good thinking, Hitomi, it just might work."

Hikaru was still unsure, but Daiki was a powerful and well respected man. He may decide to rid himself of the child rather than allowing adoption in order to protect his honour.

"I know that you will have to speak to your husband about this, but I don't think he will agree to help us," Hikaru said flatly.

"That's because we haven't asked the Lord to ready the path for us," replied Hitomi.

Hikaru was taken aback by her boldness. This formerly timid, shy, and quiet woman was transforming into a strong, courageous and bold Christian. He had never once thought that the Lord would use this trial to refine Hitomi into a fearless believer.

"If you are sure about this, why don't we seek the Lord's face in prayer and ask that He prepare the way for you."

Hitomi nodded and they bowed their heads to pray. As they called upon the Lord for help, Hikaru felt a strange surge of power fill him. In that moment, he knew with certainty that this was what the Lord had planned from the beginning. With the Lord going before them, who could stand against them?

Setsuko checked her reflection in the school bathroom mirror. In a few months, she wouldn't be able to hide her secret. Everyone at school would be talking about her, she would be shunned, and she would never be able to live with the shame. As the reality of her situation weighed on her, she wondered if she shouldn't have taken David up on the offer. Yet, every time she thought about going back to that clinic, she broke into a cold sweat. Was there anything that could be done? Why couldn't they just remove the foetus somehow and put it into an incubator like they do with chicks? "Why was I so stupid?" she moaned softly to herself. She cast another wary glance at the door, hoping that no one came in. Her chemistry class had been turned into a study period, so she took advantage of the free time to hide out in the washroom, hoping that it would calm her nerves. With shaking hands, she splashed cold water on her face.

Looking at the grim visage that stared back at her, she barely recognized herself. The once proud and strong Setsuko Fukui had been reduced to a terrified little girl. How was her mother going to fix this? Hitomi hadn't told her anything yet, and with every passing day she found it harder and harder to control her emotions. Misayo and Natsuki, as well as several others, had witnessed her meltdown and now people were starting to spread rumours. No one had correctly guessed the cause, but once her body began to change they would know exactly why. Then there was Akari. If she found out, she would use the information to destroy her. Akari was the last person Setsuko wanted to find out.

"Father's going to kill me," she whispered, wiping away her tears.

Never in her life did she ever have anything to fear when it came to her father. She had worked so hard to be the son he never had. As she grew up, things had changed. She began to despise him and his traditional values. The way her mother always bowed to commands like a good wife. She hated how his word was the law and no one dared to challenge him. How much he favoured his pet, Suzaku, and how much he demanded her to be a good little girl, get good grades, grow up and marry the man of his choosing. It used to make her sick to her stomach how she was expected to toe the line.

The thing that had scared her the most were the bruises her mother used to get when she was younger. Daiki used to beat Hitomi whenever Setsuko misbehaved, and Setsuko knew she was to blame. Setsuko had seen the bruises, and she knew, for her mother's sake, she had to be a good little girl and never allow her father to hit her mother again. For that reason, she had always longed to free herself from her father's grip, but looking at the situation now, she wondered if she had been wrong the whole time.

As much as she despised her father, a part of her still wanted his love and respect. She wished she could turn back the clock and change what she had done, to somehow save herself from the dire consequences that were sure to come when Daiki found out. Why had she been such a fool? Why had she fought so hard to be free only to find herself in this state?

"There you are," said Natsuki without preamble. "Is it true?"

"Is what true?" asked Setsuko.

"Are you pregnant?"

All the blood drained from Setsuko's face. "How? Who told you that?"

"Akari said she heard it from David before he left yesterday."

Horrified, Setsuko blew past her friend and tore down the hall towards the cafeteria. Coming to a corner she turned, colliding with Akari and her new group of friends, sending them all crashing to the floor.

"Who do you think you are?" Akari snarled. When their eyes met, Akari's anger turned to amusement as she picked herself up. "Well, well, well, if it isn't the school harlot."

The others began to laugh and many of them whispered with one another. Looking around, Setsuko saw everyone staring at her. They all knew her dirty little secret. Her school image, life, everything was over just like that.

"What have you done?" Setsuko demanded, her voice wavering between anger and fear.

"Nothing that you wouldn't have done if it were me." Akari laughed scornfully. "Now the whole school gets to know you for who you are."

The air around her grew cold and everything seemed to slow to a crawl as Setsuko felt her heart stop. It felt like some horrifying nightmare, something that just couldn't be happening, it was all too terrible.

"Setsuko, are you all right?" Natsuki asked, giving her a hand up.

"That's right, Natsuki, we wouldn't want to cause our little princess any undue stress. Not in her condition. Speaking of your condition, why don't you take this, I'm sure you will need it more than we do." Akari held out her lunch, as did several of her friends, "You are eating for two, aren't you?"

Setsuko's heart broke in agony before the force of the verbal assault. When she looked up at them, she caught sight of Misayo in the back. Misayo gave her a brief look of sympathy looking away. Unable to take the humiliation, Setsuko fled down the hall with Natsuki tailing after her.

"Setsuko, wait!" Natsuki called after her, but all Setsuko could hear was the rapid pounding of her pulse in her ears. Everyone stared at her, talking amongst themselves as she ran through the halls. One teacher called for her to stop, but she ignored him, wanting only to get away from everyone's prying eyes. As she left the school, she quickly ran past the gates and then continued to run until she was too nauseous to continue. She leant against a nearby wall of a building and, no longer holding back, wailed all of her pent-up emotions to the sky.

That is how Natsuki found her, crumpled against the wall as people walked by, giving her only cursory glances before carrying on with their day. Kneeling down, Natsuki helped her friend back up. "Come on Setsuko-chan, let's get you home."

Neither of them said a word. Natsuki supported her as they walked. Setsuko cried until she had no more tears. When they neared her home, a kindly old lady came over to see what was wrong.

"Now, why are you crying, dear," the she asked.

"She was just given some bad news at school today," Natsuki said on Setsuko's behalf.

Taking one of the flowers out of the bouquet she had, the woman weaved the stem into Setsuko's hair. She patted her on the cheek and smiled. "Now, don't let life get you down, dear, when things get tough you can always find hope. Whether it's through the friends you have, or your family, or maybe even God, if you know Him."

Puzzled by the woman's statement, Setsuko stared back at her.

"Thank you, Ohara-sama," replied Natsuki, earning a confused look from Setsuko.

"You take care of her, Natsuki, and maybe invite her to church sometime, I'm sure it will do her some good."

Natsuki nodded before continuing on their way.

"You are a Christian, too?" Setsuko was shocked.

"Yes," Natsuki replied, wondering what she meant by 'too'.

"I completely forgot. When and how did you become one?"

Taking a deep breath, Natsuki told her everything. "My mother has always been a Christian as long as I can remember. My father was Buddhist, but since they could never agree on how I was to be raised, they decided that I could choose what I wanted to believe when I got older. As you know, my parent's relationship fell apart, and they divorced when I was twelve. My father took great strides to try to train me up as his parents had, but it was my mother's gentleness and kindness that drew me to Christianity. I always found my father to be too proud and arrogant. He taught with a heavy hand and it seemed strange to me that a belief that sought for inner peace and tranquility brought out the worst in him. Christianity on the other hand, teaches that we can never find that peace my father longed for, unless we let Jesus dwell within our hearts. While my father struggled with internal battles of good over evil desires, it seemed to come easily to Mom. When Father died, it was hard on me."

Natsuki's voice began to waver, the pain of losing her father ran deep and was compounded by the fact that the last words they exchanged had been in anger. Setsuko remembered those days well. Natsuki had become so depressed she refused to speak to anyone, so they would spend their time together sitting in companionable silence. Setsuko was a good friend by simply being there, an understanding ear should Natsuki need one.

"If it hadn't been for you and mother, I'm don't think I would have been able to cope. Every day a part of me died as the memories of my father began to fade. When I saw how quickly my mother recovered from her own grief, I was angry. I couldn't understand how the pain I felt didn't paralyse her as it did me. It seemed we couldn't be in the same room without fighting. Things stayed like that for a long time, until we took the train to visit my maternal grandparents in Tsushima. As the city came into view, Mom pointed out many of the large buildings we passed, describing each one in turn, and telling me how my father had designed them. As she spoke, she began to tear up, and that's when I realised how much she loved him. She asked if I was okay. I told her 'no', and that's when she said that she still missed him too. I asked her how she was able to deal with her grief so well, and that's when she shared her faith with me. I didn't want to believe her at first, but as I watched her, I discovered that even in her grief, she had the strength to go on with her life. I then felt a strong desire to know this Saviour of whom she spoke, this Messiah who had given her so much hope and peace. It was just over a year ago that I was baptised and dedicated my life to Him."

That was the day Setsuko's adventurous, wild young friend had been transformed, right before her eyes, into someone she didn't recognize. The change in Natsuki's attitude threw everyone for a loop. Some of their former friends didn't like the new Natsuki. While everyone was trying to make up their minds about her, Setsuko knew in her heart that Natsuki, wild or not, was still and would always be her friend. It took Misayo and Akari some time, but they eventually warmed up to her.

"What did you mean by me 'being a Christian, too'?"

It took a moment for Setsuko to remember what she had said earlier, "Oh, that. It turns out my mother is a Christian, as well."

"She told you?"

"Yeah."

"And does your father know about this?"

Setsuko shook her head, "I don't think so. She seems really tight-lipped around him, and I doubt he would tolerate her new faith."

"Are you going to be all right?" asked Natsuki.

"Yes, I'll be fine."

"What are you going to do when your parents find out?"

"My mother already knows, but she told me to keep it quiet until she figures something out. At least that was the plan."

"It won't be long until your father finds out, I'm sure the teachers know about it by now, and they will be calling to confirm with your parents."

"I know," said Setsuko. The thought of what her father might do sent chills down her spine.

"What are you going to do about it?"

"About my father, I'm not entirely sure."

"No, I meant your baby," Natsuki said.

Setsuko didn't know what she was going to do. On one hand she wanted to get rid of it, but on the other hand, she felt an overwhelming fear that aborting her pregnancy would bring her an unspoken amount of pain and suffering.

"I haven't figured that out either." Natsuki looked thoughtful for a moment. "If you kept the baby, you would make a wonderful mother."

Setsuko was surprised by her words, "Really?"

"Of course! If you're anything like your mother, that child will be loved just as deeply as your mother loves you."

Those kind words brought a smile to Setsuko's face. "Thanks, I'm glad one of us thinks so."

Natsuki glanced at her watch, knowing she had better head home. "I hope I'll see you tomorrow. Let me know how it goes, okay?"

"Sure."

As Natsuki departed, Setsuko stared at the driveway that snaked up towards home. A dark cloud hung in the sky, as if foreshadowing what was to come. She started her ascent, each step becoming progressively harder as she felt the weight of the world settle upon her shoulders. When the garage came into view, she was relieved to find the driveway in front of the house vacant. Heading inside, she found her mother standing in the sitting room, looking towards the kitchen.

"Mother, I'm sorry, I didn't mean for it to happen."

Hitomi turned and was startled to see her daughter home so soon.

"Setsuko, what are you doing home?" she asked in a cautious whisper.

"They found out, Mother," said Setsuko on the verge of tearing up again. Dropping her bags by the door she went to her mother. "Akari found out from David, and she's spread it throughout the school." Tears rolled down her cheeks as she recounted what had happened. "Now what am I going to do? I can't go back there, and it's only a matter of time before Father finds out."

Strangely, Hitomi didn't comfort her daughter, but continued to look towards the hallway and started trembling.

"Mother, what is it?" asked Setsuko, alarmed by the fear she saw in her eyes. Hitomi glanced at her briefly, only to snap her mouth shut when Daiki emerged. When Setsuko saw her father, her blood ran cold.

"And what was it that Akari has told to the rest of the school?" Daiki asked coolly. Setsuko's mouth went dry, and beads of sweat appeared on her forehead. Her father's dark foreboding eyes sought to swallow her whole.

"Nothing. I just did something stupid, and now Akari is holding it over my head," Setsuko said quickly, hoping he didn't see through the lie.

"That mistake wouldn't happen to involve a boy, would it?" Setsuko felt herself grow flush and then cold with fear.

"I'm so sorry, Setsuko-chan, I had to tell him. The school called today asking if the rumours were true."

Staring back at her mother, Setsuko couldn't even begin to describe the betrayal she felt in that moment. As she stood, her father drew near, causing her take a few steps back. Standing tall with her head held high, she chose to stand up to her father's fury.

"Is it true? Are you pregnant with that foreigner's child?" he asked in a low growl.

Setsuko looked at her mother once more, and nodded. "Yes, I am pregnant with his child."

The defiance in her voice drew another growl from her father. He grabbed her by the face, forcing her to look at him.

"Do you have any idea what you have done?" he ground out as a vein swelled in his forehead. "What you have lost because of your disobedience?"

She glared back at him, tears rolling down her face and over her father's hand. She refused to wipe them away as she didn't want to show him any more weakness than she already had.

"I have worked hard to make sure I provided both you and your mother a life of comfort and tranquility most people would never know, and this is how you repay me?" Letting her go, he turned his attention to Hitomi. "And you, my *wife*, hid this from me?"

Hitomi bowed her head in shame, drawing a sound of disgust from her daughter. Furious at his daughter's attitude, Daiki turned, grabbed her by the shoulders and pressed her up against the wall.

"Do you think that this makes you any better than her?" Spittle flew from his mouth in rage, but Setsuko never flinched. "I've grown tired of your defiance, and your consistent challenging of my will, but you will obey me this time, I swear!"

For a brief instant Setsuko grew fearful of the dangerous look in his eyes. She had seen him lose his temper before, but not like this. The raw fury in his eyes terrified her.

"Tomorrow, you and I will be making a trip to the clinic and we will deal with this problem before things get worse. As it is, I don't know if Mr. Hashida will allow his boy to marry you, but if you're lucky, I may be able to salvage something from this."

"I'm not your property," Setsuko whispered.

He grabbed her face again as he held her against the wall. His face was inches from hers as he struggled to control his rage. "What did you say?"

Setsuko could feel the heat of his breath on her face. She stared back at him, unwavering in her determination. "I don't belong to you," she said.

Daiki's eyes flashed. He raised his hand and struck her, knocking her to the floor.

Hitomi ran over and threw herself over Setsuko, shielding her daughter from her husband's wrath. "Daiki, what are you doing?!"

"Get up, woman!"

"You promised me you would never lay a hand on her!" Hitomi's black eyes were snapping.

Setsuko glared at her father over her mother's shoulder as he glared back at her. Blood trickled from the corner of her mouth, and she could feel the side of her face begin to throb.

"Tomorrow morning, you will be ready at ten sharp and we will deal with this."

"No!"

"If you keep that child, I swear I will disown you and your mother right here and now!" Daiki promised.

"I'm keeping this child so that you no longer have power over me."

Hitomi gasped.

Straightening, face flushed with anger, Daiki looked from his daughter, to his wife, "This is your doing, isn't it?"

Hitomi didn't say anything as she looked up at him. Her daughter's courage strengthened her resolve; no matter what happened, she was going to save this child.

Through clenched teeth, Daiki told them, "If this is what you have decided, then know that I am no longer your father, or your husband. You are both dead to me, and once this child is born, I want all three of you out of *my* house."

"Daiki, you don't mean that," Hitomi called after him. Wiping the blood from her mouth, Setsuko pushed free from her mother and brushed herself off.

"Setsuko-chan, are you all right?" Hitomi studied her face as she framed it with her hands.

"I'm fine." Setsuko pushed her mother's hands away.

"Why do you have to always fight with him? He only wants what's best for you."

"Best for me?" Setsuko scoffed. "Is this how he shows his love for me?" Hitomi looked away when her daughter pointed at the welt on her face. "If this is how he loves me, then I am better off without him."

Setsuko stormed off to her room, leaving her mother alone in the sitting room.

Clutching her hands to her chest, Hitomi cried quietly to the Lord, "Dear Heavenly Father, please send us Your strength. Help Your humble servant speak words of wisdom and truth into the lives of those around her. Please open the hearts of my daughter and husband, and call them to Your side, oh Lord. Help us weather the oncoming storm, and give me the strength to stand firmly on Your Word."

That night, Setsuko woke up feeling thirsty. Her face still burned where Daiki had struck her. A check in the full-length mirror revealed that her cheek was puffy and bruised. She felt her anger return as she gingerly touched the swelling. She stepped into her slippers and went to the kitchen to get a glass of water. On the way back, she stopped when she saw her mother sleeping on the sofa. She walked over to her mother's sleeping form, and shook her slightly.

"Mother," she whispered.

Hitomi eyes fluttered open. She took a deep breath and shivered as she sat up. "Setsuko-chan what are you doing up?" she asked, wrapping her arms around herself.

"I was thirsty, what are you doing sleeping on the sofa?"

Hitomi looked towards her bedroom, and shrugged. "Your father made it clear he didn't want anything to do with me after today. Are you hungry? I could make you something."

Even after everything she had done, her mother was still looking after her. No matter what she said or did, nothing seemed to deter the unconditional love her mother had for her.

"I'm fine. Why don't you come sleep in my bed."

"No, it's all right, the sofa is comfortable enough. Besides, I'm sure you would feel awkward with your mother sleeping beside you."

Taking her hand Setsuko shook her head, "No, I wouldn't, Mother. Plus you look really cold, so please come and keep yourself warm in my bed. I'm sure that Father will get over it by tomorrow."

Hitomi finally relented. She nodded slightly and she stood up to follow her daughter. They found the futon to be a little uncomfortable with the two of laying back to back. Unable to sleep, Setsuko thought about what she had said to her father earlier about keeping the child. The reality of having a child at her age scared her. Setsuko started as her mother rolled over and drew her close. It was only then that she realised that she was crying.

"Setsuko-chan, are you all right?" Hitomi asked.

"I don't know, did I make the right decision?"

"To keep the child?"

"Yes," she said and sniffled, "I just wonder if maybe David was right and I should have taken his offer."

"Shush," Hitomi said soothingly, stroking her daughter's hair. "Everything will be all right, I promise. Tomorrow I will be calling in sick for you and we will go see someone who may be able to help us."

Help? Who could help them? She hoped that something good would come out of all of this.

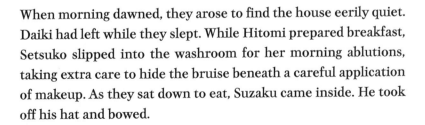

When morning dawned, they arose to find the house eerily quiet. Daiki had left while they slept. While Hitomi prepared breakfast, Setsuko slipped into the washroom for her morning ablutions, taking extra care to hide the bruise beneath a careful application of makeup. As they sat down to eat, Suzaku came inside. He took off his hat and bowed.

"Hitomi-sama, Setsuko-ojousama, Kacho told me to take you wherever you need to go." He had a peculiar look on his face as he spoke.

"Is something wrong?" Hitomi asked.

"Kacho was oddly distracted this morning, and he woke me up much earlier than expected. Also, he told me to take the car home yesterday. Did I do something wrong?" Suzaku was clearly worried by the recent activities.

Setsuko rolled her eyes, but her mother reassured him. "No, Suzaku-san, it has nothing to do with you, we just have some family issues to deal with."

"The car is ready whenever you wish to leave, I will be waiting outside for you."

"Suzaku-san, wait," Hitomi called after him. Popping his head through the door, he was as surprised as Setsuko when Hitomi invited him to join them. She shot her mother a curious look, but Hitomi shook her head and smiled, pointing to an empty seat between her and Setsuko. Suzaku tried to decline but she insisted, and he shyly sat down, making Setsuko groan in annoyance.

"I'm sorry, Setsuko-ojousama, did I bump you?"

Before Setsuko could say anything, Hitomi shot a look of warning at her.

"No, it's not you, Suzaku-san. She is just feeling unwell this morning."

Confused, Suzaku looked to Hitomi, who sighed in vexation. "Why don't we sit and eat in peace, please," she said, glaring at Setsuko.

Quiet at first, Suzaku opened up when Hitomi began discussing her ideas for the next year's garden. When they had finished their meal, Suzaku started up the car as the women got ready.

"Hikaru-Bokushi's house?" he said in surprise when Hitomi told him where they were going. He glanced uncertainly at Setsuko.

"It's all right, Suzaku-san, I told her everything."

He looked at Hitomi, still a little unsure. "But what about Kacho? If he finds out that I—"

"Don't worry about it, Suzaku-san, Setsuko and I won't say a word, we promise. Your job is safe."

He was assured by her promise, but he still eyed Setsuko suspiciously. As they went on their way, Setsuko felt her anxiety mount as she wondered what her mother had in mind. Hopefully, whatever it was would put her at ease and end her humiliation.

Suzaku pulled up to an older home that was larger than any residence in the neighbourhood. Setsuko was curious how a pastor could afford a place like this. From what she had been led to believe, pastors or priests were humble and poor.

After instructing Suzaku to wait with the car, Hitomi walked to the front door and knocked three times. A moment later, the door was opened by a woman Setsuko had never seen before.

"Hitomi!" The woman said in surprise, "We weren't expecting you."

"I'm sorry I didn't call first, Mai; I didn't have much time and I needed to leave right away. Is Hikaru-Bokushi around?"

"No, I'm afraid he stepped out for a moment, but you are welcome to join me for morning tea while you wait." Hitomi bowed in thanks as Mai let them in.

The inside of the house was plain, except for a few paintings and pictures that overlooked the spartanly furnished sitting room. Setsuko felt nervous being in a stranger's home and meeting people who may know more about her than she did of them.

Mai went to the kitchen to fetch two more tea cups. She offered some breakfast desserts that a parishioner had given them. Hitomi and Setsuko declined, but thanked her for the tea.

"This must be your beautiful daughter — Setsuko, is it?" asked Mai.

Setsuko bowed, "Fukui Setsuko, it's a pleasure to meet you."

"The pleasure is all mine, Setsuko-san, my name is Ichenose Mai, but you may call me Mai, if you'd like."

Well she's pleasant enough, Setsuko thought, taking a tentative sip of her tea.

"I take it that your mother has told you about our little congregation?"

"No, not exactly. All she has told me is that she has converted to Christianity," Setsuko replied, glancing at her mother.

"What do you think about Christianity? Are you interested, or have any questions?"

"No, none that I can think of." In truth, she had more questions than she believed Mai had answers, but she didn't really want to get into a discussion about religion at the moment.

"You are always welcome to ask us whenever you come by, or maybe you could ask your mother."

Setsuko was becoming annoyed. She didn't come here for a chat, she was here to find a solution to her problem, "What can you do for me?" she asked bluntly.

"Setsuko-chan," Hitomi chided, "mind your manners. I'm sorry Mai, she's been under a lot of stress."

Mai waved her hand. "It's all right, Hitomi. Your daughter is obviously anxious, as is to be expected under the circumstances."

Setting down her cup, Mai looked right into Setsuko's eyes, as if she were trying to see into her soul, "I promise we will do whatever it takes to help you, so don't feel pressured to make any decisions right now."

Setsuko nodded, not sure if she trusted Mai with her promise that there wouldn't be any pressure.

"Has your mother shared with you what we are considering?"

Considering? What does she mean by that? Setsuko thought. "You aren't talking about abortion are you? Because if you are, I don't know if I can do that. Even the thought of it makes me uncomfortable." Setsuko placed a protective arm over her abdomen.

"No, no, that's not what we had discussed. You don't need to worry about hurting your child." Mai placed a gentle hand over

Setsuko's. "Why don't we wait until Hikaru-Bokushi gets here and then we can all talk together?"

At that moment, a man stepped through the front door. "Speaking of which, Setsuko, I would like you to meet my husband. People call him Bokushi."

Hikaru bowed, "Hello, everyone, I hope I'm not interrupting. It's nice of you to come, Hitomi, and it's good to finally meet you, Setsuko-san. Your mother has told us all about you."

"She has, has she?" Setsuko said disdainfully.

"Don't worry. From what she has told us, you are an amazing, brilliant and, may I say, beautiful young woman. Welcome to our home, I hope my wife has been a good hostess in my absence."

"She always is, Bokushi. I'm sorry I didn't call but we didn't have a lot of time," apologised Hitomi.

"It's quite all right, I'm glad you two came." Hikaru slipped off his shoes and joined them at the table. Mai brought out another tea cup.

"Thank you, dear, now what have I missed?"

"Nothing really, we had just begun talking when you walked in." Mai filled his cup.

"Have you told her what we were thinking?" Hikaru asked looking to Hitomi.

"I haven't yet. I'm sorry, I can't figure out how to bring it up."

"Bring what up?" Setsuko asked, annoyed that everyone was talking as if she wasn't there. Hikaru took a sip of tea and cleared his throat. "What are your thoughts on adoption?"

"Adoption!!" Setsuko exclaimed in shock. "You want me to give my child away?"

She wasn't sure why, but the thought of putting her child up for adoption seemed worse than aborting it. Everyone was quiet for a moment, waiting for someone to break the tension. Hitomi placed a hand over her daughter's.

"It's not something we are taking lightly, dear. This may be the only way to save your child."

"The only way?" Setsuko slammed her hands down on the table. "Are you mad? You are asking me to give up without a fight. This is your great plan? Why didn't I get an abortion? That would have been easier."

"Would it have?" asked Hikaru. Setsuko stared back at him defiantly, like a cornered animal refusing to back down.

"From what your mother has told me, it's unlikely your father will let you keep the child. He would sooner have the child killed than let it destroy your family's honour. What we are offering may be your only option, but you need to make the choice."

Everyone looked at her in silence. The decision she was about to make would affect the rest of her life. Pushing her cup aside, she got up and walked to the door.

"Setsuko, we haven't finished talking," Hitomi said.

"You can stay, but I am done talking. You might want to give up, but I won't. I will raise this child alone if I have to." Hitomi stepped towards her but halted when Hikaru spoke.

"Do you have a plan on how you will raise this child without your parents support?" he asked.

Setsuko met his serene gaze. She mentally reviewed different possibilities, and quickly understood what he was trying to tell her. If she kept the child, her father would disown her and when she graduated from school, he would cast her and her child out. She was so angry that it had all been reduced to this choice. Her eyes burned as hot tears poured down her face. She struggled to come to grips with the reality of her situation. Hikaru got up and stood in front of her, placing a comforting hand on her shoulder.

"I understand what we are asking you is something that may haunt you for years to come. I also know that in your heart you desire to protect your child, but that may require you to go to great lengths in order to do this. I wouldn't ask you to do something that would harm you or your child, but this may be the only chance you have left. In this moment, you are surrounded by people who care for you and your child, and want nothing more than to provide for you both. As long as you are under your father's household, he won't let you keep your baby. I am asking you, for your sake as well as your child's, will you consider giving your baby up for adoption?"

Setsuko wiped away the tears, still shaking, not in rage but in sadness. "What if I choose to abort it?"

With a sigh, Hikaru took both her hands into his. "The choice is yours in the end, although I can tell you, from what my counselling experiences have taught me, the kind of emotional and physical pain you will experience with abortion is beyond description. I have borne witness to young women like you, dealing with a pain that never seems to go away. These young women have regretted the choice they had made, or were forced to make, every day and have had to deal with the emotional baggage. We don't want to see you suffer, and we want to provide a way that you can still be a part of your child's life. Will you let us help you?"

After some thought, Setsuko nodded in response. Letting go of her fear and pain, she cried. The others gathered around and, wrapping their arms around her, began to pray, asking that the Lord God Almighty would give her peace and would provide them with the wisdom to move forward. Standing there, surrounded by those who loved her, Setsuko felt a strange warmth wash over her. As hard as it was going to be, she had a feeling that with their help, everything was going to be all right.

CHAPTER 23

Hitomi waited outside Daiki's office. They hadn't spoken since the night he struck Setsuko. Daiki made himself scarce and spent a lot of his time at work, while Hitomi avoided him, and still slept on the sofa. When they did interact, Daiki was withdrawn and cold, still angry at her for what she had done. Now Hitomi sat waiting, wanting to speak to her husband in hopes that he might be merciful and help them in their time of need. While she was silent in prayer, Hitomi was startled when Daiki's young assistant called for her.

"He's ready for you, Fukui-sama."

Hitomi picked up her purse. She thanked the assistant with a courteous bow and stepped into the office.

Daiki's office was one of the largest corner offices in the building's Penthouse. The walls were decorated with plaques and many other awards of distinction. Everything had its rightful place and was in order; just the way he liked it. Daiki sat in a large leather chair, his head bowed over the paperwork on his desk.

"You have another young woman working for you, I see," Hitomi said.

The hidden meaning behind what she said didn't escape him. He looked up from his work. "I let the other one go because of her lack of attention to detail." There was a slight edge to his words. Folding his hands in front of him, he gave her his full attention. "Besides, unlike others, I don't let personal matters affect sensible business decisions."

Is that all I am to you — a business decision? she thought. Taking another step forward, she looked him in the eyes and pleaded her case. "I have come to you for help."

His eyes narrowed. "Help? What kind of help?"

Taking a deep breath, she said carefully, "We have a family that may want to adopt our grandchild, but without your help, it may never happen."

"My help? It would seem that, all things considered, I would be the last person you would want help from. If it were up to me, I would dispose of that foul thing before it destroys us all."

Anger rose in Hitomi's voice. "You may not agree with the decision, but you must realise that what you are asking of our daughter would only hurt her. Why can't you see that? You can't just simply do away with the problem without considering the consequences."

Leaning forward, Daiki rested his chin on his hands. "Consequences?" he snorted. "She should have thought about that before she went to bed with that foreign boy. Now she must deal with what she has done. Just like anyone else, what I have to offer is far less humiliating than what you have convinced her to do. If she rids herself of this now, she may still have a bright future, with a husband who will provide for her and give her as many children as she wants. Sacrifices were made, and our family's reputation lies with her. If she chooses to have that child, everything that she could have had will be lost."

"You mean everything *you* could have had." Hitomi corrected him, drawing a sneer from Daiki.

"Oh, and what exactly will she have after she allows it to live? A life as a single parent. She will be thrown to the side like any common harlot if this gets out. Is that what you want?" Daiki shouted.

Saying a small prayer in her head, Hitomi felt compelled to stand strong, as God gave her the words to speak.

"God is moulding our grandchild in our daughter's womb as we speak. Are you so quick to be rid of that innocent life that you haven't even considered what joy that child may bring into our lives? Have you become so cold and callous that you see no other way of salvaging this, other than the destruction of a child?"

Daiki glared back at her, his rage mounting. "It was a mistake allowing your poison into this family. I should have cast you out the moment I found out about your faith, and now Setsuko will suffer because of it."

"Is it because of my faith or you?" Hitomi retorted. Daiki's brows rose; Hitomi had never defied him like this. Now she stood before him, unflinching. She was no longer the shy and fearful woman he knew, but strong and unbreakable. Her faith in this Jesus infuriated him, but it was the strength she drew from it that made him curious.

As they stood glaring at one another, Hitomi feared that she had gone too far. From the look on his face, it seemed she had lost, but as they looked at one another, his expression began to change. He looked down at the reports that were sitting open on his desk, and felt a strange calm come over him. When he looked at Hitomi again, he could see that there was nothing he could say that would deter her.

"What is it that you need from me?" he asked in a low growl. Blinking in surprise, Hitomi was at a loss for words. "What is it?" Daiki barked, irritated by her silence.

Quickly realising this was her chance, she remembered what she was going to say. "We need your help, so that they can adopt."

"Why can't they go through the normal channels like everyone else?" he asked, confused at what this had to do with him.

"They can't because they aren't from here."

"A foreign couple? You want to give this child away to some foreigners?"

"Do you think this child will have any hope of being adopted here?" Hitomi asked.

She was right, of course. It was unlikely that an unwanted hafu child would find a home here as many of those children were adopted overseas. Chances were that the child would be stuck in the system for a long time. But why was this any of his concern? he wondered.

"This couple wants the child?"

"Yes, but they are from a place that won't allow them to adopt from here, they may never get the chance. That's why I have come to you."

Daiki sat back down at his desk and sighed heavily. "I will see what I can do; until then I don't want to hear another word about this adoption. Not another word, do you understand?"

Hitomi nodded emphatically. She couldn't have dreamed of this going so well, it made her want to cry out in joy. Holding her excitement in check, she produced a small bag from her purse and placed it on his desk.

"What is this?" he asked.

"Your lunch, you forgot to pack one, so I decided I would bring you something."

"And what if I had said 'no'?"

Smiling at him she bowed her head, "I would have still given it to you, because I still love you, and only you."

With that, she left his office. Long after she had gone, Daiki pondered over what had transpired, and wondered if this sudden change of his heart had anything to do with the faith his wife had.

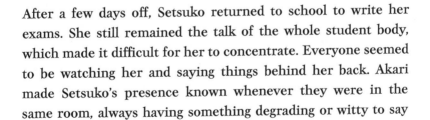

After a few days off, Setsuko returned to school to write her exams. She still remained the talk of the whole student body, which made it difficult for her to concentrate. Everyone seemed to be watching her and saying things behind her back. Akari made Setsuko's presence known whenever they were in the same room, always having something degrading or witty to say about her.

Misayo and Natsuki kept their distance, only giving her brief glances whenever they passed by her. One day a teacher advisor took her aside and asked if she had any plans on dealing with her problem. Angrily, Setsuko told him that she could take care of herself and that she didn't appreciate having someone pry into her personal matters. The advisor apologised, and gave her a number to call if she needed someone to talk to. The rest of the teachers didn't say anything, and continued on with their classes like normal.

Whenever she had a study period at the end of the day, she went home. One afternoon, Setsuko had the urge to confront David and tell him what she had decided. When class finished, she made a quick stop at the complex to see if he was still around. As she neared the door to Kyo's apartment, the door opened and Akari stepped outside.

"Thanks for coming over, Akari," said a voice from the doorway.

"You're welcome, Kyo, anytime. I am happy we became best friends," Akari said with smirk.

"Yeah, well I hope everything goes well with your exams, and I will see you at school tomorrow."

"Thank you, say hi to Tetsuya for me."

Akari began walking towards Setsuko. When Akari saw her, she grinned.

"Setsuko, what are you doing here?" she asked.

Still in shock, and feeling angry, it took a moment for Setsuko to respond. "I came to — No, what am I saying? I should be asking you, what you are doing here."

Akari's grin grew malicious. "It helps when you are friends with your boyfriend's friends, you know. It makes things easier."

"Boyfriend?" Setsuko repeated.

"What, you didn't really think that he was only after you, did you?" When Setsuko didn't reply, Akari seemed fully satisfied.

"At least he only left one of us with a little present. It seems he got what he wanted from you." She laughed, pointing at Setsuko's stomach.

A mixture of rage and pain filled her as she watched Akari walk by her and down the steps. She had sensed that he had been hiding something from her, but until now she would have never guessed it was Akari. He had played her and strung her along, while he was messing around with her best friend. All this time she had thought that he was hers. Nothing could have prepared her for this betrayal.

Deep in her own thoughts, Setsuko didn't notice Miya approach from behind. "Setsuko, what are you doing here?"

Setsuko turned and stared at her, unmoving. Seeing the look on her face, Miya realised what had transpired and she tried to console her.

"I'm sorry. He does this every time, and each time he hurts another girl. You aren't the first one to be burned by him, and you won't be the last. I wish I could have warned you sooner, but Tetsuya didn't want me to get involved. At least now you can move on with your life, and know what kind of scoundrel he is."

"He isn't here?" Setsuko asked sadly.

"No, he left a few days ago, back to America with his father. He's not going to be back for a while, or until his father has to make another trip out here. Forget him. He's gone now and you can move on with your life."

When Setsuko wouldn't look at her, Miya grew worried. "Are you all right?"

Setsuko unconsciously placed one hand on her stomach and held the other over her mouth as she cried. Miya put two and two together and gasped.

"Are you pregnant?" Miya whispered. Setsuko nodded, but when Miya came close, Setsuko pulled back.

"I'm fine, I'm just angry," she said, her voice shaking.

"Oh, Setsuko, I'm so sorry, I didn't realise. Do you need help?" Adjusting the straps on her backpack, Setsuko began to leave when Miya reached out to stop her.

"Setsuko, I'm so sorry. Why don't you come inside for a cup of tea and let's talk."

Setsuko glared up at her, eyes glossy. She pushed her hand aside. "I'm done talking. That's all anyone wants to do is talk, but talk is cheap. None of you understand what I am going through, but you all want me to make a choice. You all treat this as if it's such an easy decision to make. Keep the child or get rid of it. Well, if you are planning to give me your own opinion, don't bother, I'm keeping it. At least that's one thing he can't take away from me."

Miya's only response was a sympathetic look. Frustrated, Setsuko left in huff, promising herself that no man would ever take advantage of her again.

Angela was finally approved for surgery. As the days flew by, she was eating more and was beginning to look a little more like her old self. The first semester was coming to a close, and Jonathan was looking forward to some quality time with his wife. Pastor Hikaru would call periodically to check up on them and provide prayer or counselling when needed. When the question of the adoption would come up, all he would say was that he was still working out the details and would let them know as soon as he had everything sorted.

Since Angela wasn't able to get out much due to her health, Jonathan allowed her to make more calls home so she wouldn't feel so isolated. Their phone bills were excessive, but he considered that, if they made her the least bit happy, it was worth the expense. Back at school, many of the teachers and students gave him gifts to bring home. After they had received a few food items that made Angela feel sick, Jonathan requested that they limit the gifts to presents such as stuffed bears, flowers or hand crafted items.

On school nights, Jonathan graded exams and homework, while Angela napped on the sofa until he was ready to go to bed. On the weekends they went for walks, or visited with Kate whenever she was home. Since they missed a lot of church, they often spent time in the Word in the apartment. Angela was a little disconcerted that Jonathan seemed to show a lack of desire to lead them spiritually, but she relented, deciding that he was at least willing to spend time in worship. On Sunday afternoon, as they were preparing to go out for a walk, the phone rang.

"Hello?"

"Hello, Jonathan, it's Hikaru-Bokushi, how are you doing today?"

"Good, Bokushi, we were just about to head out for a walk, what can I do for you?"

"Are you going to be out for long?"

Jonathan looked at Angela, and wondered if this had anything to do with the adoption.

"Has something come up?"

"It may have, but I think we need to discuss it first and perhaps pray on it."

Wondering who Jonathan was talking to, Angela raised her hand to her head like she was holding a phone, and raised her eyebrows.

Covering the receiver, he responded, "Hikaru-Bokushi"

At the mention of the name Angela's eyes lit up. "Really? What does he want? Any news about us being able to adopt?" Jonathan held his hand up to tell her to hold on as he continued to speak with the Pastor.

"When were you thinking of coming over?" he asked.

"How does an hour from now sound to you?" Jonathan checked the time. That would give them time for a half-hour walk and be back in time to get ready before he arrived.

"That sounds great, Bokushi, we look forward to your visit."

"As do I. I will see you two in a bit. Oh and before I forget, I might have two more visitors as well."

Two more? Who else was he bringing? "Sure, that works."

"Glad to hear it, I will see you in an hour then. I'll talk with you soon."

When Jonathan hung up, he looked up to find Angela had disappeared from the front hall.

"Angela," he called out, "Where did you go, honey?"

"I'm in the bedroom," came her voice from down the hall. When he entered their room, she had laid out a few dresses and was holding one up against her, "What do you think?"

"I think a dress is a little too light for outside, you still don't have your full strength."

"No, not for outside, silly. I mean for when Hikaru-Bokushi arrives. I'm sure he doesn't want to see me in baggy pants and a sweater."

"But we still have time to go for our walk," Jonathan objected.

"No, we can't, I've got to get ready and you have to get the living room clean. We don't have time for a walk now."

Before he could reply, Angela walked past him to the washroom and closed the door behind her. Jonathan, knowing that there was no point in trying to talk her out of it, resigned himself to cleaning. The living room had once again become his office, with papers and books scattered everywhere. There was also two days' worth of dishes laying around the place. When he looked at it, he thought it looked like a hand grenade had gone off. While Angela finished getting ready, it took Jonathan about half an hour to get the room clean and the dishes done.

"Oh, hun?"

"Yes?" replied Jonathan, still annoyed from earlier.

"Are you okay?"

"I'm fine," he said, trying to mask how he felt as he wiped down the coffee table.

"You sound upset, are you sure?" Angela asked as she stepped into the living room while putting on her favourite earrings. Looking up from the cleaning, he caught his breath as he regarded his wife, and he was reminded just how beautiful she was.

"Does this look good?" she asked glancing down at the dress she had worn that first night they had dinner together.

"You look amazing," he replied, looking at her the same way he had back then. Blushing, Angela adjusted her hair.

"I'm glad you think so." She walked up to him, and kissed him lightly on the lips.

For the first time since she had been sick, she looked as radiant as she had when they courted, and it took his breath away. He couldn't believe how lucky he was to have such an amazing woman in his life. A simple look from her stirred something in his soul and made him hope he could spend the rest of his life just looking into her beautiful green eyes. The doorbell sounded, breaking the spell he had been under.

"Coming!" he called out.

"It would appear Hikaru-Bokushi has arrived early," Angela said. She stroked his face, and smiled. "Don't be annoyed. We will have plenty of time for us later."

Hitomi waited for her daughter to come home. She had been anxious since her talk with Daiki that morning. A mixture of joy and sadness filled her soul. They had found a home for their grandchild, but the prospect upset her. She could only imagine what Setsuko would go through when the time came to give up her own child. Hitomi had prayed day and night since their meeting with Pastor Hikaru, asking the Lord to provide them with the strength and wisdom they would need to see them through the next few months. Even with all the prayer, she still held onto a deep seated feeling of regret over the whole situation. What if she had done more as a mother? What if she had been more vigilant? Could she have prevented this, and saved her daughter years of pain and remorse over her decision? It's a little too late to dwell on that, she thought, looking out the window once more as she paced the room.

This time she saw movement, and she watched her daughter as she walked up the driveway. Relieved, Hitomi headed outside to where Suzaku waited patiently by the car as Setsuko strode up towards him.

"Where is my mother off to today?" Setsuko asked with a smidge of mirth.

"I am driving you two to meet your child's adoptive parents," he said shyly.

Setsuko eyes flashed, enraged that her father's servant knew anything about her pregnancy. "Who told you?" she shrieked.

Suzaku flinched as Setsuko reached out for him, but before she could do anything, Hitomi stepped outside and intervened.

"Setsuko-chan, what do you think you are doing?" she demanded.

"He knows, too?" Setsuko spat.

"He put it together himself, but ultimately, it was my decision to tell him. Did you think you could hide it forever? What excuse were you going to use when you start to show in the next few months? You're gaining weight."

Still infuriated by the breach of trust, she couldn't deny her mother's rationale. Suzaku flinched at her scornful look.

She rolled her eyes. "I'm not going to hurt you, you're not worth it."

"Are you forgetting something?" her mother asked as she walked to the car.

Setsuko sighed, clearly put out. "I'm sorry, Suzaku-san. All right, is that what you want to hear?"

Hitomi shook her head in vexation, "Get in the car, Setsuko, we don't have time to waste. We are picking up Hikaru-Bokushi on the way. He told the couple we would meet them in about an hour, so I would like to get going."

Suzaku opened the door for Setsuko. Setsuko threw her bag onto the seat between her and her mother and stepped inside, but refused to look at anyone. Seeing that she was in a mood, Hitomi decided to give her some space as they drove. When they arrived at Pastor Hikaru's place, he was waiting for them outside. Hitomi invited him to sit up front with Suzaku.

"Thank you," he said, "I've always wanted to ride shotgun."

Suzaku laughed at that, drawing an annoyed sigh from Setsuko. When Hikaru looked in the back, he raised his brow up at her. "Had a bad day?" he asked.

"I would rather not talk," she mumbled, still refusing to make eye contact.

"It's the hormones," Hitomi said, giving Setsuko a disapproving look.

"Oh, well. I will keep the chatter down to a minimum until we arrive, then," Hikaru said, giving Suzaku a wink.

Even with his promise, it wasn't long before Hikaru and Suzaku began talking at length. Setsuko tried to block it all out, and focussed on what was going on outside. Thirty minutes later they finally arrived. Hikaru led them up the stairs of the quaint little apartment complex to a suite on the third floor.

"Here we are," Hikaru chimed as he pressed the doorbell. A few moments later, a young woman answered the door. She gave a quick smile to Pastor Hikaru. A look of surprise crossed her face when she saw Hitomi and Setsuko.

"Hitomi, what are you doing here?" she asked.

"I have come with some news," Hitomi replied, beaming at the other woman, "and hopefully an answer to prayer for both of us."

The woman invited them in and offered to take their coats. Eyeing her, Setsuko noticed that she was a little gaunt, and looked like some of those American models she had seen in magazines with her skinny body and long, curly blonde hair. She had a gentle smile, just like her mother, but it was her sharp green eyes that made her look exotic. For a moment, Setsuko had a hard time not staring at them, until her mother nudged her.

"Don't worry, you aren't the first person who has been entranced by her beautiful eyes," said a handsome man as he walked up and gave the young woman a kiss on the cheek.

"My name's Jonathan, and this is my wife, Angela," he said, giving her a small bow.

"My name is Setsuko," she replied in English.

"You speak English, I see," Jonathan said.

"It was a mandatory course for all who had aspirations to join the student exchange program," said Setsuko, speaking slowly, as her English was a little rusty.

"I teach English in a few classes at a school nearby."

Jonathan was fluent in Japanese, just like David, but it seemed that Angela struggled with the most basic of the language, for her husband had to translate. Looking at the two of them, she could see that they truly loved one another. It made Setsuko feel a little jealous, wondering if David had ever looked at her in that way, or had he only seen her as his plaything.

"Why don't we all sit down and get this started?" Hikaru invited, making his way to the sitting room. Everyone followed him, except for Jonathan, who offered to make the tea.

"That's all right, hun, I can do it," Angela said, wanting to feel useful.

Placing a firm hand on her shoulder, he turned her around and guided her to the sofa.

"No, it's fine, I can serve everyone. You sit down here and rest."

She tried to protest, but he wouldn't hear any of it. Reluctantly, Angela sat down on the sofa with Hikaru. Setsuko took the recliner and Hitomi took the dining room chair that Jonathan had pulled over for her. They sat quietly, waiting for Jonathan to join them.

"Start without me, I will be there in a minute," said Jonathan as he set the kettle down on the stove.

Taking the initiative, Angela turned to Hitomi and asked, "This is your daughter, I take it?"

Hitomi nodded and smiled, "Yes, this is my daughter, Setsuko," she said proudly. "She is turning eighteen this year and she is planning to attend university, as long as she can keep the grades up."

"University? I attended university, but circumstances prevented me from finishing. Jonathan and I have talked about me going back when my health improves. Who knows, things may change if we have a child," Angela said, smiling at Setsuko.

Setsuko was a little curious about with whom her mother associated. As far as she knew, her mother had few friends; she was understandably surprised to learn differently.

"How do you know my mother?" she asked.

"We met at Hikaru-Bokushi's church and have been friends ever since," replied Angela.

Hitomi blushed in embarrassment. She hadn't intended to hide this part of her life from her daughter, but she did hide it out of fear of Daiki's threats. Jonathan finally joined them with a tray holding cups and the kettle of tea. He poured tea for their guests before sitting down beside his wife.

"I take it that your visit has something to do with the adoption?" he asked.

"Yes, that's why we came, but I think it's best to have Setsuko and Hitomi explain the situation first. But before we do that, why don't we open in prayer," Hikaru said as he folded his hands and waited for the others to join him.

All but Setsuko bowed their heads and closed their eyes as they all gave thanks to God for His answers to their prayers. They asked Him to lead them and fill the room with His Holy Spirit to guide them during their conversation. Setsuko watched them with a keen interest. She had never known her mother to get so wrapped up in spiritual things since the death of her grandparents. Her father, on the other hand, practiced kami-no-michi, or Shinto, which honoured and respected their ancestors and worshipped all the gods of nature, of heaven and earth.

It was odd to her that they spoke to this one god as if He was a real living being, and who somehow held sway over the matters of mere mortals. What kind of god was this that held human life with such great value? she wondered. When they had finished, Hitomi took Setsuko's hand and gave it a slight squeeze.

"Do you wish to start?" she asked. Setsuko shook her head, feeling uncomfortable about sharing something so intimate with complete strangers.

"I guess I can tell them, then," Hitomi said softly, taking her daughter's hand. She quietly explained the relationship with David that had resulted in Setsuko's pregnancy, of how both David and Setsuko's father wanted it terminated. "When I heard that you two were looking into adopting a child, I knew that the Lord had sent you during our time of need. I just hope my husband can make everything work out," Hitomi said, looking a little unsure of herself.

"I'm confused, are you saying we can adopt your child, or is there something I'm missing?" Angela asked.

Clearing his throat, Hikaru spoke up. "Adopting internationally in Japan isn't as easy as in other countries. Under the current agreements, only certain provinces in Canada are permitted to adopt from here, and as it stands, Alberta isn't one of them."

"You are saying is there's a chance we might not be accepted as adoptive parents for any child from here?" Jonathan said, sensing his wife's heartbreak by the revelation.

"We don't know yet," Hitomi responded, wanting to keep their hopes alive. "My husband has many contacts within our government. He has been known to pull strings in order to allow things that our laws would normally prohibit on many occasions. When I last talked to him, he said he would look into it, and if there is anyone who can make this work, I know he can."

"Really!" exclaimed Angela, her eyes lighting up with joy. "When will we find out?"

"It may take Daiki a few weeks before he receives an answer, so until then, all we can do is pray," replied Hitomi.

Setsuko listened silently while those around her discussed the fate of her unborn child. The reality of what they were discussing began to weigh heavily on her heart. She had never considered what it was she was really losing until now. The thought that she might never play an important part in her child's life caused her much distress. All those moments a mother shared with her child would be lost to her, a lifetime of memories gone in a blink of an eye. It felt unreal, yet here she was, sitting amongst her child's new parents and about to agree to sign over all her rights.

"Are you all right, Setsuko?" her mother asked, concerned by the expression on her face.

"I'm fine; I just need some air," she said, excusing herself. She went to the door, grabbed her jacket and shoes, and then walked out without another word.

"Is she okay?" asked Angela, worried that they had upset her.

"I think she feels a little overwhelmed. Hitomi, why don't you go and see if she needs anything," Hikaru suggested, motioning to the door.

"Is it okay if I talk to her?" Angela asked. The men were unsure, but it was Hitomi who spoke first.

"Yes, please do, I think she needs to understand where you are coming from, and that she would be giving her child to good parents."

Donning her coat and shoes, Angela went outside and found Setsuko at the end of the complex balcony, looking down over the railing.

"I'm sorry you have to go through this." She stood beside Setsuko and leaned against the railing.

"You don't know. You can't begin to understand," Setsuko choked out between sobs.

"Why don't you tell me and maybe you can help me understand?"

Angrily, Setsuko wiped away her tears. "No, you can't, no one can. No one has asked you to give up so much."

Angela thought for a moment before speaking. This young girl was about to make a decision that would affect the rest of her life. Turning towards Setsuko, Angela placed a hand over her lower abdomen and asked, "Do you know what's happening to me?" Puzzled, Setsuko looked at Angela's hand and shook her head when she couldn't think of anything.

"What is it?" she asked.

"I have cancer," Angela replied. "It's uterine cancer, and as it so happens, I have to have an operation that will remove any chance of me ever having my own children."

Setsuko looked at her, wide-eyed. "I didn't know."

"I know you didn't. Just like you may not fully understand what this means to me, I can't fully understand what you are going through, but here we are, each facing a decision that will affect both of our lives for years to come."

"I don't want to give it up," protested Setsuko, eyes red and puffy.

"Is there any way you can keep the child?" asked Angela, placing a warm hand on the young girl's shoulder.

Thinking it through, as she had a million other times, Setsuko couldn't figure out how to keep her child. If she did, her father would disown her and she would be cast out, with no support and no prospect of a future beyond what she could scrape together on her own. It was a terrifying thought, to be alone, without someone to turn to. In some small way, she was beginning to understand her mother's hesitation to stand for what she believed in. One misstep and she would lose it all, and then what would she do?

"I know that it's beyond anything I can imagine, to ask you to give up your child, and that's why I'm not going to ask." Angela looked into her eyes. "If there is any way we can help, any possible chance we can give you the support you need to raise this child on your own, we will gladly give it. I may never have the ability to have my own children, but I would never expect you to give up something so precious without considering what it would do to you."

As she regarded Angela, she could see what her mother had seen in her. Angela spoke with such sincerity that Setsuko's misgivings and concerns evaporated along with her reservations. She knew then that she could trust Angela. This woman and her husband would be the parents of her child.

"I cannot keep my child, but I can give it to you," Setsuko said tearfully. "It is the only choice I have left. If I were to do anything else, I would be disgraced. No one would want me, and I have to gain back my family's honour."

For the first time in her life, Setsuko's loathing for her family honour dissolved in that single moment. She knew the path she had to take in order to regain what she had lost. Even though it may prove to be the hardest choice of her life, she had to make it in order to redeem her family.

"I have only one request."

"Anything," Angela replied with bated breath.

"I get to pick the name of my child and you need to keep it."

Angela smiled at her tenderly. "Of course we will, I promise."

CHAPTER 24
Summer 1985

After their meeting with the Hansens, Setsuko and Hitomi went home to make arrangements with their doctor for regular pre-natal check-ups. Jonathan and Angela prepared for her surgery that was to take place in the near future. As Setsuko's pregnancy progressed, she spent most of her time studying at home and only went in for her exams. That allowed her to avoid Akari, who made it her Mission to make Setsuko's life miserable. Natsuki would occasionally walk home with her, but Misayo no longer associated with her. On her way home one day, Setsuko decided to pay Misayo a visit.

Misayo's parents owned a small bakery a little ways away from where Natsuki lived. When they were children, they had spent a lot of time there, enjoying the free baked goods Misayo's parents would give them. Their two bedroom home was located above the shop.

When Setsuko reached the shop, she hesitated at the door. As she stood outside, a customer came out with some fresh goods. The smell of bread made her mouth water as she remembered all the pastries and rolls she used to enjoy there. Looking through the window, she could see Misayo stocking the display racks while her father swept the floor. Watching her, Setsuko thought about what she wanted to say to her friend. As Setsuko stepped up to the door, Misayo saw her through the window. She said something to her father before walking to the door. She opened the door just enough to poke her head out.

"Why are you here?" she asked glumly.

Fidgeting with her backpack, Setsuko took a deep breath. "I wanted to see if you could talk."

Looking back to make sure her father didn't see Setsuko, Misayo stepped outside, quietly closing the door behind her. "I don't think it's a good idea," she said, looking a little uneasy.

"Why? I thought we were friends, we have been for years. What's changed?" Setsuko asked, bewildered and hurt.

"I can't be around you anymore, my parents said you are a bad influence."

Bad influence? Those words cut deep as a lump formed in Setsuko's throat. She tried to find the words that would convey how she was feeling inside. How much she wanted to still be friends. How much she wished that she had never met David.

"Misayo!" Misayo's mother barked as she walked up to them, "you get back inside and help your father or I promise you won't leave your room for a week."

Misayo looked morosely at Setsuko. "I'm sorry, I wish things were different."

Misayo's mother shooed her daughter inside before turning her attention to Setsuko. "My daughter has no time to waste with a tramp talking about boys. You hear me?"

Setsuko flinched as Mrs. Nagasawa wagged her index finger just inches from her face. "I'm sorry for bothering you, Nagasawa-san, I didn't mean to cause any harm."

"Then leave, before you put any more ideas into my daughter's head. Her grades in school have cost her enough, no thanks to you and her other friends. All you girls do is talk about boys and fill your heads with nonsense; now look where you are."

Setsuko bowed her head woefully. Turning to leave, she took one last look into the shop and saw Misayo staring back at her, tears in her eyes. After all they had gone through together, one mistake had torn their friendship apart.

As the last week of school came to a close, Jonathan was thankful to be home with his wife. During the weeks leading up to her surgery, Jonathan was an attentive husband. In addition to preparing for the upcoming semester, he handled the housework and shopping as well as taking Angela out on dates and, when her stomach was up to it, preparing the occasional meal.

Just days before the surgery, Angela received a call from Stephanie.

"Hi, Steph, how are you doing?"

"I'm counting down the days until summer break. I don't think I will ever look at another text book again. How are you two doing? I miss you."

"I miss you, too." Angela said, "Jonathan's on break until the next semester. He's spending too much time prepping for class, and was told to be less thorough and to try to make it through the course material. Other than that, they like him. I was worried for a bit after I became sick, but things worked out for the better."

"Speaking of sick, when are you supposed to go in?" Stephanie asked, concerned.

"I'm booked for Thursday morning. They said I will be under for several hours."

"Scared?"

"A little."

In truth, Angela was terrified, but she didn't want to frighten Stephanie. She had spent a few sleepless nights considering what would happen if she didn't come back. How would it affect everyone she knew? How would Jonathan react? It unnerved her thinking about it. As they had grown together, she was beginning to see Jonathan only wanting to go waist deep in the water that was the Lord's grace and mercy. She wondered just how much of a relationship he actually had with God, or if he even had a relationship at all. Whenever she broached the subject, it felt like he was saying what he thought she wanted to hear, or he would get upset and change the subject. The mere thought of her passing without knowing if he was a true believer scared her.

"I don't know how you do it, but you have more guts than me. If that were me, I'd be a basket case. So, how long will they keep you afterwards?"

"A few weeks, maybe longer depending upon how quickly I recover."

There was a silence as Stephanie absorbed this news. Then she asked, "Would you like to hear some good news?"

"Sure, what is it?"

"We are going to make a trip out to visit you two!"

"Really?"

"Yes, really," Stephanie huffed. "No joke. With my father back in town and possibly even staying long term, my mother decided she needed a break from the drama and asked if I wanted to go and see you guys."

"Your father's back in town?"

"More like moving back in."

"Wow, what happened? I thought he was with that young thing."

"Let's just say that Dad found out how hard it is at his age to keep up with someone who is only six years older than his daughter."

"Oh dear!" Angela said with a laugh, and excitedly jumped back to the proposed trip. "I can't wait to see you two! When were you coming over?"

"That's why I called, I want you to let us to know when you are out of surgery so we can plan our trip around that.

"That sounds like a plan." Angela said happily.

They spent the next hour on the phone, planning for the proposed visit. Jonathan didn't even complain when he noticed how long they talked. When she got off the phone, they ate lunch in the living room while a gospel album played on the stereo Mr. Matsuno had given them. It was nice to get her mind off of things for at least the day.

On the morning of the surgery, Angela had an air of anticipation and anxiety about her as they sat in the surgical waiting room. Just before she was called up, Pastor Hikaru, Mai, Hitomi and Setsuko paid her a quick visit.

"We wanted to meet with you so that we could pray and ask that the Lord guide the hands of the surgeon," said Hikaru.

"Are you nervous?" Hitomi asked.

"A little," Angela admitted. "I'm just looking forward to this all being over."

"Are they going to remove all of the cancer, then?" asked Setsuko curiously.

"We hope so, but we won't know until they test her after the surgery," Jonathan replied.

"Shall we get started?" Hikaru pressed. Lowering their heads, they joined hands and prayed. Even Setsuko held hands with the others, but she was silent during the prayer. When they had finished, a young nurse brought in a wheelchair for Angela. Jonathan didn't let Angela's hand go, afraid. He knelt next to the chair.

"What if something goes wrong? What if they can't fix it?" he asked, his voice breaking. Angela looked at him and committed every feature to memory, from the few freckles he had down the new creases on his forehead.

"It's okay, Hansen-sama," the nurse assured him in English, "We take good care of her."

Angela caressed his face and kissed him on the forehead. "I'll be back," she said smiling at him, "I promise."

Jonathan let her hand go and watched her be wheeled down the corridor.

The hours dragged on. Hikaru and the others stayed with him for the first few hours, encouraging him to talk to help pass time. When they left, Jonathan paced the corridors between the waiting room and the main entrance, stepping out often to catch a breath of fresh air. When he wasn't pacing, he was standing at the room's entrance, half-expecting a nurse to come over with the horrible news. No one seemed to notice him, and when he asked how much longer, he was told that it could be another hour and to sit down. Sitting down in the chair was like sitting on thorns. So he paced. Right when he thought his last nerve was ready to snap, the nurse who had taken his wife earlier called him over to the desk.

"Hansen-san, Shoji-oishasan will be out in a moment."

"Is she all right?"

"Yes, the surgery went well. She is in Recovery. Follow me and the doctor will see you."

He followed her down the same corridor they had taken Angela, and then into a small room. Relieved but still tense, he chose to stand as he waited. A few minutes passed before a small knock at the door announced the arrival of Dr. Shoji. When he entered, the same nurse followed him in.

"Hansen-san, I have some good news and some bad."

The nurse began to translate for the doctor before Jonathan interrupted in Japanese.

"It's okay, I don't need an interpreter."

With a curt nod from the doctor, the nurse left the room. Dr. Shoji turned to Jonathan.

"Your wife will be all right, and we are confident that the removal of the cancer was successful. As to why it took so long, we encountered some complications."

"Complications, what complications?" Jonathan asked in panic.

"We discovered she was in Stage Three, which necessitated the removal of the uterus, fallopian tubes and ovaries. Also, there were small tumours in the tissue just outside of the uterus. We believe that they were benign, but they have been removed as a precaution. We would like to run several tests to make sure that the cancer has not metastasized."

Jonathan's head spun, what exactly was Dr. Shoji telling him? "I don't understand? Does she still have cancer?"

"Our hope is that we have prevented the spread of the cancer. I'm sorry that we cannot do more for her, but as far as I am concerned, she should live a healthy life." The doctor waited for a response. When Jonathan remained silent, he continued, "I would like to keep her here for at least three weeks for further treatments, and to monitor her progress on a day to day basis. If she responds to the treatments, she will be free to go home, but you cannot have any intimate contact for another two weeks after that."

Intimacy was the least of Jonathan's concerns; he was just relieved that his wife was all right. "When can I see her?"

"She will be moved to a private room on the fifth floor for the duration of her stay. You can ask the nurse at the desk for the room number. I want her to get as much rest as possible, so you may only visit for a short time."

Jonathan bowed deeply, thanking the doctor for all his work. He was so happy to know that Angela had another chance at life, and that she may live to grow old with him. His heart soared with joy as he left the room. From here on in he was going make every moment with her count.

Angela spent the next four weeks in hospital receiving traditional postoperative treatments. She received many visits from some of the church members who came with Pastor Hikaru. Hitomi and Setsuko also came to visit whenever they could, and almost always brought her gifts.

Three weeks after the surgery, Stephanie and Mrs. Marshal flew over and joined them at the hospital. Angela was so happy to see her friend that they spent the first two days exchanging news and practically ignored Jonathan and Mrs. Marshal. When the latest test results came back, Dr. Shoji was happy to report that the tumours had indeed been benign. Everyone was relieved to hear this, especially Angela.

At the end of the third week, she was released from the hospital; to her consternation, Jonathan was back at school for the second semester. Mrs. Marshal decided to tour Japan by train, leaving Stephanie and Angela free to spend the next two weeks getting in as much shopping and sightseeing as Angela's compromised strength allowed.

The two girls enjoyed their time together after being apart for so long. Their banter and talks made Jonathan a little jealous, as they shared a bond that went deeper than friends. As always, Stephanie liked to tease Jonathan, but there was something in the way she acted that made Angela take notice. Then one night, as they stayed up late and talked, Angela decided to ask Stephanie about what had been bothering her since Stephanie's arrival.

"Stephanie, do you like Jonathan?" she asked over a glass of wine.

"I don't think I like him, but maybe the idea of him," Stephanie replied slowly.

"Okay." Angela laughed nervously, "What do you mean by that?"

"I guess he was the first guy who treated me like a person, and not like a piece of meat. Having someone treat me with respect and care made me reconsider what kind of guy I want to be with. I'm not in love with him, if that's what you're asking."

"No, I wasn't implying you were. I guess some things have been on my mind of late."

"Oh, like what?" Stephanie asked, wondering if she had behaved inappropriately while interacting with Jonathan. She would never think of taking someone so special from Angela. She also knew, by the way Jonathan looked at his wife, that he loved her deeply.

"If we do adopt this child and something happens to me, would you be willing to be his help mate?" Angela spoke those last words so softly that Stephanie almost didn't believe her ears.

"Are you joking? That's not funny, Angela. You are fine and soon you are going to be a mother. You two are going to be parents, for heaven's sake! What makes you even think of something like that in the first place?"

Angela put down her glass and looked up into the night sky, like she always did whenever she was about to reveal her deepest secrets. Yet, there was something in her eyes that made Stephanie feel uncomfortable.

"Angela, what's going on? You're scaring me."

Taking a deep breath, Angela turned to her friend and told her about the recurring dream of the graveyard. She could only recall some parts of it, but somehow things were beginning to come into focus with recent events.

"So, what you're saying is that God's planning on taking you away from us, and that He's been giving you dreams about it? You're crazy, you know that."

"I'm not joking," Angela said, this time looking straight at her. "Ever since I got sick, I've had this feeling that I may still be dying. I want to make sure that I have someone here to watch over things if I do pass on; someone like you who has similar values."

"Stop it, Angela!" Stephanie's voice shook as she tried to hold it together, "Nothing's going to happen to you. The doctors said you that were fine, and I don't care what this dream of yours shows you, you and I will grow old together and that's the end of it."

She crossed her arms and turned away from Angela as she tried to regain her composure. Her friend had never said something that struck her heart so hard she wanted to scream in anger. They had grown up like sisters and, as far as she was concerned, they would always be, no matter what.

"Stephanie?"

"What?" Stephanie asked bitterly.

"I'm sorry, I didn't mean to hurt you."

Drawing in a ragged breath Stephanie turned to face Angela. "I know, but no more talk about this dream, all right? It's just a dream. As for Jonathan, I promise I don't love him or see him as anything more than maybe a big brother, you got that? So no more. Let's just enjoy our time together."

Angela smiled faintly at her. She wished with all her heart that Stephanie was right, but deep down, she knew that the dreams were much more than just dreams.

CHAPTER 25
Winter — 1986

The months seemed to progress slowly for Setsuko. During her last semester, the school offered her the opportunity to work at home with the help of a teacher's aide. She gratefully accepted, wanting to free herself from all prying eyes and Akari's incessant ridicule and harassment. Setsuko had worked hard to salvage her grades, and once again found herself on the District's top ten list, following closely behind Natsuki who had obtained third place. The two of them had maintained their friendship and got together to study whenever they could. Hitomi busied herself with the house, as well as providing Setsuko with some helpful prenatal delivery tips.

Their home lives had returned to normal for the most part. Daiki still spent most of his time at the office, as seeing Setsuko in her delicate state was a daily reminder of the shame she had brought him. As expected, Mr. Hashida withdrew the contract of marriage, which only made things worse between the three of them. Hitomi took Daiki's absence the hardest, and Setsuko could see the strain on their relationship was beginning to wear her down. Most nights, Daiki would arrive late from work with no explanation of where he had been or what he had been doing, and asking would only invoke his wrath. Some nights he wouldn't come home at all, and she would find her mother lying in their bed, weeping.

Setsuko found that the last month of pregnancy was almost intolerable. Her belly was much bigger than she thought was normal, but the doctors told her that it was just a large amount of amniotic fluid. When she realised just how big she had become, she cried, saying this child was going to ruin her.

Hitomi snapped at her. "You will have to bear the scars of childbirth that every mother has to carry for the rest of her life. You knew it wouldn't be easy, and it's too late to go back now."

"But I look like a balloon," Setsuko groaned, staring at her reflection in the full-length mirror.

"That can't be helped now, you need to get over your vanity and realise that what you are about to give birth to is a gift. It's nothing to be ashamed of; I still carry the scars you gave me," Hitomi said, alluding to the few stretch marks she had.

"I will never look the same will I?" Setsuko pouted trying to cover her belly with the large maternity shirt.

Shaking her head, Hitomi sighed. "If you rely on your looks alone, you will get nowhere in life."

"Didn't you rely on your looks, Mother?" Setsuko asked mockingly.

Not willing to be goaded into another argument, Hitomi ignored the comment, "Get over here and help me with these clothes. You also need to get your homework done so your advisor can pick it up tomorrow."

Setsuko complied begrudgingly, still eyeing herself in the mirror from time to time.

Ever since Hitomi had stood up to Daiki, with the Lord's strength and encouragement through His Word, she had grown bolder and more confident. She could still be soft, but the more time she spent with her daughter the more she began to realise that softness was probably what got them into this predicament in the first place. As she got to know Setsuko a little better, she soon realised how much of a spoiled brat she was. Daiki had warned her that being too soft on the girl would cause more harm than good. In retrospect, she realised just how right he was.

Their daughter needed a strong hand to guide her; instead, she had acquiesced to Setsuko's demands. She wished she could take it all back, but in reality she knew that the only person who could change Setsuko was God. She prayed for her daughter day in and day out.

Daiki began to come home more often, much to Hitomi and Setsuko's surprise. One evening, he brought up the idea of having a home birth.

"You don't want me to go to a hospital to have this child?" asked Setsuko in complete shock. "But why?"

"Daiki, I don't know about this. What if something goes wrong?" Hitomi asked.

"It will prevent my daughter from being made a spectacle of, and hopefully save us from more shame," Daiki said darkly as he eyed Setsuko. "I have been told that a physician can be asked to attend to the birth, in case something does happen. I have also been informed that home births are still widely practiced. I have talked to a midwife and she has offered her assistance, at great cost I might add."

Setsuko was about to speak up but her mother shook her head, telling her to take their dishes into the kitchen. When Setsuko left, Hitomi turned to Daiki.

"Daiki, I know you are still angry at her for what has happened, but I don't know if a home birth is a good idea. I nearly bled to death after giving birth to her."

Daiki could never forget that day, seeing his wife in a pool of her own blood. Setsuko had been a large infant, and had torn her mother badly during her delivery. It had been a gruesome sight, and Hitomi had fallen in and out of consciousness. The midwife was so afraid that Hitomi wouldn't make it, that she told Daiki to prepare for the worst. It had been a miracle that Hitomi had survived at all.

"Don't you care about our daughter?" Hitomi asked, knowing immediately it had been the wrong thing to say.

Daiki stood up and excused himself from the table, telling her his mind was made up and there would be no more discussion. There was nothing else for Hitomi to do but wait and pray that God would keep them under His protection.

It was a cold January afternoon when Setsuko's water broke. They were just preparing to leave for a doctor's appointment, and Setsuko began to panic when she realised what was happening. Hitomi told Suzaku to contact the midwife and to tell her to come immediately, and to call Daiki to tell him Setsuko was in labour. Suzaku was so unnerved, Hitomi had to repeat herself several times. Once he made the calls, he hurried off to pick up the midwife. Once she had Setsuko settled on the sofa, Hitomi ran to the kitchen to prepare the hot water and towels that would be needed. When Suzaku returned almost an hour later, it was to find Setsuko crying out in the midst of a contraction. Frightened by her cries, he could only stare at her, and didn't hear Hitomi until she yelled at him.

"Fukui-sama? Kacho?" Suzaku repeated.

"Yes, Suzaku-san, don't you need to pick him up?" Hitomi asked angrily.

"Right, I have to pick him up," he said, bolting for the door when Hitomi shouted for him again.

"Suzaku-san, stop!"

"What?" he asked bewildered.

"The hot water and towels? They're in the kitchen."

"Yes, sorry Hitomi-sama, I will get those first."

When he returned, he informed Hitomi that Daiki called to say that the obstetrician would not be arriving. Rolling her eyes, Hitomi asked the midwife where she wanted her daughter.

"On the floor here, that way we have a bit more room," the midwife replied. She helped Hitomi get Setsuko from the sofa to the blankets and pillows they had laid out on the floor. "How far apart are the contractions?"

"I'm not sure, we haven't been keeping track," replied Hitomi.

Once they had Setsuko settled, the midwife patiently instructed her on how to breathe during the contractions, and told that when her contractions grew closer together and her cervix was properly dilated, they would begin the birthing process.

It was over an hour before Daiki came home. He ordered Suzaku to go home for the night and that he would be called once everything was over. Not wanting to be there another minute, Suzaku hightailed it home. The next eight hours of labour were going to be the longest eight hours of Setsuko's life.

When it was all over, Setsuko lay exhausted, tired, covered in sweat and fighting the urge to nod off. She was not prepared for the intense love and joy she felt for her newborn child. Cradling the little girl in her arms, she smiled down at this precious gift. Her little Takara was beautiful with ten perfect fingers and toes. She had Setsuko's colouring and dark hair and her nose and the shape of her deep blue eyes were David's. Setsuko could also see pieces of her parents in her. It was amazing that, not so long ago, she considered destroying this little life. Now, Setsuko would give her own life to protect her precious girl.

The moment was spoiled when her father strode into the sitting room. He didn't look at her but instead silently stared out of one of the windows overlooking the gardens. Seeing him so cold and detached shattered the calm she felt.

"You may take care of the child for now, but we must be rid of her as soon as possible." He turned to face her, but she refused to meet his eyes. "I know it will be hard, but this needs to be done, Setsuko-chan," he said more tenderly. She began to weep and held her daughter tighter, which caused the baby to fuss.

"But why can't I keep her?" she sobbed.

"Haven't you brought us enough disgrace? Is it not enough that we let the child live? Or do you wish to bring even more shame to our family?" Without waiting for a response, he abruptly turned and stalked to the door, then paused. "I am doing this for your own good. One day you will thank me."

With that, he exited the room, leaving his distraught daughter to weep hopeless tears, alone.

Daiki had arranged for the family lawyer to sign the required paperwork in the afternoon. Hitomi was dreading the meeting, and every minute leading up to the appointment gnawed away at her nerves. Even though she was exhausted, she hadn't slept all night. Setsuko was also on edge, and she pleaded with her mother to let her keep her baby. Hitomi wanted to say yes, but she knew it wasn't a possibility. There were also Angela and Jonathan's feelings to consider; Setsuko had given her word that they could adopt the baby.

When the lawyer arrived, Hitomi felt every muscle tense. He was a spindly looking older man, with greying black hair and a pointed nose. She remembered meeting him once before, but couldn't recall where. She did, however, remember how he made her feel. Like her husband, he came off as a cold and calculating man who looked down at those around him.

Daiki ushered him into the sitting room where Hitomi and Setsuko stood waiting. Hitomi greeted him as he entered. He gave her a curt nod before reaching into his briefcase for the documents.

"Here is what you requested, Fukui-sama. These documents, once signed, will legally strip you of any responsibility for the child. It will also ensure that your family fortune will stay in the family."

"What do you mean 'stay in the family'? Father, what's he talking about?" Setsuko demanded.

The lawyer stared at her coolly as Daiki cleared his throat in warning. Taking Setsuko's hand Hitomi bowed apologetically and said he could continue. Still looking at Setsuko, the lawyer continued to explain some of the details of the documents.

"With your signatures, we can have this issue resolved as quickly as possible. Now, if I may inquire, where are the adoptive parents?" He pulled out even more documents from his briefcase.

"I will get them to sign these when we meet with them later this week, Ojima-san," Daiki explained, reaching for the documents.

"But, sir, if I could get them to sign the paperwork today, it would help to expedite the process," Mr. Ojima asserted.

Daiki snarled at the man, "That will be quite enough, I do not wish to have any unwanted involvement from someone outside this family, do you understand?"

Mr. Ojima gave Daiki an apologetic bow. "I apologise for my misstep Fukui-san. Send the papers to our office as soon as they are signed. I will ensure that we will deal with this promptly."

Setsuko stared at the documents in front of her and hesitated. She looked to her mother in silent entreaty.

"Your mother can't help you, Setsuko-chan. You got yourself into this mess and now I am trying to clean it up. I let your child live, and now you must live up to your end of the bargain," Daiki said darkly, piercing his daughter with his steely gaze.

Setsuko realised her mother couldn't help and that she had no choice in the matter. She signed over her rights, and ran off to her room in anguish. Daiki and Hitomi added their signatures to the last of the documents before handing them over.

"Thank you for your time, Fukui-san, it was a pleasure working with you, as always," said Mr. Ojima as he filed the documents into his briefcase. Daiki walked him out, while Hitomi went to check in on Setsuko and the baby.

Hitomi knocked softly, and waited a moment before whispering, "Setsuko-chan, are you all right?"

No reply came, but she could hear Setsuko as she sang to the baby. Listening to her daughter's voice, everything they had gone through caught up with Hitomi, and she collapsed on the floor beside Setsuko's door and sobbed as the exhaustion and her emotions took over.

As she sat there weeping, Daiki walked back inside and approached her. "I don't want to hear another word of this, do you understand?"

Nodding in response Hitomi didn't dare challenge him; instead, she resigned herself to the fate that lay ahead of them. In the next few days Setsuko would face the most heart-wrenching task of her life; she would have to give up her child.

As Setsuko's due date drew near, both Angela and Jonathan found it difficult to relax. They were worried over the possibility that the adoption would not go through, and over their recent decision to return home. Angela was excited about having their first child, but she braced herself to be accepting should God say 'no'.

Jonathan was equally worried about whether or not he would have a job when they returned to Calgary. They had decided to tell only a few people of their plans, and those who knew had tried to encourage them to stay. Jonathan was most shocked by Mr. Kagawa's reaction. Out of all the people, he had thought that Mr. Kagawa would be happy to be rid of him; instead, he seemed to be the most disappointed. Even the students were sad to hear that Jonathan was leaving the following year, so they all pitched in and gave him cards of thanks, and gifts for their new child.

What concerned both of them most of all was the response they would receive from Hitomi and her daughter. It had to be hard enough on Setsuko to be giving up her child, but to find out that her daughter would be taken to a place so far away may prove to be too much for her to bear. They had gone over what they were going to say, but whenever the opportunity came to tell them, their courage evaporated when they saw Hitomi and Setsuko.

Hitomi called them the day following Takara's birth, and asked if they could meet that Saturday. Angela was overjoyed to hear that everything had gone well, and was thrilled at the prospect of having a daughter. She wanted to ask if they were still able to adopt, but she quelled her excitement and waited to see what Saturday would bring.

The night before their meeting, sleep once again eluded them. They sat in the living room until daybreak, staring out over the lights of the city and pondered the reality of having their first child. "What do you want to do first if we get her?" Angela asked Jonathan as they stood looking out through balcony doors.

"I'm not too sure, I guess we should get her some girl toys or something like that." He sipped his hot chocolate.

"Really, that's all you can come up with?" Angela laughed. She threaded her arm through his, and rested her head on his shoulder. "I know what I want. I want to take her for a walk through Shinjuku Gyoen, and then take a ride to the Araihama bay and look out over the ocean. We would need to pick up a camera first, but I want to capture as many moments here as possible."

Jonathan wrapped his arm around her and kissed her forehead. "That sounds like a great idea."

"Have you had any thoughts about what you will do when we get home?" she asked.

"I sent out some resumes and no one has responded yet. Professor Lang said he might be able to get me a job at the university, but I don't know if I want to go back there."

"I'm sure you will find a job, honey, just keep it up. Have you said anything to anyone at home?"

"About what?" he asked curiously.

"About us being parents, or do you still want us to keep it quiet until we get home?"

"Oh, that, I would like it to be a surprise. I told everyone to meet us at the airport, but I haven't told them why yet."

"And what if Setsuko decides to keep the baby?"

Jonathan smiled down at his wife. "Why don't we worry about that when the time comes?"

Angela nodded. It had been a long night, but it may become the happiest day of their lives.

As the taxi drove up the winding driveway, Angela gasped when she saw the large house. After a year of seeing small homes and cramped apartments all crowded together, the Fukui house with its beautiful gardens was breath-taking.

"It's huge!" Jonathan said in astonishment.

"Are you sure this is where you are supposed to be?" asked the taxi driver.

Jonathan checked the address he was given. "Yes, this is the address for the Fukui house," he said.

"Fukui!" The large, balding man exclaimed. "How do you know someone like that? He is a powerful and rich businessman."

"We are friends with his wife," Angela said, smiling as Hitomi appeared at the front door and waved to them.

The driver's jaw slackened when he saw Hitomi, and he was so entranced that didn't notice Jonathan handing him money.

"Are you going to take the money?" Jonathan asked, flashing him the cash.

"Yes, okyaku-sama! Sorry, okyaku-sama! Thank you for the ride ... I mean, I hope you liked the ride." As the words tumbled out of his mouth, the driver began to blush.

"It is fine, arigatou gozaimasu," Jonathan said, chuckling as he got out of the car.

When Hitomi guided them in, they looked around in wonder as they took in the old Japanese paintings and delicately hand-carved figurines that lined the walls of the large and spacious sitting room. To be standing amidst so many rare and exquisite artefacts made them feel out of place.

"I haven't been able to get all the cleaning done, so please excuse me. It's been an extremely trying week for us," Hitomi said, embarrassed. After seeing a home like this, Jonathan was feeling a little ashamed of his own cleaning habits.

"I will get Setsuko, and we shall get started." Hitomi bowed before disappearing down the hall.

Jonathan and Angela didn't know whether to sit or stand as they waited for her return. An older gentlemen, with short salt and pepper hair, flinty black eyes, and wearing an expensive suit, entered the room.

Jonathan greeted the man with a bow; all he received was a grunt. From what little Hitomi had told them about her husband, it, didn't compare to the real thing. He was a commanding and intimidating figure. Everything from the way he dressed to his presence, spoke of a man of stature and power. Jonathan imagined he was a force to be reckoned with. Made uncomfortable by the man's cold demeanour, Jonathan hoped Hitomi would return soon.

Angela and Jonathan breathed silent sighs of relief when they saw Hitomi return with Setsuko. Cradled in the young girl's arms was the baby. Angela inhaled sharply upon seeing the sleeping infant. She was as beautiful as Angela had imagined, and her heart ached to hold her.

"Is this her?" Jonathan asked in awe, looking down at the bundle in Setsuko's arms.

"Of course it is. Now, can we cut the small talk and get on with this?" Daiki pushed some documents and a pen across the coffee table to Jonathan.

"Shouldn't we talk about this?" asked Jonathan, taken aback by Daiki's abruptness.

"Just sign it and let's be done with this," Daiki growled.

Not wanting to raise the man's ire, Jonathan and Angela read and signed the documents and handed them back. Daiki quickly deposited them into a brown envelope and sealed it.

"Daiki, may we have a moment with them before they take our grandchild away?" asked Hitomi.

"You may take some time and visit if you'd like, but I want the child gone when I return."

Envelope in hand, Daiki walked to the door and left, taking the room's tension with him. Everyone breathed a little easier.

"I'm sorry about my husband, it's been hard on all of us," Hitomi apologised.

"It's because he's ashamed of me, and this child," Setsuko said coolly.

Hitomi gave Setsuko a sharp look which she returned with a glare of her own. Jonathan and Angela looked at each other, not wanting to get involved in a family argument.

"So, this is your little girl? She's beautiful!" Angela said as she stood beside Setsuko. "May I hold her?"

Setsuko secured the blanket around her daughter before tentatively placing her into Angela's waiting arms. "Her name is Takara," she said softly.

"Takara?" An unreadable look briefly entered Angela's eyes before she turned to her husband. "Look at her, Jonathan, she's so gorgeous. You must be so proud, Setsuko."

"Yes she is," said Jonathan reaching over to caress the little face.

They took turns holding the baby as she stared up at them curiously. When it was Angela's turn to hold her again, her name suddenly fell into place and the recurring dream of the baby in her arms became as clear as day. The grave, Jonathan and the others gathered around it, and the young girl was Takara grown up. For a moment she felt fearful and began to tremble. Gasping, she took a few steps back and bumped into the coffee table. Takara wriggled her arms out of her blankets and reached for her. In that moment they both looked at each other, and, Angela's heart was filled with so much joy, love and hope that she felt like her heart was going to burst.

Smiling down at Takara, Angela kissed her forehead and said a silent prayer. Dear Lord, I know You have plans for us, and I am thankful for every day You have given to me. Lord I ask that, with what time I have left, You grant me the ability to raise this child in the way You desire. Fill her with Your Holy Spirit, and keep her safe.

When she lifted her head, she found that everyone was staring at her strangely.

"Honey, are you all right?" asked Jonathan, concerned.

"Yes, I am." She laughed, wiping away tears of joy. "I was picturing her a little older."

"Do you still want her?" inquired Setsuko, hoping that they would say no.

"Of course we do, that's if you're okay with us taking her. She is your child after all." Setsuko looked like she was about to come and take the child from her, when Hitomi stopped her with an outstretched arm.

"We can't keep her. As much as I would love to have her in my house, Daiki will never permit it," Hitomi said sadly, giving her daughter a sympathetic look.

Looking to his wife, Jonathan felt a twinge of regret, "I guess we should get going before your husband returns. Thank you, Hitomi, for everything. And thank you Setsuko; I can't imagine what you are going through. We will stay in contact as much as we can."

"Stay in contact?" Setsuko said, startled, her eyes glistening. Angela felt horrible, they hadn't even discussed the fact that they were returning home.

"We didn't want to say anything until it was for sure, but we have decided to go back home," said Jonathan, pursing his lips.

"Oh," Hitomi said, taken aback by this new development. "When do you leave?"

Sensing the hurt coming from Setsuko and Hitomi, Angela said decisively, "You know what, we don't have to leave right away. I'm sure we could work something out and stay a while. Jonathan and I have some savings, we could extend our stay for a few months if you'd like. That way you can still spend time with your child before we take her. We didn't want to hurt either of you. It's just that with my health, and all those we left behind, Jonathan thought it was time for us to go back, but we could try—"

"It's fine," Setsuko interrupted. Everyone looked at her. She shook her head. "It's fine. You both must miss your family, and this isn't your home, so it's not fair to expect you to stay."

Walking up to Angela, Setsuko placed a final kiss on her daughter's forehead, making the little girl restless as she reached up towards her mother.

"I will miss you, my little Takara," Setsuko whispered, adjusting the blankets. With tear-filled eyes, she looked up at Angela. "Please take care of her," she implored, her voice quivering.

Careful not to jostle Takara, Angela embraced Setsuko with her free arm. "I will, I promise." She looked down at the baby, and asked, "Before we go, what does her name mean?"

"Her name means 'treasure', and that is what she will always be," Hitomi responded, trying to swallow the hard lump in her throat.

Angela and Jonathan said their goodbyes and left with their newborn daughter. As Hitomi watched them, she thought of the things she would miss, from Takara's first steps, to her first word. She thought of all of the things she would never be a part of, and now she wished she could take it back. As Setsuko walked back towards her room, Hitomi stopped her and held her at arm's length. "I'm so proud of you, Setsuko. I know this is hard, but we will make it, I promise."

Looking back into her mother's teary eyes, Setsuko shrugged, "I have to grow up some time, it might as well be now. It's not like I had much of a choice to begin with, anyway."

Hitomi let her go and watched her run off to her room. It was going to be a long road ahead, and only God knew what it would take to fill the hole in Setsuko's heart. All she could do was hope and pray that her daughter would give her life to Him soon.

The Hansen's flight home was booked for March 28th. Jonathan had declined his contract renewal and got a job with a small paper in Calgary. Angela was excited to be going home to her family and friends, but she was feeling a little sad to be leaving the friends they had made in Tokyo. The Sunday following the adoption, they announced at church they would be returning home. Everyone in the congregation expressed how much they would be missed, and Pastor Hikaru made plans for a special lunch on the Sunday before their flight.

Hitomi didn't attend church during the weeks following the adoption. She hadn't realised how deeply attached she had become to Takara, and was unsure if she could handle seeing her. Angela and Jonathan called her on several occasions; when they couldn't get through, they asked Hikaru if he had heard from her. Feeling his own sense of distress over Hitomi's absence, Hikaru made an unscheduled stop by her home to see how she and her daughter were faring.

"Hikaru-Bokushi!" exclaimed Hitomi, surprised to see him standing outside their door.

"Hello, Hitomi, how are you doing?"

Flashing a disingenuous smile, she said, "I'm fine, things have been busy around here. I was planning to come to church after next week, I'm sorry if I worried you."

Hikaru could tell she was fighting with the decision she had made. He reached out to take her hand, and said, "Hitomi you are never alone, you are part of God's family now and we are there to help support and love one another. I think Philippians 2:1-4 says it the best: **'Therefore if you have any encouragement from being united with Christ, if any comfort from his love, if any common sharing in the Spirit, if any tenderness and compassion, then make my joy complete by being like-minded, having the same love, being one in spirit and of one mind. Do nothing out of selfish ambition or vain conceit. Rather, in humility value others above yourselves, not looking to your own interests but each of you to the interests of the others'.**

"Don't abandon your spiritual family during your time of need, Hitomi. Know that you are loved. Let us help share the load and make your burden lighter."

The tenderness of his words struck home, and Hitomi poured out her heart to him. Ever since they had given up Takara, Hitomi had felt depressed and hopeless. She constantly wondered if there had been another way. Maybe there was something she hadn't considered that would have allowed them to keep her granddaughter.

"Did I do the right thing? Was it God's will that we give her up?"

"I have always found that in life there are times that, no matter what decisions we have made, whether good or bad, can be used for God's glory. Every decision we make comes with its consequences. Sometimes these consequences can aid us, or discourage us. In the end, even when we answer God's call, we will have moments of doubt and reservations. And there are instances in life when God doesn't give us clear answers. I think that this was one of those cases. You could have kept your granddaughter, but lost the relationship with your husband and faced more hardship than you have ever known. In this I know it would have been hard, but I am sure, that with the support of the church, you and Setsuko may have come out stronger, but the consequences to that choice would still be great. Instead, you chose to entrust Takara to a godly couple who will love and support her. I think that, no matter what choice you made, God will be there to help you through your struggles."

Hikaru could see that she understood what he was trying to tell her. It warmed her heart to know that God put so many caring people in her path who would love and provide for her. She was thankful for them, and thankful for the fact that God allowed her friends to adopt her grandchild. She wouldn't need to worry about Takara's safety or spiritual welfare.

"Thank you, Bokushi, I sometimes don't know what I would do without other believers' support."

Giving her a small bow, he smiled. "You can thank Angela and Jonathan. They were the ones who had asked about you. Are you planning on seeing them off on Friday?"

Hitomi nodded, then brightened. "Yes, I will be there. I want to say goodbye to them, and to my granddaughter."

The Friday of their departure was a sorrowful one. Kate helped Jonathan and Angela pack their belongings and prepare for their flight.

"I'm really going to miss you both," she said after they had exchanged addresses and contact numbers.

"We are going to miss you, too." Angela gave her a hug.

"It's going to feel so lonely without you guys around. I really wish you wouldn't go," Kate said, looking forlornly around the empty apartment.

"I know, but I think the family is getting a little stressed after everything that's happened, and want us to come back. I have to admit that, as much as I didn't like the idea of coming here, I've grown to see this place as home. I already feel a little homesick thinking of all the people we are leaving behind." Angela adjusted the blanket around Takara and picked up the baby carrier.

"She's so cute," Kate cooed as she stooped to peer at the little bundle.

"I know, I can't believe that we are parents. It feels a little surreal every time I pick her up. I can't wait to see how everyone's going to react when we get home."

Kate picked up Takara's rattle and shook it playfully, eliciting a smile from her. "Seeing her makes me want to have one of my own."

"My husband has a cousin back home who's free. He's a little bit of a clown, but I'm sure you would have no problem reining him in."

"No, thank you," Kate said throwing up her arms, "I don't want to raise two children."

They both looked at each other and laughed. Jonathan came back inside after loading the last of their bags into the Limo. "Are we ready to go?" he asked.

"Well, my friend, I guess this means goodbye," said Angela, giving Kate one more hug.

"Call me as soon as you can, and let me know how everyone reacts to your little bundle."

Angela she rifled through her bag and pulled out her Bible. "I want you to have this. Please treasure it as I have."

"I will, Angela, I promise."

Jonathan and Angela waved a final goodbye as they got into the vehicle. The air was filled with a sense of anticipation. When they arrived at the airport they were met by Pastor Hikaru, a few of the church members, Mr. Matsuno, and some of the students from Jonathan's class, all wanting to exchange contact information and give their final farewells.

As Jonathan checked in their bags, he noticed that Angela seemed disheartened as she watched their friends leave. "Are you missing it already?" he asked.

"I was hoping to see Hitomi before we left," she said wistfully, saddened that their friendship had seemed to end with the adoption.

"I think it's been hard on her. Hikaru-Bokushi said she was extremely upset the last time he saw her. Maybe she just couldn't handle seeing Takara again," Jonathan said. "Let's get going, honey, before we miss our flight."

He shouldered their carry-on bags and led them to departures. A voice calling out over the hum of the crowd caught their attention. They turned to see Hitomi moving quickly towards them. Handing Takara off to Jonathan, Angela ran to her and gave Hitomi the biggest hug she could muster.

"I thought you weren't coming," Angela said, fighting back tears.

"I couldn't let you leave without saying goodbye," replied Hitomi, eyes glistening. She looked over at Jonathan, and then at Takara. She carefully took her granddaughter out of the carrier and held her in her arms. Takara kicked and squealed as Hitomi stroked her face. "I will miss you, my little treasure," she whispered.

"We will take care of her, I promise," said Jonathan, with a nod of affirmation.

"May I sing to her?" Hitomi asked.

"Of course," Angela said, standing beside her husband as Hitomi cradled Takara in her arms.

Hitomi choked on the words of the song as she struggled with her emotions. Wiping away the tears. Hitomi cleared her throat and began again, singing in Japanese. When the song ended, Hitomi pulled Takara to her, and kissed her lovingly on the head.

"That was beautiful," Angela said in amazement, "What song was that, it sounded familiar?"

Hitomi smiled, handing Takara back to Angela, "'Jesus Loves Me'. It is one of my favourites."

Angela took Hitomi's hand in hers and looked at the woman with adoration and love. "We will call you as much as possible, and we will try to come back when we can."

Hitomi clasped her hands over Angela's, "I know. Thank you for taking her, I know that she is safe in your care."

Hitomi presented Takara with a teddy bear that she had lovingly made for her. She asked if Jonathan could take two Polaroids of her and Takara. Hitomi gave them one to take with them. The women hugged, crying as they said goodbye one last time. Hitomi watched them leave, then went to watch their plane depart.

When Angela and Jonathan boarded, Angela took the window seat and looked out, hoping to catch a glimpse of Hitomi. When she saw her she waved, even though she knew Hitomi couldn't see them. Cradling Takara in her arms, she looked down at her daughter and grinned.

"Our journey begins, little one," she said softly, "Everyone will be excited to meet you."

Takara reached out and grasped Angela's finger. She giggled, her eyes wide and face smiling as she stared up at her mother. As the plane took off, Angela took one more look out the window, and committed what she saw to memory. She would always remember this place, the friends she made, the good times they had, and the hardships they had endured. After all they had gone through, she was thankful for all that God had done for them. Now was the beginning of a new chapter in their lives, and the beginning of Takara's story.

NAME PRONUNCIATIONS AND DEFINITIONS

Daiki Fukui (D-AHiy-Kiy) (Fhu-Khu-ee)
Hitomi Fukui (HHiy-TuwMiy)
Setsuko Fukui (SEHTSuwKow)
Akari (AA-Kaa-Riy)
Natsuki (NAETSuw-Kiy)
Misayo (MIY-Saa-Yow)
Suzaku Ikeda (Soo Za Koo) (Ih k ai d ae)
Mr. Asato (Ah-Sah-Toh)
Mr. Takeda (TawKeDa)
Hikaru Ichinose (HHIY-Kaa-Ruw) (Eechee-Nose)
Mai Ichinose (May)
Tetsuya (TEH-TSuw-Yaa)
Kyo (Key-oh)
Miya (MIY-Yaa)
Mr. Michio Hashida (MIY-CH-iy-ow) (Hha-Shee-Dah)
Ryota Hashida (RAYOWTaa) (Hha-Shee-Dah)

Wabori Tattoos — Traditional Japanese Tattoos.
Bokushi-sensei — Title of a Pastor
Kamidana — In Shinto, an altar or high shelf for enshrining a kami in a quiet place in the house of a Shinto believer.
Taiyaki — Fish-shaped Cakes
Nerima-ku — A centrally located Tokyo suburban neighborhood
Kurasukuri — Style of Japanese home architecture

Ojousama — Is the honorific for girls from a very well-to-do family.
Sama — How to refer to the boss's wife
Kacho — Boss/someone in authority
Genkan — Japanese vestibule that is a traditional entryway and most of the time it is a combination of a porch and a doormat. It can be seen in the main entrance of a house and it somewhat connects the outside world to the inside of the house.
Getabako — Is a shoe closet located in the genkan
Itadakimasu — Is a prayer said as a thanks to the plants and animals that gave their lives for the meal you're about to consume; I humbly receive
Putaro — Tramp
Hojokyoyu — Teacher Assistant
Okyakusama — Guest or customer
Hafu — Is used in Japanese to refer to somebody who is biracial
Kami-no-michi — He native Japanese words meaning 'the Way of the Kami', corresponding to the Chinese shen-tao (Shinto) as the designation for the indigenous religion of Japan.
Arigatou Gozaimasu — Polite way of saying thank you.
Oisha San — Doctor
Kijo — Witch

Printed in Canada